AN ANCIENT ENEMY RISES AGAIN

Desperation was taking hold in the dragon's heart when there came a brilliant flash of bright green light. Suddenly the passage resounded to the thunder of hooves and a great white horse clattered up. It bore a tall knight in shining armor. Imps scattered out of the way. The bewkman stood back. The knight brought the horse to a halt and threw up his helm. Revealed was the steely perfection of feature that marked the elven lords of antiquity.

Bazil had turned to face the knight, but now the steel-clad figure raised a hand and uttered words of power that froze his minions in their places.

"Never can revenge have been so timely and so sweet." He drew his great sword, and it emitted a chill green glow. "To arms, Great Worm! I, humble Waakzaam, I will take up the challenge. Prepare to taste my steel!"

THE DRAGONS OF ARGONATH

THE DRAGONS OF ARGONATH

CHRISTOPHER ROWLEY

A ROC BOOK

ROC
Published by the Penguin Group
Penguin Putnam Inc., 375 Hudson Street,
New York, New York 10014, U.S.A.
Penguin Books Ltd, 27 Wrights Lane,
London W8 5TZ, England
Penguin Books Australia Ltd, Ringwood,
Victoria, Australia
Penguin Books Canada Ltd, 10 Alcorn Avenue,
Toronto, Ontario, Canada M4V 3B2
Penguin Books (N.Z.) Ltd, 182–190 Wairau Road,
Auckland 10, New Zealand

Penguin Books Ltd, Registered Offices:
Harmondsworth, Middlesex, England

First published by Roc, an imprint of Dutton Signet,
a member of Penguin Putnam Inc.

First Printing, February, 1998
10 9 8 7 6 5 4 3 2 1

Cover art by Daniel Horne

Printed in the United States of America

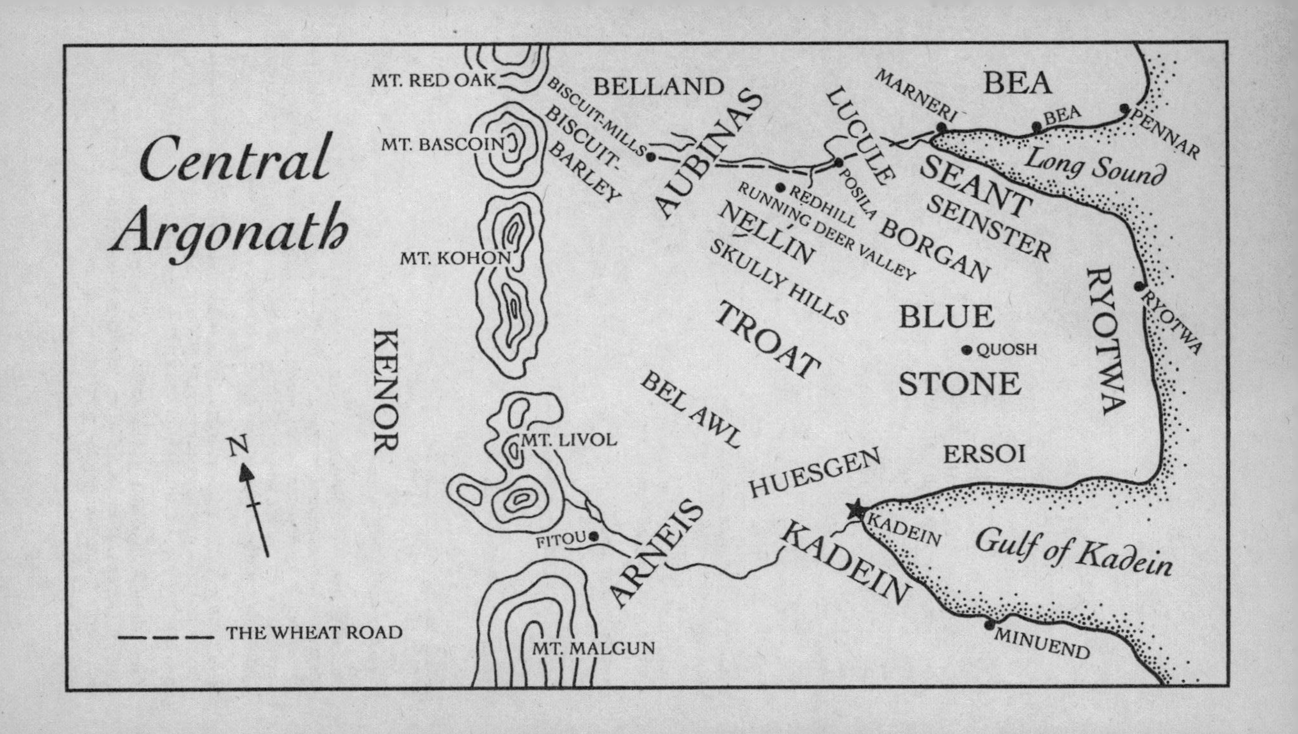
Central Argonath
MT. RED OAK
BELLAND
BEA
MARNERI
BEA
PENNAR
Long Sound
BISCUIT-MILLS
BISCUIT-BARLEY
AUBINAS
LUCULE
MT. BASCOIN
POSILA
REDHILL
RUNNING DEER VALLEY
NELLIN
SEANT
SEINSTER
BORGAN
MT. KOHON
SKULLY HILLS
RYOTWA
RYOTWA
BLUE
QUOSH
STONE
TROAT
KENOR
BEL AWL
ERSOI
MT. LIVOL
N
HUESGEN
KADEIN
Gulf of Kadein
FITOU
ARNEIS
KADEIN
MINUEND
THE WHEAT ROAD
MT. MALGUN

Chapter One

It was the custom in the vale of Valmes for the farmers to harrow their fields in the spring, after the plow and before they planted. They used teams of two or four horses to pull the great steel-toothed harrows, combing the ground and smoothing it out ready for the seed.

When seen from a distance, or even while passing along the lane, harrowing seems a perfectly tranquil part of farming life—a scene for a pastoral painting, a poem to the glories of the annual round. But for the small inhabitants of the fields, the harrow is the most dreaded event of all, for there is no escape from its fifteen-foot-wide comb of steel points, dragging through the topsoil. For mice and voles this is bad enough, but these little fellows are swift-footed and might yet escape. For toads, slow-hopping, crawling toads, it is certain death.

Thus in Valmes, as in much of old Cunfshon, there was another custom. The old witches, including all the retired crones, would scour the fields to gather the toads. For the farmers of Cunfshon, with their fine-tuned husbandry, were acutely conscious of the beneficial effect of toads, which consume insects in considerable numbers every growing season.

This was but one of many ways that the old witches, who had gone into the mystic or simply retired from active service, paid for their upkeep. Of course, they also fashioned spells to encourage crops and animals, and they used their arts to drive away flies from house and stable. The benefits of this last activity were enormous, and many of the diseases that plagued the world were virtually unknown in Cunfshon.

In Valmes, the witches were aligned to various farms from time immemorial. Thus old Lessis, now in retireme was at work that day in the field of Gelourd, still farmed by folk of that name after seven centuries.

She put a shoulder bag occupied by two dozen disgruntled toads over the wall and into a barrow. In the next field over, Bertain's, she could see the old witch Katrice working with an assistant, hauling a cart full of toads toward the road. It was a fine day, warm enough to require only a simple shift and sandals, but not so hot as to work up a sweat. Ah, the toads, the fine rapacious toads, Lessis blessed them silently. She felt their confusion, they were afraid, poor things, but they were toads that would survive the morrow, when the harrow would tear through these fields. The day after that they would be returned to their fields, a simple task that farmworkers would perform, since all that was required was to open the bags and dump out the toads, carefully.

At lunch she rested sitting on the stone wall above the field. Behind her the ridge rose up in a long dun-colored mass. Spread before her was the town of Valmes, spires and roofs visible amid the trees. The graceful stone tower of the temple was due north, and the long spine of the temple roof was visible just behind. It was a well-sited town, with centuries of concern taken with every detail of place and road. Some black cattle were being moved up a lane about half a mile distant. Farther away sheep dotted the hillsides of Big Bank and Chalk Hill. In the sky were a handful of soft white clouds.

Farmer Gelourd sent out fresh-baked bread, cheese, and fruit to all the workers in his fields. With the toad collectors he was always free with the best in his cellar. A good Valmes Reserva was uncorked and poured into Lessis's plain tin cup. She washed down the good bread and the soft white cheese, and then ate an apple. The wine was rather too good for her old tin cup, but Lessis decided that was part of Farmer Gelourd's homage to his toads—the "worthy little folk" of every well-kept field, who would annihilate crickets, beetles, and caterpillars.

Lessis enjoyed the moment and gazed over toward the town with peaceful detachment. She had found retirement even easier to enjoy than she had imagined. Just worrying about the roof of her house, and the flowers and fruit trees was enough to fill some days. Add in such duties as the gathering of toads or the blessing of crops, and she found she had limited time to devote to the study of the mystic.

Suddenly she noticed a small node of change strike the pastoral scene. Someone, walking very fast, emerged from the trees on the west farm road. The figure was instantly at odds with the peace around it, a dot that emitted a field of tension.

It disappeared from view when the road went around a bend, then came back into sight, pulling hard up the long slope. At the crossing it turned onto the lane running up to Gelourd's fields.

Clearly whatever message impelled this person was important.

Now the figure was close enough for Lessis to see that it was exactly what she had feared, a tall girl in novice blues.

Lessis studied the girl as she came closer and saw a long face, a determined set to the shoulders, dark hair tied back in a novice bob. The clothes seemed too big for her, but maybe she would grow into them.

The girl approached her. Lessis's concern grew. Everyone knew that she had retired. She had served for five hundred years and more, that was enough. There were other witches with skill. Irene and Melaan could take up the slack. Lessis had sent enough men to their deaths.

"Excuse me, Lady," the girl curtsied clumsily. She was a little gawky.

"Yes, what is it?" Lessis did not welcome this intrusion.

"Message came for you. Prioress said it was important. Sorry to trouble you."

A long, long moment of silence. Lessis heard the wind soughing in the tall grass on the slopes above. The gentle clouds continued to float in the high blue sky.

"Yes, that's quite all right, child. What is the message?"

"Here, Lady," the girl handed her a pouch containing a tiny scroll, the specialty of the Imperial message corps. It must have been brought on the wings of a seagull.

Lessis opened the scroll and read it in a moment. Ribela, the Queen of Mice, begged her for help. There was something she must do. People she must visit. The toads squirmed in the bag on the roadside, and Lessis squirmed at the thought of engaging once more with the world's troubles. She had set that aside. After five centuries she had earned a decade's rest before a peaceful death.

But no, it was not to be. Circumstances were not in her favor. Now Ribela herself, the very Queen of Mice, had begged her to intercede, and Lessis could not refuse.

Chapter Two

Situated down in the Blue Stone country, Cross Treys camp was an old legion post, so old the palisade was rotting away in places. The corner towers were too dangerous to occupy and could fall down in the next stiff gale. Someday soon a decision would have to be made whether to keep Cross Treys going or abandon it.

But the main block was still functional, and the Dragon House, though small, was known to be famously warm in the winter and cool in the summer. The plunge pool was outdoors, of course, as in most outposts, but it was paved and the water never got muddy.

That summer Cross Treys was host to the 109th Marneri Dragons, along with sixty men of the Eighth Regiment, Second Legion and a party of twelve youngsters who were completing their pre-legion training in the youth Pioneers.

Cross Treys was regarded as a restful posting, a place for convalescence. Nothing much happened in Blue Stone that required legion interference. A minor incident with a troll owner now and then, or an old vendetta in the western hills might flare up. Bandits occasionally attacked wagons on the road in Ersoi on the coast, but mostly it was just a quiet routine of work in the woodlots and helping parties of Imperial Engineers to build and repair roads and bridges. Dragons actually looked forward to these projects. They didn't last long, not with ten dragons helping, and wyverns didn't mind a certain amount of heavy work. It even felt good to dig and haul stone for a few days. But mainly they liked it because the Imperial Engineers always had a huge budget for beer. On that score the dragons were well pleased. Blue Stone brewers specialized in summer wheat beers that were very popular with the dragons.

Another pleasant aspect of building a new bridge was that the local people would vie to feed the dragons. Pies, roasts, huge platters of ham, mounds of hot bread and cheese, the cooks everywhere tried to outdo each other in feeding the dragons. This could be an expensive process, though not nearly as expensive as hiring gangs of laborers.

Throughout the Argonath lands, the roads were now paved and usable year-round. Clean water flowed to every city and town. Sewage was dealt with sensibly in all major towns. Bridges, walls, canals, ponds, docks, wherever possible the Imperial Engineers were at work, assisted often by dragon labor, which made heavy work go very swiftly indeed. Ten wyvern dragons, equipped with gigantic shovels and steel beams to use as picks and prods, could cut two hundred yards of canal, ten feet wide and eight feet deep in a few days, depending on the nature of the ground.

When there wasn't any work, the dragons just lazed around the camp. They exercised regularly, of course, and worked with their weapons. There was a drill session at least once a week. Dragon Leader Cuzo insisted on this. But there was always the plunge pool when they got hot. And in the evenings there was legion dinner, plain but plentiful, and with it some legion brew. It was a restful life at Cross Treys.

And it would have been for the 109th, but for the growing rivalry between dragonboys Swane and Rakama.

Big, long-nosed Swane had been the bully boy in the unit for years. The brown-haired fellow was well over six feet and solidly built all the way down. He could whip any of them, except Relkin, who he had never fought. The two had always fenced around, but had never come to serious blows. Swane respected Relkin and was jealous of him at first, but over the years his respect had grown and the jealousy had faded.

Now the hierarchy was challenged by the presence of Rakama, a pug-nosed chunk of muscle from the Blue Hills town of Mud Lake. Rakama was a scrapper and more, he had trained in fighting school. He had a powerful upper body and a terrific straight right hand. His hand speed and coordination were dangerous.

Swane was the taller and twenty pounds heavier, but from the beginning Rakama thought he could take him on.

Swane was never one to ignore a challenge like that, and

so the two had had several run-ins. Swane had prevailed so far, but none of these fights had lasted more than a minute or two before being broken up by others. Even though he'd been pushed around in these short exchanges, Rakama had hit Swane plenty and hurt him. They both knew that, which had changed the equation slightly. Now Rakama was even more eager to fight Swane, convinced that if a fight ran on past the first furious two minutes, he would hammer the bigger youth. Swane fought well, however. But Rakama had a natural hand speed that made his stinging right hand too much for anyone but a trained boxer. Indeed, he had been chosen to represent the Eighth Regiment in the summer games at Dalhousie in the light-heavyweight division.

If Rakama could get through Swane's first rush, then he felt sure he'd start getting in punches that would take the steam out of Swane very quickly. Swane had a sneaking suspicion that this might be true and knew that he had to level the Rakbrat with his first charge, keep him down, and whop the hell out of him on the ground.

A serious fight would come soon, it was clear. Rakama and Swane were constantly after one another, and there were brushes every day. Finally it came from a silly incident between their dragons. After a five-mile march one afternoon, the dragons headed for the plunge pool, and Vlok accidentally tripped Gryf. Rakama said something nasty about Vlok. Swane told him to apologize. They bounced up against each other and had to be ordered apart by Dragon Leader Cuzo.

"Later!" they both growled.

That evening the camp was quiet enough. Men had eaten and were sitting around before sleep claimed them. Bazil and Relkin were actually at the far end of the camp, giving legal depositions, again, in the case of Marneri vs. Porteous Glaves. A pair of scribes from Marneri, one hired by Glaves and one from the crown attorney's office, took down their responses to questions from a judicial assistant.

They had answered the questions two or three times before, during earlier stages of the marathon trial of Porteous Glaves, who had once commanded the Eighth Regiment. Yet again Glaves's case was being appealed to the Marneri high court.

It was while they were absent that Rakama and Swane

finally got down to it. They met in the hallway behind the refectory. The only other boys around were the newbies Curf and Howt, and neither of them wanted to tangle with the older boys.

Rakama spat on the floor and muttered something at Swane. Swane charged and booted Rakama into the wall. He crowded in and started pounding left and right, pinning the smaller youth for a while. Rakama head-butted Swane to break out. Swane came right back with a body tackle that slammed Rakama back into the wall and crushed him there. Swane held him there and went for the body, two heavy shots, but Rakama finally got a right to Swane's head that propelled him away and gained enough room to kick clear.

Rakama shook his head to try and clear it. There was blood running from a cut on his forehead, and his mouth had taken a solid whack, but Swane's whole face and chest were crimson from the blood running from his nose. The first adrenaline blitz of fighting had begun to ebb. Now it was down to guts, training, and skill. They sparred around trying kicks and punches, feints and ducks.

Rakama, floating on his toes, was recovering every second. Swane rushed in, but Rakama's right hand snaked out and Swane staggered back, shaking his head. Rakama moved closer.

Swane moved to stay clear of the right hand. He was beginning to fear that punch. They kicked at each other and blocked and swerved. Rakama was trying to edge closer, trying to get Swane into an exchange of punches, and Swane felt a sudden strong twinge of concern. It seemed he'd caught a bear here. He didn't feel that confident of getting through Rakama's defenses without getting knocked silly in the process.

He wondered what to do. Both were tiring. They had been battling for more than four minutes straight. Their breathing was starting to come hot and heavy.

Swane suddenly found the wall at his back. Rakama came in, and Swane snapped a desperate left and then a right to keep him away. Rakama dipped, dodged, and came up inside, and the right hand slammed Swane's head off the wall. A tooth popped out. Swane hauled him down to the floor, and they wrestled. Swane rammed Rakama's head into the wall one time, but Rakama got him back with an elbow in the face, and they both reeled away for a few seconds to recover their wits.

There was blood everywhere now, mostly from Swane's nose, great splashes of it on the whitewashed walls. Rakama sensed victory. Swane was afraid of him now, afraid of that right hand, which was still way too fast for the bigger boy to block. Rakama came in again, ducked Swane's frantic left with a confident twist of the head, but then ran into a short right hand that stood him up straight. Swane got a knee into Rakama's midriff, then connected with a big left hand to the jaw and Rakama went spinning away, out of control and his careful fight plan in ruins.

None of this was without cost. Swane felt like he'd broken his hand, and Rakama's jaw was going to ache for a week. Rakama came up against the wall and clung there, shaking his head vaguely to clear it. Swane pushed himself forward, determined to finish it while he had the advantage.

And then he heard a voice in his ear telling him to stop. He ignored it. It was time to finish this bastard Rakama. This had been coming a long time.

Relkin had come in through the refectory door and heard the fight at once. It was what he'd been expecting and dreading for days. Swane and Rakama had really hurt each other, blood all over. He didn't hesitate, waving the other boys to help him as he stepped in and took Swane down with a low kick into the back of the knees. Swane fell backward with a startled cry. Curf and Howt jumped on him and pinned him down.

Rakama lurched off the wall and would've kicked Swane on the ground except that Relkin was there to block him.

"No more."

"Get out of the way," snarled Rakama dizzily. "This ain't your fight."

"It's over."

"No way . . ." Rakama didn't hesitate. He knew that Relkin had a reputation as a fighter, but the other dragonboy was too slender to worry him. He snapped out that quick right hand and moved left, just as he'd been drilled, but Relkin had read the move and was already out of range. Rakama went a little out of balance and hung there for a moment. Relkin was fresh and took the opportunity, planting a foot so deep in Rakama's midriff that the bigger boy dropped like a stone and stayed there, struggling to get a breath.

Swane was trying to get to his feet despite the efforts of Curf and Howt. Relkin pushed him back down.

"Stop, Swane, listen to me!"

Swane's big nose was definitely broken. Relkin had broken his own just a few months earlier and knew all about that. Swane would be having a few bad days up ahead.

"Swane, stay down, I swear I'll kick you down if I have to." Curf and Howt grappled with Swane again, who struggled in their grasp.

"Shut up, Quoshite! This is my business."

"No! It's all of our business. You two have been going at each other for months. It's got to stop. Dragons are feeling it. We're all tired of it."

"He'll be tired, when I'm done with him."

"You should see yourself. You're both gonna be up on charges as soon as Cuzo finds out. And you're going to be under medical orders for months."

"Look, this kid's been asking for it ever since he came up. You weren't even here then!"

"Then, you're gonna fight it out in the ring under rules."

Rakama finally got back on his feet. His face had gone white, then slowly it turned pink again. Relkin worried for a few seconds there, afraid he'd done some serious internal injury. That foot had gone deep.

"S'not over," he blurted.

"It's over, Rakama. You fight Swane in the ring, or you don't fight just Swane, you fight me."

"You?" Rakama snarled, and lifted his head. His eyes locked on with Relkin's, and after a while they fell again. There was something in Relkin's eyes that promised more than he could handle. Suddenly Rakama understood something about the quiet youth. Relkin knew about killing.

"Fight's over. If Swane attacks you, we'll take him out; if you attack Swane, you're in it with all of us, you got that?"

Rakama stared at him, shocked by his little discovery. Then he gave a sullen nod.

Relkin turned to the others.

"Just maybe, if we all get to it hard and quick, we can clean this up before Cuzo sees it and save these two idiots a charge."

Curf and Howt nodded enthusiastically.

"Get hot water, get brushes and soap." Relkin looked down at Swane, now a blood-soaked mess. "I'll get the others. You"—he pointed at Swane—"get cleaned up, you're a disgrace right now."

Swane nodded slowly, accepting the situation. Damn that Quoshite, he was always right.

"And start rehearsing some excuse. Make it simple 'cos Cuzo is gonna be damn curious about how both of you are messed up at the same time."

Chapter Three

Unfortunately dragons have minds of their own, and they are all individuals, all different. Most unusual of all, by common consent, are hard greens. These are wyverns with a slim body build, unusual height, and deep, dark green skin. They have a reputation for being difficult to work with, of carrying grudges, and sometimes going so far as to kill a dragonboy in anger. Still, they are often very skilled with dragonsword, providing the most fluid movements, balletic spins and turns, amazing for beasts weighing two tons.

Rakama's dragon was Gryf, a young hard green, from Mud Lake. When Gryf heard the story of the fight, he was upset by Relkin's interference. Rakama would probably have won, in Gryf's view, and so Relkin had taken the victory from his dragonboy. Gryf found this a bad thing in principle, and he complained loudly in the Dragon House on his return from sword practice.

"Dragonboys fight. That is natural. Why not let Rakama finish the job?"

The others ignored him. Bazil was in the plunge pool and out of earshot, but the Purple Green's eyes took on a dangerous tinge. The Purple Green of Hook Mountain was unique in the legions, a wild dragon who had joined the legions after losing the power of flight. The Purple Green had had several run-ins with Gryf already, and the smaller wyvern dragon had been saved again and again by the intervention of the others.

"Vlok! Where is Vlok?" called Gryf, eager to make his point to Swane's dragon.

"This dragon is Vlok," said the leatherback from his stall. He emerged a moment later with a question of his own. Vlok might appear dim, but in his own way he often hit on certain truths.

"Dragonboys are hurt," he said. "This fight go too far. Why waste dragonboys?"

"Listen to Vlok," sneered Gryf. "My boy beat your boy. That is the truth of it."

"By the fiery breath," roared Vlok.

"My boy will beat yours, you know it, he knows it. I know it," Gryf said loudly.

"Enough!" hissed the Purple Green. "We all tired of you and your boy."

"Who was talking to you? Not me, that's certain."

"Well, I am talking to you, and that too is certain." The Purple Green rose up to his full massiveness. Gryf's shoulders came up and a snarl escaped him.

"You stupid thing, wings cut, useless, can hardly wield sword!"

There was a brief moment of shock as this insult hung in the air, and then the Purple Green charged. Gryf tried to dodge, but was caught up in giant arms and swept back against the wall of the Dragon House, which shook under the impact. The Purple Green had returned to his atavistic nature. His huge jaws snapped down on Gryf's shoulder, which fortunately was still encased in leather armor from his work on the sword butts. Gryf roared in pain no less for that protection.

The building shook. Shouts of alarm rang out as men ran for the stairs throughout the central block. Two-ton wyvern and four-ton wild dragon grappled briefly on the wall, and then Gryf escaped the wild one's grip and broke away. The Purple Green came after him, but stumbled over a dragonboy stool that disintegrated to matchwood in the process. With a second to spare, Gryf now drew his sword from the shoulder scabbard.

Suddenly the incident had escalated into truly dangerous territory. A dragon with sword in hands became the most lethal thing in the world, and Gryf was in an insane place, black eyes flaring in mad battle rage. Unarmed, the Purple Green seemed doomed. Dragon murder hung in the air.

Then Vlok interposed his sword, "Katzbalger," and in a moment there was a fearsome flash of steel on steel. Gryf and Vlok were engaged in sword battle, right in the middle of the Dragon House.

Dragons tumbled out. Eventually Vlok too spilled out, defending himself desperately from a Gryf gone completely berserk. Vlok barely deflected the blows that were coming, any one of which could have slain him instantly. He was forced back across the yard, Gryf swinging with a speed and skill far beyond that of poor, old Vlok, who had never been much more than a middling hand with sword and shield.

Bazil Broketail, a leatherback of a little more than two tons, heard the commotion and rushed out of the plunge pool. He could see that Vlok was in a perilous state, outmatched and only just fending off Gryf's assault. But there was no sword to hand, and Bazil watched helplessly for a moment as dragon blades rang off each other just a few yards away. Then his eye caught on the nearest wooden butt. Huge pieces of the sword butts were constantly being cut away when dragons exercised upon them. Bazil grabbed up a hefty slab of wood six feet long and ran at Gryf from the side.

The young green never noticed him, too intent on finally getting through Vlok's guard. Bazil swung, but not too hard, and brought the balk of wood down on the back of Gryf's head and neck. The green was bowled over in a heap.

Unfortunately this didn't quite do the job. Gryf was a hard-headed wyvern, so he rolled over, sat up, and let out a shriek of rage as he started to get back on his feet.

Bazil instantly regretted holding back. He should've swatted Gryf with everything he had.

Vlok was standing nearby, panting, struggling to get a breath after that defensive struggle across the yard. Bazil reached over, grabbed Vlok's arm, and pulled him close.

"What you want?"

"Sword," said Bazil, twisting Katzbalger out of the other leatherback's astonished grasp.

Gryf was back on his feet, and his sword "Swate" was coming up in front of him. Bazil shoved Vlok away and moved to engage.

Gryf swung again and again, and was parried with a neat efficiency vastly unlike Vlok's hurried strokes. Once more Gryf came on, but Bazil parried and then turned Swate with a deft move, forcing it to the ground. Bazil struck on the rebound, and Gryf was forced to stumble back. The situation had changed radically. He wasn't fighting Vlok anymore. Bazil hefted Katzbalger in his hand. It wasn't the magic blade "Ecator" by any means, but it was well made, and light for its size. He came on at Gryf with speed and precision, and the hard green was forced back, helplessly on the defensive.

Gryf roused himself twice, coming close to regaining the initiative, but each time Bazil responded with a trick or two that absorbed Gryf's energy and kept the situation as it was. Finally Bazil came overhead, their blades rang together and the leatherback and green came belly to belly. They struck at each other, but Bazil struck the quicker and his forearm scored a solid smash that sent Gryf wobbling. For a second or two the green was virtually defenseless. Katzbalger came around in a flash and struck Gryf's forearm with the flat of the blade and knocked Swate loose.

The green gave a shriek and tumbled backward, clutching his arm. The other dragons seized Gryf and subdued him by brute strength. They dragged him over to the pool and dunked him headfirst to cool him off, then they escorted him to the infirmary. Along the way they let him know that if he wanted to survive in the 109th Marneri, he would never draw steel on a dragon again like that. Next time he would die.

Gryf was silent under their chastisement, his head hung low. The enormity of his folly was coming home to him.

Later the old core group of the unit gathered by the pump house to talk it over.

"This can't go on," said Bazil. "Trouble every day. That green is just the worst of it. We're all getting grouchy."

"I know, I have occasionally wanted to draw steel on the Purple Green myself these past few days," said Alsebra, the green freemartin renowned for her skill with dragonsword.

The Purple Green just glowered at her, but bit back his retort.

Bazil noted the wild one's restraint.

"You are quiet, this is unusual."

The Purple Green exhaled slowly and ominously. Sometimes Bazil could easily imagine the wild dragon venting the fiery breath of the great ancestors.

"I am insulted, but I understand. She is right. We are all upset."

"Does the Red Star ride high?"

"Not yet."

"Is Gryf unstable?"

They shrugged. Greens were all a little odd. The Purple Green hunkered down.

"This dragon tire of Gryf and sharp tongue."

"We've noticed," said Alsebra, who had broken a few things over the Purple Green's big head to stop him from attacking Gryf.

"We have to make Gryf part of the squadron," said Bazil. "He not fitting in yet."

"The other new dragons are fine. Churn is a good brass, very strong," said Alsebra.

"Ah, this dragon see," gurgled the Purple Green. "You have the eggs to fertilize. You wish to go to the mountain-top with young Churn."

Alsebra flushed somewhat purplish herself, then swung to Bazil with wide, staring eyes. The most sensitive thing to any infertile female dragon, known as freemartins, was her lack of eggs.

"You see?" she said. "He provokes me."

Bazil shrugged in sympathy and turned harsh eyes on the wild dragon. "Alsebra has no eggs, she freemartin, you know that. Why upset her? She take sword and kill you right quick. She very good with a sword, as you know."

The Purple Green withdrew into himself. His sword work, though improved over the years, was still crude, but his vast strength and utter ferocity had compensated. He had burst clean through lines of trolls with his mighty shield alone. Still, he knew that in a sword fight with Alsebra, he could only lose. Along the way he had learned to be quiet sometimes. This had not been easy for the former Lord of Hook Mountain, but this he recognized was one of those times when he was better off keeping quiet.

Bazil sighed, glad to see his wild friend withdraw. "Gryf remains a problem. Good with a sword and bad with his temper. Perhaps this time he learn a lesson."

"He knows now that he isn't the best dragon with sword in this squadron," said Alsebra. "Maybe he learn a lesson from that."

They all nodded in agreement.

"Good thing that Cuzo didn't see."

"Very good thing," agreed Alsebra.

"So much trouble and why? We have nice quiet life here. No marching, no fighting, very quiet. Food is adequate."

"Maybe that's the problem," said the freemartin.

"I think she right," said the Purple Green. "We bored."

"Good legion food. Good beer."

"Bah, legion food is bland. Noodles day after day. Not enough akh."

"I want to eat horse again."

"Oh, no, not that again. We ate horse."

"It was good. I had never had it roasted before. This roasting of meat is best thing men ever invent."

"That's why the ancestors had the fiery breath. They roasted their own meat on the spot."

The Purple Green looked at Alsebra with astonished eyes.

"I think you are right."

The bell was ringing to announce the first boil of the evening. They set off for the refectory in a group, the ground shaking beneath their heavy tread.

"Never enough akh!"

Afterward, in the stall, while Relkin worked on the seams of Bazil's new joboquin, which was now broken in and had started breaking up, Bazil sharpened Ecator's edge on the whetstone.

"So how did Gryf bruise his arm?" asked Relkin. "Rakama's working up compresses like crazy."

"Vlok did it."

"Oh, really? Vlok?"

Relkin worked on for a few moments.

"So Gryf picked a fight because of Swane and Rakama?"

"Are there seals on the ice floes?"

Relkin shook his head. "We've got to put a stop to this fighting. Thank the gods that Cuzo was busy and doesn't seem to have connected it all up. Yet."

"Swane has broken nose?"

"Oh, yes. They're both pretty seriously beat up. Rakama has a broken rib."

"Mmm."

There was a rap at the entrance, and the curtain was pulled aside to admit little Jak.

"Have you heard the news?" he said with a conspiratorial smile.

"About what?"

"Marneri, we're going back to Marneri in a week's time."

"Mmm, and then?"

"And then we're going to ship out to Kadein."

"You know what that means."

All three youths were suddenly glum.

"That's going to be a long march."

If they were shipping out to Kadein, it could only mean they were being sent to the siege at far distant Axoxo. They would be traveling for months, and then they would have to endure a winter in the appalling conditions of the White Bones Mountains.

"Maybe it will help settle down the unit."

Jak left them to spread his news among the rest of the Dragon House. Relkin turned to Bazil, a determined look in his eyes.

"We better ask for special leave. We can't miss the opportunity while we're down here."

"We go to village? Have good dinner!"

"The dinner of our lives probably. We haven't been back to Quosh in years. The village has become famous because we were at Sprian's Ridge. Earned them a few bonuses too."

"We pay our way."

"Have to go back, see the farmers and the families."

"It is only over the Rack Hill. We get there in four hours' march."

"Right. I'll ask Cuzo. It's a good thing that you weren't involved in the fray with Gryf, right? He's got no good reason to say no."

"Very good thing," said Bazil with a twitch of the tail tip.

Chapter Four

The fortified city of Andiquant was the nerve center of the Empire of the Rose. Here too was the headquarters of the little-known Office of Unusual Insight. In a shabby back room in a nondescript office building, two women of markedly different appearance met to drink tea and talk.

"You visited them?" said the one dressed in a black velvet grown trimmed with silver mouse skulls. Her long black hair was pulled back behind her head. Accentuated with cosmetics, her eyes appeared enormous. A sense of shadowy power was about her at all times.

"Yes. A pleasant house, very nice surroundings." The other, clad in plain grey garb, shift, pantaloons, sandals, and a robe, was a slender, unremarkable woman of indeterminate age. Her hair was a stringy grey-white, her face slightly haggard. "There's a road down to Ilka Park from there. So beautiful, Ilka Park."

"I know that. But their story?"

"It is what we have feared. What you have long predicted."

"He makes his move at last."

"This evil has hung over the world since the beginning, since before the coming of man."

"The Sinni have warned us. They can do little more. They too fear the Dominator."

There was a long silence. They exchanged a long frank look, black eyes boring into grey eyes that accepted and melted in understanding.

"Then, I must return to service." There, it was said. Lessis felt the huge burden sag back onto her shoulders. For a few precious months she had been free of it, now it was back. She groaned as she felt the weight of the world once more.

"You must. I have come to realize, dear Lessis, that you are far better at running the Office than I could ever be. I underestimated your abilities, my dear, and humbly crave your pardon."

The Queen of Mice inclined her head in a bow to the Queen of Birds.

Lessis smiled. "Pardoned," she said quietly, and allowed herself the pleasure of accepting this apology.

It had rankled, all those years, those centuries of providing swift efficient service from the central office, and never, ever to have it appreciated, or praised, or even understood. Well, at least the grand Ribela now understood what was involved.

"I found Prince Evander very convincing," she said. "Yourself?"

"Yes. I have no doubt that he and Princess Serena were catapulted between worlds. The Old Red Aeon has left many dangerous relics. This wizard that haunted the city of Monjon was the same gzug that was driven from the magic isle by our dragons during the voyage to Eigo. He was a cruel, monstrous creature, grown contemptuous of all life."

"He will repay his debt a thousandfold. They have made of him a most powerful thymnal, strong enough to raise the city and set a million lamps aglow."

"Yes. I've always wondered what one might be able to do with a thymnal. Such power to work for the good of the world. But now I think I will do without; they are dangerous to acquire."

They exchanged a small smile.

"The prince and princess, though, they are an even more precious relic. They have seen the world of Orthond crushed under the feet of the Dominator, and by a miracle they have returned to warn us."

"I imagine the Sinni were involved somehow. But they dare do nothing overt."

"Have you told the emperor?"

"He has been informed. He intends to make an Imperial Progress through the nine cities. It has been many years since an emperor visited all the cities; perhaps it is time. There are considerable tensions between Kadein and the rest."

"It is a hideous risk." Lessis was aghast.

"We must see to security."

"Does the emperor know that I am here?"

"No, dear Lessis, but he will be glad. He finds it difficult to deal with me. In truth, we have mutual difficulty. I find it hard to accept that he must rule, that he must make the decisions. Sometimes he will not do what must be done."

"He is concerned also with the people. He must represent them. If he goes too much against their will, his rule is weakened. The people cannot be ridden like a mare, they can only be guided with a gentle hand. Since Eigo, I am sure he has been overly cautious with the legions. But it is to be expected, we took terrible casualties there. It is not easy to send men to die in such numbers." She paused. "He must rule, because he is of the people in a way that we no longer are. We have lived too long."

"I know this with my head, but not with my heart. You are far better for this role than I."

"And how does Irene fare in your old shoes?"

"She has learned much, I believe. In time she will know enough."

"In time?"

Ribela grinned mirthlessly. "Considerable time."

"She will return to her old position strengthened by her experiences in the higher planes, I'm sure."

"And you, dear Lessis?"

"I will return to office. This threat cannot be ignored."

Chapter Five

Cuzo made him wait outside the squadron office. Relkin had applied for special leave after breakfast. He'd pointed out that they were only twelve miles from the Broketail's home village, and that both he and his dragon were way overdue a visit to their home village. Cuzo told him to return at the fourth-hour bell for his answer. Relkin was there when the last echoes were still fading away.

There he waited outside the door, standing at attention while others came and went. Cuzo was telling him something, and Relkin knew what it was. Cuzo was dragon leader, not Relkin, even though both of them knew that Relkin should have been a dragon leader by now. With any justice in the world, Relkin should have had command of the 109th Marneri, the unit with which he was so identified by the world.

But there was no justice in the world, and Cuzo had been given the post when dragon Leader Wiliger resigned his commission and returned to civilian life. At that time Relkin was thousands of miles away and presumed dead. Thus went the missed opportunities of life.

So Relkin waited.

Finally the door opened, and Cuzo waved him in.

"Stand at ease, Dragoneer." Cuzo sat behind the big pinewood desk. He toyed with a stencil, gave Relkin a long, slow inspection. It was a moment that both of them knew was important, even though Relkin had been back in the unit for months and he and Cuzo had already formed strong impressions of each other.

Cuzo dropped the stencil, crossed his hands, and pursed his lips.

"All right. I was inclined to say no when you asked me

this morning, because I heard that you were involved in these fights that took place yesterday. I had the medical reports at breakfast. Swane has a broken nose. Rakama is swathed in bandages. Gryf has a bruised arm. The list is long, and I was very angry."

Relkin sighed inwardly. Sometimes it seemed he was always cursed with Dragon leaders who hated him. They always found a way. There'd been Turrent, then Wiliger, now this new man, Cuzo.

"But I wasn't satisfied with just the initial reports. I know how things go in a squadron. I served five years as dragonboy."

Ah. Hope flickered briefly.

"So I did some digging. It wasn't easy, but finally I put it all together. Swane and Rakama have been butting heads for a while. And being dragonboys, with the collective wit of one flea, they did this outside the ring, outside supervision. Thank the Mother they didn't resort to weapons; that is the only consolation we can take from this debacle. And you, young Master Relkin, you broke it up."

Relkin eyed the dragon leader with mingled apprehension and curiosity. This was not taking quite the expected route.

"Gryf, on the other hand, was the Broketail's work. I ought to order him detained to the fort; no dragon may strike another outside the combat ring. It's virtually the same rules as for men; you know it. We have to enforce that, just to keep order."

Relkin began to worry again.

"But I know that Gryf's a green, so I asked some questions, and I finally got the truth about Gryf going for Vlok. That was bad. Can't have that. It's one thing when the Purple Green loses his temper but he never goes for the sword. Can't have dragons drawing steel on dragons."

Relkin coughed.

"Permission to speak, sir."

"Granted. Dragoneer."

"Takes awhile to settle a new green down. They're a little crazy, always."

"Mmm. So you agree with the orthodoxy on this issue, Dragoneer Relkin. I know this is what the old hands say. Give a green just a little longer to adjust. But this was close to murder. He might have killed old Vlok."

"He's impressive with the sword, for a youngster that is. He will be a great sword dragon, given time."

Cuzo stared at him hard for a long moment.

"I see. Well, I understand you, I think. And I concur. And we will erase all mention of the Broketail's stroke from the record." He paused.

"You and the Broketail have three days leave to visit your home village. Three days, understood? You must be back by nightfall, third day. We're going to Marneri next week."

"Marneri? Sir?"

"Don't pretend, I'm sure you all know. And you probably also know that we're shipping out to Kadein soon after."

"Kadein?"

"Well, you know what that means. A long trip and a cold winter ahead of us at Axoxo."

"Axoxo." There it was. Confirmation of the worst possible duty. A winter on the siege lines around the enemy fortress at Axoxo. A winter spent in the White Bones mountains, with howling snowstorms, freezing nights under the stars.

"Right. So when we get to Marneri, we're going to make sure that everyone has a double ration of warm clothing. Freecoats will be inspected for wear and tear. New ones will be ordered. I will be a real zealot when it comes to equipment. I want everyone to stock replacements, and that means armor too."

"Yes, sir!"

"Dismissed. Have a good trip home, Dragoneer, you deserve it."

Relkin took the news to Bazil with considerable satisfaction. It seemed they could actually live with Dragon Leader Cuzo. He was humane, rational, and most important of all, somewhat knowledgeable about dragons.

Bazil was pleasantly surprised as well. They'd had some difficult dragon leaders the last few years. Relkin packed some bread, filled his water bottle, and slung his bow and hunting quarrels over his shoulder. There were always rabbits on the Rack Hills.

The next day dawned cloudless. They breakfasted and set off soon after, heading west from the camp on the narrow cart track to the village of Felli. The track climbed steadily up the long straight slope of Rack Hill. They passed scrub oak and pine in clumps, with blackbirds, scrapes, and robins all in great numbers. Above circled half a dozen hawks and farther away a larger shape that might have been an eagle or a vulture.

Relkin kept his bow ready, for rabbits would be wary with the hawks above. They wouldn't show themselves for long. In good spirits they continued the climb. The trees gave way to heather and open grass. Exposed rock began to show here and there.

They reached the pass over the Rack, just below Old Baldy, the tallest of the knobs. The Roan Hills were visible across the valley. They turned south on the ridgeline trail, which wound between rock outcrops across the top of the scarp slope.

Moving through this high country, they saw occasional sheep and rabbits, but none close enough for a shot. At noon they were far south, approaching Beggars Hill. Below them were spread out Brumble Woods, Quosh Common visible just past the woods. In the distance, beyond the commons, rose the tower of the temple at Quosh, a tiny jut from where they stood.

They paused while they wolfed down bread and drank a little water. The wind brought up a soft breeze from the valley, filled with the scent of trees and grass.

"We'll go down through the dingle, then across the common. Have a beer at the Bull and Bush."

"I always like the Bull and Bush. Though I never understand the name. There is no bull there, nor any bush. The common is flat enough for boys to play football. No bush grows there without risking destruction."

"Don't ask me, Baz. I only grew up there. Nobody ever told me stuff like that. When an orphan asks questions, he doesn't usually get answers."

"Dragonboy is born with excuses coming out of mouth."

"Yeah, well I remember things coming out of mouths too. I remember when we came up here on that long day hike, on your tenth birthday."

Bazil stiffened. "I have no memory of that."

"You stuffed yourself with brackberries and then you got a bellyache."

"You didn't have to remind me of that."

"What an afternoon we had, all the way back to the village."

"Enough!" Bazil clacked his long jaws angrily.

"Yeah, enough." Relkin turned away with a smile. His eyes lifted to the Roan Hills on the far side of the valley coated with purple heather. The green valley below, the purple hills, and the distant tower of Quosh Temple all awoke memories of the former life. He had sat here many times before, but that had been before he had seen the outside world. Back then he had wanted to escape. The hills were like the bars on a cage. Now he saw them as sheltering walls, enclosing the valley so green and peaceful. Keeping it safe from the dangers that haunted the world. From here to the Ersoi they'd rambled all their young lives until they'd finally taken the Borgan Road with that contract with the baron.

That damned contract with the baron! It had turned out to be nothing but trouble, especially with those illegal trolls the baron kept. He'd thought at the time that it would make the ideal start for them in life. They'd learn on the job, make a little money and then go on to Marneri and apply for acceptance in the Legion Dragon Corps. Instead they'd had to hurry out of Borgan with the baron's imprecations at their backs. Still, once they'd got to Marneri, they'd found a place in the legions, and the rest was history.

The world had seemed a bright place back then, inviting and challenging when they'd set out from Quosh and marched up the road to Borgan. Now it seemed as if it had been in another lifetime.

"We've been around the world and back, Baz."

"We have traveled farther than this dragon ever dreamed possible."

"Doesn't seem to have changed much."

"Peaceful life down here. Glad we left."

"I wonder what old Macumber's doing."

"I too. Sat here many times with master Macumber."

"I'm sure. He always told me that you would be one of the best wyverns Quosh ever produced. Glad to say he was right."

"Eh?" Bazil swiveled a large eye to check Relkin's face. A joke?

"You are the best wyvern they ever came up with, really."

Bazil's eyes blinked. He rumbled happily in his chest.

"This dragon please to hear you think so. Dragonboy not often this kind to poor old dragon."

"I'd say old Macumber should be plenty proud of you."

More contented rumbling indicated approval of this concept.

"Seems long ago that we went up that road," said Bazil, pointing to where a line of poplars marked the Borgan Road. In the distance Kalcudy's heights loomed like a lion's head above the River Saun.

"Someday I'll have to bring Eilsa here to see this. I think she'd like it. It's not that different from Wattel Bek."

At length they stirred, they set off down the steep path that lead through the rock-strewn dingle, with its huge blocks of stone fallen from the cliff face above. In places this could only be done by climbing and working one's way through the giant puzzle of the blocks of stone.

At the bottom they left the rocks, crossed a low stone wall, and walked beneath the dark leaves of the woods. Soon they were on the lane that ran along the north side of Quosh Common. The spire of the temple was straight ahead. On their right the ground rose up to Birch farm, a cluster of whitewashed buildings on the top of the rise.

The woods thinned, and they saw across the common to the village, with its brick houses along Brennans Road, and the larger buildings farther off, such as the Blue Stone Inn. Behind the houses on Brennans Road rose up another long slope with Pigget farm at the top with its red barn.

They crossed the common. The folk of Quosh came out of their doors to stare at the wyvern battledragon, dragon sword carried in the shoulder scabbard. At the sight of the strange kink in his tail, they grew excited. Only the handful of folk who had traveled to Marneri had seen their famous Broketail dragon since he'd left to join the legions!

Children ran out in droves. The word had flickered around the village like lightning. Customers came out of the Bull and Bush, and an excited crowd soon gathered at the corner of Green Street and Brennans Road.

This was indeed the famous pair, Bazil the Broketail and Dragoneer Relkin. A general round of clapping began as the two reached the corner of the green and stepped into the street.

Rustum Bullard, a huge man with a bald red head,

emerged from the Bull and Bush with two cellar lads, hauling out a cask of ale.

Tarfoot Brandon was there, the town clown, his nose redder than ever. And there was Nurm Pigget and his brother Ivor, and Mrs. Neath, the grocer's wife, and Lorinda Keen and old Martin Pueshatter and a dozen more. The children were whirling around in ecstasies of excitement.

More and more people came running up Brennans Road as the word got out, and then came Farmer Pigget riding down from the opposite direction on his great grey gelding.

The folk began singing even as Rustum Bullard broached the keg and poured a few pints before dedicating the rest of it to the thirst of a dragon returned.

Bazil gave a great happy roar that shook the roof tiles and hoisted the keg and let the good Blue Stone ale go foaming down his throat. The crowd cheered him, Relkin was the center of a back-slapping frenzy, and the rest of the village downed tools and came out to welcome them home.

Chapter Six

Before long they were drinking the kegs dry at the Bull and Bush, and Rustum Bullard had to close up and send everyone down to the Blue Stone Inn.

There they were met by Avil Bernarbo and his family, who had hastily prepared the beginnings of a feast.

Three sides of beef had been brought up from the butcher and were set to roasting in the inn's big kitchen. Pots of meal were on to boil. The pastry man at the inn was working furiously with both his assistants to turn out a slew of cakes and tarts to cap off the meal.

A hat was passed in the inn for contributions, and everyone present gave generously. If ever there was the right time for a grand celebration, it was this night, with the return of the prodigal pair Bazil and Relkin.

Old Macumber came down from the Dragon House with his two young candidate dragons, Weft and Fury. Both were leatherbacks, though Fury had some gristle in him. They brought a wagon loaded down with stirabout and akh. Bazil lifted old Macumber up and put him on his shoulder for a round of cheers from the people. Then he toasted the new dragons.

"To the new blood in the Dragon House of Quosh."

Another roar swept the inn and the street outside, which was packed. Folks were even coming in from the farms up past Barley Mow. Word had reached Felli and Twin Streams, and folk from those villages would be down presently. The whole valley enjoyed feeling responsible for producing Bazil the Broketail.

Trestle tables were set up by Neath the grocer. Soon they were passing out plates from the inn, laden with roast beef, roast potatoes, meal porridge, and cabbage. The inn's best ale was sent around to lubricate the throats and keep the conversations roaring.

The dragons ate their dinner in the courtyard of the inn. Bazil held court in the center, and parties of the good folk of Quosh came up to visit him and wish him well. Wyvern dragons have prodigious memories—one area where they score better than men—but still he found it a little tricky, since so many people had grown up or grown old while he'd been away. Recognizing the brood of Nurm Pigget and his wife Iua was hard because they'd all shot up to be blond giants, six feet tall, with Iua's outland looks, since she was a maid of Kenor.

Everywhere it was the same. What had been babies were tall children, tall children were young adults, and those who had been adult had become white-haired in some cases. Such sights brought on a certain pang of melancholy in both Bazil and Relkin. They too had grown older, even while they'd been fighting battles all over the world. Both had a sense that their youth was slipping away, they were in the last part of their legion service now.

At some point Relkin caught Bazil's gaze, and between them there flashed the same sensation. They'd lost something, something they'd never realized they'd had. The golden years of late adolescence, which for them had been compressed entirely within the legion life and too many campaigns to want to think about.

Then the glee-club band took up their instruments and launched into the first of the classic dance tunes of Blue Stone, "The Stepper's Old Sheep." Tarfoot Brandon set down his ale pot for the first time in hours and took Verina Pigget's hand and lead her out to dance on the courtyard. Tarfoot's red nose was aglow as he did the hidy-ho with the wife of Farmer Pigget, Quosh's leading citizen.

"Oh, the stepper's old sheep, the steppers old sheep
The stepper's old sheep are they
But the stepper's old sheep, the stepper's old sheep
They're shaved real close in May."

Farmer Pigget wasn't going to stand around grumbling in such a situation. In a trice he'd found Luchea Brandon, Tarfoot's lovely young daughter, and was dancing the Stepper's Jig with her in a fine exhibition of toe-and-ankle motion. Then Lavinia Pigget and Wil Felber stepped out, along with everyone who could find a partner. By the last chorus of "The Stepper's Old Sheep," the whole center of the village was a whirling mass of dancing folk calling out with many a wild whoop and a holler.

With barely a moment for a mouthful of ale, the fiddlers stepped up again, the bagpipes came to life, and old Chester Plenth, the ostler, raised the grand old rhythm of the "Blue Stone Waltz" on the drum. And away they went again.

There was a bonfire lit in Brewery Yard, with old barrels, corn duff, and rotten wood out of the old brewery roof that Avil Bernarbo had set aside to be burned at Fundament Day. Children danced gleeful and wild around the fire while the elders stood in line, arms entwined, swaying gracefully to the ancient song of "Bluestone Hills."

"Away to the Bluestone Hills my love
Away while still we can
Away to the Bluestone Hills my love
Away with your handyman."

And so it went, and on into "La Lili La Loo," "A Fine Young Man from Marneri," "The Kadein Waltz," "Daniel Went a-courting," and even a round of "The Kenor Song," in which the dragons came in on the choruses and sent the volume up so loud you could hear it all the way to Twin Streams and more.

Then came a hammer of gongs as the pastry makers emerged from the inn, pushing out a huge cart laden with cakes, puffs, and tarts. The children converged on the cart with a collective scream of delight, and the fiddlers paused for refreshment.

Farmer Shon Pigget wiped the perspiration from his brow with a big red handkerchief and took a mug of ale in the large front room of the Blue Stone Inn. Around him gathered the informal court of the village. Tomas Birch, Avil Bernarbo, Farmer Haleham and old Macumber from the Dragon House. These were the largest producers and the largest consumers of the valley's wheat and barley.

Surrounding them were the lesser lights: Ivor Pigget, the Dorns, Farmer Tallo, Dernck Castilion, who was the proprietor of the other village inn, over at the Bridge House.

Together this informal group effectively governed the village, with reference to custom and occasionally to the Great Weal of Cunfshon, the constitutional texts that underlay the governing structures of the Argonath. Of course, matters of law were settled by the justices and matters of religion were settled by the temple.

"And so, how do you find your prodigy, Macumber?" said Farmer Pigget after he'd taken a wet.

"He has come through it all very well. The two of them make a fine team. You can see they have worked together for a long time."

"We had high hopes for them, I remember. The leatherback was quick and supple, clearly very good with the sword."

"Oh, yes, he was always good with the sword. But there was more to Bazil than just a sword fighter. He has that good soul, the very best trait of our wyverns."

"That boy was a scapegrace as a lad, but I always thought he'd make a good soldier," said Tomas Birch.

Farmer Pigget chuckled. "I seem to recall a time when you found your orchard just about stripped."

Birch pursed his lips and nodded. "I'd have taken rawhide to him if I'd have caught him that day!"

"Well, here's to them," Farmer Pigget raised his mug. "They've saved the village from legion taxes for many years now. They've served us all very well indeed."

The mugs were raised high, then drained.

For a while the talk was of more parochial things, the state of the planting after the heavy rains of the week before. Farmer Pigget was concerned about the bottom end of his main field.

"They should never have taken the elms out along the south road. It always gets muddy down there now."

"They were too old, Farmer Pigget, too old. There's young ones in there now. Give them a decade or so. It wasn't done right in your father's day." Thus spoke Farmer Haleham.

Pigget nodded at this criticism of his sire. "Aye, Haleham, I'm afraid you're right about that."

"Lukam up at Barley Mow has a wagon for sale," broke in Trader Joffi. "It's almost new, a Kadein make."

"I'm not yet ready to go buying wagons from anyone up

at Barley Mow," groused Tomas Birch, who was known for his ungenerous opinions of the nearby villages.

"It's a fine wagon. Made in the wagon shop of Postover in Kadein."

"From Lukam at Barley Mow? You've got to be joking with me."

"Not at all. By the Hand, will you listen now. It's a fine wagon, and not that old at all."

"Would you talk of the devil," said Tomas Birch, pointing as Relkin entered the front room of the inn intent on refilling his mug.

A general caw of acclaim came up from the circle in the center of the room. All around the periphery other heads turned. Relkin felt the influence of so many eyes upon him and felt that odd unease again. His recent experiences in the mad elf-city of Mirchaz had left him rawly sensitive on the psychic plane. He could feel all these people staring at him and filling him with their preconceptions, their concerns, their desires. Their hungers seemed to burn him, as if he were too close to the flames. He could not satisfy these people. He was just a dragonboy, a good one perhaps, but no more than that. Not even a dragoneer or dragon leader yet, he thought a little bitterly. What these people wanted he didn't have, no answers to their questions, no balm for their wounds. He had to wall off their thoughts to keep his own turning smoothly.

Now he was drawn into their circle and made to shake hands with all the great men of the village. He thanked them with a grave bow. In his previous life here, he'd been just an orphan boy, paired with the dragon; the dragon was far more important than he. He'd been unlettered, unschooled, raised in the orphanage and then by Macumber in the Dragon House. Macumber wasn't bad. He was stern, but kinder than he seemed on the outside. His bark was much worse than his bite. And he had a lifetime of dragon lore to impart to a dragonboy who could sit still and listen.

But it remained the fact that in the old life Relkin had been outside society's walls, wild, hardly schooled, viewed with suspicion as a potential criminal. Now things were changed. It took a bit of getting used to. They were eager to know him now, where once he'd gained no more than curt little nods from such as Farmer Pigget or Farmer Haleham. Now they were beaming at him. Now he was the hero of the hour.

He gave an internal shrug. And so he was, he acknowledged to himself. Enough of bitterness, he and Bazil had earned their night of adulation. They'd fought their way across the world and back and accounted for themselves pretty well. Relkin decided that he could take this sudden elevation in his social status as his due. After all, he and Baz were known to a few kings, queens, and elf lords, and after such lofty connections, what were a few prosperous country yeomen?

"I thank you, kind sirs. Bazil and me have seen a few knocks in our time, but you know a lot of those stories. We had the luck, or the misfortune, to be in at the cutting edge of the war on more than one occasion."

"Aye, lad, and you two were at Sprian's Ridge."

"Sprian's Ridge!" They all raised their cups in memory of the battle that had saved the Argonath.

"Well, we made it through all that, and we're glad to be back home tonight."

"We're happy to welcome you home."

"And is it true you have to return tomorrow?" said Farmer Pigget.

"No, sir, we have tomorrow in the village, and we must be back the evening of the day after."

"Splendid!" said Demck Castilion of the Bridge House Inn. "Then, will you honor the Bridge House Inn by attending a luncheon tomorrow, beginning at the First Hour."

Relkin hesitated.

"Does that include the dragon?"

There were smiles. Trader Joffi giggled when he imagined a dragon devouring the fine viands that came from the kitchen of the Bridge House Tavern.

Dernck swallowed. "The dragon is invited too, of course."

"That's wonderful. Nothing he'd like better. And I would be honored, of course, Master Castilion."

"Good, that's settled, then." Castilion glanced around the group. "And may I extend this invitation to everyone present. We will fill the ballroom for luncheon tomorrow."

There were happy shouts of acceptance. Even Pigget nodded when pressed.

"Field's too damned wet to work anyway."

"I'll be there. The kitchen at the Bridge House Inn is justly famous," said Farmer Haleham.

"Excellent." Castilion looked back to Relkin. "I must go and start the preparations. There's much to do as you might expect." He left them, and the conversation resumed.

"Well, that was a bit of a surprise," murmured Farmer Pigget.

"I'll say," said Tomas Birch. "Don't see the Bridge House Inn thrown open like that very often."

"Dernck Castilion still has the first penny he was ever given."

"Oh, will you stop that!" snapped Avil Bernarbo

"It's true," protested Joffi. "I've seen it. He keeps it nailed above the bar in the saloon at the inn."

Bernarbo blew air noisily through his teeth. "Bah."

"I had heard that rumor too," said Pigget.

"Well, 'tis true the prices are high, but the kitchen is excellent. Castilion has won the prize in Brennans three years running."

"Castilion should be running a restaurant in Marneri. Down in Blue Stone we don't pay those kind of prices."

"Ha!" snorted Joffi. "Castilion should go to Kadein. they would pay his prices there."

"Ah, prices—why do we spend our lives thinking about prices?" said Pigget.

"Aye, 'tis a rotten shame," agreed Birch. "What with the price of wool this year, we'll be lucky to put anything away."

Pigget sighed. "But wheat prices are high because of the Aubinans. That will help. We've got the makings of a grand wheat crop this year."

At this they all nodded. The Aubinans would help to keep the price of grain sky-high in Marneri this year.

"And yet that makes me feel guilty," said Birch. "We all owe the white city on the long sound a great deal. Our lives even."

Once again Sprian's Ridge rose up in their minds. The thin margin that had halted the likely destruction of their world in rapine and fire under the swarming mass of tens of thousands of imps and trolls.

"We owe the legions our lives. We owe the cities for much of our prosperity. Marneri has been a good market for our grain, enough to provide for all in our village."

"Aubinas has a short memory."

"Is Kadein behind the Aubinans?"

"No. This game is not in Kadein's favor either. The price of grain will hurt the poor in the great city."

"It makes one fear for the future of the Argonath, all this talk in Aubinas of a rebellion."

"The future must be faced, no matter what it brings."

"Whatever we do, we must try and provide for the future."

"And so we are governed by the prices of things. If we were to abandon all thought of the future, we could spend like princes."

"My wife already spends like a princess."

There was a grim chuckle.

"Ah, we all fare well enough," said Bernarbo. "The emperor is a good one, things go well in Blue Stone. We have been preserved, thanks be to the Mother."

" 'Tis correct," said Farmer Pigget. "But we must still invest in the future. There will be an issue of consols this month. Will you be taking any?"

"I am in the long bonds at the moment. I have wondered about the consols. The last issue did very well, I understand."

"Remember that it is a fine line between fair business and avarice," said Birch. "Ho ho, who preaches the temple line now?" responded Bernarbo.

"One must be careful with money," said Pigget. "You leave it in gold coins in a box under your bed? Of course not. You put it in a bank in Marneri. The bank is far more secure and is regulated by the Imperial Service. The bank can also lend out money and make a profit. We do the same when we buy bonds or consols."

"Farmer Pigget, you're absolutely right, and what we have to do is to get the wage earner, the small farmer, the small holder, even the laborer, to invest part of his wage."

"This is unlikely, they are improvident. Few see beyond the needs of the moment."

"True," said Bernarbo, "they drink their money at the bar and then complain that they were not paid enough."

"That is the way of the laboring classes . . .".

Seeing Relkin absorbed in their words, they turned to him.

"And how about you, Dragoneer Relkin," said Birch. "Have you saved your money while in the legions?"

Relkin pursed his lips.

"We have indeed, sir. We put our money in the consols, and also in the amalgamated."

"By the Hand!" exclaimed Farmer Birch.

Shon Pigget and the others merely stared, surprised at such financial sophistication from a dragonboy. Avil Bernarbo gave a hoarse chuckle.

"I see that we have a financial prodigy on our hands, gentlemen. Dragonboy Relkin, where did you learn about such matters?"

"Dragonboys are encouraged to invest their money, sir."

"Ah, this is legion policy."

"Yes, sir."

"An investor for a dragonboy! Sensational news. Well, Macumber, how d'you answer for that!"

"I've always tried to teach them careful management of their resources."

"Well, it appears to have been taken to heart by Master Relkin," said Pigget.

"Bah!" interrupted Haleham. "What about that thief Pixin? And that one last year? I forget the name. Stole a calf right out of my barn."

"They're more thieves than investors these days!" said Birch.

"What about this lad Pixin, Macumber? Caught stealing apples. Now it's candles. What next, gold?" Bernarbo pressed.

"They aren't bad at heart, Master Bernarbo. They just don't receive very much in their lives. Little in the way of comforts, small change, not much love."

"Bah, Macumber, you mollycoddle them down there. Don't try and tell me different."

"Avil's right," chipped in Birch. "Five dragon boys in five years, sent to jail for theft in the village. It's got to stop, Macumber."

They had forgotten Relkin for the moment. He turned away and found himself face-to-face with Farmer Pigget.

"You know, we came up to Marneri for your funeral, lad."

Relkin smiled politely. He'd heard all about his funeral,

held at the memorial service that dedicated the monument to the fallen on the expedition to Eigo.

"I'm sorry you had to go so far for nothing."

"Don't be. It was good for us all to be there. The country came together then. Aubinans stood with the rest of us. It's easy for us to forget, kept safe and sound in this lovely land, that we owe our safety to the heroism of boys like yourself, and dragons like the Broketail."

"I thank you for your words, Farmer Pigget," said Relkin.

"And I was especially glad to hear that we were wrong to have written you off. We should've known that the Broketail and his dragonboy would survive somehow, even on the dark continent."

"Well, it was close, I can assure you. I called on the old gods, though I don't know whether they still listen."

"Ach, you young devil," said Tomas Birch. "Put away those ancient gods. The goddess is all there is. All there ever has been."

"So they say, Farmer Birch," said Farmer Pigget. "But whatever it was, whether the gods or the goddess, they brought our prodigies home, and we are thankful!"

They drank to that.

Chapter Seven

Relkin would have slipped away, but Ivor Pigget insisted on a toast in his honor, and they drank it off. Then Trader Joffi suggested a toast in honor of the 109th Marneri Dragons! And they drank that off too.

"Some day, young Master Relkin, I'd like to talk with you about what you plan to do come retirement," said Farmer Pigget.

"No secrets there, sir. We plan to retire in Kenor and take up land grants. I even know where."

Pigget chuckled. "Remarkable. And your investments, they will help you there."

"We plan to buy as much as we can afford. Land is still not expensive in the Bur Valley. The soil is good, but there's no way to ship downstream yet. It's still wilderness there, so we will clear land and supply the hill tribes with wheat and barley. They can only grow oats on the fells."

"You've thought it all out, have you?" said Pigget.

"Well, sir. I happen to know that there's a plan to put in an Imperial chute system on the Bur. Take heavy goods quickly down the rapids at the Lion's Roar."

"Oh-ho, and so you'd be sitting pretty . . ."

"We hope so."

"Have you thought about taking a wife, Dragoneer Relkin?" said Haleham.

"Oh yes, Farmer Haleham. In fact, I am affianced. With a young lady of fine family in the south of Kenor."

"Oh, are you now? Well, well, and might we know the young lady's name?"

"Surely, Farmer. 'Tis Eilsa Ranardaughter of Clan Wattel."

"The clan that stood at Sprian's Ridge?"

"The same, sir. Eilsa was there that day. She fought beside her father to the end."

Farmer Haleham's eyes grew round as he listened to this.

Just then there came a commotion at the door, and the Pawler brothers burst in. They were huge men, with wild hair and wild expressions, their skin reddened from a life spent on the hillsides with the sheep. Ham Pawler and his even huger brother Roegon stood in front of the bar. Ham was distraught, there were the marks of tears on his face.

"Something's been worryin' the sheep!" he hissed. His eyes were filled with pain.

"By the Mother's Hand, but it's terrible up there," said brother Roegon.

"What has happened?" said Pigget.

"Forty, fifty dead, just torn to pieces."

"Torn? Not cut?"

"Torn, twisted, as if they were killed by giants, maybe trolls."

There was a collective intake of breath. Feral trolls had long been feared in Blue Stone, ever since the Baron of Borgan had employed some on his property. Some had run off up into the hills back then, and not all had been recaptured.

"Mother preserve us."

"The dogs?"

"Gone. Not a trace."

"That is weird. It'd be a quick troll that could catch a dog."

"I left my dogs, Tonko and Trot, up there last night. Good hounds, will kill a wolf if it comes too close. But they were gone today."

"Off chasing wolves?" said Tomas Birch.

The Pawlers frowned and shook their heads.

"The Borgan pack sometimes roams this far south," said Farmer Haleham.

"We've not heard from them in years," protested Pigget.

"There's a pack in the Ersoi," said Ham Pawler, "but we've not had trouble with them in many a long year either. This is new, and I don't think it's wolves. They'd never take the trouble to kill so many."

"Are trolls that avid?" said Bernarbo.

"Who can say?" replied Haleham. "Who has studied the creatures?"

"Not me, that's for sure," said Trader Joffi

"Not an occasion for mirth, Trader," murmured Pigget.

"By no means, Farmer, by no means."

"Come," Pigget was decisive, as he generally was. "There's no help for it, even with our two prodigies celebrating their return, we shall have to rouse ourselves. We must look into this at once. I will fetch my hounds. Birch, will you bring yours?"

Birch nodded and set his ale pot down.

"Call the constable," Pigget directed Benarbo. "We should send word down to Brennans tonight. Let the sheriff know and get out the alarm across the hills."

"I'll send my boy Lenott, he has a fine horse."

"My apologies, Dragoneer Relkin, I hate to leave at this point when there's still some dancing to be done, but this matter does sound rather serious. I'm sure you would agree."

Farmer Pigget set down his glass and left the inn.

In ones and twos the others soon left as well, and Relkin was finally set free to take his mug, refill it, and slip back into the big inner courtyard, where the dragons had dined. They were still sitting there in a happy circle, drinking from a keg of mild ale. From the sound of it they were gossiping. Relkin smiled fondly at the sight. Bazil was now the acknowledged champion of the legions, and he was overdue some company with his kin and old friends. Bazil and he had been through some hard times together. Relkin hoped this celebration was a taste of the sort of life they would eventually live. Just a few more years, and they'd be free.

Relkin quietly climbed the outdoor steps that lead up to the first-floor gallery. Out in the street was the roar of the party, down below in the kitchens and saloon room there was further noise, but up here it was cool and peaceful.

Relkin scratched his face, stretched his leg muscles. It was a moment for reflection. Here in the old village there was the illusion of safety in a normal world. Here was everything that he'd left behind when he joined the legions. But Relkin knew too well that the illusion rested on the strength of the Imperial Legions. And he also knew that he and Baz didn't belong here anymore, not really. They were battle-hardened veterans, indeed they were heroes. For some reason this thought didn't mean as much as he might have expected. You could be a hero and still have a stomachache. He was still Relkin of Quosh, still just an orphan boy with no one in the world except that big dragon over there. He was still the same person he'd always been.

Or was he? He felt a little shiver of unease. Since the last days of Mirchaz, since that strange and terrifying experience as the anointed agent of the Mind Mass, he had had to face the thought that perhaps he wasn't who he thought he was. Something had stirred within him that he didn't understand, and it might lead him to places far from anywhere he wanted to be.

One day he'd tried to will a strand of hay to move by his thought alone. Of course, nothing had happened. He had no magic powers. Only . . . right at the end, when he was about to give it up, he thought he saw the blade of straw give a shiver and twitch.

The wind, of course, it was just the wind. Except there was no wind that day.

He felt that shivery cold feeling again. That way lay the path to sorcery, and everything he'd seen about sorcery had shown him that it was dangerous and corrupting and led men to become most foul and hateful. One would start off doing only good. Being just and kind to the world, a good wizard Relkin. But then would come the thirst for power and control over whole worlds, and with that would come the corruption of the heart until all was black and stinking and dead inside.

He wanted none of it. He spat on the step as if to exorcise the thought, then sipped his ale. The Grey Lady had gone into retirement. Things were relatively quiet on the military front. With a little luck, maybe he would be spared any further exposure to the eerie world of magic.

That turned his thoughts away to Eilsa, and the Clan Wattel. He'd hoped for a posting in the Lis Valley, or Dalhousie at least. From there he could hope to visit Wattel Bek once in a while and work at demonstrating to Eilsa's family that he was more than just a dragonboy.

After Mirchaz, he and the dragon were set up pretty well with gold. Part of it was banked, part of it was hidden, and one way or another they were both set for a good life in retirement when their legion contract expired. Gold wouldn't make all the problems of life disappear, but it sure made them easier to bear.

During their four months of special leave, Bazil and Relkin had spent time with the Wattels, and he was more keenly aware than ever of the peculiarities of their position. Eilsa remained Ranardaughter and had to perform her function in the clan, until she was wed. The pressures on her to wed within the clan were strong, but so far she had fended them off and remained true to Relkin. Others in the clan were obviously unhappy about this.

Eilsa had made no demands on him, nor quizzed him overmuch about his adventures on the dark continent. She had seen that there had been a great change in him, he had been exposed to things that had altered him forever. And yet there was still the feeling between them. That had always been there since that first moment they'd met, on the fells near the Bek. One day they would be together, somehow.

Relkin sat there quietly until the dragons finished their keg. They lifted their huge bodies and moved off to their beds at Macumber's Dragon House. Bazil shifted to a bed of straw that had been made for him in the stables, and Relkin joined him there for a sound night's sleep. Relkin had been offered the best room in the inn, but a dragonboy never leaves his dragon.

Chapter Eight

In the late afternoon of the following day, there came an astonishing sight on the road to Ryotwa, just seven miles southwest of Quosh. With hooves and wheels rumbling, a swift moving column of cavalry surrounded two sleek coaches, each drawn by a team of eight horses. A string of sixty spare horses brought up the rear. Everything about the column spoke of speed and haste.

First came a pair of scouts, men in grey mouse skin with visored caps riding fiery grey horses, a breed known as Talion Runners. Then pounding along at a steady trot were twelve troopers from a crack Kadein cavalry regiment in green field uniforms, flat black hats and boots. Behind them came a dozen other men, in soft greys and blacks, who just by a certain presence in voice and manner gave hint that they were dangerous. All rode superbly, as well as the troopers. These were the private guard of the Emperor of the Rose, Pascal Iturgio Densen Asturi.

In the center of the column came the two coaches, jet-black, with curtains at the windows. A driver and guard rode on top. The teams kept up a steady quick trot that ate up the miles between Kadein and Ryotwa.

In the leading coach the emperor had put his feet up on a cushion on the front seat and was looking out the window in a relaxed manner. The countryside here was charming. The late afternoon sun had bathed everything in a golden glow. Neat fields of green, tidy woodlots, and occasional stone-built farmhouses covered the lower ground. The use of poplars to line the roads gave many intriguing quirks of perspective to the landscape.

The emperor enjoyed the view and went over in his thoughts the events of the last few days. Things had gone well. He had arrived in the Argonath quite suddenly, with just three days notice of his arrival. This was by careful design. In the city of Kadein, the greatest of the nine cities of the Argonath, he had ridden in state up the Grand Avenue and then greeted the crowds from the balcony at the palace. King Neath and the Kadeini royal family held a grand dinner and ball in his honor, all organized at short noticed by the king's impeccable staff. He had gone on daylong rides through the provinces surrounding Kadein including Arneis, where he had visited the battlefield on Sprian's Ridge, which had become a shrine of sorts. He had then visited the smaller city of Minuend and toured its fruitful provinces before swinging back through Kadein for one more parade in state. He then made a secretive exit for the next city on his Imperial Progress through the Argonath.

Everywhere he'd received the same ecstatic response, instinctive and openhearted. The surprise of his sudden visit seemed to bring out the best in the folk of the Argonath. In their hearts they knew full well that the Empire of the Rose underlay the success of the great cities, even that of Kadein, which had become by far the greatest of them. The emperor was sometimes thought of as remote, a distant figure always demanding more for the war effort in distant lands. But here he was, among the people, moving out to greet them and speak to them as if he were one of them, truly an emperor with the common touch. The Empire of the Rose was a new thing in the history of the world, an empire that was not imposed from the beginning by conquest. The emperor was showing them that not only did he claim to feel their pain, but he was here among them in person. Pascal had found the experience uplifting. The feelings of fear and delusion he'd suffered in the past had faded. It was good to get out and walk among the people and share a mug of ale with them in the town squares.

Among the nobility too he had found a healthy, goodhearted response. Of course there were the holdouts, like those who wanted independence for Arneis, but for the moment these had been thrown back on the defensive. Their grumpy faces were hardly noticed among the joyous crowds.

While the Emperor toured Arneis, the Imperial Party made sure that the benefits of belonging to the empire were enumerated to the common people. They had no vote except in local elections of mayors and sheriffs, but their broad opinion was in the end vital in the equations of power.

Many people were aware that the empire restrained the power of the wealthy merchants of Arneis, a group that thirsted for vast riches and influence. The common folk were apprehensive when they thought of this small group taking Arneis into independence.

In the gloom-ridden aftermath of the mission to Eigo, where so many men had died, such things had been forgotten. The divisive campaign for independence had gained influence. Now Pascal was doing something to restore morale to the other side of the argument. He contented himself with the thought that it was a much better approach than just sitting out there at Andiquant, safe but remote.

In the second coach rode the three grey muses, as Pascal liked to call them. Clad in black cloth was the man Wysse, who had been Pascal's secretary for a decade. His eyes perpetually mournful, like some overgrown bloodhound, his hands always ink-stained, Wysse was a man of documents. Next to him rode Doctor Orta, a round-faced man who wore white robes with the grey stripe of the Office of Insight. Orta was fanatically devoted to the health of the emperor. Everything that Pascal did had to be monitored and evaluated and inspected and carefully considered. Orta was the man of the vegetables.

Finally there was the slender woman of indeterminate middle age with lank white hair cut to her shoulders. Her pale complexion and grew eyes matched the uniformly grey shift, tunic, and shawl that she wore. She sat on the other seat and looked out the window, lost in thought. She was Lessis of Valmes, the Grey Lady, a Great Witch of Cunfshon. She was known to be more than five hundred years old. Lessis was the woman who brought heartaches, at least to the Emperor Pascal.

The outriders clattered into the small village of Sunder.

There was a knock at the emperor's window. Commander Grant was there, leaning down, earnest concern on his face.

"Your Majesty, this is a small village about a mile or so from Cailonne. The water here is very good. I suggest we change horses here, rather than in Cailonne."

"Good. We'll stop here a moment, then."

The emperor stepped down. All around him, at a distance, a screen of hard-faced men in grey and black moved purposefully about the village, their eyes peeled for the slightest sign of danger.

The occupants of the other carriage got down too. Wysse and Orta seemed a little stiff, but Lessis moved with a light spring and a playful jump that belied her age.

The emperor pulled his purple cloak around him, and strode out on the open ground in front of the village's only inn. He gazed off up the road, which wound away with a curve to the northeast. To the right loomed the purple hills of Ersoi, a wild and rugged area that was once famous for bandits. To the left, a pair of curiously round hills hummocked up from the fertile green valley bottom. Everything was clothed in golden late afternoon haze. He sighed with pleasure. At last he was beginning to feel like himself again.

There was a cloud on the horizon, however. He was aware of her presence, he always was. Without turning around he spoke.

"We will continue through the night. When do you think we'll reach Ryotwa?"

"By late morning, perhaps by the tenth hour."

"There! We will have gone from Kadein to Ryotwa in two days. The speed of a courier! I told you we could do it."

Lessis did not respond. Pascal continued to admire the round hills that glowed in the evening sun. The forests on their upper slopes were lit up with golden light.

"The country here is splendid, is it not?"

"This is Blue Stone, Your Majesty, famous for its natural beauty and its dragons." Pascal pointed off to the right. "There are the Ersoi Hills, am I correct?"

"Indeed, sir."

Pascal swung around. Wysse and Orta were out of sight. The worn horses were removed from the shaft and fresh horses were being lead up from the string. Beyond the horses the hills were a series of purple masses, dark beneath the setting sun.

"Tomorrow Ryotwa. We will tour the palace with the king and greet the people from the balcony. Before our enemies can even begin to organize anything against us, we will be finished there and ready to move on."

Lessis nodded. "Of course, Your Majesty."

Local people, led by the village mayor, were gathering

to meet the emperor. Pascal roused himself. With a smile and a firm handshake, he dove in among them. Now was the opportunity for the people to see and speak with their emperor. To see that he was a genuine person, who understood their lives and their troubles.

He clutched at their hands, kissed a proffered baby, hugged an old woman who brought him a glass of wine, and greeted as many as possible with a personal smile and a nod.

A few minutes later he extricated himself, while the men in grey and black watched with flinty eyes, and returned to his coach. He signaled for Lessis to join him.

With joyful waves to the astounded locals, they rolled out of Sunder and down the road.

"We are to dine in Cailonne. Apparently the food here is very good."

"The ale is famous throughout the land, Your Majesty."

A silence fell over them.

"Well? I sense your disapproval, Lady."

"Your Majesty, I have been troubled since this progress began. I will continue to be troubled until it is over."

"And as chief of your office, I suppose that is to be expected. Still . . ." He gestured vaguely out the window.

Couldn't she see that they were succeeding by boldness? Here they were, pounding down the highway, actually ahead of the news of their coming. What could be more secure than that?

"I thought we did rather well in Kadein. Didn't you think things went well there?"

"They did, Your Majesty. Undoubtedly there will be new heart in the forces of the governing party. King Neath will survive. Perhaps the grain factors can be turned back."

Pascal nodded at her words, a smile of satisfaction creased his face.

"There, doesn't that sound like a job well-done? This visit was necessary! After Eigo the wound was deep."

"Still, Your Majesty, treachery could have come at any moment. As it was, I doubt that our security was good enough to completely mask our departure from Kadein."

"We travel as fast as any messenger, unless they've taken to riding those bat things."

"There are other ways of sending messages, Your Majesty."

"The grain factors are not sorcerers, Lady."

"They are wealthy. Not all sorcerers are so blessed."

He threw up his hands. "If I were to listen to you witches, there would come a point at which we would become so scared of our own shadow that we would not dare to go outside."

Lessis smiled. He had a point. The emperor was still vigorous, chafing against the restraints of his position. It was up to her, once again, to play the sorry old voice of caution. She sighed inwardly. Retirement seemed far away now. She missed thinking about simple things, like the health of her pear tree, or the rabbit that was raiding her lettuces. Now all that had been snatched away, and she was back in the eye of the hurricane, riding beside the emperor himself, sick with worry.

"Of course, Your Majesty. This progress through the cities is good politics. And in other times it would not concern me nearly so much."

"You cling to the thought that we are in deadly danger."

"We have had information of a disturbing nature. You know what I'm speaking of."

The Emperor Pascal frowned and looked out the window.

"The concepts are difficult, hard to believe perhaps."

"But true, nonetheless. The situation is unclear, and highly volatile. We have a new enemy, a shadowy foe who will not reveal himself until his victory is assured. He has forged some kind of alliance with the Four Masters still in Padmasa. He is a known master of the arts of manipulation. He will seek to ignite civil wars and internecine struggles among his enemies. On many worlds he is called the Deceiver. On others simply the Dominator."

"What motivates such a monster?"

"There are great mysteries here, that hark back to the very beginning of the world. This one was sent to infuse spirit in the world, but failed his duty. The thirst for power can be very strong, Your Majesty. It can unhinge even the greatest minds."

They clattered over a bridge into a small town.

"Where are we?" Pascal called up to the driver.

"This be Cailonne, Your Majesty. Next town is Brennans."

"And what do they do in Cailonne?"

"They grow barley and wheat here, sir," said the guard. "The ale is good too."

"We shall stretch our legs here, and perhaps take a quaff of the famous ale."

They pulled up. The market square in Cailonne was dominated by the red brick Hotel Cailonne. Out of the carriage, Lessis walked behind the emperor, allowing the bodyguards free rein. The emperor never moved, but he was covered by two or three men at all times. A pair of archers stood behind the carriage and scrutinized the upper windows all around the square.

Pascal, who was not oblivious to all of this, was determined to meet the people. Word had already flashed through the village that some very important personage had suddenly pulled up in the market square with thirty men, two carriages, and a huge string of spare horses.

He strode through the crowds as men went ahead proclaiming the presence of the emperor, Pascal the Great.

Outside the Hotel Cailonne he was greeted by the manager, the mayor of the town, and several prosperous farmers. A silver mug of the best ale was brought out on a silver tray, and the emperor ostentatiously drank it and called for another. There was a roar of applause. Meanwhile Secretary Wysse paid for a round of ale for everyone present, and a cheer went up.

A quick meal of cold meat, fresh bread, and steamed vegetables was produced in a few minutes from the kitchen of the Hotel Cailonne. The emperor dined with the mayor of the town and twelve of the leading citizens and their wives. Pascal did not stand on Imperial protocol. With the first clink of the ale pots, he told them to treat him as one of themselves, to tell him what they really thought of things.

To some extent they actually went for it, and for half the hour they spoke of their fears concerning the Aubinans, and their sorrow after the Eigo campaign. Two men from Cailonne had gone to Eigo and not returned.

Pascal nodded somberly. His hair had gone from black to grey the night he'd sat up with the casualty lists from Eigo. He paid his respects to the fallen and explained that the mission to Eigo had been vital to save the world. In their eyes he saw the sorrow give way for a moment to a broader understanding.

As the emperor headed back to his coach, he fell in alongside Ambassador Koring of Ryotwa, a short, distinguished-looking man, who even at the age of fifty-five could still ride a horse all day and night.

"Join us, Koring, until we reach the next town."

"Of course, Your Majesty."

Koring signaled for his horse to be tied to the emperor's coach and climbed aboard. At the sight of the witch, he swallowed and licked his lips. She stared out the other window after giving him a cool nod. She would listen but not participate.

Koring was a man with little direct knowledge of the Imperial witches. He had met other witches, of course, but they were not reputed to be able to turn themselves into animals, or to fly like a bat under the full moon like these Great Witches. It was said they were immortal and had lived for centuries. People whispered that their appearance was a fraud, that they were actually hideous, ancient, withered mummies wrapped in fell magic. Koring shivered. In Ryotwa the witches lived quietly, and contented themselves with the work of fields and family. They did not surround the king and his court as they were rumored to do in some cities.

The emperor sat heavily on his seat, looking forward. His face was flushed. He had been in a shell for months following the news of Eigo. Now he was breaking out again, seizing the initiative and regaining his grip.

The horses were whipped up, and the coach began to roll. Pascal waved to the crowd in the square outside the Hotel Cailonne. Then the town was behind them, and they rolled out into the darkened countryside.

The moon had not yet risen, the stars were shining bright.

"We'll be in Ryotwa tomorrow morning, Ambassador, so let us go over the political situation there once again. King Ronsek is a fierce old fellow. I expect he'll try my patience."

Koring laughed tightly. It was all too likely.

"Well, Your Majesty, the king is very keen to have a decision on laying the keels on two new white ships. The builder yards in Ryotwa are in need of the work."

"Yes, of course. Wysse has kept me informed of this matter. The keels will be laid in Ryotwa, as promised. The money for them has been a little hard to find, that is all. Remember that there are a great many projects for the empire to take on. Wherever we can, we seek to improve transport, sanitation, irrigation, throughout the realms of the Argonath as well as on the Isles themselves. All across Kenor we're putting in basic engineering for the new towns that are springing up there."

"That is wonderful news, Your Majesty, the king will be overjoyed. The matter of the keels had preyed on his mind lately."

The coach rolled swiftly on into the night.

Chapter Nine

The miles rolled past, and the country outside grew wilder. Ambassador Koring did his utmost not to drone on and on, but it was difficult. The emperor asked such exacting questions, requiring such detail, that it was necessary to answer at length. Koring was surprised, then amazed, and finally awed by the emperor's appetite for knowledge and his ability to remember detail while piecing together the complex picture of Ryotwan politics.

Koring also concluded that when it came to the dominant problem of the day, the movement for secession in Aubinas, the emperor was exceptionally well-informed. Emperor Pascal clearly lived up to his reputation as a most formidable sovereign.

"Ryotwa is a small city, Your Majesty, and Ryotwans are simple folk. We lean toward the sea. We look out across the world, where our white ships sail. Our Ship Builders Guild sees a threat from the Aubinan grain magnates, for more expensive grain will lead to less shipping. It's as simple as that with them. But this simplicity is modulated by another feeling, which is our envy of Marneri."

The emperor was nodding. Encouraged, Koring continued.

"Consider how powerful Marneri has grown. She has great provinces, Aubinas just the richest of them. Look at Ryotwa with only the bare bones of Rueda, Selceda and Lacustra. Places of rock and wind, where fishing villages cling to the coastline and potato patches fill the scant fields. Many Ryotwans think Marneri could afford to let the Aubinans go. They think that Marneri could be improved by being reduced in size and power."

The emperor nodded slowly. "Kadein is even mightier

than Marneri, but it is toward Marneri that they cast their anger, not Kadein."

"Ryotwa has barely a tenth of the population of Kadein. To us there can be no competition. Instead we focus our envy on Marneri. It is not a charitable trait in our people, I fear."

"Indeed, Ambassador, it is something we must overcome. Ryotwa and Vo are the smallest city-states in land area, but they serve our cause well, nonetheless. Their folk have always been sailors, and they maintain strong links with the folk of the Isles."

"Absolutely, Your Majesty. Between Ryotwa and Cunfshon there is greater traffic than with any city other than Kadein. Many of our leading families have their roots in the Isles, more than in any other city, I believe. This, in part, is what drives our animus against Marneri. Ryotwans feel somewhat separate from the rest of the Argonath. We are linked to Cunfshon and the oceans rather than to Kenor and the western lands."

"In Cunfshon they hold Ryotwa in high regard. The 'trusty' city they call you. Ryotwa with its grey stone towers across the sea, the eternal friend of Cunfshon."

"Long may our two cities reign over the Bright Sea that lies between them."

The emperor pressed his hands together. "And so, the opinion of the people is against Marneri, rather than in favor of the secessionists of Aubinas."

"Yes, Your Majesty. Ryotwa feels independent in its own way, and we see Marneri as too overweening. On the other hand, there is no great love here for the grain factors, and it is widely understood that it is the grain factors who really seek independence for Aubinas. Still, things are seen through the prism of our dislike of the arrogance of Marneri."

"And thus King Ronsek must seem to maintain neutrality of a sort."

"Certainly, yes, Your Majesty. The king will tell you himself that he wishes he could be more publically supportive of Marneri. He believes, however, that he must strike a carefully modulated tone of neutrality in the struggle. Ryotwa has historically sided with attempts to break up the provincial structures of the nine ruling cities. Ryotwa never received its fair share of lands. Blue Stone, for instance, should be part of Ryotwa, but it turns to Marneri instead, although Marneri is five days' journey from here. Thus our king must hew to that tradition; it is expected of him."

"Yes, of course, the web of tradition is a necessary part of our civilization. Still, innovation can be just as rewarding sometimes. Perhaps this will prove to be an opportunity to press for change. Ryotwa believes itself slighted by the greater glory of Marneri, which outshines all the other cities, even Kadein. Oh, Kadein is the big city, the cosmopolis of the empire, but Marneri is the heart of our great enterprise in the Argonath. And let us make no mistake, Ambassador, for I know you are a perceptive man, it is Marneri that carries the banner of the empire. Marneri that has given the most and fought the hardest. Now, that said, Ryotwa too has given in generous measure of her resources. I have sailed in Ryotwan ships, and there are none finer.

"Still, the glory has shone on Marneri so much in recent times that folk in Ryotwa have succumbed to envy. We are all but mere men and women, making our way through the world as best we can with the guidance of the Mother's Hand. We can do no more than that. Envy is ignoble, but we are weak. We can do no better.

"But we can try! Damn it all, we can still try! We can ask Ryotwans to confront this feeling in their hearts. We can say, stop for a moment and think of what Marneri has given to our sacred cause. For you and I know, Ambassador, that no other city has given so much from such a small population. They have raised two legions, and built almost as many great ships as Ryotwa! And those legions of theirs have handled more than their share of the fighting."

Koring had to agree. "True, Your Majesty, I know, but the people have their prejudices."

"The people can be challenged. Their prejudice is ignoble and beneath their dignity. We shall encourage them to try and rise above it."

The emperor smiled and folded his arms across his chest.

"If the people of Aubinas seriously wanted independence, then I would work to give it to them. Let us be clear. The strength of our empire rests on its elasticity. We must rule with flexibility. No great province should remain bound to a city if it feels it would be better off independent. Provinces should love their capital city. The capitals must love the empire. That is the only way we can be different from any other power in the world. That is the only way we can hope to defeat our monstrous enemy in Padmasa.

"But it is not the people of Aubinas who wish independence. It is the grain magnates. They have whipped up every grievance they could find, and still they have support from no more than one third of the people. The rest are terrified. The grain magnates wish to free themselves from Imperial controls. They would like to hold grain off the market and force up prices. I can have no sympathy for them. In a time of war, with our very existence constantly threatened by the power in Padmasa, we cannot indulge their desire for further augmentation of their wealth."

"Your Majesty will be pleased to know that in Ryotwa there is a significant group that shares your thinking. The Ship Builders Guild is with you, of course, but so are others with less obvious interests at stake. Opinion can be swayed."

"Exactly, my dear Ambassador Koring. This progress is long overdue. I think we can reawaken the people's understanding of our real problems. They will see that we love them, that we come among them to show them that we are men, as they are, but men working all their lives in their service. That it is service which is the spirit of the empire. We show them that, and they will turn back the minions of the grain magnates."

Eventually, however, even Pascal Iturgio Densen Asturi had had enough of political talk. He thanked Koring and sent him back out to ride his horse. Pascal drew the curtains and put his feet up on the farther cushion and went to sleep with a brief prayer.

Lessis remained silent in the corner. Her thoughts were far away, reviewing what she remembered from a chilling visit to a house in the suburbs of Cunfshon. Ribela had sent her to meet with a prince and princess from the western lands, by name Evander and Serena. They brought a grim warning and spoke a name that had not darkened the air of Ryetelth in many an aeon, the name of the Deceiver, the Dominator of Twelve Worlds, Waakzaam the Great.

The house they'd been given was a pleasant, two-story place, built of the grey stone they built everything with in Cunfshon. There was an herb garden and a curving drive up to the front steps.

A curious little man, a midget no more than three feet tall, had met her at the door. It had been an astonishing experience, she grinned at the memory. He had been immaculate, hairless, with a noble set of fine features. He moved like a dancer, and he treated Lessis very rudely, remarking in a loud voice that she had no business coming to the front door of the house, since she was dressed like a servant and should go to the servants' entrance to be let in. Vexed, she had responded with a spell and discovered that it was hard to keep it in place. The little man was a magical construct of quite fantastic power. Awed just a little, Lessis had given up any attempt at reining it in. She had to explain twice who she was and what she wanted. The amazing tiny man had then made her wait in the hall while he disappeared to find Prince Evander.

Fortunately for Lessis, Princess Serena appeared after a few minutes, having been warned by someone else that there was a visitor in the hall. She explained to Lessis that the servant was an unusual little person, much older than he looked and very cranky. Lessis had accepted the explanation and passed off his rudeness with a laugh. Her awe had given way to intrigue. How had these young princelings from Kassim come to possess such a fantastic creature for a servant anyway?

The princess, a laughing brown-skinned girl with handsome eyes, led her down a passage of polished brick, through a small garden, and into a pleasant whitewood room that looked out over a pond covered with lily pads.

The room was furnished in lovely old wooden things from the Cunfshon Foresters workshops. On the wall was a painting by one of the famous Czardhan painters, possibly Giltoft.

The prince had been working on a watercolor of the paddies and the pond. It rested on an easel to one side. Lessis could see that the prince had some skill with the brush.

They had sat there, while a more cooperative servant came in with some hot kalut and a selection of small cakes. The prince and the princess had then told their story.

In a few moments her long-dreamed-of retirement had been laid to rest. Such a mad saga was related that she was by turns torn by sadness, ripped by pity, and then left frightened, more afraid than she had been in a long time.

Swayed by the rhythmic motion of the coach, Lessis murmured a prayer to the Great Mother for her guidance and put her head back and let sleep claim her. The coming day would be another nightmare as the emperor put himself about in the city of Ryotwa. Security would be fragile, an assassin might strike at any moment, Lessis would be on duty all day. Some sleep now would be a good investment.

Chapter Ten

Sleep ended with a sudden eruption of noise. A tremendous crack broke along the bottom of the coach. It came to a staggering stop amid a mad tangle of rearing and screaming horses, and the emperor pitched off his seat with a muffled curse. A fierce green light beat down from the sky above them. Lessis noticed that it threw stark shadows, even inside the coach. Men were shouting all around them.

"What the hell is this!" roared an enraged Pascal as he struggled to extricate himself from the space between the seats. Wide-eyed in apprehension, Lessis opened the door, her other hand resting on the long knife hidden within her robe. The light shone down on them as if from a giant's lantern. Arrows flashed past, she heard them distinctly through the rest of the noise. Then, ten yards distant, she glimpsed things approaching at a lumbering run, huge creatures like nothing she had ever seen before. At first glimpse they looked like bears, but then she noticed they had human heads with faces like those of pigs. One of them was clearly carrying a sword.

She pulled back. Questions crowded in her thoughts. Was this a new kind of troll? And how was the light projected? And from where? She looked up for a moment into a blinding dazzle that shone down from nearby rocks. Then she shut the door again and turned back to the emperor.

The other side!

He needed no more warning. Opening his door, they tumbled quickly out.

There was fighting all around them, more screams, the ring of steel on steel. Men rode past at the gallop. The driver of the coach fell in front of Lessis with a thud; an arrow jutted up from his throat.

The emperor had his short sword out and ready. Pascal had drilled every week for most of his life in anticipation of an emergency like this. He was ready to fight. Lessis, however, was only concerned with getting away. She knew that this ambush had to be by an overwhelming force; nothing else would have been contemplated by their enemies. They had to hide, then make an escape from the scene.

And how was that damned light projected? It was so bright, it hurt the eyes and threw shadows far away across the moor.

Just then the coach rocked under a terrific, crunching blow. The next moment it was turned over. The horses screamed as they struggled in their harness. Lessis tugged on the emperor's arm, who came, unwillingly. The bearlike things were smashing the coach with huge hammers. The blazing light made them seem like giant men, burly-chested with fierce, hog-like features.

A trooper spurred forward and thrust his lance home into one of the monsters. It coughed angrily, bent double, and dropped to its knees. Imps came out of the dark to thrust spears into the trooper when his horse pulled up. He screamed and tumbled, and the imps swarmed over him. The hammers continued to smash the coach. If anyone had been inside, they would have been broken like an egg.

More imps came screaming past, bandy-legged imitations of men, wielding swords and round shields, products of an evil magic. The emperor ducked a blow, whacked an imp to the ground with his shoulder, and then stabbed down with his sword to end it. Another was about to attack the emperor from behind when Lessis thrust her knife into its back. It gasped, straightened, and then sagged. She toppled it away from herself.

Two of the emperor's guards, Thorn and Blade, had materialized beside them, with swords drawn and eyes bright. Blade was a giant, a head taller than most men, exuding strength. More imps came up but were almost instantly slain.

For a moment there was an empty space around them.

"Run!" said Lessis.

The emperor stared at her hard-faced, eyes questioning her tone.

"Your Majesty, you must not die here. To those rocks, we have to get away."

Pascal's eyes were wild, and his mind filled with dangerous thoughts, but Lessis's words struck home. The empire could not afford to lose its emperor at this crucial moment in history. He had to accept the need for self-preservation above all else.

"Where?" he croaked.

A trooper shrieked behind them as one of the bearlike things ripped his head from his body.

"That way, to the rocks!"

Lessis almost tripped over a rope set at knee-height across the road. There were more, arranged down the road. So that was how the coach had been brought to such a dead stop. These huge creatures had pulled the ropes up under the coach as it rolled by. The horses had fallen, the wheels had jammed.

A dismounted trooper ran by, blood running down his face. His forehead was cut wide open, to the bone; the blood had stained his vest bright red. Pascal put out a hand to steady him. The trooper's look flashed wide in recognition.

"Your Majesty," he exclaimed, and fell in beside them.

They slipped farther away, out of the pool of light. The main body of imps had missed them in the confusion. Lessis glanced back. The coaches had been smashed to flinders, and there was still fighting up and down the road. About a hundred feet above the scene on the opposite slope among the rocks, several figures crouched around the source of the powerful light.

She slipped into the bushes with the others.

"Up here," said Thorn, indicating the darkness beyond. "There is a gulley deep enough for us to hide in."

Brush cloaked the ground along the gulley, and they stole away quickly up the rocky slope and were soon out of view from the ambush site.

"Quickly," whispered Thorn. "There's a way up the hill here."

"What were those things?" asked the emperor.

"I have no idea, Your Majesty. I have never seen anything like them."

"Where are we, then? Anyone have any idea?"

"This is Capbern's Gap, Your Majesty," said the trooper with the bloody head. "Brennans town is a few miles away. The town of Quosh is over there."

"Quosh, did you say?"

"Yes, Lady. I believe that is what it's called."

Lessis nodded, as if this knowledge confirmed something of great import.

"They meant to kill us by crushing the coach with us inside it," she said.

Pascal had a haunted look in his eyes.

"You were right, Lady Grey. I underestimated our enemies' urge to kill me." He took her slender hand in his large, powerful one. "Still, all this will play strongly to our advantage in the Argonath. We will rouse the nine cities with the tale of our escape."

"Your Majesty, we will only have the chance to do that if we escape and we aren't safe yet. The pursuit will not be long in coming."

Pascal looked back. The fierce light was visible, tinging the trees pale and stark. Imps and other things were milling around while harsh voices yelled orders. A search party was being organized.

"Yes, of course."

Thorn waved them on, out of the gulley and across a flat area of bare rock, with patches of tiny gnarled trees and thick clumped moss. The light was suddenly extinguished.

"Those things, were they some new kind of troll?"

"Possibly, Your Majesty," replied Lessis. "But I have never seen their like before. They moved more quickly than trolls."

"Hush!" whispered Blade.

There came the clatter of hooves, and a horseman came riding by. The horse was panting heavily, and the man was hunched over his pommel.

"It is Ambassador Koring," said Thorn.

"Ambassador!"

Koring pulled up.

"Your Majesty! You are alive, thanks to the Mother."

"Thanks to the quick reflexes of those who protect me."

"You must get away at once, Your Majesty. The enemy has dozens of those things. They will soon learn that they failed to kill you."

"What are they?"

"I don't know, but they are eating the fallen."

"That is what trolls do . . ."

"What caused that light? It was brighter than the sun."

"Powerful magic," said Lessis. "We face a new enemy, and he has many powers beyond those we possess."

"Come, lords," Thorn was anxious now. "We must not linger."

They went on, toiling over the rocks, following a winding path through heather and cliff. The Emperor of the Rose, titular overlord of the Isles of Cunfshon, the Argonath city-states and the land of Kenor, had been reduced to a fugitive, scurrying through the wild dark.

Chapter Eleven

On their second and last morning in Quosh, Bazil and Relkin rose early, not long after dawn. They breakfasted at the inn and then washed up at the village pump house. There they said hellos and farewells to as many folk as walked by, which was about half the village by the time they'd finished, for the word had gone out quickly that the famous Broketail was taking a good scrub at the pump. Everyone who could take the time made a beeline for the spot. By now the famous pair had become used to the gracious attentions of those who would barely have nodded to them in the old days, and they replied to everyone with good humor and manners.

A large lunch, packed in two hampers, was waiting for them at the inn when they returned, talked out and very clean. One hamper, designed to be carried by a donkey, held a pair of choice hams from Farmer Pigget and his wife, plus a smoked turkey, taken off the bone, a bushel of potato salad sauced with akh, and a dozen country pasties. There was also a small hamper with a country pie, more akh, and some sausage and cabbage pickle. Relkin also carried six long loaves, fresh out of Baker Matuseis's oven and bound with string.

They set out around the ninth hour, under a patchy sky with towering cumulus riding up from the south. Ahead loomed the Rack, five knobs of bare rock standing up like the vertebra of a long-dead giant. The most northerly knob, known as "Old Baldy" or "Baldermegi," was famous as a place haunted by fairies. Descending southward, and growing smaller came Little Baldy, Thick Neck, Big Rack, and Beggars Hill.

They would go back the way they had come. Across

Quosh Common into Brumble Woods, then ascending through the Dingle to the Cutback Valley, which offered a good route past Beggars Hill. The trail here was narrow, used mainly by hunters out for the abundant rabbits. Beyond Beggars lay the pony trail that ran up from Barley Mow. The road bent northward there and traveled along the flank of the hills to join with the cart road that led over the Rack and down to Cross Treys camp. With good weather Relkin was sure they would easily make it back to camp in time for the evening boil, something that would be very important to a certain leatherback dragon. If they made good time in the morning, they'd have lunch on Neck Hill.

They said their farewells to the folk who gathered along the Market Way and Brennans Road until they reached the Bull and Bush. The regulars poured out to surround them and sing a fare-thee-well from the old song book. Then Bazil thanked them and was applauded for doing so. At last they set off across the common, still accompanied by a few younger boys and dogs. After a mile or so the youngsters dropped back, and a little later so did their dogs, with a last cluster of mournful barks.

Relkin's stride was cheerful and confident that morning. The visit home had been a great success. He felt something strong and deep had been renewed for him. Perhaps he really did belong, despite his orphan status. He and his dragon had become village heroes, and it felt good. Of course, he checked himself, he wouldn't want to be treated like that all the time, but it had been nice for a day or so. Every pretty girl in town had been keen to talk with him, and many had flirted outrageously, unlike when he was younger. Then they had been haughty little princesses, secure within their families, and would have nothing to do with any dragonboy.

He laughed to himself. The dragon raised an eyebrow.

"What make boy laugh?"

"I was just thinking about how things have changed. . . . How it used to be in the village, and what it was like on this visit."

Bazil chuckled, a deep rumbling sound, and snorted a little. He too was enjoying the morning.

"The innkeepers never volunteer to feed this dragon before, that for certain."

Relkin laughed aloud, recalling the luncheon in their honor held at the Bridge House Inn the day before. Bazil had gone through a side of beef, buckets of ale, and a tremendous tart, filled with cheese and tomatoes. Castilion had planned to cut the tart in small pieces and sell it to the village folk outside his Inn, but Bazil had devoured the whole thing in the matter of a few minutes, while adding more akh with a liberal hand from the tureen on the table. Castilion, to his credit, had endured the sight with a brave smile.

"Still, they were spared a lot of taxes because of us," said Relkin.

"They do well."

"So do we."

Relkin thought of the gold tabis and doubloons they'd brought back from Eigo and deposited in banks in Kadein and Marneri. For a dragon and dragonboy pair, they were exceptionally well set up, even wealthy.

The dragon, by dint of great mental effort, had finally come to grips with the human concept of money, or at least the idea that pieces of shiny metal were exchangeable for considerable supplies of food.

He clacked his jaws happily at the thought of all the food they could buy. Relkin laughed, knowing exactly what Bazil was thinking.

Up through Brumble Woods they went, climbing through stands of hemlock and pine to flatter areas covered in oak and beech. The day continued fair, with towering clouds passing northward through the blue sky. After a while the woods began to thin on the higher ground, and they could glimpse the cliffs of Beggars Hill looming above, a series of grey limestone faces thirty to fifty feet high.

Soon they came to the bottom of the dingle, a steep-sided canyon cut into the limestone by a strong spring. There were slabs and blocks of tumbled stone stacked like giant childs' blocks all the way up. For the agile and fit, it represented a good shortcut up onto the higher slopes of the Rack. For Bazil, after two nights and one whole day of eating and drinking, it was something of an ordeal, and he was huffing and puffing loudly by the time they reached the top. Relkin was waiting for him, discounting the complaints about dragonboys that pushed old dragons past their limit and the like.

"You didn't have to eat quite so much for dinner last night. And three kegs of beer? Isn't that a little too much?"

"Dragon cannot drink beer in the afterlife."

"Afterlife?"

"You think dragonboy is only creature that goes to heaven?"

Relkin raised his hands, palms up.

"I don't know if they take dragonboys in heaven. Maybe you have to believe in heaven before they'll let you in."

"Well, take it from this dragon, there's no beer in heaven."

Relkin had to agree that this was probably very likely. Heaven didn't sound all that heavenly sometimes. He wondered if a dragon boy who still called to the old gods would be granted admission to heaven. Then again maybe not going to heaven would be a blessing. Relkin liked a certain amount of peace and harmony, since there'd been a pronounced shortage of them in his own life; however, nothing but peace and harmony, forever and forever? He wasn't sure about that. And no beer? Very dubious proposition.

From the top of the dingle they took a rocky path along the side of a steep bank. The path angled upward along the cliffside, and soon they were atop the cliff, walking in open heathland. The sky offered patches of blue, but away to the south, past Pawlers Hill, the Ersoi glowered beneath heavy clouds. Relkin had a premonition that they might get a soaking before they got back to Cross Treys.

Just his luck, he thought as he considered the way fate always seemed to arrange these things for him. Just when everything was going well, you got soaked. Being someone who tended to look for hands on the tiller of fate, Relkin always wondered whether someone much greater than himself had it in for him.

Suddenly there came a strange, quavering cry echoing off rocks above them. Relkin spun around.

"What was that?"

Bazil had stood up on his hind legs and raised his head to stare around himself.

"This dragon never heard that before."

"The something that was worrying the sheep over on Pawlers Hill?"

"Not wolf. No cat that I know of either."

Together they carefully scanned their surroundings, but

failed to locate any sign of the creature that had made the noise.

"Bear?"

"Never."

"Yes, you right. That not noise of bear."

The cry was not repeated.

They moved on, alert to anything unusual in the hills around them. Nothing showed itself, and though the clouds to the south were slowly thickening, Relkin was beginning to believe that they might get all the way to Cross Treys before it rained.

Suddenly they both became aware of a rumbling sound also coming up from the south, but it wasn't thunder. Relkin put his head to the ground.

"Riders, many riders."

"A posse from Farmer Pigget?"

"I don't know."

The rumble grew much louder suddenly. Some sixth sense made Relkin uneasy.

"Get down," he said. The hooves were drawing closer. Rolling up from the south through the heather behind them.

"Get down!" Relkin tugged on Bazil's arm. The dragon chose not to argue. He ducked down into a cut in the rock, using ancient dwarf pine trees for handholds. Relkin dropped down beside him, then scrambled up to peer over the edge.

A moment or two later the riders came into view, first three men, clad in black leather, then other figures, smaller, squarer than men, riding horses. A dozen of them, then more.

Relkin sucked in a breath with an involuntary oath.

"Imps!" he said in a harsh whisper.

"Imps never ride. Forbidden to them."

"Well, these do."

"Never seen that. They don't do that at Padmasa . . ."

"But, wait a moment, what is this? Imps on the Rack? How could imps get all this way without being detected?"

"Maybe they land from sea, down in Ersoi."

The riders, twenty strong, rolled on over the open ground at a canter and disappeared downslope heading north.

Dragon and dragonboy looked at each other.

"Need cavalry for this."

Without more ado, Relkin strung his bow and readied a set of arrows.

"Got to get to Cross Treys and pass on the information. They ought to send a cavalry patrol down here. Something is definitely wrong."

"This dragon not like to see imp in these hills."

"Then, we better step up the pace." Relkin loaded shafts into the bow.

"Why not take hunters trail? Go over Big Rack way past Lion Rocks."

"Then down to Touzan and Minden. Get on the north road there and save an hour or more."

"Boy thinks it out."

"Well, well, here's one dragon who knows how to plan ahead."

"Thank you." There was a loud wyvern jaw clack. "This dragon learn to think for himself."

They set off northward, uneasily following in the trail of the imp riders. The riders had gone along through the heather then down a sheep track, where they'd had to go in single file. They were now below Bazil and Relkin, moving along a lower trail that ran up to the ford across the Inth Stream. When they reached the place where the upper trail split in two, the two caught sight of the troop of imp riders, passing under the trees toward the ford, several hundred feet farther down. Here the trail they were following started to zigzag down toward the ford. The less used fork in the trail was a hunters' trail that ran on to higher ground heading eastward. Eventually it would take them up the row of nobs that represented the crest of Big Rack Hill. Past the Big Rack loomed the mass of Old Baldy, by far the biggest of the nobs that made up Rack Hill.

They left the ford and pony track to the imps and turned east on the higher trail. The heather thinned out, and the rock grew more barren, and there was just the dwarf forest of bent and contorted pines. Wood flox, bright pink and yellow, were in bloom all around them.

They passed a rock wall that had been carved in some dim antiquity with the figures of men and lions, a time, perhaps, when lions still roamed the primeval forests of the Argonath.

After the rocks they left Beggars Hill and descended into the upper part of the Inth Vale. Here it was a shallow bowl, and they dipped down through the dwarf pine forest into a belt of bigger trees along the creek and then back up on the next ridge.

Now they gained a view of the wider lands to the east. Below, in the near distance, lay the woods of Kroy. Just to their south the Curling Stream made its way past the woods to the green rectangles of Lurnow's famous fields, the most fertile wheat fields in all Blue Stone, or so it was said. And away to the south was the small town of Brennans, visible by a smudge of smoke from the brick kilns there. Brennans was the capital of the region, about twice the size of Quosh or any other village. Relkin had thought about going there with word about the raiders, but that would just slow the process of taking the alarm to Cross Treys. And Cross Treys was the only place that could mount an effective response.

"Look!" Bazil pointed down.

There, crossing the Curling Stream on a logging bridge, was a party of imp riders much like the one they'd seen earlier on the other side of the ridge. Relkin felt the hair on his neck rise.

"Not the group we saw before."

"Yes. Something big is going on." They were effectively cut off from the trail down to Barley Mow in the west and the trail to Brennans in the east.

"Too many imp."

"I think we want to get to Cross Treys as fast as we can."

"Better pick up the pace."

They hurried on the hunters trail along the ridgelines, climbing toward the three rock knobs of the Big Rack.

It was about halfway up the slope toward the rocky nobs that they came across the trail of blood. It slanted up from a gulley on the eastern side and then went on up the trail ahead of them.

Bazil sniffed the air cautiously.

"Men pass here, not long ago."

"Imps?"

"No. This is man blood."

"Someone is bleeding pretty badly, and being helped along." Relkin studied the ground closely. "See there, a foot dragged. And there's several footprints back there where the ground is soft."

They both drew their swords, Bazil resting Ecator lightly

on his shoulder as they cautiously went on over a hillock and down into a small swale. There they suddenly came on a small group of men gathered around one of their own, who was lying on his back. The men started up instantly, and swords flashed in their hands.

And then there was a shout, and one of them came forward, calling out, "Relkin and Bazil!"

Relkin recognized Lessis the witch with stunned eyes. She wore finer clothes than was normal for her, but they were the usual uniform grey.

Bazil recognized her too.

"By the fiery breath of the ancients, this dragon knows we in hell of a lot of trouble now."

Chapter Twelve

Bazil and Relkin were quick to comprehend the situation, the presence of the Lady Lessis concentrating their minds with remarkable rapidity. In their lives she had always managed to live up to her nickname of the "Storm Crow." The huge man lying on the ground was a member of the Imperial Guard. He had a severe chest wound and was plainly dying. The emperor had survived an ambush. Imps and strange new trolls had been involved. Imps on horseback had been seen. A major operation had been launched to try and slay the emperor, and it was still going on.

Indeed, the emperor himself was standing nearby, and at the appropriate moment Lessis introduced them. The emperor was a powerfully built, middle-aged man with white hair and grey beard. He had kept his figure, bore no signs of a paunch, and seemed quite unafraid despite the desperation of the moment.

Relkin was awed, if only for a moment. He had never dreamed he would actually meet the Emperor Pascal himself. But now he saw that the emperor was still just a man, albeit one with an aura of strength and power. Bazil was less awed, but still impressed, despite dragonish disdain for the trappings of human hierarchy. Bazil had heard often enough about the emperor, who dwelt far away in the Isle of Cunfshon. From spratlinghood he had understood that he trained and would eventually fight in the emperor's name.

Then Relkin remembered his manners.

"We have food, Lady," he said, gesturing to the packs they'd put down on the trail.

"Food? That is wonderful news, child. I swear that your steps have been guided by the Mother herself."

They were interrupted by a screech above their heads, and a crow came flapping down to land on Lessis's outstretched arm. It rested there for a moment to report, and then flew away. Relkin had seen Lessis among her birds before. Relkin had seen Lessis do things that could make it hard to sleep nights if you thought about them too much. Trooper Loder, on the other hand, had only heard legends of this sort of thing, and he was plainly awed.

Lessis spoke quietly to the emperor and Thorn, informing them of what the crow had told her. Neither seemed surprised by this turn of events. Relkin watched them and assumed that they too had witnessed Lessis's magic before and were almost immune to surprise now.

They shared out the meats and the bread for a quick meal. Everyone in the small party was ravenous after walking all night and day.

Taking a turkey leg and a hunk of bread, the emperor sat beside Bazil and asked questions about dragon life in between bites. Bazil did his best to reply truthfully, as the emperor had requested. It was the first time anyone had ever asked him to sum up certain aspects of the life he had known.

And, in truth, he had enjoyed his term of service, despite the dangers he'd been exposed to. He knew he had achieved great fame. Certainly he'd seen enough hard fighting to pay his way in the world. And now, thanks to their travels to faraway Mirchaz, they had gained riches. Old Macumber damn well ought to be proud. As a sprat, Bazil had been quite average, and he'd grown up to become a leatherback of ordinary girth and weight. But with the great sword in hand, he had cut himself a position in the history of the Argonath that was quite unique.

His answers gave the emperor a unique and invaluable window into the world of the wyvern battledragon.

The wyverns fought because the Padmasa enemy were Enthraans of the death magic, and they lusted to use the deaths of dragons for their mightiest sorcery. The wyverns had been hunted almost to extinction when the men of the Isles had come to teach them how to fight back. The wyverns were virtually the equal of men in intelligence, and though they were a conservative breed, they saw the wisdom of an alliance. The dragons had entered the legions willingly, seeking survival and revenge. Their complaints about the service were few, but widely held. Mostly they hated boredom and the bland food. There was never enough akh! This was a burning question for every dragon in the service. There was usually plenty of noodles, plenty of bread, but never enough akh.

"Dragon never have to sleep on empty stomach in legions, but food needs akh."

The emperor absorbed Bazil's words with a calm, serious expression, and then promised to look into the persistent shortage of akh. Bazil fell silent as he concentrated on one of the hams. It did not last long in the hands of a wyvern dragon.

Elsewhere Koring sat by the prone figure of Blade. Lessis came to take another look. Relkin knelt beside them.

"He will not last long," he said.

"Correct, Master Relkin," said Lessis. Ambassador Koring's eyebrows shot up. She actually knew this youth? "The wound passes into the pulmonary processes, the left lung is collapsed. He has lost too much blood. I do not think great Blade will awaken again. The world is a little less safe as a result."

Relkin had to agree. Blade was a natural warrior and a giant, well over seven feet tall. Not Katun of Mirchaz, or Kreegsbrok of Padmasa would have cared to match swords with Blade. Not even Thorn would have enjoyed such a contest.

Sadly they stood up and moved away, leaving Koring beside the fallen giant. Thorn approached, hastily swallowing some bread and sausage. He had several questions for Relkin concerning the surrounding countryside.

"You lived here as a youngster, I believe."

"I did."

Thorn had a general idea of the terrain all along the route of the Imperial Progress, but Relkin had the knowledge of a local. And Relkin bore the unmistakable mark of someone that had seen a great deal of combat. Thorn sensed it immediately.

"So what's the quickest way out of these hills?"

"If we go on up to the Big Rack, we can cross over on this same trail and go on down into Minden."

Thorn nodded. "There's a legion camp up there somewhere, isn't there?"

"Right, that's Cross Treys camp. We're actually on our way there right now. We need to get back by dark, or we're in trouble with Dragon Leader Cuzo."

Thorn's lips twisted into a smile.

"Then, we'll go there with you. The emperor should be safe there."

"There's a whole squadron of dragons there, if that's any help."

"Dragons? Good. The enemy has a new monster, something we've never fought before."

Relkin was instantly alert. "What are they?"

"Don't know, not as tall as trolls, but quicker, and they wield sword. About the size of bears, I'd say."

"Wield sword, you say. Sounds bad."

Thorn nodded. He understood well the dynamics of combat between troll and dragon. Dragons were always outnumbered; they needed their speed and intelligence to overcome the enemy.

"We can be up to the Big Rack in about an hour, get down to Minden in maybe three, maybe four."

"It's steep?"

"Part of the way, but nothing the dragon can't handle."

Ambassador Koring informed everyone that Blade had just that moment died. Thorn knelt beside his comrade to check his eyes and then his pulse.

"It is true, great Blade has passed on. May the Mother care for him in the afterlife."

The emperor came to kneel briefly by the body of the giant who had served in his guard for so long and so well.

"We will all miss his strength and courage."

"We don't have time to bury him," said Thorn.

"We will come back for him. There is nothing else we can do," said Lessis.

Relkin thought that Loder, the Kadein cavalry trooper with the huge slash across his forehead, needed treatment. He mentioned this to Lessis and indicated his pouch, in which he always carried needle and thread, plus antiseptic in the form of Old Sugustus stinging lotion.

"It is a good idea, but you must be quick. We should not linger here; the enemy searches for us. The crow reported riders to our west. Probably one of the groups that you reported seeing."

Loder submitted to having the wound cleaned and stitched shut. He winced a few times, but made no outcry as Relkin cleaned the wound and then sewed the skin together. It took twenty stitches, some of them too big for Relkin's taste, but they could be redone later. For now it just had to hold together for the march.

Dragonboys had to be fast, it was a prerequisite of performing surgery without anesthetic, and the stitches were in place in a matter of a few minutes. A dressing took another two or three and then Loder was able to stand up, a little unsteadily, but no disgrace to the honor of the Kadein cavalry.

They discussed trying to disguise Blade's body as that of the emperor, but were dissuaded by Lessis. They will know that Blade, of all men, is not the emperor. Blade stood a head taller than any other man alive.

Thorn was growing anxious.

"We ought not to stay in one place so long. The pursuit cannot be far behind."

Thorn took point, Bazil and Relkin brought up the rear, Bazil moving on all fours and trying to keep to cover wherever possible. They moved through thick heather and dwarf montane forest along the twisted cuts and traces of the trail as it wound up the ridge to the knobs of the Big Rack. The sun had reached his zenith, but the clouds were thickening and the sun was hidden much of the time. A cool breeze blew out of the south. The Ersoi Hills had become dark and ominous-looking.

Around them it was still a beautiful day, and the sun broke through occasionally to light up the knobs of bare rock above, turning them a bright ocher. The shoulder of the hill was streaked with green where the forest grew thicker along the watercourses and purple where the heather was in flower.

They climbed steadily. For Relkin the day had taken a surprising turn, but that always happened whenever the witch Lessis showed up in their lives. The wind blew steadily out of the south. Several times they saw hares darting away from them. A hawk spiraled down to report to Lessis, completely ignoring a rabbit that sped away.

Lessis was immediately concerned by what it told her.

"Animals that have never been seen before are moving along the eastern side of the hill. Also there are riders."

Concern mounted in Thorn's eyes.

"Can we get past them and down to Minden?"

"I will send a crow to check. Crows are better at the details."

The emperor and Thorn exchanged a look. Lessis whistled, and a crow appeared within seconds. She whispered to it, and it flew away again.

They had reached the high point of the trail, the bare knobs of rock just above. Now they looked down over the eastern flank of the hill and Kroy Woods, which were spread out below.

The crow returned in a hurry with disheartening news. Soon afterward they were able to see black specks appear in the distance, coming down from the knobs of the Big Rack.

"Twenty, thirty or more imps. and the other things, that look like bears but aren't."

"How could such large parties get here without being detected?"

"They must have come by sea," said Lessis. "They landed on the Ersoi shore."

"How could they have known where to set the ambush?"

"They must have been informed soon after the planning of the Imperial Progress was completed."

"Treachery at such a high level? But who . . . ?" The emperor was plainly disturbed.

"Your Majesty, just as we strive ever to place spies within our enemy's councils, so do they try to do the same to us. Many men and women had some knowledge of the progress. It was inevitable. Questions had to be asked concerning shipping, and to arrange the meetings with local royalty and nobles. Your day-to-day business in Andiquant had to be put off. Special arrangements for swift communications between the Argonath cities and Andiquant had to be made. Enough partial reports, no matter how slight, could allow them to deduce many things."

The emperor nodded. "Yes, of course, I see." He had blinded himself to the risks, determined to make the progress.

"We must go south, then," said Thorn.

"And quickly," said Lessis.

They turned and hurried back down the trail, glad of the cover provided by the dwarf forest.

"What now?" said the emperor as they went. Thorn calculated distance, dropped back to talk to Relkin again.

"What lies off there to the southeast? Past the woods."

"That's Brennans, the biggest town around here. They'll have horses there."

"If we left the trail past the place where we left Blade, can we get down to those woods below?"

"Yes, there is a little trail, very steep in places. Goes down to the Kroy Woods and the Pike Pool. We get past there, and we'll soon be in Lurnow's fields. Brennans is just a mile or two farther than that."

"Good. But we must hurry. Can the dragon keep up?"

Relkin grinned. "Bazil is a legion dragon, I bet he can march just as fast as you can."

Thorn's eyes narrowed momentarily, then his hard face broke into a wintry grin. "Yes, I suppose you're right."

Now they swung down the trail at a smart pace through the taller trees of the saddle, and came on the place where they'd left Blade. He lay as they'd left him, covered in his robe, although there were vultures circling over head by now. Lessis immediately cast a spell and banished all the carrion birds from the area, except for one that was ordered down to report to her on what had been seen in the vicinity lately.

The vultures streamed away to the south, where other corpses had been spotted. One only was left to spiral down to Lessis's arm, where it crouched for a minute or more. Lessis soon reported to Thorn that parties of imp on horseback had been seen on both sides of their position. Strange animals had been seen to the north, coming down the trail toward them. Thorn's face knotted with concern.

"We have to get out of these hills. We'll try for the town of Brennans."

"We could not approach it before."

"Because the riders were all strung across Capbern's Gap. It sounds as if they have moved up to cover the hills."

The emperor was ready to try it, so Lessis agreed. Indeed, what else was there for her to do? They left Blade's resting place and went down the main trail for a quarter mile. Relkin pointed off down to their left where a narrow trail, not much more than a goat track, went down through heather and bare rock to the woods below.

The trail was steep as well as narrow, and there were places that were difficult for a dragon to negotiate, but Bazil had rambled on these rocky hills all his youth, and he knew how to make his way through almost anything.

They surprised a family of deer browsing in a glade of hawthorns and wild rose. The deer bounded away through the tangle of vines and brush.

Now they pushed through deeper thickets, and progress slowed. There were bogs and hollows and then places of bare rock, but the trees of the Kroy Woods were a lot closer.

At last they were in the true woods, surrounded by aspen, birch, and pine. Thorn called them to a halt. Lessis sent out a crow to scout ahead, but before it had left their sight, they heard an uproar below. Hoarse shouts and uncanny wailing were followed by the sound of horses in motion. Then a dull sounding horn blared out.

"Imp horns!" Relkin muttered, who knew them all too well.

Chapter Thirteen

The imps were coming up slope, their horses crashing through the brush. And now, to complete their despair, hounds bayed in the woods below. It was almost as if the enemy had been lying in wait for them here. They had read Thorn's move, perhaps because it was one of such a small set of possibilities.

"What now?" said Lessis in a quiet voice, doing her utmost not to stir Thorn to defensiveness. She need not have worried.

"We go back. Have to try another way." Thorn wasted no time on ill feeling, and they turned to climb back up the steep, difficult trail that they'd just descended. Back through bogs and hollow, back over the bare rocky parts and into the tangles of vine they went.

There was an eager edge in the calls of the hounds, for they had smelled the dragon and were aroused to fever-pitch by this unknown scent. If there'd been time, Lessis would have composed a confusion spell that would have kept the hounds busy, but the enemy were too close for that.

Emperor, Great Witch, ambassador, and the rest all redoubled their efforts so that they trotted on the flatter stretches of the trail. They scrambled up the muddy slide and pulled themselves up with roots and stems to climb the rocky breaks. A trace of desperation had added itself to their flight. The pursuit did not gain, in fact, they lost a minute or so when they had to leave their horses behind and continue on foot, but the imp horn kept calling, which would inform the other enemy groups that were roaming the hills that the quarry had been seen. The emperor was in flight.

At last they reached the top of the small trail to Brennans. Once more they were on the hunters' path that ran along the north side of Beggars Hill. They headed west along the trail, moving as quickly as they could manage.

"We could try the dingle," said Relkin. "It's real steep, but the dragon can climb down pretty fast. That comes out in Brumble Woods. We go west, and we'll be in Quosh village in no time."

"Quosh?" said Thron.

"Quosh is an old dragon village. Macumber is the trainer; he has two leather backs and a brass there. And there's older dragons too. Of course, most of them are females, so not used to fighting."

"You foresee a fight, then?" Thorn studied the dragonboy carefully.

"We know what they hope to do. We've seen a lot of imps. Then there's those critters up the hill. With all that force at their disposal, why wouldn't the enemy press to the very last?"

Thorn nodded. "I'm afraid it makes sense."

The emperor pursed his lips, listening.

"Are all dragonboys so versed in warfare?"

"Probably not, Your Majesty," said Lessis quietly. The emperor met her gaze with thoughtful eyes. She knew this lad, knew him well. He turned back to look again at Relkin.

"Quosh is where me and the dragon grew up," said the dragonboy, seeing the questions in their eyes.

"Ah!" said Thorn, enlightened at last.

Then came the sound of a horn close by and the baying of hounds.

"Hurry!" shouted Thorn. "They are upon us!"

Bazil gave his big head a shake as he caught up to Relkin.

"Hurry? We haven't done anything, but hurry since we met them."

Relkin had to agree. The day, which had begun so splendidly, had become an expanse of hidden danger. There were literally hounds on their trail, and they'd had to give their lunch to the emperor himself.

Whenever the trail allowed, they ran or stumbled over the shale and bare rock. The heather and dwarf pine trees surrounded them, a welcome source of cover that hid them from the pursuit. The calls of the hounds grew fainter.

Now the dark clouds from the south slid overhead and obliterated the sun. Soon after that a gentle rain began. When they emerged into the open heathland that covered the western side of Beggars Hill, the sky was heavy and black, and they saw lightning strike spectacularly three times in a row in the distance on Pawlers Hill. The rain started falling harder, and the wind picked up as they skidded and slithered down the sloping trail beneath the grassy bank overlooking the entrance to the rocky dingle.

Thunder cracked across the sky, and lightning flashed stark and purple-white nearby. Even the dragon winced as the thunder broke again. It felt so close as to be almost a physical blow. They scuttled along under the rain, which was driving down hard and fierce now. Again lightning struck on Pawlers away to the south and west, and for a moment they could see the wide valley light up, to show woods and fields and a distant tower, the temple at Quosh.

The footing was less than ideal on the trail, and more than once Lessis slipped and fell. She was up at once, unharmed, but she had to admit that her lovely old Cunfshon boots were not adequate for this sort of wear. Across smooth, wet rock and through dark puddles and rivulets they stumbled. The entrance to the dingle was close now, like a dark maw surrounded by misshapen rocky teeth.

"There!" shouted Ambassador Koring, pointing to the south. They looked up and saw a party of imp on horseback with men at their head, pressing up the track toward them in a cloud of spray and mud. They would intersect just above the dingle.

"Come on," cried the emperor, setting off at top speed for the clash.

"No, Your Majesty!" Lessis cried weakly, too late.

He was gone, Thorn and Trooper Loder behind him. Relkin and the dragon were in motion too, the ambassador passed her, and she ran at last, drawing her long knife and holding it ready. She tried not to think of the consequences if the emperor were to die here. How they could ever have risked this progress, once they knew the identity of the new enemy in Padmasa, she would never understand.

They closed on the open space around the dingle entrance, a flat plane of limestone, pocked here and there by erosion. The imps charged, pressing their tired horses into a semblance of speed.

Relkin had his bow ready, and sent an arrow into the leading rider. Bazil drew Ecator and stepped forward to meet the horses. The imps lowered their spears and ran at him as if they were going to stick a bull. Bazil had no shield, but he had trained for this situation for many years. He waited until the imps were almost upon him, and then he blurred into action. Ecator came up and whirled through spears, horses, and imps in a lightning-fast forehand and backhand riposte. Horses and imps crashed to the ground on either side of him; the others spurred past and onto the waiting swords of Thorn and the others. Relkin's bow hummed again, and he shot a second imp from the saddle. Lessis had placed herself at the emperor's side and was trying to persuade him to come into the dingle, before anything could happen to him.

Pascal had his sword out and his eye on the nearest imps. He had no intention of running from the fight. He too had trained all his life for this moment, but unlike Bazil, he had never been allowed to wield the sword in combat. An emperor was too precious for that, but part of him had always desired to see battle for himself.

The imps came on straight into them. Thorn knocked up the lunging spear of the first and ran it through. Ambassador Koring tried to do the same with the next, but missed and came within a hairbreadth of being spitted; luckily the spear took an upward wobble and passed over his shoulder. He was knocked aside by the charging horse a moment later and sent to his knees.

The spear passed through where the emperor had stood, but Pascal had already shifted, and now he hewed the imp from the saddle. The horse ran on riderless. His stroke was efficient and well executed. His trainers had done their work well, and he had lived up to their expectations.

Screams followed the mighty swings of Ecator as Bazil dodged spears and chopped down imps. They watched him cleanly cut an imp from its horse with a smooth forehand stroke. A moment later the lightning struck Beggars Hill and lit up the dragon, a frowning colossus, with Ecator raised high.

"Back!" said Thorn. "Back into the rocks."

Some of the imps were dismounting, running up with swords and spears. A horseman in the black uniform of Padmasa rode among them, cracking his whip to drive them on. Trooper Loder engaged a pair, drove them back, knocked one of them over, but then had to retreat as several more came in around him.

Bazil shifted position, swung, returned with the backhand, and took down another spear-wielding rider. Then he danced sideways, and his tail whipped around to surprise the black-clad Padmasan and knock him off his horse.

Ecator whipped through an imp and came back in a spray of scarlet and then flashed high and came down on the Padmasan mercenary before he could evade. Relkin saw the emperor's eyes pop at the sight.

Suddenly there was an empty space around them. The imp troupe fell back, disheartened by the casualties and the ferocity of the dragon. It was hard, even for imps crazed with the black drink, to throw oneself within the range of that dragonsword, that shining ribbon of lethal steel. With the leader dead, there was no one to terrify them and urge them on. They grew passive.

Relkin was familiar with the pattern.

"Now would be the best time to start down the dingle. They've lost heart. They won't follow for a few minutes."

Thorn nodded. The dragon boy knew more about actual combat than he did.

"A good idea."

They began the descent. The rain had lessened temporarily, but the rocks were wet and somewhat treacherous. More difficult was the darkness, which made finding the safe places to put your feet very hard. Relkin led the way down, showing them the easiest route through the huge blocks of stone and the narrow cracks between them.

Bazil and Thorn came last. Bazil moved quickly once he was on the rocks. He knew the way as well as the boy. There were a couple of tight spots though, and one had to remember carefully the series of movements that were required to thread a two-ton body through the narrow crack.

They went down, and the minutes ticked away until at last they heard the imps above roaring together to get up their courage. By then they were halfway down the steep staircase of boulders. Another couple of minutes, and they would be safe.

Screams from the head of the dingle informed them that the imps were coming. And now the imps that had met them by the dingle had been reinforced by the imps that had pursued them up from Kroy Woods.

Imps came leaping down the boulders while spears flashed overhead and caromed through the lower passages. Bazil was lucky at the place called the Turnkey, where a narrow break in a rock curtain was the only good way through. He squeezed through the space just before a spear rang off the stone where he'd stood. Bazil had a healthy respect for spears. Without armor, a spear could end a dragon's life just like that.

The imps above them made weird chilling cries as they came on. More spears clattered in the gap by the Turnkey rock. After the Turnkey the passage widened, but there was a cavity big enough to take a dragon. Bazil flattened himself to the rock in the dark, and was hidden.

The imps came to the Turnkey. One passed through, yellow eyes ablaze with black drink. It snorted back to the rest, and several more came through.

Then Bazil erupted from concealment. They shrieked, and some made play with their swords, but he seized the leading imp in both huge hands and swung it like a living weapon and bowled over the others. Then he took them one by one and smashed them on the rocks and stuffed their corpses back into the Turnkey passage, partially blocking it.

Bazil went on down the dingle as quickly as he might, letting himself slide down the Slip Rocks to the Accordian stone, where he almost flattened Relkin.

"Hey, watch it, or you're gonna have to cut your own claws."

"This dragon in a hurry, we all in a hurry, correct?"

"Correct."

"Then, even dragonboy must get out of the way."

There came yowls and groans from above. The imps had found the remains of the scouts that had gone through the Turnkey passage. They argued among themselves over who was to put his head through the passage next.

"They'll need quite a bit of encouragement to get through the Turnkey after that," said Relkin.

"Hate imps. Let's hurry."

Now Relkin and Bazil were on the last lap of the trail. The emperor, Lessis, and Ambassador Koring were already stepping out into Brumble Woods. Thorn had gathered up a few spears on his way down. Relkin took one, so did the emperor and the ambassador.

Fortunately the woods covered them from the view of the enemy on the cliff top. They stole swiftly away into the woods as quietly as possible. For a while they ran on, down short banks and across the little bogs, breathless in the wet woods in late afternoon.

The rain had slackened somewhat and left the woods filling fast with a rising mist. The light was gray, the sun hidden in banks of clouds. Birds were busy in the trees, migratory thrushes were gathering slugs and snails, small hawks were busy stalking the thrushes.

And then they heard the nervous barking of the hounds. The imps were down the dingle. With Relkin and Thorn in the lead, they ran through the wet forest, keeping to the broad trail that ran from the dingle down to Quosh Common. The horns behind them had grown to three or four in number as other groups had joined the first two. The horns were leading a small army of imps toward the peaceful village of Quosh.

Thinking that spellsay on the run was getting hard to do now she was in her sixth century, Lessis mumbled a spell as she tried to keep up with the nervous warriors ahead. They had to warn the village, or at least stir it to life. She thought of trying another spell, to confuse the dogs, but realized it was too late. The imps had their trail now and would follow no matter what.

The spell took a minute or so of hasty recital, the volumes were very hard to handle while running like this, but at last it was done, and she released it.

An eruption of crows, starlings, and hawks rose up from Brumble Woods and flew toward Quosh with cries of alarm. On this occasion thrushes were left to their snails, for the Queen of Birds favored the sweet songsters from the south, and this was the season when they raised their young in the woods of the Argonath and needed every moment of the day.

Once they were in the village, the birds flew low through the streets, croaking and calling. Since such a thing had never been seen before, ever, the folk soon poured out of their houses. Even the hardened bunch lurking in the Bull and Bush emerged to stare at the flocks of black birds that were making such an outcry.

"What ails them?" cried Farmer Pigget.

In the woods of Brumble, the emperor, the Great Witch and the ambassador of Ryotwa ran for their lives beneath the wet leaves. The rain had died away to almost nothing, leaving everything dripping, the mist thickening. Their boots sloshed in the wet muck.

Harsh triumphant shouts broke out not far behind them, and the baying of the hounds grew loud.

Away in the village, people heard the hounds and the sullen horns, and they turned to each other with wonder in their eyes.

"The birds have gone mad, and now there are hounds in Brumble Woods?"

"Call out the militia," bawled Tarfoot Brandon. "Something's up."

"Remember what happened on Pawlers Hill," bellowed Nurm Pigget, coming out of the Bull and Bush and standing in Brennans Road.

"Call out the militia, don't waste any more time."

Nurm Pigget brought out the bell from the Bull and Bush, and started ringing it in the street. Rustum Bullard brought out the Great Horn used to spread the alarm to the farther parts of the village. He tried to blow it, but could only get a few fitful squawks from it.

"Here, give it to me," said Nurm Pigget. Nurm had a huge chest, and he made the horn give a bright, brassy blast that would be heard in Barley Mow. Or even on Pawlers Hill.

Certainly they heard it in Brumble Woods, and the hearts of the fugitives leapt at the sound, for this was the Great Horn of the Argonath. The village was awake, the guard was being summoned. The emperor and his party were encouraged to pick up their pace, and it was good that they did, for now coming on after them were some of the new monsters that had smashed the emperor's coach to flinders. They emitted guttural growls as they shambled in the manner of bears on all four legs. With these beasts there were men and imps, almost a hundred strong now, and they were driven onward by the black drink and the furious will of the Great One that had brought them into this land.

Amid the wailing of the hounds, this small army came on at a great pace, and gained steadily on the small group of fugitives up ahead.

The mist thinned ahead, and they crossed a lane and saw the open space of Quosh Common ahead. To the right, the tower of the temple soared above the trees. Beyond the common lay the village.

"Run for your lives," shouted Thorn.

Chapter Fourteen

The breath came harsh and hard in their chests as they pushed themselves to keep running, to keep planting one foot in front of the other and lurching forward across the open meadow of Quosh Common.

For the emperor this experience was a vindication of the hours and hours he had spent jogging to stay fit. He had never particularly enjoyed exercise for its own sake, but he had persevered, not wanting to ever become the immobile sort of emperor. Not like old Mikalus the Obese.

Now Pascal ran across the wet grass, and his lungs were searing and his heart felt as if it might burst out of his chest, but he continued running at this insane speed, which might have been fine if he'd been twenty years younger. And yet he was keeping up, Thorn only a few feet ahead of him. He risked a look back and saw the dragonboy, looking fresh and running easily with his bow in hand. Ah, youth! Farther back loomed the dragon, a great grey shape, loping along on two legs, his body bent low for speed and his tail outstretched behind. A true monster of war, thought Pascal.

The Emperor Pascal Iturgio Densen Asturi was not the only one astounded by what their legs were capable of. Lessis was grey in the face, literally, but somehow, she too was keeping up with Thorn. It was amazing that her ancient body could actually do this, sprint along like some forest hind. By the Hand of the Mother, she had not run like this in centuries! What would the other Great Witches say if they could see her now!

Even the portly ambassador was running flat out across the common, though he was purple in the face and his breath came in stentorian gasps.

There came a chorus of harsh calls from behind them, and they knew that the imps were out of the woods and in pursuit. Hounds bayed on the left, the imp horns sounded almost directly behind them.

Ahead lay the only chance, the village of Quosh, which was now looming out of the mist. The distance was perhaps a quarter of a mile, straight across the flat ground. It seemed impossible that they could stay ahead of the charging imps. They would surely falter and be overtaken and hacked down, despite the presence of the dragon, for once the imps were close enough to engage, they'd be mixed too inextricably for the dragon to wield the sword upon them without killing those he sought to protect.

And then on their right came another sound, a bright-sounding horn. From across Temple Lane, down from Birch's farm, rode Farmer Birch and his sons and their men, some twelve in all. They were all mounted and most had swords, a few even had spears, snatched from Birch's front hall when they'd first heard the alarm horn blow at the Bull and Bush.

"To rescue, to rescue!" they shouted as they spurred their mounts up the bank from Temple Lane and out onto the common.

A dozen tall riders, coming to the rescue of the Argonath in the person of its emperor. Relkin greeted them with a whoop, and Thorn followed suit. Then the rest joined in despite their lack of breath, and the riders acknowledged them with shouts of their own and waved swords while Tomas Birch blew his hunting horn.

Their mounts were fresh and eager, and they came by with hooves digging into the meadow as they galloped under the horn. They raced past the fugitives and crashed into the oncoming imps.

The imps tried to avoid the riders, intent as they were on slaying the emperor, but Birch and the others rode them down or spitted them from the saddle. The imps scattered, and scattered farther when they saw the dragon turn back and come at them with Ecator whirling. For a few moments the pattern changed.

The fugitives, staggering now and slowing from the sprint they'd made out of the woods, had gained a hundred yards, but many imps had passed around the riders and the dragon, and were racing after them with swords and spears at the ready, spread out in a line a hundred yards from end to end.

Bazil was forced to sheathe the sword and give chase, and with him came the farmer and his men, for they were simply too few to stop the enemy. The imps had got past, but they had still won crucial space for the fugitives.

As he got up to speed again, Bazil felt an arrow lodge in the back of his neck and another one strike the skin of his shoulder. Neither went deep, but still they told him it was time to retreat even faster, so he dug into his reserves and increased his pace.

Bazil came suddenly through a drift of mist upon a small group of imps, bunched together by the pursuit. They whirled in alarm as he came up on them. He drew Ecator with a fluid, practiced maneuver, but they scattered with a collective shriek before he could slay them. Bazil felt another arrow whack into his shoulder. This one had gone deeper. Clearly it was time to move. He ran, dodging as he went, for without armor he was vulnerable.

The mist thinned away to nothing, and they were running across the green toward the Bull and Bush and the row of houses that fronted onto Green Street. Beyond rose the bigger buildings of the village. A crowd was visible in the Brennans Road, staring across the common, watching them run.

The emperor, the Great Witch, the ambassador, all lurched along, still running, urged on by Thorn, who darted back and forth behind them to ward off any imp that might catch up. None did, however, and it was clear that they would reach the crowd ahead of their pursuers.

A few more strides, and they were there. The emperor was staggering a little, and now he slowed to a halt and stood there gasping for breath. Lessis was glad to do the same. The ambassador came a moment later and promptly fell flat and lay there like a fish out of water.

"Imps are coming!" shouted Thorn to the crowd.

The news was received with incredulity. People shifted uneasily.

"Imps?" said a chorus of voices. "Imps, here?"

"Remember what happened on Pawlers Hill," said a voice.

"There be imps in them hills. I've always said it," said Tarfoot Brandon.

"Shut up and help build the barricade. We need to block the street."

"Look!" screamed a voice.

And out of the mist loped imps, not in ones and twos, but in fives and sixes. They were bronze-skinned brutes with small heads and bulging eyes and huge teeth, grinning in hungry mouths, and they bore swords, round shields, and spears.

"By the breath!" muttered Rustum Bullard.

"I don't like the look of those," said Tarfoot Brandon.

"How the hell did they get here?"

More imps were coming, and then there was a roar-scream. The imps scattered, and Bazil the Broketail came up behind them.

"It's the Broketail!"

"Build a barricade, block off the street!"

The folk were already in motion. The regulars from the Bull and Bush were pushing a couple of wagons across the road. Other men were running up from the village. The cooper was coming they said, with all ten of his workers. Crates and barrels, even an empty bathtub were dragged out of the alleys and flung into place around the wagons.

Then Chester Plenth, the ostler, came clattering up on his horse along with good Martin Pueshatter.

"Where are the enemy?" called Plenth. "Clear the street, let Chester Plenth through."

"No, Chester, there's too many of them."

"Too many, you say?"

"Dismount and join us at the barricade!"

"There's an army of them!"

And this was true, for now there were more imps pouring out of the woods, and it was plain that there were hundreds of them. Chester Plenth saw the imps, and his jaw dropped. Martin Pueshatter helped him down from his horse. With trembling hands they drew their swords and took their places at the barricade.

Rustum Bullard had ordered the potboy to bring up some water, and the emperor and Lessis took a few gulps. Then they splashed some on the ambassador.

"Welcome to Quosh, excellencies," said Bullard, not knowing quite who it was that he addressed.

"I thank you," said the emperor with a gasp.

An outbreak of shrieking and horn blowing just fifty feet

away told them that the enemy had not given up. The imps were still coming, pouring out of the woods. There were three hundred at least on the common, and now there were some of the other things, huge brutes running easily through the crowd of imps.

The temple bell from across the common started ringing in a frenzy. The priestesses had realized the town was under attack. That bell could be heard as far as Barley Mow, even in Brennans on a good day, and the men would heed the summons.

The dragon came up and accepted a few buckets of cold water. Relkin clambered up his shoulders and worked on the arrows that had lodged on his head and neck and shoulder. Two were easily dug out, the third he had to cut out carefully, since it was too deep for an easy pull. Bazil muttered and hissed in discomfort until it was done, and then poured a bucket over his head, soaking his dragonboy in the process.

"To the barricade!" went up the cry, for the massed imps were now being goaded forward by horsemen in black leather at the rear. The dull horns of Padmasa sounded across Blue Stone for the first time since the Demon Lord of Dugguth had marched this way long before.

The imps jogged forward to the attack, and with them came three of the bearlike brutes. They wore leather aprons and shoulder armor, drew long swords and uttered harsh war cries as they advanced.

At the sight of them the defenders uttered thin wails of fear.

"What in all the hells are they?"

"They're not trolls, they move too quick."

"What can we hope to do against them?"

But Thorn jumped up on a wagon and shouted.

"If they move, then they're alive! And if they're alive, then we can kill them!"

This put some heart back into the men of Quosh, and they roared out their own challenge to the enemy.

The imps shrieked back at them and bounded up onto the wagon, where they exchanged blows with the first line of defense. Other imps tried crawling under the wagons or pushing their way through the spaces between.

The sound of steel clashing on steel, of cursing men and screaming imps became a general roar, into which the monsters came with a special shriek of triumph. Their big swords burst asunder the line of men, and Odis Shenk was slain, cleaved from neck to crotch. One wagon was heaved up on its side, and in a moment it would have been thrown back on the men behind. Then they were roughly shoved aside, and the huge figure of the dragon came up and put his shoulder to the wagon and heaved it back, almost crushing the monsters.

They barked at him in rage, and their eyes, which were yellow with black pupils, dilated with their fury. They rushed at the wagon with their swords waving high. Bazil responded with Ecator. The first to reach him engaged. He parried the thing's thrust and knocked the sword aside. With smooth precision he riposted and drove Ecator home, spitting the brute through the chest. It gave a gurgling cry and sagged down on its knees while dark blood bubbled from its mouth, and then it was gone, trampled by its fellows as they assailed Bazil from either side.

The wagon was all that lay between them, and it was taking a beating from the giant swords: shards of wood flew and the wagon buckled in the middle.

Bazil deflected a blow from the right and just managed to simultaneously twist aside from a thrust from the left. He actually felt the flat of the enemy sword slick against his belly.

The one at the right struck again and again. Bazil hacked its weapon aside and brought Ecator over in a hurried stroke to trap the left one's sword before it could stab the dragon's side.

These damn things were just too quick. They were smaller than trolls but had twice the speed, and were therefore deadly.

Bazil defended himself with desperate strokes to right and left. Without a shield he was perilously close to being overmatched. He grabbed desperately at a broken brass bedstead that had been thrust into the barricade, and hauled it out and used it to defend against the thruster from the left while he engaged the one on the right.

Ham Pawler and his brother Roegon jumped up with spears in their hands and thrust them home into the breast of the one on the right as it was defending itself from Ecator. It stiffened, gave a coughing grunt and doubled over.

Ecator came down a moment later to decapitate it, and it collapsed.

The bedstead broke asunder at the same moment, and the brute on the left got up on the broken wagon and thrust for Bazil's throat.

By a near miracle, a barrel hurled by Thorn and Tarfoot Brandon together interposed and spoiled the stroke. Bazil jerked his head out of the way.

Relkin stepped under Bazil's arm and hurled a spear into the brute, piercing its chest and driving it off the wagon, which further disintegrated.

Imp archers filled the space with arrows, and Bazil sprouted new shafts on his shoulder and chest. Relkin felt an arrow zip unpleasantly close to his ear, and he ducked down.

Tarfoot and some other men responded with a rain of cobbles, pulled up from the Brennans Road by the women and children. The cobbles struck imps and beasts, and forced them back. The imp archers lost their aim and fell back as well.

The men of Quosh gave up a big cheer. They had held the barricade, thanks to the Broketail dragon.

Chapter Fifteen

The cheers died away slowly. The enemy milled beyond range of their rocks and spears, but occasional arrows flew. Tenzer Haleham gave a sudden gasp of surprise and fell backward dead, an arrow sprouting from his open mouth. Everyone kept their head down after that.

"We need more stuff on the barricade" came the cry, and groups began moving furniture and barrels out of the houses on Schoolhouse Street and adding them to the pile stretching across the road. The enemy held the common and most of the green.

Thorn squatted down beside the panting form of the emperor.

"They are driven back for the moment, Your Majesty."

Rustum Bullard heard those words, and his eyebrows rose. He glanced at the slender woman in the grey robes. A witch? It had to be. And who was the other one, in the fine wool overcoat? And what were those things out there?

At that moment Thorn finally informed Rustum Bullard just who the fugitives were, and Bullard paled.

"The emperor?"

Pascal Iturgio Densen Asturi had recovered his breath and some of his poise.

"I am," he said simply.

Bullard floundered for a moment, then bowed and frantically summoned his servants to attend the emperor.

"Here, lads, 'tis the emperor, himself. Needs our help!"

The potboys stared goggle-eyed for a moment, and then sprang to assist the barrel-chested man who was still getting to his feet.

The emperor did his best to assume his Imperial posture, chest out, head back, eyes level and calm, despite his shortness of breath and the wobbly feeling in his legs. Then he saw Koring struggling to get to his feet.

"Ho, Ambassador, how are your legs?"

"Weary, Your Majesty, I never would have thought I could run like that."

"When you've got the devil at your heels, Ambassador, there's no limit to what one can do!"

"Indeed, Your Majesty, indeed."

Pascal looked into the eyes of the men standing close around him. He spoke in a stronger voice, much more like himself.

"And now we can take the fight to the enemy, for we are in the stouthearted village of Quosh."

More men had thrust their way through to surround the emperor, and their eyes blinked as they learned his identity. Gil Haleham, Tenzer's brother, and Avil Benarbo were at the front, and they took it on themselves to speak for the village.

"Welcome to loyal Quosh, Your Majesty," said Bernarbo, bowing low in what he imagined must be the etiquette of the Imperial Court in Andiquant.

"I thank you, and all the true folk of Quosh. I am sorry only to have to meet you in such conditions. I'm afraid I have brought great trouble to you."

Their response was steady as a rock.

"Quosh is ready to fight to the death for the Argonath and the Empire of the Rose, Your Majesty."

The emperor clutched his hands together and shook them to the folk of Quosh.

"Then, we shall fight and die together, for your emperor will not shirk the battle." His words brought a flush to the men's cheeks, and Pascal enjoyed seeing the effect he'd had, but purposely avoided Lessis's eyes. He knew that she would do everything in her power to make him stay out of the fighting, if it came to that.

"We need to send a message to Cross Treys camp," said Thorn.

"Good idea," rumbled Bullard. "Where's Pip Pigget? He's got a fine horse."

In a few moments young Pip Pigget was clattering up the north road past the pump house on his way to Felli and the road over the Rack up by Big Baldy.

Three men pushed forward with a captured imp between them.

"Kill that thing," snarled someone.

"Hold. We got him to talk. Listen."

One of the men grabbed the imp by the chin and spoke to him. "Here, you tell the good folks what those things are, the beasts like trolls."

The imp had a slightly dazed expression. The black drink was wearing off.

"They are bewks of Waakzaam. They are mighty fighters and will kill and eat all of you," the imp said.

"Bewks?"

"Yes."

"A strange, fell name. And who is Waakzaam?"

"Hush, Thorn, do not speak that name," said the Lady in a quiet but commanding voice. Thorn turned to her in surprise.

"Bewks?"

"The enemy mixes life in his vats of evil and produces monsters. Most are slain. A few are bred for improvements. These are his latest offering."

"Bewks, then."

"Whatever they call them, they can still be killed," said the emperor in a loud, commanding voice.

"That's right, Your Majesty," rumbled old Bullard while the other men nodded and waved their weapons.

Now there came a sudden outburst of cheering down Market Street. Dragons were swaying down the street with Old Macumber at their head. They wore leather plate armor and helmets, and carried full shield and sword. There were the young brutes from Macumber's Dragon House, Weft and Fury, plus several older dragons who now lived close to the village and worked in the fields for a living.

Among this group were Zambus and Big Eft, both massive brasshides retired from legion service. And then there was old Edda and some other females, like big Bejja and Osteoba, carrying long spears.

"The dragons, the dragons are coming!" came the cry, and more and more people came out to greet them. A drum was beating somewhere, and a distant voice shouted that the emperor was in the village of Quosh.

Macumber's assistants were carrying a shield and some leather armor for the Broketail. Relkin ran out to help them, anxious to get Bazil into some kind of armor as soon as possible.

Macumber greeted the emperor with a legion salute.

"More dragons are coming, Your Majesty. The message has gone up the road to Barley Mow and Felli. Gompho and Belo will come soon, and the men from Barley Mow will be with them," said Macumber.

The female dragons were not trained for combat, but they were just about as powerful as the males and able to fight with a spear. They took places behind the highest parts of the barricade. There was now a good crowd there, so much so that Thorn was beginning to worry about its vulnerability to arrows and spears coming over the barricade.

Suddenly groans and cries of disgust rang out. Smoke was rising from some of the houses on Brennans Road just outside the village. Old Ma Fowles house was the first to burn, then went the Potishars' place. Gelmey the Pigman's, which was closer to a hut, caught at once and burned like a torch. Gelmey's swine, however, had broken free at the back and were running up Pigget Lane toward the farm. Old Ma emitted piercing wails of horror at the sight of her home going up in smoke. But her plight was only a small fraction of the disaster facing the village.

The imps had lit fires on Brennans Road down a ways from the barricade, and were sending fire arrows into the roofs of the houses along Market Street. The thatch above the Bull and Bush began to smolder. With a scream of outrage, Rustum Bullard ran inside through the side entrance on Market Street. His potboys ran after him with buckets in hand.

Then came the sound of more bright horns as Farmer Pigget came riding up the south lane with all his men, a force of more than twenty. Gelmey's swine scattered with shrieks of alarm as the men on horses came through the lane at a gallop. Even as the echoes of Pigget's horns died away, there came more horns as Farmer Birch and his men took up the call from the northern end of the green, where they had regrouped to aid the defense of the temple.

More riders came up through Temple Lane to join them, men from Dorn's farm, Offler's farm and the other northern homesteads along the road to Barley Mow. Their numbers had grown to thirty by then.

The smoke along the south side of Brennan's Road was

thick now as the houses caught and blazed. Rustum Bullard appeared at the loft window of the Bull and Bush, and threw out a bucket of water, then another. That put out the fire, but then arrows flashed, and Rustum Bullard gave a cry and vanished inside.

More fire arrows arced across the sky.

Here and there a man came up with his hunting bow and started shooting back at the imp archers, but they were outnumbered ten to one and could do little to suppress the imp fire.

The group around the emperor was forming into an ad hoc command center. It moved around the corner into Schoolhouse Street to be out of the line of flight of the imp arrows, which were falling regularly in Market Street. The emperor, with Thorn at his side, was quick to assume control. It was a time for firm leadership, and the local men had indicated that they were ready to fight.

The emperor raised a hand and then introduced Thorn, as the man in charge of the fighting.

"Thorn has my utmost confidence. He has seen more fighting than any of us."

Thorn flicked a glance across the street to where Relkin was helping his dragon get the unfamiliar leather armor on. Thorn wondered if they oughtn't to be placing the dragonboy in charge on that basis.

"It's simple, friends. They intend to fire the town and then assault us again," Thorn said. "We need to organize ourselves quickly. We need a force to hold the barricade, but we need men to guard the houses along the street fronting on the green, for the enemy will try and come through them."

Farmer Pigget had ridden up and dismounted. When told the emperor himself was there, his big, round face had gone pink with amazement. He was introduced to Thorn and suggested that they signal to the riders bunched at the north end of the common that they should attack the imps massed on the common. When the riders charged, the men and dragons would break out from the barricade and advance. With a little luck they could panic the imps and drive them from the field. Imps were notoriously unstable, and a sudden shock could break them.

Thorn agreed. A rider was sent galloping up Schoolhouse Street to Temple Lane, where a right turn brought him to the north end of the green. The men from the farms were massed there, at least thirty strong, and most had a weapon of some sort to hand.

The message was received, and Birch blew a sharp pair of notes to signal their agreement. Then the riders moved out onto the green. Ahead of them was a two-hundred-yard stretch of flat ground to the first trees and bushes of the common. The enemy was clumped along Brennans Road and in the fringe of bushes where the common met the green.

The horns at the barricade signaled that the men there were ready. Farmer Birch raised his horn, blew the charge, and away they went. Quickly their horses sped to a gallop, and they were flying along, thirty men on horseback, swords in the air as they rode toward the imp masses.

Now the force at the barricade gave a shout and surged forward, ignoring the arrows that fell among them. They charged over the barricade and into Brennans Road, sweeping past the shattered front of the Bull and Bush and over the corner and into the imps.

The battle broke out along the line of impact with a savage, hacking fury: imp sword and shield against all manner of weapons in the hands of the men of Quosh. Then the dragons lumbered up, with arrows sticking out of their armor and shields, and the imps broke and tumbled back rather than face dragonsword.

But there were the bewks, the new monsters of the enemy to contend with, and though smaller than trolls, they were significantly bigger than men and almost as quick as men. They formed a line, swords ready to engage the dragons. Their faces were those of giant pigs, with sharp staring eyes. They clashed their shields against one another and uttered a communal roar.

The dragons came on with a will, and the men behind them shouted "Argonath!" as they drove in against the beasts. Immediately huge swords flashed in the late afternoon sun and terrible blows rang across the green.

The young leatherback Weft clove a creature in half in the first moments. To his right the other leatherback, Fury, parried a blow and then smashed a bewk down with his shield, trod on it, and drove home his sword. Next in line, Zambus knocked aside more swords and spears and cleared a rank of imps, sending heads and shoulders asunder from their torsos.

Bazil, now wearing hastily donned leather armor on shoulders and belly, with a worn but serviceable shield on his arm, tore into the line with Ecator flashing on high. Several of the creatures engaged, and Ecator wove between their swords, while Bazil used the shield to parry some strokes and worked to heave the bewks back. They were devilish, strong brutes for their size, and it was quite as difficult as it was with trolls. Worse still was their speed, which was the equal of his own. It made it hard to engage more than two at a time, and even that was difficult. These monsters knew well how to wield a sword. It soon became apparent that the dragons were outmatched, the bearlike bewks were just too numerous and too well trained.

Just when the tide seemed sure to turn against the men and dragons, the horns of the horsemen blew sharp and clear, and they came thundering down into the imps on the right of the enemy array.

The imps did not panic, however, for now on the common came more horns. But those of Padmasa and a troop of forty imp riders broke out of cover and galloped onto the green, crashing into the farmers' flank.

The imps steadied, turned in their place, and put their spear butts to the ground, holding them like pikes. The farm boys had no idea how to deal with this, and while they struggled to turn their horses around the imps struck them from the side. Several went down at the first shock. Elvyn Birch fell then, an imp sword in his side, blood gushing from his mouth. In moments a whirling melee developed as imp and farmer went at it from the saddle.

Now the imps on foot took up their spears and started thrusting at the farmers and their horses. In a moment they took more victims. Young Phelan Birch died then, spitted from behind. And Ginais, one of Birch's old tenant farmers, was brought off his horse when the poor brute was hamstrung from behind. On the ground Ginais fared poorly, and the imps hewed off his head and stuck it on a spear.

On the other front of the fighting, the battle had swung farther over, for the main mass of imps had steadied behind the line of bewks. A quick round of black drink had been passed around them, and now they came back, moving through between the ranks to assail the men and dragons.

Overwhelmed and out of breath, old Zambus was speared and forced to retreat; blood poured from his belly. Weft too was wounded and wounded again as he struggled to extricate himself. He emerged with a spear thrust through his tail. The bearlike creatures snarled and roared and thrust forward. Their swords beat down on the dragons and men like hail upon the wheat. A dozen men fell then, and with them fell Fury, cut down by a bewk and then decapitated by another. His head soon rose above the yelling horde of imps. Now the imps were heartened immensely by the death of a dragon, their greatest enemy, and they came on with wild abandon.

There was nothing to be done but to give ground and return to the relative strength of the barricade. Giving ground became a rout, and they fled in disorder for the barricade at the mouth of Market Street, beside the old Bull and Bush, which was on fire now, flames visible in the thatch. The imps took a toll, harrying them from behind and cutting down many a man before he reached safety. Last of all came the dragons, hewing their way out of the swarming imps and bewks.

The wagons were held apart until the dragons were through, Zambus staggered and collapsed once he was through. The female dragons hauled the wagons shut with a crash, and piled up the barricade again. The men of Quosh had to rally themselves and form a stout front behind the barricade, for the imps came on now with a harsh shout and charged up onto the wagons, clambering over the barrels and crates and pitched into the men on the line. Behind them came the stolid masses of bewks, huge and ominous. The battle flared up more fiercely than ever.

Parts of the roof of the old Bull and Bush were collapsing as the fire took hold. All along the Brennans Road the houses were ablaze, and a vast pillar of black smoke was rising into the sky.

Chapter Sixteen

The fighting hung there in the balance, poised over the barricade under the flashing swords and axes as the men of the village fought for their lives. Central to the struggle were the remaining dragons: Bazil, the big females, and Weft, who was still fighting, despite his tail. The bearlike creatures could only come at them a few at a time because of the constriction of the street, so the dragons had the classic advantage of defenders of a narrow space. With Ecator and Weft's sword "Diune," they also had an advantage in reach of a foot or more, and they used that as much as possible while fighting over the width of the wagons.

The females fought with the long spears from the Dragon House, stabbing across the wagons whenever bewks or imps tried to mount up on the far side.

To help protect the dragons, Relkin had hurriedly organized a squad of men and youths with swords, one with a spear. Any imps that got through the line and broke out behind the dragons had to be slain at once before they could stab the dragons from the rear.

That's how they started out, but things soon grew more desperate. Relkin found himself in the thick of hard fighting as he moved from group to group, wherever the imps seemed on the point of breaking through. Smoke from the burning buildings cloaked everything and made it hard to see.

Some imps wormed their way through the stuff jammed in beneath the wagons. Others stormed over the wagons, risking the dragonswords and hurling themselves onto the line of weary men that stood on the other side. That line broke more and more easily as the men of the village, civilians used to a comfortable life, died on imp swords and spears.

The dragonboy and his ad hoc crew were too busy to really take care of the dragons as they worked in front of them, battling imps that had gotten through the line.

Ecator hummed through the air above their heads with a heart-stopping quality. Relkin kept shouting to the Quosh boys to keep their heads down, but they hadn't the training, and he knew sooner or later someone would lose his head as a result. Bazil didn't have time to worry about them, he was dueling hard with the new trolls, the bewks of Waakzaam on the other side of the wagon. They kept trying to mount the wagon or break it apart, and they had to be stopped.

An imp wriggled out from a space beneath a wagon and got to his feet just as Relkin tackled him from behind and brought him down. The imp twisted under him like a huge greased eel. It stank of filth and sweat, and wriggled around and struck at him with a thin black dagger.

Relkin jerked his upper body aside and felt the dagger slide along his ribs. He cut down with the edge of his hand and knocked it away while he brought his sword across and drove it through the imp's throat. Another imp landed on his back, and he twisted desperately to break the grip around his neck. He caught a wrist as it came down with a knife meant for his neck, and struck out blindly and caught the imp in the belly. It fell with a groan, and he sprang back onto his feet in time to deflect a spear driving at him and then run his sword through its wielder. More imps, Bazil had missed some since he was fighting two of the bear-creatures now. Relkin caught one by the foot and jerked it off the wagon. A big lad from Quosh named Derri was there to finish it with a sledgehammer. Another imp kicked away Relkin's sword, and there was a hard blow to the head that made him see stars. Another imp fell on him, but Derri caught the imp by the back of the neck and smote it with his hammer. Relkin was back on his feet, still a little blurred, but fighting without conscious thought, purely by training and instinct. An imp with a sword held high came at him, but he caught the arm, dug his hip into the imp, and tossed it over his shoulder. It bounced off another imp and both fell to the street. Bazil stepped on one, and Derri hammered the other.

Then Derri gave a soft groan, staggered, and sat down. A pair of arrows had suddenly sprouted in his chest. His young eyes went very wide, and he slid back, quietly going into oblivion.

Relkin had no time to say a word to the dying youth. He ducked a sword sweep, felt a hard punch land in his ribs, and then a shield rammed his chest and knocked him back a step. He bounced off the dragon's leg and went down on his hands and knees. The imp launched itself, spear first, but Ecator flashed and took its head and shoulders. Relkin had time to pick up his sword, lurch back onto his feet, and parry a sword thrust from an imp that had wriggled under the wagon. He punched the imp in the face. When it staggered back for a moment, Relkin took the opportunity to run it through.

An arrow flew past his face, missing by no more than an inch, but he took no notice and struck down again and again into the imps on the ground.

And then Thorn was there beside him, fighting with a measured, practiced fury that was awesome to contemplate. Thorn had a stabbing sword in his right hand and a long dirk in the other. He kicked one imp's head almost off its shoulders, and decapitated another with the sword. A huge snarling bewk swung at them, and they dove low as the big sword clanged off their end of the wagon. Then a dragon's shadow passed over, and Ecator whistled around in a savage sweep that knocked the beast right off its feet. Bazil put a foot up on the wagon, tilting it way over while bits of the barricade rolled away as he jabbed down at the fallen bewk. The bewk was no oafish troll, however; it wriggled like an eel, knocked Ecator's thrust aside with its own sword while lying on its back, and rolled out of range. Bazil was left impressed once more by the speed and quality of these new monsters of the enemy.

For a few minutes more the battle seesawed back and forth across the barricade and then two more dragons, big old brasshides Belo and Gompho, came running up, short of breath and purple-faced after coming all the way from Barley Mow. They were carrying dragon-size scythe and sickle, the tools of their trade as mowers. They'd been mowing a meadow for Farmer Lyle and had come straight from the field when they'd heard the bell going like crazy in the temple. Then on the road down from Barley Mow, they'd met young Pip Pigget riding a big white horse and spreading the word. They'd run ever since, and were breathing very hard when they arrived. But they were in time to wield their scythes on a final thrust by the imps, and took a dozen heads while Bazil took a couple more. The imps fell back in screaming disorder, and the bewks finally lost heart too as the enemy horde flowed back from the barricade. A lull fell over the scene.

Relkin and Thorn looked around themselves. Smoke swirled through the streets. There were dead and wounded everywhere, casualties had been heavy. Imps were mounded up below the wagons. There were dead men aplenty too. The men of Quosh were not soldiers. They were not ready to battle a horde of imps like this.

"We held them!" said Thorn with a note of triumph in his voice. He had not seen actual combat in a long time, and his confidence was renewed.

There was a crash from the corner where part of the Bull and Bush had fallen in, and the flames burned up even brighter.

"Yes," said Relkin, "but they'll be back."

Relkin noticed the emperor standing there, face blackened by soot, clutching a bloody sword in his hand and looking a little dazed. And there was Farmer Pigget, leaning exhausted on a spear. He too had the shocked expression that Relkin had seen on many a battlefield.

Thorn put a hand on Relkin's shoulder.

"We beat them, thanks to you, young man. You and your dragon made the difference."

"It's not over yet," insisted Relkin.

The ambassador was lying against the side of a house, blood seeping from a slash wound across the side of his head. Lessis knelt beside him, trying to staunch the bleeding.

Thorn stared across the barricade, which had suffered considerable damage. The wagons were listing, barrels smashed to staves.

"I know, lad. They haven't given up, they intend to kill the emperor. They've put too much into this to give up now."

Relkin pointed past the burning Bull and Bush.

"They'll go through the houses next."

"You're right, lad, good thinking." Thorn spun away to

organize resistance. Calling to the men huddled in Schoolhouse Street, he moved to the door of the nearest house.

They had to huddle down by the barricade, or retreat into the doorways along Market Street, for arrows were still flying in from the imps. The collapse of the Bull and Bush and the intense heat from the fire made that side of the barricade impossible to man. The wagons were all right, but some of the rubbish at that end had caught fire too. Meanwhile the houses along Brennans Road blazed furiously.

The emperor lurched across to squat down beside Ambassador Koring. The ambassador was purple in the face from coughing against the harsh smoke, and the wound on his head was still bleeding despite Lessis's efforts.

"They'll see this smoke in Brennans, help will come."

"Your Majesty, you fought well. It was an honor to stand here today."

Pascal threw back his head and laughed.

"Well, I thank you, Master Koring, and I would beg to return the compliment. I saw the way you spitted that damned imp that was going for the dragon's back. Damned fine stroke, that."

"We held them."

"We did, we did, though to be honest we couldn't have done it without the dragons. And there, I'm afraid, we've paid a price already."

Indeed poor Zambus, dragged out of harm's way into Schoolhouse Street, was dying, and Fury's head was stuck on a pike out there on the common.

"We are not out of this thing yet either," said Lessis quietly.

"Indeed, Lady, we are not." Pascal sounded resigned but resolute.

And then there came a savage clamor from the back of the houses on Market Street. There was fighting going on in the backyards, where Thorn and his men had met imps and a couple of bewks. The sound of steel, the screams and roars of combat soon escalated to a new level of commotion. When Relkin ran back the short distance to Schoolhouse Street corner, he found a mob of people running down the street wide-eyed in terror. One of the strange creatures was smashing its way out of the front door of one of the houses in the street.

"Quick!" he called to Bazil.

Another door burst open, and imps came tumbling out. One of them caught a little boy by the back of his head and thrust home with a long knife. The child's scream was high and piercing. Then a bewk burst out behind him and took the shutters right off a window as it came. Relkin watched the little boy fall, blond hair in the gutter.

Women and children were running for their lives up the street in the distance. They'd stayed far too long in their houses, not dreaming that the tide of war could ever invade the kitchens of Quosh. Now they ran from the nightmarish sight of imp warriors running loose in Schoolhouse Street.

Relkin and Bazil called the other dragons from the barricade and turned up Schoolhouse Street, swords in hand. Bazil's roar-scream brought the enemy's heads up. The bewks rushed to engage, but Bazil's blood was boiling. No pair of enemies, whether troll, monster, or even the terrible mud men of Dzu, could have withstood his fury then. Ecator sang, and there was just room enough in the street for Bazil to wield the blade freely. The enemy made play with their swords, but Ecator was the quicker and the deadlier blade.

Relkin kicked an oncoming imp in the chest and bowled him over. The next he met sword to sword, and he caught the imp's knife thrust and kneed the imp hard in the crotch. It doubled over, he cut down with the sword, and it fell.

Thorn stumbled by, bleeding from a head wound, clutching his hand, with blood running down the fingers.

"Too many for us, I'm afraid."

"We have to clear them back, build more barricades."

"You're right."

Thorn was in a slight state of shock. Relkin could see him struggling to clear his thoughts and concentrate.

Meanwhile the fighting raged. Bazil slipped the guard of one of the creatures, and a moment later he clove it to the waist. The other hewed at him, but Weft was there to engage from behind the Broketail and the stroke never landed. The bewk was shoved back, smashed into the wall, and almost beheaded instead.

Relkin tried to stay out of the way of dragonsword on the back strokes, not to mention the dragon tails, which moved violently from side to side as the great beasts balanced themselves.

The emperor appeared at his side. Relkin pulled him

down a foot with an urgent tug on his elbow, and Weft's sword hummed over their heads.

"Duck the tail!" Relkin shouted. The emperor saw it coming from the corner of his eye and joined Relkin in bobbing underneath it.

"What do we need to do?" he asked Relkin from a half crouch, acknowledging frankly that in warfare the youth was the one with the greatest experience.

"Need to pull the barricade back to this corner, block off Market Street here, and put defenses in the houses up Schoolhouse Street."

The emperor scrambled away to try and organize things. The fires along Brennans Road had consumed much of the houses there, but clouds of thick acrid smoke still rose into the twilit sky.

More men came up, having ridden from Felli and Barley Mow. They immediately went to the fight in Schoolhouse Street, joining the dragons in stemming the imps and then forcing them up the street. With the bewks beaten back, the men could shift forward of the dragons and confront the imps. The dragons could cut at the imps from over the heads of the men in front of them. This forced the imps to give ground.

Macumber was working with the female dragons, and they dragged what was left of the wagon barricade up the street. The pile of debris seemed skimpy in the new location. Then somebody opened up the gate to the undertaker's yard, and they hauled out the big hearse. That completed the span. More stuff was piling up fast as people hurried down with barrels, chairs, bits and pieces of wood dredged from their homes. Soon the barricade stretched high across Market Street at the corner with Schoolhouse Street. The defenders crouched behind the new barrier, and waited, while the dragons and the new arrivals drove the remaining imps out of Schoolhouse Street and back into the houses and backyards on the eastern side.

The dragons could hardly push through human-scaled houses, so they could do no more. Thorn and the emperor judged they'd done enough.

Schoolhouse Street connected Market Street and Temple Lane. On its eastern side it was a row of houses. On the west there was the big mass of the bank at the southern end, then came the opening to Bank Yard, an alley that ran all the way to Pump Street between the buildings at the back.

Thorn and Avil Bernarbo put together a force of twelve men, and sent them to hold the passage into Bank Yard. Another ten fellows, some of whom had just arrived from Barley Mow, were sent to hold the northern block, where Schoolhouse met Temple Lane. There were six houses on that block, and these families were now fleeing down the lane into the northern part of the village. Between these houses and the southern block lay Bank Yard.

The bank had no entrance in Schoolhouse Street, which helped fortify the street. If they could keep the enemy out of Bank Yard, they could hold that flank of the barricade.

To the south of Market Street, Schoolhouse was lined on the west by outbuildings of the Blue Stone Inn, with the inn's big courtyard within. This position would be held by Bernarbo and his men, with the addition of an old dragon, Chutz. Weft went up to the barricade built across Bank Yard. The last six houses at the top would have to be defended from within. Men started fortifying their doors and windows as best they might.

Communications had now been lost with the men under Farmer Birch, who were trapped around the temple. But the temple bell was still ringing furiously, so they knew that it had not been captured by the enemy.

The evening light was failing now, and Lessis climbed to the roof of the inn, where she communed with a pair of blackbirds. The birds had flown quick sorties over the enemy positions and brought back their impressions.

She hurried back to rejoin Thorn and the emperor, who were sheltering behind an overturned wood skip outside number seven Market Street, which had been in the process of renovation prior to the battle. Thorn wore a bandage on his right arm and carried his sword in his left hand. He had trained for such a situation, of course, though he would never be as skillful with the left as he was with the right.

"The enemy has massed another force on the common."

"Ah, you are so good at bringing that kind of news, Lady." The emperor looked over the top of the skip toward the barricade, and the men hunched below its shelter.

"I wish I didn't have to, Your Majesty."

"Where can we retreat to?" said Thorn, who was thinking on the same lines as Lessis. Their job was to keep the Emperor of the Rose alive at all costs.

"The roads south and west are watched. The road north goes to some little places in the valley until you reach Borgan. The enemy will harry us all the way if we go down that road."

"We will stay here and make our stand," said Pascal Iturgio Densen in a firm voice.

"I was afraid you might say that," muttered Lessis.

"We will hold Quosh to the last." The emperor sounded immovable.

Lessis had to admit to a degree of vexation. Good sense dictated a swift flight northward on the best horses in Avil Bernarbo's stable. Getting the emperor to safety in Borgan or over the Roan Hills to Querc was the highest priority. Her gaze met his, and she knew he would not retreat.

"How long until they get the news at Cross Treys?"

"Not long now. Our message went hours ago. We have to hold them through the night."

A man nearby gave a gasp of horror. "They're burning Pigget's farm!" he said.

Farmer Pigget lurched up from his place by the barricade.

"The farm!" he cried in grief, for it was true, flames were rising from the roofs of the farm on the hill.

And then the enemy's horns blew, and there was no time for grief, for the far end of Market Street had suddenly filled with the enemy.

"Too late!" cried Lessis. "They are coming."

Chapter Seventeen

They held the enemy once more, but only after a hard struggle during which the barricade was pierced and almost captured, while Schoolhouse was the scene of desperate fighting, and the men in the northernmost houses were slain and those houses were set ablaze. This left the defenders without any effective control of Temple Lane.

They held, but the casualties were high. Brezza, a big old grandmother dragon was killed by a spear thrust to the eye. Luther Pigget, nephew of the farmer, was cut down by the imps, but so were a dozen or more men at the barricade and many more than that on Schoolhouse Street. High or low in birth, it meant nothing on the point of an imp's sword.

Wendra Neath was weeping over the body of her husband Pedo. The town's potbellied greengrocer was dying, run through by a spear. Not far from where Pedo lay was the small form of little Ianno, Fury's dragonboy, who had been slain in the last moments of the fighting.

Night had fallen before the enemy finally withdrew, the fire from the black drink subsiding in their veins. In the square they left a drift of dead imps, bewks, and men. Further down the street the Bull and Bush had collapsed in on itself in the inferno. The wind tore at the pillar of smoke, acrid eddies drifted through the streets. Men and dragons' faces were blackened, their eyes and mouths forming pale dots and lines against the soot. The darkening eve was reddened by the flames, which were rising high at the northern end of Schoolhouse Street, where the entire block was ablaze. A few imps were visible up there, holding part of the street and firing arrows into the houses on the opposite side.

An exhausted Thorn sought out the emperor, who was lying in the portico to the Neath home on Market Street, number three. Pascal had received a cut on the thigh, which required a field dressing. He submitted to the ministrations of old Macumber, who still wrapped the best dressings in Marneri, after twenty years of training dragonboys in the art. The emperor was exhausted, but he still rode the dreadful energy that came with battle. As Thorn came up, Pascal raised himself in his seat to clasp hands and embrace his bodyguard. They had fought together at the barricade, side by side, and each had saved the other. Indeed all the men had fought bravely and well, even those who had fallen at the barricade.

"Well met, old friend, but I see you took a wound or two as well."

Indeed Thorn had his right arm bandaged, and there was another bandage wrapped about his head.

"In the melee, Your Majesty, anything can happen."

Thorn wished fervently that he could persuade the emperor to leave the fighting and seek safety in the rear. Pascal was not having it.

"Not while we have dragons like the Broketail fighting for us. It's no wonder the imps reek of the black drink. How else could they nerve themselves to attack?"

"True."

The dragons had fared better this time around, for only Brezza had been killed, although there were many wounds on the big dragon bodies, despite the leather armor and helmets and shields. The fighting with the bear-creatures had been a close run thing. Bazil had slain three of the brutes before they'd finally given up. Now their huge forms were piled on the barricade, except for one monster that had broken right through the line. It lay by the overturned wood skip outside number seven, the head at an unnatural angle and the huge, hoglike eyes staring down the street.

Thorn sat down on the soot-blackened step. Weariness overcame him for a moment. He took a few deep breaths.

"The witch took a knock."

"Proves they don't have eyes in the back of their heads."

"Will she live, Your Majesty?"

"They say her head's not broken, but she's unconscious, so I don't know. We must pray for her."

Pascal Iturgio Densen Asturi contemplated a future without the Grey Lady at his elbow all the time, and then he prayed that she would live. She was the one who was absolutely indispensable, if the enemy only knew. They could find another emperor, even if they had to go outside the Asturi family, but another Lessis did not exist.

"Can we hold them if they come again?"

"Yes, I think so. But it will be close."

"How long do we have before they attack again?"

"They must rest like we do. It is harder to attack than to defend, and it requires more of a man's emotional reserves. Even imps have emotions, they will be exhausted now. We have an hour or two, I think, before they can attack again en masse."

"Where is the dragonboy?"

Thorn smiled. "With his great beast." Thorn struggled for words. "Your Majesty, never have I seen the like of this. That dragon is terrible in the extreme. He kills them by the dozen. You can see why our legions are so hard to defeat. The battledragons are the lords of the battlefield."

Thorn's eyes were those of one exposed to a miracle. The emperor nodded. It had been an education for him as well. He still wondered how the imps found the courage to charge the dragons, for he knew that he could not imagine trying it after seeing Bazil and the others in action.

"Invaluable experience, Thorn, but we must survive to employ it. We need reinforcements."

"Yes, Your Majesty. Help will come."

"May it come soon."

Thorn shrugged, knowing that it would be hours yet before any significant assistance could arrive.

Pascal sighed as he contemplated the distasteful.

"We need to think out where we can retreat to if we have to give up the barricade." Pascal raised a hand. "No, it has to be contemplated. We are heavily outnumbered."

Thorn nodded somberly. It was better to plan for even the worst eventuality. The emperor was not finished, though.

"We held them, Thorn. I can sense it. Even though they have the numbers, I feel we can still defeat them right here and send a message to their dreadful masters that the men of the Argonath will fight to the death for the things we believe in."

"Yes, Your Majesty."

Suppressing any misgivings, Thorn moved on down the street to discuss the situation with Dragoneer Relkin. Thorn had found that Relkin had a store of battle experience that far exceeded his own. Thorn had spent most of his life as a bodyguard, not a soldier. He had never fought beside dragons.

"How is the dragon?" Thorn nodded to the vast recumbent beast lying inside the alley behind the bank.

The big head came up, and one eye focused on him.

"He's doing well. He's hungry, what else?" Relkin said.

"Dragon is very hungry, you forget 'very,' " said Bazil. Despite the grim situation, Thorn felt a grin break across his face.

Sometimes Thorn still found it hard to accept being addressed in ordinary verio by a wyvern dragon, but that sense of oddness was fading. Strange as it was to hear speech from that big mouth, lined with daggerlike teeth, it was not as strange as it had been at first. Thorn was growing accustomed to dragons.

"Then, we must get you some food. I will speak to the innkeeper."

"And plenty of akh."

"Of course." Thorn turned to Relkin.

"Pip Pigget had a good horse. He'll be past Felli by now."

"It's a long march in the night. We have to hold them off until tomorrow morning."

Thorn nodded, eyes downcast. "I pray we have the strength." He rose to his feet. "I'll go and ask about that food. I think we could all use something to get our spirits up."

Privately Relkin thought it was unlikely they could hold out until morning. If the enemy attacked every couple of hours as they had before, then in the end they would be worn down and overrun. The enemy was prepared to press the issue in almost suicidal fashion, and he had considerable numbers, several hundred imps at least. Plus a dozen more of those strange new monsters.

Relkin turned back to cutting down the shafts of imp arrows to fit them for the Cunfshon bow. He had used up all his own shafts long before. The situation was desperate. They would have to retreat from the village and fight their way north up the road, or they'd have to perform a miracle and hold out until reinforcements came.

A miracle! He glanced down the street to the inn, where he knew Lessis lay, still out cold from that blow to the head she'd taken. She could not perform any miracles for them now.

It seemed they were out of options, except for one thing, and that was the one that left Relkin very disturbed. His palms itched, and he started to sweat just thinking about it. His stomach turned fluttery with panic. The Lady Lessis was not, perhaps, their last source for magic. Relkin had seen it, he had felt those strange powers awake inside himself. He had gazed into the abyss they represented, and he had drawn back, genuinely terrified.

Ever since the moment of his possession by the demon of the Ten Thousand, he had lived with this terrible knowledge. When Mirchaz fell and the demon was released and the Mind Mass of Mirchaz finally knew itself, then were the channels laid bare for Relkin to see and never forget.

Then had come the power, surging through him in such shattering volume that when he laid his hands on the gates of the city, they were shattered in a flash of light and thrown asunder. The air stank oddly afterward, his hair stood on end for hours, and there were black spots across his vision that took days to fade, but for a moment he had been a god.

Oh, yes, he remembered those channels. He had visited them before that, but blindly, driven to it by the agonies imposed by the mad elf lord Mot Pulk. But now he knew where they lay, and he thought he knew how to open them. And that terrified him.

Relkin wasn't the sort of person to be easily terrified, not after all he'd lived through in his career with the legion. Yet this frightened him deeply, for he suddenly could see that other life in which he gave in to these powers and became a sorcerer. There was a corruption there that could devour the spirit. He well knew how great was the discipline of the witches. Lessis and Ribela possessed powers that could easily give them command over empires, but they chose to serve the Empire of the Rose. They took no interest in material pleasure or possessions. They were rather frightening in their dedicated single-mindedness. But he doubted that he possessed such strength himself. The wielder of great powers of magic could take what he wanted from the world. That godlike feeling again. But with it came the corruption. Relkin had seen the effects of that corruption. He had seen what it had done to the great Heruta, Gzug of Padmasa, and he had witnessed the dreadful senile corruption of the elf lords of Mirchaz. Could he avoid such pitfalls? Could he remain himself if he allowed himself to fall into the abyss where the magic powers winked and gleamed in the dark?

That way lead to madness, he was certain. The old gods would never forgive him, and if they still lived to govern the heavens, they would doom him. He would be consumed by the magic. He would lose his soul and become something fell and evil.

Thus he had resolved to never open those channels again, for anything. It was better if he forgot all about them. He had told only one person in the world about the experience, Eilsa Ranardaughter, his beloved and wife-to-be. She had counseled him to beg the pardon of the Mother and never, never enter the magic realm again. Among Clan Wattel there was a strong prejudice against sorcerers in general. In the old days they'd burned them at the stake.

Relkin had done his best to forget the powers he had glimpsed. And now he was faced with a terrible choice. More than his own life, more than the life of his dragon, hung on this choice. They might even lose the emperor himself. Relkin didn't have more than the common knowledge of the political situation in the Argonath, but he was sure that the murder of the emperor would not be good for justice or stability. Or for solving the problem posed by the Aubinans. The empire itself could be at stake here.

Did he dare to tread those abyssal deeps once more? Could he make himself go into that state? Was there any alternative? Wasn't it his duty?

And what else was he going to do anyway?

The dragon noticed that Relkin was sunk into himself, but being too tired to care about anything except a meal, he let his head fall back and closed his eyes again.

A few minutes later they awoke to see the happy sight of Avil Bernarbo and his family wheeling a cart down the street laden with a big pot of sweetened corn stirabout. They gave Bazil the biggest spoon in the kitchen and poured in an entire pot of akh.

There was hot kalut, bread, sausage, and pickles for everyone. More carts came down from the inn. At least there was absolutely no shortage of vittles.

Relkin took kalut and a half loaf of bread larded with cream cheese, and sat in the shadows. Bazil finished the stirabout and then stretched out with a happy groan.

"Now if we die, we at least die on a full stomach."

Relkin didn't respond.

At that moment one of the bear-creatures came forward and hurled something high over the barricade. Men went to look and gave cries of anger and woe. It was the head of Pip Pigget.

No message had gone through past Felli. They were alone.

Bazil grunted after a few moments. "So you have realized that we cannot keep them back all night?"

Relkin looked up.

"Boy have no choice, but to try. I know you have this power. Dragon can feel it."

"I'm afraid, Baz."

"We die otherwise."

Chapter Eighteen

In the Dragon House at Cross Treys, the day was drawing to a close. The dragons had eaten their dinner, taken a plunge in the pool, and finished their allotment of ale. Then they trundled off to their stalls for sleep.

As usual they slept with thunderous snores, particularly from old Chektor and the Purple Green. Dragonboys made last-minute kit checks before they too turned in to sleep. This came easily, despite the curious whoops and hirrups, blurps and zuzzes that came from snoring wyverns.

There were a few exceptions. Swane, Manuel, and Jak met out front to talk.

"It's not like Relkin, not these days," said Swane.

"Something must have delayed them. Probably they ate too much yesterday. Can you imagine what kind of a party they probably had down there?" Manuel tried to be the calming influence.

"Yeah, and I can imagine the kind of party they're gonna get from Cuzo when they get back."

They shared a grim chuckle. Cuzo could be a right bastard when he thought you'd tried to take advantage of him. Being made to look foolish by Relkin would really turn him purple.

"Swane's right, though," said Little Jak. "They wouldn't have wanted to get on the wrong side of Cuzo. I mean, imagine old Wiliger letting them out on leave like that."

"Never would have happened." Swane was emphatic. "Trouble for Cuzo is that Relkin ought to have been made dragon leader. We know it, and Cuzo knows it, but Relkin wasn't here when Cuzo got the step."

"There's some politics behind it too," said Manuel.

"What? In Marneri?"

"Yes. There's those who have it in for Relkin, and the Broketail too."

"The Aubinans?"

"Right," Swane nodded heavily. "It all goes back to Commander Glaves. They'll never stop trying to get Relkin. A real pity if this turns Cuzo nasty, just as he was easing up."

"It doesn't seem right that Relkin didn't even send a message." Manuel sounded thoughtful. "But whatever the reason for it, they're in hot water with Cuzo already."

"By the Hand, did you see him at dinner call?" Jak puffed up his cheeks and turned himself pink in imitation of their dragon leader.

They laughed, but it was laughter tinged with sad certainty that Cuzo's wrath would fall hard and heavy on their friends when they eventually presented themselves at Cross Treys.

Eventually only the snores of wyverns shook the air of the Dragon House.

Little Jak slept on his bunk, high up on one side of Alsebra's stall, and Alsebra lay stretched out on a mound of fresh hay. The freemartin dragon's sleep was not the noisy process of the Purple Green; she scarcely snored at all and normally she hardly moved from eye shut to eye open—except for an occasional stretch and a wriggle down the back to the tail tip before laying down again in a new position.

From next door came the rumbles and whirs of the Purple Green. Though Jak had grown used to them, he still wondered sometimes how Manuel managed to sleep while actually being in there with the snorer. Jak wondered how anyone could live with the wild dragon. He took up half the stall as it was with that huge bulk, augmented by the wings. There were some postings, like up in the Blue Hills, where they'd had to knock down a wall and give the Purple Green a double stall. And when he snored, it was as loud as he was big. Jak sighed and turned over and pulled the blanket over his shoulder.

Despite it all, Jak slept soundly.

Alsebra too was in her normal relaxed sleeping state, laying on her side with tail drawn around her head. An occasional light flutter came up from her as her side rose and fell.

But then after an hour or so of sleep, something changed. Alsebra's rhythms were off. She began to snort occasionally or to clack her jaws, a sure sign of agitation. And indeed Alsebra was having a most peculiar kind of dream. She kept seeing Relkin, but a weird, blurry Relkin, as if he were a ghost. He was trying to talk to her, but she could not quite hear or understand. As if the words were being swept away in the wind. And she strained to understand, strained so hard that her head hurt, but she could not quite get it.

Alsebra twitched and moaned in her sleep. She rolled over and hissed and shrugged, and turned over again and again and then finally she woke up and sat up straight.

Jak had woken by then, disturbed by her agitation. Blurry-eyed, he stared at her.

"What is it?"

"Dream. Strange dream. I saw Relkin. He said things, but this dragon could not understand." Alsebra had the strangest look in her eyes.

"Weird." Jak was fully awake now. He got up, lit the lantern, and gave Alsebra a cursory examination. The look was gone. She stared back at him with huge, haughty black eyes.

"Do you feel hot, or cold?"

"Neither. It was just a dream, but it seemed more than a dream too. This dragon does not understand."

Jak blew out the light and got back into his cot.

"Better we get back to sleep; be morning all too soon."

The dragon curled up, he turned over, and they sent themselves back into the arms of sleep.

But it was not to be. A few moments after they'd both dropped off, the curtain twitched aside and in came Curf carrying a small lamp. He went to the crib and shook Jak awake.

"What the hell!" said Jak, groping for a knife as he came up out of a deep sleep for the second time.

"It's me, Curf."

It took a few seconds for this to sink in.

"Curf? What you want, Curf? Isn't it a little late, Curf?" Getting woken twice like this was getting to be annoying.

"Listen, Jak, do you know anything about dreams?"

"Huh?"

"I just had the strangest dream I ever had. Relkin was

talking, and I could only just hear him. It was like he was far away, and his voice was very weak."

Jak was sitting up by that point.

"What is going on?'

Alsebra had woken up at the sound of voices in the stall. One huge eye contemplated them from over her tail.

"Relkin said that he needs help." Curf gestured with the lamp. "He needs us all, in Quosh. There's a fight going on there. Desperate fight."

"You heard Relkin say that in dream?" said Alsebra.

"Yes."

"I have same dream, but I not able to hear the boy's words."

Curf's eyes got wider, and his eyebrows vanished under his hair.

"You had the same dream?"

She nodded.

"Then, it must mean that it's true. If two of us had the same dream, me and a dragon!"

"We better tell Manuel."

A few minutes later a dazed Manuel was listening to the story. He quickly cleared sleep from his brain when it all fell into place, and he saw the picture.

Then came the capper. The Purple Green himself arose from straw, seeming to fill the space.

"I had dream too. I saw dragonboy, he rode on a horse that I wanted to eat. I flew above and wanted to make the kill, but the boy was on the horse. Then he said something, but I could not hear him."

Manuel was convinced.

"Magic, some kind of magic. Relkin's involved in something, and he needs our help."

"We've got to tell Cuzo!"

Manuel shook his head after a moment of sober reflection. "No. That won't work. He'll never understand. We just have to go. And trust that Relkin really is in trouble."

"Won't that be mutiny?"

"Yes, but if it's enough of an emergency to get Relkin involved in some kind of heavy magic, then it's serious enough to risk it. If we get there and we're wrong, then we'll face some kind of aggravation, but at least we won't be risking not going and finding out that Relkin and the Broketail were killed because we didn't go."

Curf and Jak needed no further encouragement. In a matter of minutes they had woken everyone in the unit, except Cuzo, who slept in his own private room at the end of the Dragon House.

When the story went around the Dragon House, it received confirmation from some of the other wyverns who had also seen Relkin in a strange dream. All the dreams were different, all had been vivid, and in them the common thread was that the wyverns could see the dream Relkin, but they could not hear him.

The only dragonboy who had had such a dream was Curf, and he had heard the message clearly though distantly. To the dragonboys this was just evidence of the difference between the dragon mind and the human mind. Equally they understood that Curf was the one who had the dream because he was a rare daft fellow, more into his music than the real world. So naturally it was Curf who was sensitive to this weird magic. And, of course, all were aware that Relkin had been unwillingly involved in magic over the years. He was a friend of some of the weirdest witches alive, even the Queen of Mice. So with Relkin anything was possible, or so they thought.

No one, not even Swane, mentioned doing anything other than just getting up, taking down their swords and shields, grabbing helmets and chain mail, and moving out to form up outside in the parade ground.

The dragonboys studied the situation at the gate. Cross Treys was a quiet post, the night guard was rarely more than two men: one at the main gate, and one on the south tower. Another ten men slept in cots inside the gatehouse, but nothing had happened in this part of Blue Stone province in so long that the watch was not well kept. It was no secret that Captain Bandar, who ran the night watch at the gate, was too fond of whiskey. Sometimes the men took advantage of this.

Alas it was not to be so easy. Bandar was drinking all right, with a couple of cronies in his office in the gatehouse. But on guard was Jasben Darthold, a relatively wakeful member of Bandar's detail.

It was important to steal away and not arouse a fuss. Pursuit would come in the morning, but by then they'd be close to Quosh. Darthold had to be neutralized. Swane and Rakama teamed up to do the job.

Jak went down to the gate, ostensibly to check the tally sheet for the next day's expected deliveries. While there, he engaged Darthold in a conversation about the weather, which was awful, with the rain still coming down hard.

The sound of the rain drumming on the roof of the gatehouse also helped to muffle Swane and Rakama's approach. Darthold didn't realize something was wrong until Rakama grabbed him around the chest, pinning his arms as Swane pulled a sack over his head and jerked it down. He struggled, but Rakama held him and they worked the sack down to his waist. The struggle got quite intense for a while, and Swane was forced to whack Darthold over the head with a spear to quieten him.

Breathlessly they waited. Would Captain Bandar investigate the noise?

Bandar opened his door and shouted something unintelligible in query.

Swane bit his lip and then shouted something back that was also unintelligible, but soothing.

They waited another tense second, then Bandar's door closed, and the voices in his office went back to their normal drinking chatter.

"You're coolheaded for an orphan, Swane," murmured Rakama.

"Let's go."

They trussed and gagged the unconscious Darthold, stashed him in the back of the hay storage at the barracks stables. No one would find him there until dawn at the earliest.

The gates swung open, and the 109th Dragons slipped out, moving as quietly as wyverns can. The gates swung shut again, and they moved quickly down the curving road that lead from the fort to the crossroads and the ford over the Killjoy Stream. Not until they reached the ford would they be out of sight of the gate tower.

It was a long two minutes as the dragons trotted down the curving gravel road, but no call came from the camp, and when they reached the ford, they broke into murmurs of victory.

They splashed across the stream and went on up the narrow road into the Rack Hills. It was night, and the moon was hidden. The rain came down in gusts, but they marched and made good speed, keeping in two files, marching at a steady rate.

They knew the road, which they had used for a dozen or more training marches. They had been over the Rack to Felli and back too many times, in fact. They hadn't done it in pitch-darkness before, but they could sense the mass of Baldy on their right, and the slightly smaller hill of Little Baldy on their left. Rakama, Jak, and Swane carried lanterns to light the road ahead, and that was enough.

Once they got to Felli, they would turn to the left, get onto the bigger road that ran down the valley from Borgan. If they marched hard, they could be in Quosh well before sunup. And if there was trouble there, they'd deal with it. Whoever was causing it would have to face the fighting 109th of Marneri.

Chapter Nineteen

Lessis awoke to a deepening nightmare. She found herself in a room filled with the groans of the wounded. When she moved, she thought her head would split in two. She put her hand up to her head, and found a bandage swathing her face and crudely tied below the jaw. There was crusted blood on her hair. The wound had been treated superficially and would need more work later. The important thing was that she had survived it.

She didn't even remember how it had happened. All she remembered was the desperate fighting at the barricade, then imps almost breaking through and a momentary melee in the whole street. And then she was here.

Lucky to be alive, she concluded.

She pulled herself up and took a good look around. A dark place, smelling of horses and sour beer.

A room in the brewery, then. She nodded, they must have won the melee too, or she wouldn't have been dragged up here. Slowly she hauled herself to her feet. Things went woozy for a moment, and she had to grab a timber for support. Then the dizzy sensation passed, and her head began to clear.

She became aware that the background din was very loud, sounding almost as if it came from just outside the building. She stumbled through a low-slung door and came out into another, better lit room. A couple of women were standing by the window. Lessis could see that they were terrified. Steps down to the floor below opened out at the farther end of the room.

There was a sudden loud scream of agony just outside, and a tremendous smashing noise. More screams followed, and then came a weird, piercing bugling roar.

The women turned to her with ashen faces.

"Old mother, you did wake up," said one of them.

"I did. What is happening?"

"The end of the world," said the other woman.

Lessis looked out the window. The noise below was horrifying and very loud. She saw that she was on the second floor of the building and that several of the monstrous creatures with hoglike heads were fighting in the street with a dozen desperate men. Imps were waiting at the heels of their allies for the opportunity to get in among the men as soon as they were softened up enough.

There were flames across the way, and smoke billowing up from them. The battle had clearly moved on past the barricade. The men were taking a beating. Two men were down, cut to pieces by the huge bewk swords. The imps were yelling insanely and blowing their dreary horns.

The men fought from behind a makeshift barricade, just a few benches and barrels dragged out into the street. It was clear that they would not be able to hold this for long against these huge brutes with their heavy swords. By the sound of it, the enemy might capture the brewery at any moment. Lessis thought of all the wounded lying in the room behind her. If these imps got in among them . . . They had to be moved. If the roof was set afire, they'd all be burned to death where they lay. Which might be preferable to what would happen if the imps got in among them.

Lessis took a deep breath.

"We have work to do, sisters," she said while she wove a quick spell that boosted their spirits and brought a martial feeling to their matronly hearts. A fire came into their eyes, and their backs straightened.

Lessis set the women to sorting out the wounded and getting the ambulatory ones moving toward safety. They had to get out of this building and go much farther back, possibly out of the village altogether. The women leapt to the task as if transformed.

Then Lessis darted down the steps and came out into the wort room. Mash tuns and tubs were set across the space. Spent grains were spilled into an enormous heap at one end.

Imps were smashing at the gate at that end. Lessis felt her heart sink. It seemed the battle was lost.

Then she heard another sound, one that to Lessis had

become instantly identifiable, the terrifying roar-scream of a battledragon. She hobbled as quickly as she could push her ancient body across the courtyard. At the gate there was a fight raging between a handful of men and a dozen imps. Swords and spears clattered off shields and helms, the men were holding the imps off. Then over their heads she glimpsed a dragon, with fragments of leather armor hanging off his huge body, go surging past and pitch into the bewks at the flimsy barricade.

There was a great growling and an almighty crunch, then screams and roars and the ringing of enormous steel blades upon one another. She saw men come staggering back, bent as low as possible. Some crawled on their hands and knees, and she glimpsed a flash of white fire as the dragonsword whirled over them. To Lessis, that fire was a gleam of hope.

She ducked into the next building. There were several women there, with a group of children. Ah, poor lambs! Lessis was stricken to see such little ones caught up in this horror. They were all too terrified to move. She summoned familiar verses from the Birrak and set to lifting their spirits.

It was the work of a moment. Their eyes came alight, even the littlest ones were changed.

"Arm yourselves," she bade them. "Go to the kitchen for knives, cleavers, pokers. Whatever you can find. We are going to fight for our lives."

The women and children ran for the kitchen.

Lessis opened the doors to the next room and was astounded to find a group of older men, lurking by the window. From their clothes she took them for wealthy fellows, and by their guilty air, she had caught them hiding from the struggle. Lessis roused them up with a spell, and sent them to the task of defending the village. With looks of bewilderment the men, who'd been looking to sit out the battle, left the room and ran down to the blacksmith's in search of weapons.

Lessis reached the street entrance, the gates were open, a crowd of men were bunched there. She joined them and got a glimpse out into the street.

The dragon's intervention had smashed the attack. Two bewks had been hewed down, and the rest had run from that furious assault with Ecator. The men who'd survived the earlier fight went out to lean against the wall. Other men arrived, including the five older fellows who'd been lurking in the pot room. They had armed themselves with hammers, tongs, pokers, and a long pitchfork.

Bazil came slowly back from the barricade, and the men filtered forward to surround him. More material was being wheeled up for the barricade. A few arrows flew over from the imps, who had advanced to the corner of Brewery Lane from Schoolhouse Street. It was the schoolteacher's house that was burning, although from the glow in the sky beyond the roofs, Lessis knew there were other fires in the village.

Men hastily piled things onto the barricade, while sparks and embers flew up from the schoolteacher's house.

Bazil found a sheltered spot out of bow shot, and lay down with a groan. Relkin was already at work on the worst cuts, a slash on the right shoulder and a deep chop in the left flank. There had been fierce fighting that night, and Bazil had been in the midst of it from the beginning. Relkin thought he'd not seen fiercer fighting, except at Sprian's Ridge.

The wound in the side was bad because it cut through old scar tissue, and the dragon's hide was already weak there. Still, it had not bled that heavily, and Relkin was hopeful that it was still only in the fat and had not gone through to any organs.

He lacked sufficient bandages to bind it up, though, and could do no more than clean it and treat it liberally with Old Sugustus, just like the other cuts and scratches.

Bazil groaned and shuddered from the sting, but was too tired now to grumble.

Lessis came up on them out of the smoke. Bazil saw her first and grunted a welcome. Relkin looked up.

"Lady! You live."

"You didn't expect me to?"

"That imp laid you out with a mace, a pretty clean blow."

Lessis waved a hand at the sky, ignoring the throb in her head that this set up.

"The Mother won't let me finish my term of service," she said.

Relkin nodded to himself, it was the only explanation for someone living through a blow like that. The goddess must have intervened. Relkin knew that this seemingly ordinary older woman was, in fact, a strange, sometimes terrifying sorceress. It was not impossible for one such as she to be on terms with the gods. Relkin had felt the breath of the gods himself, of that he was convinced. He wished he hadn't.

"They said you were not likely to live."

"The way my head feels, it might be better not to." She managed a faint grin. "But tell me, child, what is the situation? If anyone here can tell me, it will be you."

Relkin took the compliment in stride.

"Well, they took the main barricade. We slew them in droves, but they just kept coming. The imps got over and pushed us off the barricade, and we could not hold them. The men lack legion training. Same with the local dragons, and Bazil was just too weary then to make up the difference."

Relkin paused for a breath, and then coughed a moment on the smoke that swirled through the street.

"Then they broke into Bank Yard and then came behind the bank. We were taken in the flank, and we had to fight our way back up this street. We held them here, but they've captured the eastern part of the town."

"And the rest of the village?"

"The temple bell is still ringing. That's about all I can tell you."

"The emperor, child, have you seen him?"

"Not since the barricade fell, but he is not dead, I am sure. He was standing and still held a sword."

Lessis looked around uncertainly in the smoky murk of Market Street.

"When will help get here?"

"I don't think it will. The rider that was sent to Cross Treys did not get through. More riders were sent, but they won't get there until it's too late."

"We must have help."

"I tried," he stopped, unsure of himself and looked down.

"Yes, child?"

"I tried to find the magic way and send a message. It didn't work."

"Ah, well, young man, you are not schooled in it, although you have tasted the power. It takes much training to control it."

"So I have learned, Lady."

Lessis left them and went down the street. Relkin turned back to his work.

The witch found the Emperor in the parlor of the inn. He was lying on a table wrapped in a blood-soaked cloth.

His head was pillowed, and there was a pair of young women on hand to care for him.

"Your Majesty!"

His eyes lit up at the sight of her.

"Lady Storm Crow, how good it is to see you!"

"Your Majesty, where is your wound?"

"My back, lady, and along my side."

Lessis saw the blood and the crude stitches someone had made.

"You need stitching. Send for the dragonboy."

"We sent for the town doctor, but he was killed at the barricade."

"May the Mother protect us, in all her mercy. I grieve to hear of the loss of the good doctor, but when it comes to stitching wounds, dragonboys are the best."

"Then, send for him."

Thorn came hurrying into the room. His right arm was bandaged, but he seemed little affected.

"Your Majesty, Lady. It is good to see that the reports were wrong."

"Only just, Thorn," she spoke more lightly than she felt.

"Your Majesty. I came to report that we've stabilized the line and thickened the new barricade outside the brewery."

"I can hear the temple bell still ringing."

"Indeed, Your Majesty. They have held out there. In truth, I think the enemy throws all his weight against us; he knows you are here."

"Then, he would have pursued us wherever we went. We made our stand. We have not fallen yet."

"Indeed not, Your Majesty."

"Your Majesty," said Lessis. "Could you accept the need now for retreat? We have fought the enemy, but now you should retire and seek medical attention. We should return to Kadein."

"Lady, we made our stand here, and here we will stay! Until they cut me down and take my head, I stand in Quosh."

Lessis could not help thinking that this was the wrong approach.

"Your Majesty would be of more use to the empire alive, fleeing up the road, than dying here in Quosh."

"I stand here, Lady. I will not move. We will beat them, they have lost twice as many as we have, and they cannot continue such losses. Their force is finite. We can win yet."

"Your Majesty, the battle depends on the might of one battledragon, the great Broketail. Without him it is lost. Thus you stake the Empire of the Rose on the life of a single dragon."

"No finer beast could there be for such an honor! I have seen him fight. It terrifies me, and I'm on his side . . ."

His eyes caught hers and bored in ferociously.

"And we will stand here in Quosh and defeat our enemy!"

Lessis saw that nothing would move him. But if the enemy could spear the Broketail dragon, then they would soon overwhelm the defenders of Quosh and achieve their aim. Pascal would die a martyr to the cause of the empire, and indeed there would be a political bonus from such an event. But Lessis feared the shadowy moves around the throne of the Asturi. This new enemy was known to be a subtle foe, capable of arousing treacheries within the tightest cabals. What evil might break out, what hidden moves for power might be made by those who would seek the aid of the enemy to further their ambition?

She saw that she would just have to make the best of it.

"Yes, Your Majesty, I see." She stepped back with a bow.

Pascal continued to glare after her with the fire of battle in his eyes. After a life of conducting war at a distance, Pascal Iturgio Densen Asturi was finally an initiate to the life of the warrior. Something had broken and re-formed in his heart during the process. Lessis noted the marks of an epiphany of some sort, and though she deprecated the very thought of an epiphany brought on by armed combat, she had to recognize that it might exist.

Thorn came back from the door with more good news.

"They have pulled back; we have had word from the northern end of the village. There was fighting there, but it stopped awhile ago. There are just a few skirmishers in the Schoolhouse Street."

Lessis gnawed her lower lip.

"He has not given up. They must be gathering everything they have left for one final assault."

"Then, we shall meet them!" Pascal growled.

They were interrupted by the arrival of Relkin with his tools and a big bottle of Old Sugustus that had been fetched from the Dragon House. He winced at the sight of the emperor, lying on the table.

He examined the wounds. Three cuts required stitching and further cleaning. There was a two-inch-long stab wound in the thigh, a slicing cut along the bottom of the rib cage, and another shallow stab in the back.

"I think I can close all these wounds. The one I worry about is the thigh, for it went deep. Sometimes we use honey to dry a wound like this before we sew it. If treated with Old Sugustus, a dry wound will generally not infect and corrupt. But we don't have the time for such a treatment. So I'm afraid that I can only do a temporary stitch on that wound. It will have to be treated again once the fighting is over and we have the time to properly clean it."

The emperor smiled at the solemn tone of Relkin's voice. A proper doctor of physic he sounded, and yet he was just a dragonboy. No one noticed that the witch had slipped away, as quietly as a bird leaving its nest.

The wound above the waist was in almost the same place, relatively speaking, as the deep chop into Bazil's side. Relkin remarked to himself on this similarity as he strung clean gut on his needle and ran it through his fingers soaked in Old Sugustus. The needle was clean and very sharp; it was his smallest and was used for tidying up dragon cuts.

"Your Majesty, just to reassure you, if it will, I have sewn up wounds on men many times, not just dragons, and the needle is small and very sharp."

"I thank you, Dragoneer."

"Your Majesty, this will hurt a great deal. I will work very quickly, but it will still be painful. Many men prefer restraints, would you?"

"I shall not take restraints, but I thank you for your consideration, Dragoneer."

"First the wounds must be cleaned again and treated with Old Sugustus. It will sting."

Pascal Iturgio Densen Asturi nerved himself.

"Begin."

At the western edge of the village stood Tumblejack Woods. There stood Lessis, calling to the owls. She relaxed into open bird sensation, drinking in the sounds and smell of the wood. Among the trees, in holes at the base or in nests here and there, she sensed the living animals. She called again.

And soon she had one, a great grey owl. He flew in with

soft beats of enormous wings coated in tawny down, and landed in a young tree by her head. She spoke to him in the language of owls, which is a variant on the language of the raptorial birds. Then she put a message scroll out for him to grasp in one mighty foot.

"You know the place."

The square thing, man thing.

"Do not drop the scroll."

Not drop the thing he grasped in one talon. It was smaller than a rat, harder than a mouse. Not to be dropped.

"Go!"

His wings opened, and he was away.

Chapter Twenty

The commanding officer of Cross Treys camp was Commander Geilen, an older officer who had been seconded from the Third Regiment, First Legion of Marneri, to run Cross Treys for the last few years of his military career.

Geilen had succeeded in making his tenure at Cross Treys one of unsurpassed quiet and efficiency. What bandits there were had been apprehended and sent to Marneri for justice. Wood was cut and cured and shipped out to the contracting customers. Units came down from Marneri for a restful period at Cross Treys with calm regularity, and returned there equally peacefully.

Until this night. This night all hell had broken loose at Cross Treys camp. Specifically sometime before the midnight hour, the entire 109th Marneri Dragons, a famous unit that had enjoyed a good long rest up to this point, had suddenly absconded into the night. At the change of watch their absence was discovered, and the alarm raised. At least eight battledragons and their dragonboys had marched out of the camp without anyone being the wiser.

Commander Geilen thought of the humiliation his name would receive as he became the camp commander that lost a dragon squadron. Then his face went pink, and he renewed his frantic efforts to locate the missing dragons. Every lamp was lit, and every man awoken and set to searching.

Patrols went out at once in every direction. When they returned, they were grilled by the commander personally.

It soon became apparent that the missing squadron had marched out in proper formation and gone straight up the narrow road running into the Rack Hills.

"So they've literally run off into the hills?"

Dragon Leader Cuzo merely stiffened where he stood.

"I take a very dim view of this, Dragon Leader. I have commanded units of every size during my career in the legion, and I have never encountered such a debacle. Your entire squadron is absent without leave. Steps will have to be taken."

"Sir?"

"What is it, Dragon Leader?"

"I had given one dragon, the Broketail dragon, leave to visit his home village, which lies just over the hills in the valley. A three-day pass, enough time for them to go home, visit, and come back. The dragon and his dragoneer failed to return on time. As you know, sir, the other dragons have an enormous respect for the Broketail, and they were obviously concerned for him. I think that something must have happened, something which we men cannot comprehend, that would have disturbed them enough to do this."

"We cannot have entire dragon squadrons absenting themselves from their commands without leave. You know this, I know this, and we both know that we will have to arrest these dragons."

"You will send to Marneri?"

"I will send for two squadrons of dragons to be sent down here to capture the fugitives."

The cost of such a move was enormous. Dragon Leader Cuzo winced.

"Sir, could we not try reasoning with them first? I am sure they can be brought to see the error of their ways. The 109th has an enviable reputation. These are seasoned veterans, most of them."

"Seasoned or not, they're not here and that is what I have to deal with. I will send to Marneri. You will try to find the dragons and talk them into getting back here as soon as possible so I can cancel my request for a huge squad to arrest them."

Cuzo swallowed.

"Yes, sir."

There came a knock at the door. Lieutenant Loran entered. He had a decidedly flustered air as he came to attention and saluted.

"Sir, I have to report that there's an owl, sir."

"A what?"

"An owl, sir."

"An owl. So?"

Lieutenant Loran struggled for a moment.

"It's brought a message, addressed to the commanding officer."

"What are you babbling about? I have a whole dragon squadron gone missing, along with all their dragonboys, and you are wasting my time yammering about owls?"

Commander Geilen began to take on a dangerous countenance.

Lieutenant Loran swallowed heavily.

"Here is the scroll it brought."

Commander Geilen stared at the lieutenant with stony eyes. Then he snatched the little scroll.

"I don't know what this is about, but if you jest with me, Lieutenant, you will regret it."

Loran was so glad to get that witch scroll out of his hand that he hardly worried about Geilen's threat.

Geilen examined the seal under the lamp. An elfin rune, the letter "L" and the symbol of the Queen of Birds. Geilen paled.

"An owl, by the gods," he murmured softly, but loud enough for Loran to hear. The lieutenant drew heart from this. The focus of blame would be shifted, at least.

"The sentry claims that the owl brought this scroll in its claw and dropped it. Now it's sitting on the roof of the gatehouse. Hell of a loud owl."

"Mmm." Geilen realized he could no longer put off his sudden impact with the witch-ridden side of the empire. "Well, I'd better look at it whether it was brought by an owl or a band of pixies."

Geilen opened the letter and read it with mounting astonishment. It was written in a fanatically neat and tiny script that was easy to read. The signature was equally clear: "Lessis" was all it said.

But he knew it was the Grey Witch, the semi-mythical Queen of Birds; it could be no other. Commander Geilen had an instinctive queasiness concerning sorcery, and like anyone else in the army, he had heard the legends of the Grey Witch.

But the message was very clear. There was a battle raging in the village of Quosh and he was commanded, in the name of the emperor himself, to take his entire command and march at once to Quosh and attack the enemy force. He was to bring all the dragons he could because there was a new class of troll in the enemy party. He was urged to hurry; the emperor's life was at stake.

"Thank you, Lieutenant, you may go."

Geilen turned back to Cuzo. Astonishment was giving way to relief, strange as that might seem. After all this, it was good to have some idea of what had been happening.

"I don't know what's going on, but all of a sudden I think we have the answer to our mystery dragons. They have gone to Quosh. And now we are summoned to Quosh, so we will go. And perhaps when we get there, these mysteries will be more fully explained."

"Quosh?"

"Everyone, the entire command, now. Now!" Geilen raised his voice as he hadn't done in ten years or more. "We're going to Quosh, and we're going to fight. Tell my orderly to come in when you go. Round up all the dragons left in the fort; we'll need them, it says here."

Within a half hour the various units that had been on relaxed duty at Cross Treys were scrambling out through the gate, still belting on weaponry while their officers and sergeants bellowed at them to get a move on.

The rain was still coming down, but not as steadily. The men marched through near total darkness up toward the hills.

In the ruins of Quosh, the fighting had flared and died down again. The enemy's pressure was repulsed once more. With some of the others, Relkin dragged himself back to the gateway to the inn. His arm was numb, his brain fogged in exhaustion. Once again they had held the enemy and driven them back down Market Street, but the second barricade had irrevocably fallen. They had lost the brewery and were now fighting for the Blue Stone Inn itself, the center of the town. A third barricade had gone up: The delivery drays from the brewery, Wendra Neath's little blue coach, and anything else that could be moved, like the tables from the inn, had been piled up across the market between the Neaths' house and the inn.

"We held them, Baz, we held them again."

The dragon was too puffed to talk, but he nodded a vast slow nod as he laid his weary bones down inside the gate.

Relkin noted the exhaustion of the other men around him, including Ham Pawler. They were hollow-eyed, slumped over with exhaustion. They had been plucked from normal life and thrown into this horror. They were not in the physical condition of soldiers, and the hours of battle had exhausted them. They were close to collapse.

Relkin sagged back against the wall beside the dragon. Bazil had been magnificent, but even his great heart was wearing down now. They could not go on much longer, and the enemy was gaining heart, you could feel it. The imps knew it was only a matter of time now.

When the brewery was lost, most of the patients had been moved, but a few badly wounded men fell to the imps, who dragged them away to roast slowly over fires. Their agonized screams floated in now from the dark, a dreadful howling that tore at the men's nerves while the imps beat their drums and roared their war chants.

Relkin swore to kill himself before falling into the hands of the imps. They could eat his body if they liked, but his spirit would have gone to Gongo in the shadow land, and he'd be spared their torments. They'd get no pleasure from tearing out his tongue and eyeballs.

He saw Thorn go by. He was still at work, in between bouts of combat and organizing the defense. Relkin's admiration for him had grown through the hours. Thorn was extremely steady, and Relkin respected that in a battle situation, where many men became panicky. Thorn stopped at the sight of the dragon and came to squat beside Relkin. He might be the emperor's top guard, but he didn't stand on ceremony, not in the least.

"How are you, Dragoneer?" Thorn's arm had been rebandaged before the last fight, but it was a mess again, and he had some fresh scrapes on his forehead. There had been some difficult moments with the bewks at the barricade.

"We held them, Thorn, that's all I can say."

"We will hold! Twenty men came in from Cailonne just now, they rode up as soon as they got the news. More are coming. Help will come from Cross Treys."

Relkin nodded somberly. Help would come, but never in time.

"The emperor?"

"Is holding steady. That was beautiful work you did. The emperor was most impressed."

"He was a good patient, hardly moved, though I know it hurt."

"How is the dragon?"

"He's tiring. Needs food."

Thorn nodded. "I'll see what I can do about that." Thorn rose and slipped away.

Relkin got a second wind and started up to see if he could find some water, or better yet, some beer for the dragon.

A figure stepped in beside him.

"Relkin!"

That voice, so soft and quiet, yet penetrating, it was unmistakable.

"Lady. How are you?" he motioned to her head.

She slipped off her customary grey cowl to reveal that they had shaved her head and redressed the wound with a relatively clean bandage.

"Did they use Old Sugustus?"

"The stuff that stings like fury?"

"Yes. That's how you can tell it's doing the job."

"They did, and it stung all right. I appear to be surviving. And I'm glad to see both of you are still able to fight. You held them at the barricade."

"Bazil killed three of the new beasts."

Lessis shook her head slowly with that sense of terrible wonder. War was a fearsome thing, but she had seen the ghastly beauty in the way of the battledragons. Their energy and zest for combat was an awesome thing to behold.

"We have been drawn together again, child. There must be a purpose in this, but I do not perceive it. The stitches of Her Hem are beyond my reckoning."

"Many things have happened, Lady. Not just this fight, but others . . ."

"Yes, I can see that. You have grown, Relkin. Indeed you are no longer a child at all, and I shall not address you as such."

They fell silent, then Relkin spoke again.

"I have seen things, things that were terrible."

"You were in Mirchaz," she said. "What did they do to you, young man, those tired old creatures, wizened in their evil ways?"

"I was taken to the elf lords. I learned much, Lady. I learned of the ancient sorcery. I saw the Great One arise, the New Being, that which was the slave of the Game Lords. Ten thousand of them, welded together like bees in a hive, Lady. And now they are one. I felt its power within me, I have not been able to forget that feeling, Lady, even though I have tried. I have prayed to be forgotten and to forget. But I cannot forget, no matter how hard I try."

"It is a hard thing, Relkin, when a mind is exposed to the great power of high sorcerous magic and is not prepared for the experience. Without the training and discipline of years of work, the power cannot be controlled, nor can it be summoned at will except through extraordinary means. The young mind can be damaged, even destroyed by such powers."

"Lady, I can readily believe you. And you are right. I cannot use the power, I cannot even summon it up. I tried to do that tonight. I wanted to try and reach out to the thoughts of the men in Cross Treys. I thought perhaps I could speak to them in their thoughts in the way that you have spoken to me in mine."

"It was always easy to reach you, Relkin. I know the high ones must have marked your path."

"But, Lady, I cannot use the power. I could not make it do the thing I wanted."

"Without training in these arts, you can do nothing."

"But I have felt the power and seen things, seen such fantastic things that you might go mad at the thought of them. I saw worlds, whole worlds, created for the pleasure of the Game Lords. I dwelled in one and was seduced by its spirit."

Relkin paused for a moment, his thoughts whirled whenever he remembered fair Ferla in the grotto of Mot Pulk. But all that was gone, lost in tears of long ago.

"I feel the lure of it, Lady, and I fear it. I have seen too much, and I cannot forget."

"You have endured much, young man."

Indeed, she thought, his whole life had been spent at war or preparing for war, and he was only now grown to manhood. What more might he be called on to do? Like it or not, he had been recruited into the high struggle that went on across the very sphere board of destiny.

"But, Lady, I felt the power of the New Being in me. I, Relkin, orphan, nobody but a dragoneer. Then suddenly it was as if I was a god. I went to the great gates of the city, and I put up my hand and smote them. They were blasted asunder and laid open and thus the city fell to the slaves."

"Mirchaz is no more." The world had changed, their evil game was ended, for which Lessis was thankful.

"It is a new thing, Lady, the giant that was born there, and we will meet it again, I am certain."

Lessis sighed. Ribela had confirmed that something strange and awesome had taken place in Mirchaz when it fell, but beyond that had said little. Lessis thought that she was hiding something. Ribela had her pride.

"I hope we can learn from it."

"Lady, there are gods and then there are other gods, false gods. You told me of the Sinni, and I saw the elf lords. They were not gods, but they wished to be. They were corrupt and cruel. I was the ludo Faex. I was . . ." He put a hand up to his forehead and leaned back against the wall, too exhausted to speak suddenly.

The dragon watched them with huge black and yellow eyes. Bazil was lost in a cloud of fatigue. He labored, just sucking in air and expelling it from his huge lungs. He had no energy left for contemplating the strange things that had happened in Mirchaz.

"Relkin, put your trust in the Mother, she will hold you up."

"I will try, Lady. But the world is not the place I thought it was. It's like a stage set with another world set up behind it, and our actions are not entirely ours to control. There are other powers pulling the strings, and we are but puppets. These gods and demigods confuse me, Lady, and I wish I had not been chosen to endure all this."

"You are a survivor, Relkin, that is the truth of it. You survived the volcano—"

"I survived the new god, the one that was born there in Mirchaz."

"By the Hand, Relkin, we should not speak so lightly of the gods. It was not a god, and the Sinni are not gods either."

"The Sinni, they are friends?"

"They are, but like us they are in the Mother's Hand, for we are all Her children. Sinni, elves of olden days, even the horrible old wizards of the Red Aeon, all descend from the primordial force in the world, all were nurtured by mothers. In this we all share, all that live."

"We had fathers too!" Relkin murmured, protesting as

he had since he was about nine and started not to believe the stories they read to the children at school.

"Indeed, but the paternal interest is not always as strong as the maternal interest. Sometimes it is strong, sometimes it is weak. It is all the way of nature, and in this we can see the Hand."

And in your case, child, isn't it obvious? Orphaned in a village like this one.

"Trust in the Mother, Relkin. We shall talk of this again. You should receive the training if you so desire. These talents are precious and rare."

"Lady, I fear these things, these sorcerous powers that I can feel. They hover in my mind sometimes like ghosts. I wish I were just a dragonboy again,."

"That wish has not been granted you, Relkin."

There were dull horns blaring, and the imp drums were louder.

"They come."

The dragon roused himself wearily onto his feet.

"We are ready."

Chapter Twenty-one

In front of the inn, they made their stand. There were less than thirty men now, and only a handful of dragons, most of them too old for this work. But they fought alongside the Broketail dragon, who held the middle of the line. The enemy knew him and the power of his terrifying sword now, and they had to be filled to the gills with the black drink to face him.

Still, they came, their dull horns blaring and their drums thundering, despite the dead that lay so thickly in the street.

Bazil watched them come through eyes reddened by smoke and fatigue. His arm ached from weariness, but the great sword still quivered in his hand with anticipation. How it loved this work. Such a strange thing was this sword, inhabited by its own fell spirit. Bazil had sensed it many times as it awoke to its work. Strange but deadly, more so even than his first blade, great "Piocar," which had been lost long ago in Tummuz Orgmeen.

Let them come!

Relkin had twenty arrows ready, all cut down from long imp shafts and fitted to his Cunfshon bow. He waited at the side of the barricade, behind a table on its side stacked against a pile of broken chairs and a heavy wooden post. The imps came forward, a mad snarl on their faces and their voices a whooping war chant. Behind them loomed the bewks.

Relkin aimed carefully and shot the imp nearest him through the throat. It gagged and sank to its knees. Arrows flashed and flickered around the barricade as imp archers farther back let loose another volley. A man staggered back from the barricade with a sharp cry. He fell to his knees.

Women rushed up and helped him away, the shaft sticking up from his shoulder.

The bewks made their growling roar as they came, and now behind them Relkin could see men on horses, blowing horns and urging on the hordes in front of them. Always it was thus, these men who sold their hearts to the enemy were the commanders of these dreadful battalions. His hate was strongest for men like these. Carefully he drew aim, but the smoke was thick and swirled up higher when a beam collapsed in the house across the way. The rain had started again, and it was damping down the fires, but sending up enormous clouds of steam and smoke.

Bewks stamped forward through the yelling imps. Relkin put arrows into them, trying for their eyes, but missing. Bewks with arrows sticking out of their thick-skinned skulls came on and broke into the barricade. Relkin used up the last of his arrows on a huge brute that wielded a two-handed sword which was almost as big as a dragonsword. The bewk did not seem to notice. Relkin dove through the legs of the table as the big sword chopped down and broke it right through the middle.

Close, much too close. He rolled and stood up and almost got crushed as another dragon, big old Essa, thrust in with her spear at the bewk.

Essa was old and untrained in war. Her thrust was avoided by the agile brute, and she fell off balance into the barricade and stumbled to her knees. The bewk needed no encouragement, and it hewed into her with the sword. She twisted away with a shriek, blood spraying from her neck. After a couple of steps she collapsed.

Bazil had his hands full with a pair of bewks, one of which had forced its way almost through the barricade. Bazil kept whipping the sword back and forth between them, but both were wily and quick and had avoided his blows.

The bewk that had slain Essa stormed through the rest of the barricade, and men rushed it, bowling over the imps in the fury of their attack. But the creature's sword was too heavy, and it broke other blades and sundered shields and sent heads spinning from their bodies.

Relkin slid under the broken table, wriggled forward under it, and came up behind the bewk. He stabbed home with his sword, deep into the monster's back. It roared and thrust an elbow at him instinctively and knocked him flying. As he got back on his feet, an imp swung in and would have gutted him if he hadn't caught the wrist and kneed its owner in the crotch. The imp's stinking breath washed over him as he dug his hip into its side and tossed it over his leg into a broken wood crate.

Relkin had his own sword up in time to defend against the next. A scream of warning made him duck as the bewk hewed at him from behind. The bewk was on its last legs, but it had turned to find the man-child that had done it such harm. Its sword took the heel off Relkin's left boot as he dove for safety under the ruined table.

He scrambled and the table was smashed as the bewk stove it in. Relkin rolled out and flung himself sideways. The sword missed him by a hairbreadth.

And then Thorn arrived and drove a spear deep into the breast of the bewk, and it went down at last with a gurgle of helpless rage. Other men surged past and threw the imps back over the barricade or slew them on the spot.

Bazil drove the bewks back and knocked one silly with a crack from the hammer he carried in his gripping tail tip. The bewk fell backward, rolled over, and got up slowly. Bazil had time to deal with his other immediate opponent. He caught its next thrust, whipped Ecator down, and shattered its shield.

It gave a moan of astonishment, and the next moment Ecator went deep from neck to crotch. The monster slid away in blood-soaked ruin.

The battle met once more at the midpoint, hovering over the barricade. It did not remain static for long. The imps came back, and then flanking movements began around the inn. They had broken the line north of Market Street and were sweeping into the rest of the village. But now there were only twenty-three men in front of the inn, and the women of the Bernarbo family, still occupying the windows of the inn, hurled rocks down on the imps as they milled below.

More arrows were lofted at the windows, and fire arrows at the thatch. But the Blue Stone Inn refused to burn so easily, and the women threw buckets of water on any arrow that lodged and burned.

In the yard at back Farmer Pigget and twelve men plus old Zignus, a huge, slow-moving brasshide that had never been bright enough for the legions, were keeping the imps and bewks out. Zignus was so strong he fought with a wheelless wagon that he picked up bodily and used as giant swatter to smash imps, bewks, and anything else that got in the way. The only problem was that he was slow and the imps were quick.

Nor was this the only small group. Others existed in pockets within ruined houses, fighting desperately to hold onto the entrance to an alley or just an isolated house. There were also two small barricades around the pump house, where a lot of wounded men were lying on the floor.

Yet desperate as the situation was, the survivors still fought on in the hope that help would come soon. By now the folk in Brennans must be aware of the battle. They would have smelled the smoke long since, and if they climbed up Durn's hillock, they would have seen the fires in Quosh.

And still the enemy came on. There were hundreds of imps, and with the black drink to fuel them, they would fight until they dropped dead.

Once more Lessis implored the emperor to seek safety in flight. There was still the open west road. They could get across the Roan Hills and down to Querc. From there fresh resistance could be organized.

Pascal Iturgio Densen Asturi, Emperor of the Rose, was wounded, sore, and bloody, but he was determined to fight to the death. He would not leave.

"We will stand here in Quosh and defeat the enemy!"

The enemy horns began to blow, the drums to thunder. Another round of the black drink, gulped thirstily from canteens made of human leather, was investing the imps and bewks with hellish energy. Their war screams became general, and they came on again with a wild will and the cry of war.

The men at the barricade rose to meet them, and once again everything from swords to mattocks was employed in the fight. The hellish clangor rose to the rooftops, mingled with the smoke of the burning village. How long the defenders could last was in doubt, but surely the end would come soon.

And then there came another sound, a harsh singing, huge voices roaring together in song.

"Oh, to be in the land of Kenor, green grassland so far away.

"Oh, to be in the land of Kenor . . ."

"Dragons!" went up the cry, and it was caught and repeated down the street to the inn. And the hearts of the men of Quosh rose up like a high flame, and they renewed their assault on the helm and shield of their enemy.

"Oh, to be in the land of Kenor, green and grassy and faraway. . . ."

A gust blew smoke from the guttering ruins, and with it came the distinct sound of heavy steel biting into sword and shield.

Bazil started roaring the words of the "Kenor Song." Zignus picked it up and threw his hoarse bellow into it. Then everyone in the inn took up the refrain and sent it high and lovely and unafraid over the roar of battle and the stench of the burning.

Shouts echoed from Pump Street, and there were screams and then a few imps ran full tilt into the market, in flight from that which came behind them.

Then the Purple Green of Hook Mountain, with Alsebra close behind, burst into the Market with a bewk stumbling ahead of them, its arms cartwheeling as it tried to increase its pace.

"One hundred and ninth Marneri dragons are here now!" roared the Purple Green.

The men at the barricade gave up a great shout, and there came an echo from Pump Street as men from Felli and Barley Mow came pouring in carrying everything from swords and spears to scythes and flails to join the weary few at the barricade. The tempo of the fighting surged. Meanwhile the great dragons embraced the Broketail and urged him to stand back, help was at hand. Then they turned and rushed the barricade with a collective roar that scattered everyone that had their wits about them.

Little Jak discovered Relkin leaning against the wall of the inn. Bazil was lying stretched out in the courtyard while Pessana Bernarbo and the other girls were pouring water on him.

"Relkin!"

"Jak," said Relkin looking up. "Thank the gods!"

"Curf heard you in a dream, Relkin. Curf and the dragons. You said come to Quosh. So we did!"

Relkin's eyes got very wide. It had worked! Somehow or other, even though he had no idea what he was doing, he had gotten through to them. The enormity of it came home to him.

Swane was coming over, a big smile on his simple features. Relkin took a deep breath.

At the barricade the fight soon turned. The Purple Green borrowed Zignus's idea and took up a battered delivery wagon, using it to flatten a group of bewks. The rest scattered, and the dragons went over with their swords at the ready.

Behind the dragons came the men of Felli, fresh and hot for battle. The imps broke and ran, the bewks lumbered after them. The men who commanded them could do nothing to stop their flight, not even when they slashed at them with their whips, or even their swords.

"It seems like a miracle," said Thorn, standing there for a moment while the smoke rose over the ruined village.

"By the Hand of the Mother, we have witnessed an amazing thing." Lessis looked over to where Relkin stood with little Jak.

"The emperor was right to make his stand here!" Thorn looked defiantly at the witch. Lessis looked back with a neutral expression.

"It would appear that he was," she said, unable to force herself to be completely enthusiastic.

"We stood here and we held them, and somehow these dragons got here in the nick of time."

Lessis's eyes slid across the street to where she saw Relkin standing listening to an excited babble from another dragonboy that she knew well, little Jak. They were joined by another, and more were coming, while enormous dragons moved off down the street in pursuit of the enemy, who had now fallen back to the village green past the smoldering remains of the old Bull and Bush.

Relkin sensed something and looked up. For a moment their eyes met.

Lessis made a mental note that Relkin had not been interviewed concerning his experiences in Mirchaz. The boy had crossed the lands of terror, and wandered through the most secret places in the world. Ribela should have seen to his full interrogation by the skilled questioners of the Office of Unusual Insight. But Ribela had behaved oddly following what happened to her on her astral projection to Eigo. She changed the subject whenever Relkin's name was mentioned and seemed quite uncomfortable with the topic of dragonboys in general. Ribela was a mystery, that was all you could lay it to. Lessis had served in the older witch's pathway for all her own enormously long life, but never had she fully pierced all the veils of the Queen of Mice. Whatever the case, this odd failure concerning the dragonboy would have to be corrected and soon. It appeared that something very strange had happened there.

The great green freemartin Alsebra emerged from the smoke that swirled thickly on Market Street, carrying her bloodstained sword flat on her shoulder.

"Greetings, Lady Lessis," said the dragon.

"Well met, great Alsebra. You came just in time."

"Almost too late, you mean. We smelled the smoke when we were in Felli. All the men came with us. They're cleaning out the other end of the village now."

"It was very well-done, a wonderful thing. Our enemy almost succeeded in his great aim, but by your aid he has been thwarted."

Jak came up, eyes searching for any cuts or damage to the joboquin.

"Everything's fine, not even a scratch," Alsebra hissed.

"What are they doing down there?" Lessis nodded to the smoke-filled street.

"Running, if they got any sense at all."

"Yes, indeed." Lessis stroked her chin.

"Tell me, Alsebra, why was it that you all left camp together and came here?"

"Easy," said Alsebra turning and pointing to Relkin, where he was standing with Swane, Manuel, and another boy Lessis didn't know.

"We all have dream of Relkin. Worthless boy Curf say he hear Relkin tell him to come to Quosh. Since we all have similar dream, we decide we better do it."

Lessis was rocked. It was what she'd expected, but to hear it from the dragon herself was still amazing.

Chapter Twenty-two

A few hours later under sullen grey skies, Commander Geilen and his command marched into the smoldering ruins of Quosh and found a massive effort underway to care for the wounded, prepare the dead for burial, and begin work on clearing the ruins prior to rebuilding.

The dragons of the 109th were not there, having gone with a large party of men from Brennans, who had shown up about an hour after dawn, in pursuit of the enemy. A message had been sent back to say that a few of the new-style trolls had been captured in Brumble Woods, apparently abandoned by their masters. They were said to be quite tractable, now that the black drink had worn off.

The Emperor of the Rose was in Quosh, wrapped in bandages, but still hale enough to sit in a chair and receive such as Commander Geilen on the pavement outside the Blue Stone Inn. A heavily bandaged guard stood by the emperor's side. Geilen thanked his lucky stars that he had obeyed the message brought by that owl.

"Your Majesty, we came as quickly as we could after receiving the message. Even though it was a little unusual."

The emperor chuckled.

"I know, I know, sometimes these magical things are necessary, no? But it's a damn good thing you came as you did. I want you to take your men and head straight up into the hills. There were still a couple hundred imps alive and some of these new creatures called bewks. The dragons are chasing them now."

"Of course, Your Majesty. Just a few minutes to water the horses, and we'll be on our way."

"You must move the men along at their best pace. I

know they are tired, but there are lives at risk here. We don't want small bands of imps getting loose into the hills."

Geilen nodded. It was true. Imps were naturally vicious, of weak dispositions, easily addicted to the black drink and prone to kill under its influence. He stepped back and bowed. The emperor clearly didn't want any sympathies wasted on his Imperial person. Wounds were not to be considered.

"This must have been a hell of a fight," he said as he straightened up and surveyed the charred ruins along Market Street, which were still sending smoke skyward. Steam and smoke still eddied through the streets, along with groups of people carrying stretchers. In the inn's courtyard they were laying out the bodies. At least eighty men were lying there, along with more than a dozen women and fourteen children, the youngest being Inky Peltwine, six.

"It was exactly that, Commander. And the people of this village have earned the undying respect of all their fellows in the lands of the Empire of the Rose. Such courage and gallantry has been shown here this past night as will live forever in song and saga."

"May I offer my congratulations, Your Majesty, on your victory. This fight will always be remembered by men who love freedom under a just law."

"Thorn here will get some food for your men. I expect they're taking a drink about now."

Geilen's men were indeed busy at the pump house slaking their thirsts. They had marched for fourteen miles at a rapid pace, most of them ducked their heads in the pond, filled the helmets with water and sloshed it over themselves. The horses were obviously nervous. They drank, but the smell of blood and dragons unsettled them.

Shortly they were gathered in the marketplace eating stirabout out of communal tubs brought out from the inn.

Geilen took a mug of hot kalut and toasted the emperor. The men roared out their allegiance. Then Geilen toasted the village of Quosh. The emperor was plainly pleased by that. He called out in a loud voice, and his guard helped him to his feet. The men roared their approval at the sight.

The noise finally brought a woman out of the inn. The moment Geilen clapped eyes on that slender figure in grey cloth, he knew she was the witch. Fascinated, he couldn't help staring. This was the creature that had sent the owl, this was that legendary witch who sat behind the Imperial Throne and advised emperors.

Lessis felt the interest in Geilen's eyes. She knew the look of one who was captivated by the magic world. She caught his glance and charmed him with a smile and a simple spell, then bowed to the emperor and inquired calmly as to how he was feeling.

Pascal had actually sat down again. Standing was too much. There was a pain that could be fairly called searing from that wound above his hip.

"I guess I'm about well enough to sit up," he said.

"The dragonboy commended your fortitude, Your Majesty."

"A very deft hand on that boy, I have been wondering if there oughtn't to be a scholarship for dragonboys who complete their terms of legion service. They ought to be inducted into the college of surgeons."

Lessis imagined how upset the college of surgeons would be when they heard this proposal come down from Andiquant. They spent many years in pursuit of the right to practice. How would they take to dragonboys coming off the battlefields to work among them? Not well, she judged. She changed tack.

"Your Majesty has been informed that we have captured some of these new creatures?"

"Yes."

"We shall have to investigate them carefully. They must not be slain if it can be helped."

"It is hard, considering the carnage they have wreaked here, but they will be kept alive, as will the men we took prisoner. They will get their trials, and then I expect they will hang." The emperor gave her a sharp look, as if daring her to disagree.

"They will be interrogated thoroughly first, I trust" was all she said. "There is always intelligence to be obtained from such men. They have seen more deeply into the belly of our enemy than we can ever hope to."

"Of course. And then they will hang. The people will not accept any other sentence."

Lessis shrugged. "I would not expect any. Such men have turned their backs on the rest of human folk. They cannot expect mercy in return."

"Well, Lady, we did it!" said Pascal with sudden fierceness. He wanted his due.

"Yes, Your Majesty. We did." She bowed deeply.

Geilen continued to stare at her, drinking in the presence of a legend and wondering at the slightly fierce nature of the emperor's voice.

"Well done, Commander," she said. "You came quickly once he found you."

"He?" Geilen was startled to be addressed. "You mean the bird, the owl?"

"Of course. Who else?"

Geilen swallowed heavily. "Yes, of course."

"I thank you for coming so quickly, despite such a strange message bearer. Fierce wasn't he?"

"Would that we could have come more quickly and been here before the battle ended."

"The dragons came in time. They had a strange dream and responded to it."

Geilen pursed his lips. A dream? Geilen hadn't even known that wyverns dreamed at all. All along the way down the valley from Felli, they had heard tales of the passage of the 109th Marneri Dragons before them. At the time Geilen had been relieved, he'd guessed right about the dragons' destination. He'd ordered his men to pick up the pace. They started to smell smoke before they got to Barley Mow. Then they'd really cracked on, and Geilen knew that he'd done the right thing to obey that message from the owl.

"The first we'd known of all this in the camp was when those dragons just upped and vanished. Had us all worried sick when we found out."

"It has been a very strange couple of nights for all of us. A relatively enormous enemy force has been active in the Ersoi for days, but no word of it leaked out."

"Ah." Geilen was suddenly able to imagine the scope of the inquiry that would inevitably descend upon him. As commander in Cross Treys, he had some sort of responsibility for the Ersoi Hills.

"We had no news of it in Cross Treys, I can assure you. If we had heard of it, we would have been out of camp in a moment and after them. There's little enough to do at Cross Treys, you know."

"I am sure you would have," she said.

He had finished his kalut. It was time to be off.

He bowed, strode out to the middle of the market, and mounted his horse, leading the men and dragons down Market Street into the clouds of steam and smoke. Geilen hated to admit it, but he felt shivery inside. He had met both the emperor and his tame witch! He, poor old Jod Geilen, who was in the twilight of his career and would never rise above the rank of commander. He had exchanged words with the emperor and then with that strange witch. She looked so plain, so ordinary, like a pale, worn woman who might have been a laundress. Not a scrap of color on her, just a single ring on her finger. By the Hand, she looked no more than fifty, but they said she was hundreds of years old. Geilen shivered again.

He looked up sharply when huge shapes loomed out of the smoke. Two dragons were shepherding a group of five strange creatures. They were bizarre-looking beasts, these trolls, with shaggy bearlike bodies and huge heads with piggish faces. They were disarmed, and their wrists were bound behind them. Geilen stared after them, wondering what they were and how they'd been produced.

The marching men from Cross Treys made room for the oncoming dragons and their captives. There was considerable chatter among the men about these new monsters. The dragons from Cross Treys hissed greetings to the duo herding the bewks—Churn a young brass and Gryf the green.

Then the men passed the smoking ruins of the houses on Brennans Road and were marching onto the common, heading up to Brumble Woods.

Back in the yard of the Blue Stone Brewery, Bazil hissed loudly as Relkin tended to his wounds. There was an arrow lodged in his left wingstub, and it hurt like the devil to have it cut out. The wingstub was a massive knot of muscle, redundant muscles in a wyvern, located in a girdle below the shoulder blade, and it was a tender area.

The gates suddenly filled with dragons, and then with the bewks. Bazil snarled, and reached for his sword.

"Hey!" Relkin jumped back, almost losing his balance.

Bazil was getting to his feet, on the point of unsheathing Ecator, when Relkin climbed up to his shoulder.

"Baz, they're prisoners. You can't kill them."

"Prisoners," hissed the dragon.

Gryf and Churn loomed up. Rakama and Howt were behind them.

"We have captured some of these things. The witch wants them," said Gryf.

Bazil snorted. "For what?"

"I do not know," said Churn. "I would prefer to kill them."

Bazil suddenly chuckled.

"What is funny?" said Gryf sharply. Gryf was still a little sensitive around the Broketail dragon.

"The Purple Green will want to eat at least one of them."

Even Gryf found this thought amusing.

Chapter Twenty-three

By the time the 109th Marneri had marched back to Cross Treys, they had developed a clearer picture of the ambush and subsequent Battle of Quosh. The enemy force had indeed landed on the Ersoi shore. A shepherd was found, a solitary fellow who lived in the southernmost hills, who had seen boats landing from two ships that heaved up beyond the breakers.

Those ships were already the focus of a gathering search by the Imperial fleet. Message birds were winging their way to and fro about the Empire of the Rose bearing this news. Frigates and sloops from every port in the Argonath were already putting to sea to hunt down these intruders.

Most of the raiding party had been accounted for, although there were some tracks leading from Capbern's Gap up into the Ersoi that were followed for a while and then lost by the Pawler brothers and their dogs. A watch was put on the hills and warnings posted out to all the shepherds and woodcutters and anyone else who would be working in out-of-the-way places.

The dead and captured bewks were in the process of being examined, dissected, and described scientifically by a team of surgeons summoned up from Kadein. They worked under Lessis's keen eye, while a pair of scribes and an artist from the Office of Insight took down commentaries and made drawings.

The Purple Green's inevitable request for one of the things to roast and eat was reluctantly denied by the witch, who said they had all to be interrogated and then investigated scientifically. It was necessary to ascertain just how strong, how fast, how intelligent the brutes were so that adequate countermeasures could be taken. She regretted being unable to donate one to the cause of dragon gastronomy and promised to come up with some other reward in that line.

The captured men, eleven in all, were taken under guard to Marneri for detailed interrogation. Lessis sent birds to Marneri with messages that were to be sent on to Andiquant. She ordered Bell and Selera, witches of the Office of Unusual Insight, to travel to Marneri at once and there to take over interrogation of these men. They were to peel them down to the bone. Then they would go to trial.

Lessis had some specific questions for these men too, such as what had caused that extremely bright light that had shone down on the ambush scene and blinded the emperor's guards. There was a power exposed there that she had not seen on Ryetelth before.

And if, as she suspected, this was the new enemy, then he had struck with considerable skill. This had been a swift, well-conceived attempt to decapitate the Empire of the Rose, and it had come very close, much closer than Lessis liked to contemplate. It had only foundered through their good luck in meeting with a battledragon and his boy. And if the enemy had succeeded, what then? The empire would be shaken by the resulting struggles. The succession was still a matter of debate. There was no good candidate within the Asturi clan at this juncture. There was a cousin, Keffad, who showed promise, but he was only nine. Too young for an effective emperor. There was also the problematic Furnido, half brother of Pascal, who had groused for years that he had been unfairly passed over for the Imperial Throne. Around Furnido swirled a motley band of malcontents and would-be intriguers.

Lessis wondered what maneuvers might have begun already back in Cunfshon and Andiquant. The fact that Pascal had survived would have squelched them at once, of course. However, it was possible that this whole ghastly thing could have a beneficial consequence if it exposed any movements within the Asturi or their related clans.

The 109th Marneri Dragons were unconcerned with these finer details of the situation. They returned to Cross Treys and rested up while dragonboys worked on wounds and scrapes and all their equipment.

It was an uncomfortable first parade under the angry eyes of Dragon Leader Cuzo, but he had received several messages from both Commander Geilen and the witch Lessis to the effect that the 109th had responded to "special orders" and had performed wonderfully in a crisis situation.

The fact that they had completely broken legion rules—had in effect mutinied by breaking out of the camp and going absent without leave, especially bearing arms—was to be set aside.

"Just what were these special orders, Dragoneer Relkin?"

"Not allowed to say, sir. Told to tell you that you must ask that question of Captain Kesepton."

Cuzo found this all very hard, since he was a stickler for the rules. He strutted around them, looking hard for the slightest piece of equipment that was out of place, out of shape, or lacking a suitable shine. Little Jak got hauled over the coals for some splashes of mud still visible on Alsebra's joboquin. Curf got similar treatment for the state of his boots.

When he came to Bazil and Relkin, Cuzo looked particularly hard for some infringement. The leatherback dragon had lots of fresh stitching and bandaging, at which Cuzo picked to be sure of freshness and at the same time to convey his disapproval of such damage to a valued asset of the squadron. Relkin, however, had learned long before that fanatical attention to the kit was essential to survive the ire of dragon leaders. There was nothing amiss, and so Cuzo passed on, reluctantly, and chewed out Rakama for the state of the metal filigree on Gryf's rather too fancy scabbard.

Finally Cuzo ceased prowling through the formation and addressed them from the front.

"You have all been recommended for a combat star and a battle medal for your part in this fracas. I congratulate you! The Battle of Quosh they are calling it. An Imperial medal so they say! So it will be extra special."

Dragons clacked their jaws quietly. Dragonboys swelled with pride, especially the new boys, for this was proof that they had been blooded while serving with the famous 109th.

"When I joined this unit, they warned me that the 109th had a tendency to throw itself into battles. Now I find that they were right, and I'm proud of you, damned proud."

Despite his words, Cuzo was clearly still furious, in part from missing the fight and in part from anger at their insubordination.

"However, our orders remain what they were before this sudden adventure. We will be marching to Marneri shortly, and after a little time there, we'll be shipping out to Kadein. After that we can expect to march to Axoxo for the winter."

The dragonboys shivered collectively at that thought. Even the dragons nodded a little apprehensively. The winds out there in the cold western mountains would be harsh.

After that parade, however, the dragons were informed that courtesy of the Lady Lessis, they were to receive an enormous meat pie, and with it a double hogshead of fine ale. The dragons perked up considerably and happily moved on to the Dragon House for dinner.

There they were dealt out enormous portions of pie and side orders of noodles slathered in akh, their universal condiment made of peppers, garlic, and onions. The hogsheads were broached, and the ale foamed into their cans. Dragons were never happier.

Relkin took himself back to the stall and went to work assembling all the equipment. He worked on a list of things he would need to obtain while they were in Marneri.

He'd just begun when Curf stuck his head in at the curtain.

"Relkin, got a moment?"

Curf had been trying to have a conversation with him alone since the battle. Relkin had been trying to avoid it.

"Sure."

Curf nodded to the scroll he was writing on.

"Making your winter list?"

"You got it. You already have yours?"

"Cuzo's orders. Even down to wool leggings—three pair, wool socks. You think it's really gonna be that cold out there?"

Relkin looked up. "You trying to be funny, Curf?"

"No."

"It's gonna be colder than you've ever imagined. We served a winter at Fort Kenor, right out by the edge of the Gan. That was cold. I wore two freecoats, one over the other some days, and still, half froze to death every watch. Fort Kenor's cold, but we're going to be way up in those White Bones Mountains. You know why they call them that?"

"Something to do with the bones of lost travelers?" Curf was ever the romantic.

"That's in one legend all right, but the real reason is they're always covered in snow. It's always cold there, and in the winter it's like being in the arctic."

"Brr, sounds like I'd better be sure to get an extra of everything when we're in Marneri."

"Yeah, do that."

Relkin wrote down "extra wool leggings, extra wool socks, buy pair of good gloves."

"Uh, Relkin, I wanted to ask you something, about that dream and all."

Relkin grunted. He'd known it was coming, still he did not welcome it.

"Yeah?"

"It was so vivid, Relkin, like I could see you in my dream just like I'm seeing you now. You just floated there, and you talked, and it sounded like you were very small and far away. But I understood you clearly."

"Yeah." Relkin was noncommittal.

"Absolutely, Relkin, I heard you, but you was in Quosh, and I was here in camp."

"Yeah."

"So?"

Relkin said nothing for a second or two.

"So what?"

"So how did you do it? By the Hand, Relkin, that was mighty magic. How did you make that dream?"

Relkin sighed. For a second he had a glimpse into that weariness that he sometimes detected in the Lady.

"Curf, listen to me. There's some things in life that you don't want any more of than absolutely necessary. This is like that."

"Is this something you learned in that elf city?"

"I don't know if 'learned' is the right way to describe it. Let's say it almost killed me. It's too strong for me, Curf. It's too strong for anyone who hasn't had the training. You've got to learn so much before you can handle that stuff with safety, and I don't know anything."

All I know is war, he thought with a trace of bitterness.

"Yeah, but, well, surely you must have learned something, else how could you do it? You know all the dragons saw you too. Even the Purple Green!"

Relkin heard the heightened interest in Curf's voice with concern. This thing could get out of hand, start turning into a legend. Then he knew he'd be besieged forever. Whoever had an illness that couldn't be cured, or wished to transmute hay into gold, they would come to Relkin of Quosh. He didn't think he could face that prospect.

"I heard. Look"—suddenly he glared fiercely at Curf—"I didn't know what the hell I was doing. It was just that everything was completely desperate; we had to try and get help fast. Otherwise we were all going to die. So I tried to do it, but I had no control of it. I don't know even how to describe what I did."

Curf looked down sadly, disappointed more than anything. Curf might easily become one of the legion of amateur potion and enchantment fanatics.

"Oh, I see."

"Well, I wish I did. But believe me, Curf, you're better off not knowing."

The flap lifted again, and Swane came in.

"Hey there, Quoshite! Heard the word?"

"What's that?"

"We march to Marneri in two days' time. They've accelerated the schedule."

"Hope we can be ready in time."

"There's more." Swane wore a happy smile. There was nothing he loved more than being the one bearing the hottest, latest words of rumor.

"Well, don't keep us waiting forever."

"There's a parade at the Tower of Guard, and they'll give us our medals there. They're making this into a big, la-dee-da thing, it seems."

"Ah."

"Great! All the girls will see us!"

Curf's sudden excitement brought a grim smile to Relkin's lips. Watching Curf was like watching a version of yourself from a few years earlier. And then something that Lagdalen had said once came back to him. They'd been talking about the Lady, and why Lagdalen was glad to be leaving the witch service and going back to civilian life.

"For the Lady, it has all happened before, so many times. She's seen everything, heard everything, seen millions of people born, grow old, and die, and millions more replace them. She wants to die, Relkin, but she cannot. She is protected by some great magic from the beginning of the world. They say she is five hundred years old, but I tell you that I think she is much older than that. She has been cursed by the great magic that they practice. I want nothing to do with that. I want to live a normal life and see my children and grow old and die eventually and return to the Mother's Hand. That is where peace lies, not in the magic arts. In those doctrines you only find hard bargains. For what they give, they ask a heavy price."

Those words had stayed with Relkin since the morning he'd seen Lagdalen in Marneri, shortly after they landed, back from Eigo alive if rather tardy. They had confirmed what he had already decided, the life of a sorcerer was not for him. He wanted to farm and live with Eilsa and Bazil and raise a family. He wanted all the things in life that he had never known. He didn't want to know about having blue fire shooting through his body or sorcerous worlds inhabited by seductress demons that could ravage your heart and disappear in the blink of an eye if so willed by their creators.

Swane was grinning wildly.

"Quoshite's thinking those deep thoughts again."

Relkin came back to reality.

"Well, at least I can, more than can be said for some of us."

"You must be talking about Rakama."

"Oh, no," groaned Curf.

"What is it this time?" said Relkin, strangely pleased at the chance of hearing about the latest tussle between the two bull-headed big guys in the unit.

Chapter Twenty-four

It was a small room, thickly carpeted and hung heavily with fabrics to muffle all sound. There was a small blackboard on one wall, and the single window was hidden behind thick curtains, blocking out all daylight.

The only illumination came from a pair of lamps set on the witches' desks. Relkin was being interrogated by two witches, Bell and Selera, a bright-eyed pair who missed nothing. They had none of Lessis's faded look, in fact, they had all the energy in the world. They asked questions, endlessly, and scribbled notes in heavy ledgers set before them. At the end of each session they closed and locked the ledgers. Relkin was then blindfolded, led from the room and released in an antechamber close to the central staircase of the Tower of Guard. All he knew, therefore, was that this was the fifth floor of the tower, a place of mystery and secretive bureaucrats.

Relkin sat on a hard chair. He'd been sitting there for days now, from the ninth hour of the morning to the third hour of the afternoon, and sometimes there had been a second session, from the fifth hour to the seventh hour of the evening. He was tired of the room, tired of the hard chair, and tired especially of answering questions. The witches were tricky and quite merciless, boring in on sensitive areas that he preferred not to discuss.

His time in the wild southland of Eigo had brought him into some complicated emotional and romantic territories. There were things that had happened that he simply could not verbalize, could barely comprehend, in fact.

The witches did not seem to care much for his feelings in the matter. Indeed they sometimes took a lofty tone to him that implied that the doings of dragonboys were unimportant in the great scheme of things.

In that case, he wondered, then why the hell did they need to take up his time with all these questions after so much else had happened?

He did his best to answer truthfully, but it was difficult at times. Especially when they wanted to hear his views on things like the magic systems of the elf lords. How could he, a mere dragonboy, know anything about that?

"The elf lords are dead," he said for the umpteenth time. "Those who didn't die when their worlds died were burned by the slaves in the rebellion. I don't know how they made their magic worlds."

"But you visited the worlds, Relkin," said Selera. "You are the only one who we can question about the experience. You must understand that this is now a state secret of the Empire of the Rose. We have to know everything."

Everything took a little time to tell, and Relkin had long since grown impatient with the process. Today they were pressing him on his relationship with Lumbee, the Ardu girl that he had traveled into the deep interior with. The witch Bell, with her handsome open features and soft brown hair, was the tricky one. Selera, who was paler than parchment with deep-set dark eyes and bright red lips, was more direct. Selera usually carried the conversation, but Bell was the one who would dive in on something sensitive and start probing.

"Relkin," said Bell in her soft, deadly voice, "you spent several weeks on the boat alone with the Ardu girl."

"Bazil was there."

"Yes, Bazil was there, but there was no other human presence."

Just the two of them and a thousand miles of strange, alien forest.

"Yes."

"The two of you must have thought about the sexual aspects of the situation. Didn't you ever feel like reaching out to her and giving her a squeeze, or perhaps a kiss on the lips?"

Once he might have blushed at being asked a question like that by a handsome woman. No longer. Still, he wished they wouldn't ask.

"Well?"

They were staring at him with those bright eyes that didn't miss a trick. He knew there was no way he could successfully lie to them, these trained witches from Lessis's own outfit.

"Why should that matter?"

Bell ignored his question and just bored right in.

"Well, did you?"

"Ah, well, yes, now that you mention it."

"And so you acted on these impulses, didn't you?"

They just wouldn't leave it alone. They wanted to know what he'd done when he and Lumbee had been alone so long. It wasn't their business, but they said it was.

"So what if we did!" he burst out at last.

"So you must tell us more. The Ardu are a people quite unlike our own, they are the only tailed humans there have ever been."

"What?"

"You must tell us everything about Lumbee, Relkin."

"You don't have the right to ask this, we were in love."

Selera and Bell pushed themselves back and looked at each other. Selera nodded, Bell's eyebrow rose.

"Actually, Relkin," said Selera with a friendly smile. "That makes it even more important that we question you. If a no-tail man can fall in love with a tailed female and vice versa, then there are many potential complications if, and when, the Ardu come into more permanent contact with the outside world."

"In short," said Bell, "it is essential for the continued existence of the Ardu people. Unless we can prepare the peoples that live around them to treat them with respect and not to react with atavistic hatreds, the Ardu face a bleak future. They will be exterminated."

"Oh," said Relkin, his mind reeling at the implications of this. Trust Bell to know how to pluck his strings.

"They will be seen as freaks, anti-god, the incarnation of demons, and they will be destroyed. We must protect them."

Glumly he settled in for a long inquisition about things that he felt were innately personal to himself and Lumbee, and nobody else's damn business at all. It was excruciating, and time and again he wanted to jump up and run out of that room and never come back.

When it was over late in the afternoon, he was led out blindfolded from the hidden Office of Unusual Insight and left in the anteroom to the Imperial administration offices. When the blindfold was removed, Bell was standing there.

"I'm sorry, Relkin, that we have to question you so exactingly. I think it is unfair in its way to you and your lovely Lumbee, but the basic point remains. We are enjoined to care for all living things on the world, and this will help us to care for the Ardu."

Relkin tore out of the offices, skipped down from the upper floors, and left the tower by the main entrance, making his way quickly to the Dragon House. Inside the looming mass of the house of wyverns, he was met with the familiar steamy atmosphere, redolent of dragons, sweat, and Old Sugustus.

He found Bazil in the plunge pool, cavorting with Vlok and Chektor. Romping beasts with a combined weight in excess of eight tons was rather more than anyone human-size could be expected to handle, so the pool chamber was devoid of people. Relkin left Bazil to the fun. Since the leatherback had healed quickly following his wounding at Quosh, there seemed little danger of his tearing the stitches, and a bit of roughhousing might do him some good. He was also going through some interrogation, but his was about the events of some years before in Ourdh.

They were going to be called to testify again in the same old case against Porteous Glaves, onetime commander of the Eighth Regiment in which they had served. Bazil had been scathing.

"This dragon told them all they need to know three years ago. And also before that. How many times they need to hear same thing?"

It was foolishness, human foolishness that was all, and all designed to make a wyvern dragon fret. It was also guaranteed to make his dragonboy worry. Both of them had given their testimony in the earlier trials of Porteous Glaves, and yet now there was another trial.

Relkin had been grilled by the high barristers of the Marneri court before, and he remembered it as being an unpleasant experience. Now they'd both have to go through it again. And this was on top of all these days under the scrutiny of Bell and Selera. Damned right it didn't seem fair.

In particular it annoyed him because the unit was busy preparing for the trip to Kadein and then on to Axoxo.

There were a lot of important little details in the matter of kit and supplies that needed his attention. Being tied up in court hearings was going to leave him dependent on the kindness of others, and that made him uncomfortable. It didn't pay to have to depend on other dragonboys too much.

Relkin turned in to the stall he shared with Bazil and found a message scroll from Kenor waiting on his cot. Relkin's heart leapt, and he tore it open. What news?

At the top of the message were the arms of Clan Wattel, and his eyes leapt to the message in mixed dread and hope.

The dread evaporated. Eilsa was riding to Marneri on quick stages and would be there in the next couple of days. The scroll had been posted in the north and had come through the frontier lands of the River Bur.

Eilsa was coming! They would get one more chance to be alone, or almost alone, before he set off for Axoxo. Of course there were always chaperones. Eilsa was unwed, despite great pressures from the clan. She would bear the heir to the clan leadership, and so all her movements were tightly monitored. Clan Wattel had a veneer of respect for the Great Mother and the witches of Cunfshon, but basically the clan still harked back to the old gods of Veronath. Such folk did not give as much respect to women's freedom as did the folk of Cunfshon and the citizens of the Argonath.

Still, Eilsa was coming! They would have to celebrate . . . a night out at one of the city's best restaurants . . . A party for her with his other friends in the city, Lagdalen, and Captain Hollein Kesepton.

And somehow, somewhere, they would snatch a few moments alone and consume one another in kisses, hot, stolen kisses hidden from the eyes of the wretched aunties sent to keep Eilsa chaste. They did not care for this outland orphan, a dragonboy in the legions with not an acre of land to his name. Oh, but Eilsa did!

In a trice Relkin's concerns had faded, pushed aside by a warm feeling of joy. Since that first moment when they had met after his return, Relkin's love for Eilsa had rekindled and burned more fiercely than ever. She had waited for him, she had turned down the offered hands of three young men within the clan, men of good family, with lands and many flocks of sheep. She had stayed true to him.

He wished he could say the same of himself, but in Eigo he had fallen not once, but twice, and in circumstances so strange that he had never been able to tell Eilsa about it. He had imagined that somehow, he could tell her so that she would understand that these affairs, far away, were virtually in another life. But, in fact, he had never mentioned them. He realized he could never tell her without wounding their love, perhaps fatally. He could not describe to her Ferla, the lovely, magical demon of the grotto of Mot Pulk's world. Nor could he tell her of Lumbee, the Ardu girl with whom he'd made the great journey into the interior, into the ancient lands of terror, ruled by huge animals of elemental ferocity.

No, Relkin knew there was no way he could marshal the words to tell his love about these things, and so he was left with guilt—and perhaps a glimmer of wisdom.

Chapter Twenty-five

Relkin looked up at the dome of the court for the thousandth time. It was cool and white and restful, but Relkin did not feel rested after looking there. The high court of the city of Marneri was in session. Relkin was in the chair of testimony that day and had already been questioned for two hours by the barrister for the prosecution, Master Bushell.

Bushell had carefully led him through his testimony. It concerned a vital moment in the campaign in Ourdh, several years before. Relkin described how he had gone with Captain Hollein Kesepton and a band of volunteers, including some dragons, to find and destroy the demon in Dzu. On the way they had taken the ship *Nutbrown*, which had been seized by deserting troops from the Kadein Legion. After a fight of a few minutes duration, the Kadeini had fled, realizing that dragons were aboard. In the captain's cabin they had found Porteous Glaves and his personal guard, Dandrax. They had brought them out on deck and cuffed them. It was common knowledge at the time that Glaves, then the commander of the Marneri Eighth Regiment, Second Legion, had deserted from the legion force still holding out in the city of Ourdh during its epic siege. The deserters' assault on the *Nutbrown* led by Glaves and Captain Rokensak of the Kadein Legion had been witnessed by many others. Relkin described the Glaves he remembered, sitting on a bench, jaw slack, eyes staring, stunned by the sudden reverses he had encountered.

Further questioning by Bushell brought forth the information that Dandrax had informed Hollein Kesepton, within Relkin's hearing, that indeed, yes, Rokensak and his men had committed piracy and taken the ship *Nutbrown* by force and killed Captain Peek and Shipmate Doon.

Bushell had already painted for the court a harrowing portrait of the siege and the whole campaign in Ourdh. Great battles, epic marches, and the dreadful siege of the great capital city had all been described. Now he concluded Relkin's testimony and sat down on the prosecution bench.

The attorney for the defense, William Gentello, arose. Gentello was a famous litigator with enormous presence and a loud voice. He strolled up to the testimony chair, where Relkin sat within a rail of worn and polished wood.

"Dragoneer Relkin," began Gentello, as if he were reading the name off a list. "You are from the 109th Marneri Dragons, an excellent unit, I am told."

It was not a question, Relkin looked blankly at him. The rules had been hammered into him through his previous round of trials, in the matter of the death of Trader Dook. One only spoke when asked a question.

Gentello continued to orate, using an arm as if he were conducting some unseen orchestra. He described the 109th in glowing terms and mentioned that they had been on the field at Salpalangum and again at Sprian's Ridge, the two greatest battles of their era.

"So, Dragoneer Relkin, it would be fair to say that you and your dragon have been held up as good examples to the youth of the nation?"

Relkin looked up to the judge, Tuva of the Tarcho. She made no comment.

"I don't know. Not by me."

Gentello rocked back and gave Relkin a careful look, pantomiming for the jury.

"Not by you, eh? You know something you haven't shared with us, don't you?"

Relkin felt uncomfortable. There had been dicey situations in his past, things that could easily be exploited to darken him. Was Gentello going to rake up everything that had happened since he joined the legion? But no, the advocate moved on.

"So, Dragoneer, you were there on the deck of the *Nutbrown,* and you saw that Commander Glaves had been ill-used. He was in shock, it might be fair to say."

Gentello nodded broadly to the jury, who stared back at him stonily.

"Maybe. Maybe he was just frightened."

"You, of course, you were not frightened. You are a hardy man of war, are you not?"

"At that point there was nothing to be frightened of. The Kadeini had swum for it; we had possession of the ship."

"Weren't you all on your way to Dzu, a most desperate venture?"

"Yes. Everyone was afraid of that, of course."

"So there was a general feeling of fear."

"Well, I suppose you could call it that."

"So, Dragoneer, you had been made aware of the scurrilous rumors that had been broadcast concerning my client, the right honorable Porteous Glaves, of Aubinas. That he had deserted from his post and that he had turned pirate?"

"I had heard that, yes."

"So when you saw Porteous Glaves onboard the *Nutbrown,* you saw him as dazed and frightened."

"Yes."

"Which would have conformed to your beliefs, your prejudices formed by the vicious rumors that had been perpetrated against my client."

"What?"

"Because, after all, Dragoneer Relkin, your mind was made up. You had heard the rumors and assumed that they were true."

"Dandrax confirmed the rumors, in my hearing."

Lawyer Gentello flashed Relkin a look of annoyance.

"Ah, the scoundrel Dandrax, who planted the blame on my client. You venture his name into our discussion."

"Ahem," broke in the judge. Gentello looked up, Relkin looked sideways. Judge Tuva pursed her lips for a moment.

"Advocate Gentello, we are not here for a discussion. Please ask direct questions and cease this beating around the bush."

Gentello wished to protest more, but was gaveled to silence.

"So, Dragoneer Relkin, where were we? Ah, yes, you found my client, the accused, Porteous Glaves, to be dazed and frightened. He said nothing when asked direct questions?"

"Not in my hearing."

"Now, Dragoneer Relkin, was there anyone else in Dzu at the time of this venture, who might also be sitting in this court?"

Barrister Bushell objected. The judge ruled Gentello's line of questioning allowable for the moment.

"This had better lead to something worthwhile, Advocate," she said.

"Yes, of course." Gentello loaded his words with oily assurance.

"Now, Dragoneer, would you point to that person and announce her name if you know it."

Relkin pointed to Lagdalen of the Tarcho, who was at the prosecution bench.

"So the very person who is prosecuting this trial was also in Dzu. What was her role?"

Relkin hesitated. This was difficult territory.

"I don't really know, and I don't know if I could say it if I did know."

Gentello reacted as if he had struck gold.

"What is this? Explain yourself."

Bushell objected again and asked to approach the judge's bar. There he pointed out that Lagdalen had been an assistant in the Office of Unusual Insight during the mission to Ourdh. That entire aspect of the case would have to be kept secret. Testimony would have to be given in camera.

Judge Tuva nodded. She had been warned of this eventuality.

"Advocate, you will have to pursue this line of questioning in camera with only the jury and myself present. You invoke an official secret."

"Ah, secrets!" Gentello was triumphant. "That will not be the last time we shall hear the word 'secrets' before this case is done."

"Would you like to go on with something else and hold this line for later, perhaps tomorrow morning?" said the judge.

"I would like to ask these questions in the full light of day with the eyes and ears of the citizenry opened to them. Not in a secret court ruled by witches!"

There was a sharp intake of breath. The Aubinan campaign had surfaced already in the trial, and here it was again.

"I think we have heard enough of your opinions, Advocate. Take it up with the law committee. Nothing is set in stone concerning standards of secrecy. We operate under the conditions of war, as you well know, with a treacherous and powerful enemy. There are reasons for secrecy."

"That's what they always say," said Gentello with a weary wave to the jury.

"And what does that mean?"

Gentello realized he had gone too far and was in danger of contempt of court.

"I apologize to the court. I was out of order. I will continue my questions when the court has withdrawn into private camera."

Judge Tuva adjourned for the day and announced that court would reconvene in the morning with no one but the jury, judge, lawyers, and witness.

Relkin conferred briefly with Bushell, who commended him for his calm answers to questions. Relkin shrugged, he'd been through it all before.

He strolled out of the courtroom and found Eilsa waiting for him. The sight of her brought a lightness to his heart. He took her hand and would have kissed it, but for her hiss of, "No!"

She pulled away while she rolled her eyes to indicate her chaperon. Relkin sighed. Of course, there were always chaperons watching the heir to the chieftaincy of Clan Wattel.

"By the gods, it is hard sometimes, Eilsa. I just wanted to hug you, but we cannot do more than touch hands."

The thought brought back some of the gloomiest feelings from his visit to the land of the Wattels during the spring.

"Not until we are wed, Relkin, when you retire from the legions. Either that, or I must renounce the claim of the line of Ranard to the chieftaincy of the clan. My family would just die, if I did that."

"Your family wishes that I would just die, and that's a fact."

Eilsa had a small smile. "Don't say it, I'm afraid it might be true."

She looked up.

"Ah, Lagdalen is here. She looks perfect in her advocate's robe, don't you think?"

Relkin thought Lagdalen looked uncomfortable in the heavy, floor-length brown and black robe, but he kept that thought to himself.

Lagdalen came up to them with a smile. She embraced Eilsa.

"It is so good to see you here again. Thanks for coming."

"I could not stay away when Relkin was due to testify."

"Of course. So where are you staying?"

"We have taken rooms on Foluran Hill."

"Ah, excellent. You must come and dine with us. This week there will be the Festival of Shoes, why not then?"

"Well, it would be an honor to dine with the Tarchos. But my chaperon will insist on coming too."

"Excellent, we'll plan on it, then. And Relkin, will you come too?"

Of course he would, though he would have to get leave from Cuzo.

"I will have an official invitation issued. Not even Dragon Leader Cuzo would want to overrule that!"

They walked together up the hillside on winding Water Street to where Lagdalen's law offices stood. Behind them came Aunt Kiri, the stern-faced chaperon, wearing traditional Wattel costume. She hardly said a word, but was fiercely determined to keep Eilsa Ranardaughter from losing her honor to this ruffian dragonboy. Like many in the clan, Aunt Kiri was sternly opposed to the idea of a match between Eilsa and a scruff like this.

It was a fine day, and there were many other people out on the street, all happy to see some sun after the long rainy spell. There were still pools of water here and there they had to hop across. Water Street was a very old street, and parts of it were in need of repair.

"So how did I do?" he asked Lagdalen.

"Very well, Relkin. You've testified so often now that you're becoming a professional witness."

"It brought up a lot of memories, none of them good."

Lagdalen nodded. "You went through a lot with the Dook case."

"Best part of a year, one way or another. By the gods, it was boring sitting in court day after day. I don't know how you stand it, Lagdalen."

She laughed. "It isn't boring for me, Relkin. I follow every shift, every pattern. It's a battle, not unlike a duel with knives. We have to parry the other side's thrusts and drive home our own."

"I don't think I could stand it. I have to get outdoors more."

"That's one thing we don't get enough of, we devotees of the law."

Outside Lagdalen's law office they said farewell to her. Then they went on up the zigzag of Water Street where it climbed the steep slope to the plateau of the upper city, near the Tower of Guard.

The afternoon light shone on the tiled dome of the temple off to their right.

Eilsa was allowed to walk beside Relkin, and to talk with him openly, but they were not allowed to touch again apart from the initial handclasp. Not within the view of Aunt Kiri, anyway.

"I had another letter today from my uncle Stoom. He says I must consider my role in the Clan Wattel before anything else."

"Then, he hasn't changed his mind. We didn't expect him to, though."

"No, we didn't. They will all fight our wedding until it is over, and even then they will fight. The closer it comes, the harder the struggle."

Relkin shook his head sadly. "Seems unfair, really. This is the Argonath; you have the free woman's right to marry whom you will."

Eilsa hushed him with a finger to her lips. "Don't let auntie hear you say that. She'll take it as a threat against my virtue."

Relkin grumbled.

"Yes, of course," she went on. "Under Imperial law I have that right. But I am of Clan Wattel, and we have been here all through the ages. We remember a time before the nine cities. We knew a long time when there was no Imperial law."

"True, Clan Wattel has a long history. But now great changes are coming; all the lands of old Veronath are free, and people are streaming back to them. Clan Wattel will change too."

Eilsa sighed. "I hope so, for our sake, but it seems to me that the clan wants to wait out the time of the Argonath. They believe in their hearts that the Argonath cities will fall and that the dark forces will return. In their view the enemy always comes back, and victory is never complete."

Relkin could only shake his head in dismay. Such stubbornness could only make things more difficult, especially for himself.

"We'll just have to show them another way. Did you know there was a big dance on the day after the Festival of Shoes?"

Eilsa's eyes lit up. Like all her clan, she loved to dance.

"It's always held after the eldest daughters in every household put on the new shoes they were given at the festival."

"It sounds like fun, Relkin."

"Great fun. Will you be able to come?"

"Oh, yes, but Aunt Kiri will come too."

Aunt Kiri's dour face had grown thunderous at the idea. But she would come, for Eilsa Ranardaughter had a will just as powerful as that of her chaperons.

Chapter Twenty-six

The next morning there was a light rain falling on the city from grey, leaden skies. At the appointed hour, wearing a freecoat with collar turned up, Relkin was waiting outside the law courts. He expected to undergo a relentless grilling from Advocate Gentello with many attempts to trip him up and shake his testimony. He comforted himself with the knowledge that he'd said it all before, over and over, and it wasn't really that complex.

Relkin noticed Advocate Gentello among the crowd. The advocate for the defense was holding a conference with four gentlemen in wide capes and tall rain hats. Relkin felt an instant dislike for Gentello, whose voice he was going to have to listen to for hours to come. The morning's proceedings would be held in secret, however, with no members of the public allowed in. Gentello's oratory and booming voice would have only the jurors to sway.

The public might not be allowed within the courtroom that morning, but the public was still there. A group of Aubinan supporters of Glaves were murmuring together at the edge of the portico, readying their protest slogans for the moment the doors were opened to admit the advocates and the witnesses.

Lagdalen passed by, head bent in earnest conversation with Bushell, too preoccupied for any pleasantries. They knew they had a difficult day ahead of them, but at least they were sure about what to expect.

Except that quite suddenly, through the crowd, came a small squad of legion soldiers, four men and a corporal. They marched up in formation and crashed to attention in front of Relkin. The corporal stood forward. Rain dripped off their hats.

"Are you Dragoneer Relkin, Marneri 109th?"

"I am."

"Then, I must advise you that you are under arrest. You are to come at once to the Tower of Guard."

Relkin was stunned for a long moment. What strange dice had the gods come up with now? What was old Caymo doing to him here?

"May I ask on what charges?"

The corporal sniffed and pulled a small scroll out of a pocket under his cloak. Shielding it with a hand, he read the docket.

"You are charged under legion regulation, code number 545, with illegally possessing stolen goods, to wit, gold bars brought home as loot from Eigo. You are further charged with banking said bars, along with other articles of gold and silver in the Royal Land Bank in Kadein. There are several further charges relating to these first two."

Lagdalen and Bushell protested. Relkin was due to give important testimony that morning. There had to be some mistake. Couldn't the arrest be put off, at least for an hour or two?

It could not. Corporal Genny's orders were simple and straightforward, and allowed for no deviations.

While Bushell and Lagdalen still argued, Relkin knew it was pointless. If a charge had been officially laid, then the process would have to take its course. Relkin had been in the legions long enough to understand the bureaucratic imperative. He just shrugged and fell in surrounded by the four unsmiling members of the Marneri First Regiment, First Legion, the famous Double Ones. With Corporal Genny at their side, the group marched away from the court and turned up Water Street toward the Tower of Guard.

As they went, Relkin's thoughts were in a whirl. He'd never heard of the regulation involved. Beyond the first couple of dozen regulations, and a few amendments that had become important down the centuries, nobody knew them except military lawyers, and even they had to refer to books.

If pressed on the point, Relkin would have been the first to admit that the gold tabis were loot of a kind. He'd found them hidden in the wall of an elf lord's house in Mirchaz. Their city was burning as the slaves rebelled, toppling the elf lords from their cruel thrones. Relkin had felt perfectly justified in taking the fat gold tabis, like little pillows of gold. He would also have to admit that he'd banked some of them, though not all.

Being of a cautious nature, Relkin had actually split the tabis in three piles, one of which he'd buried under a rock out by the third milestone from Marneri on the Blue Hills Road.

The "other articles" involved were gifts of gold from the great king Choulaput of Og Bogon. They were the foundation for the collective fund that Relkin had set up for the 109th Marneri Dragons as a group. All the survivors of the mission to Eigo, who fought at Koubha and helped liberate the land of Og Bogon from the menace of the Kraheen army, were included in the fund. The value of the banked gold had been put into bonds and stock in limited companies registered in Kadein, Marneri, and Talion, the three premier cities of the Argonath.

None of this was a secret. Relkin had even filed the customs documents that were required by the city of Kadein to bring ashore such articles of treasure. He had also investigated the position relating to taxes in the city of Marneri and paid those taxes in full.

But now there was this strange regulation that he'd never heard of.

They marched into the Tower of Guard and took the steps down to the detention cells.

It was quiet there. Indeed, it had been a relatively peaceful period in the city the past few weeks. The cells were almost empty, except for a few drunks and a burglar caught on Foluran Hill. Relkin waited, twiddling his thumbs for an hour or so. Then Lagdalen appeared, accompanied by two guards who stood by the outer door while she spoke to him.

"The charges were filed by a certain Commander Heiss, an Aubinan officer in the First, Firsts."

"Aubinan? Oh, great." The implications sank in. Relkin was now a pawn in the struggle between Aubinas and the empire.

"The charges are related to several obscure clauses in the legion regulations code. It is the definition of 'loot' that it all depends on."

"Oh, of course." He had a problem. The gold tabis were

definitely loot. The rest had been given by the great king. Relkin thought about it for a moment.

"Well, then," he said. "Messages have to be sent to Og Bogon and to Mirchaz. Ask them there if we deserve the gold. Ask the great king. He will say we took nothing! Ask the new rulers of Mirchaz if we deserve the gold tabis we took!"

Relkin felt a flash of bitterness. He should've buried all the gold. That was what the dragon had advised. Relkin had come on all superior, talking about banks and compound interest. The dragon dismissed it all as "bear on the ice," which translated roughly as "pie in the sky." Damned dragon was right. Something that happened too frequently.

Lagdalen groaned. "It will take time to do that, and that's what they are counting on. Damn them! You see that's what this is all about, Relkin, making us take months, even years to clear your name. In the meanwhile, your testimony will be tainted. They will bring up the charges against you while they cross-examine you in the Glaves case. I have to say this is very dramatic of them."

Meanwhile Relkin's reputation would be ruined. Promotion to dragon leader would never come if he were a criminal. Marriage to Eilsa Ranardaughter might also be threatened.

"You still have Bazil's testimony. He was there too. Hell, there were others."

"Right, so they don't have a hope of changing the verdict. They're desperate, Relkin. We've been through trial after trial, and we have always won guilty verdicts. But the Aubinans won't accept it. Glaves has become a symbol to them of the independence they want."

"Will I have to testify again?"

"After cross-examination, I think not. We will depose the dragon and then put the other witnesses on the stand."

"Right, the dragon's all ready. He knows this stuff better than I do."

"Then there are the other men who we have as witnesses. No, it's going to work out the same. Your testimony was only part of the case, and even if the defense damages it, the rest of the case is overwhelming. So Glaves faces another guilty verdict quite soon."

"And there will be more trouble."

"I would think so."

"Meanwhile, I have to face these charges?"

"I'm afraid so. As you know, once the wheels have been set in motion, they have to go through the full process."

Lagdalen explained that they should be able to free him right away so he could return to duty. They would also try and speed up any court date. But the 109th were due to ship out soon for Kadein and Axoxo. Relkin might wind up detached from his unit. The dragon might have someone else for dragonboy, probably Curf.

Relkin winced at the thought of Curf working over Bazil's kit. Curf was a long way from being a proficient dragonboy.

Then she left with a few final words of encouragement.

"Look at it this way, Relkin. We have to get you out. We have a whole party arranged in your honor for tomorrow night at the Festival of Shoes."

He waited another hour, and then Eilsa Ranardaughter came in, accompanied by Captain Hollein Kesepton and Aunt Kiri.

Kesepton, Lagdalen's husband, was also in Marneri to give testimony in the Glaves case. He was presently posted to a regiment in Dalhousie, up in Kenor, and was just visiting the city briefly to testify.

Eilsa's distress at the sight of Relkin in a cell brought on something like tears in her eyes. Despite Aunt Kiri, she put her hands through the bars, cradled Relkin's head, and kissed him.

Aunt Kiri was shocked and made a face. Eilsa ignored her.

"Oh, Relkin, what is all this? Why are you in here?"

"It's a political thing, Eilsa. It's the Aubinans. They're trying to discredit my testimony. It doesn't mean anything."

"But it was a legion regulation."

"An obscure one I never heard of."

From behind her Kesepton agreed. "An obscure one hardly anyone's heard of."

Eilsa was still a little teary, but she did not actually cry. Instead her face was rapidly clearing as her practical side rose to the surface. Her mind was going to work on the ramifications of it all.

"This is not going to help matters at home, though."

"Yes," agreed Relkin, "I expect you're right about that."

Relkin had spent two and a half months in the land of the Wattels that spring, searching for sites that he and Eilsa could build their future home on. He had visited with her enormous, extended family. That had been hard going. There was a profound suspicion of the outsider that just didn't go away no matter how polite Relkin was. In fact, it reminded him all too much of the rejection he'd suffered from the Ardu folk in distant Eigo, even after he'd rescued them from slavery. There the prejudice was based on the fact that Relkin lacked a tail. Here it was just that he didn't come from the Wattel Hills. He'd always felt he'd win them over somehow. Except that now he had a lot more problems with the elders of Clan Wattel.

"Wish I'd never seen that gold now." He tried to say this as if he meant it, but it wasn't easy.

"I wish I could laugh about it," Eilsa's exasperation surfaced. "Things are going to be really difficult for us."

"But these charges mean nothing. They haven't proved I did anything wrong. I declared the gold to the customs, and I paid landing taxes on it in Marneri. I filed all the forms."

"Those old heads up there in the hills don't care about whether you're actually guilty. They just want to discredit you and force me to abandon the idea of marrying you."

He dropped his eyes.

"They must think I'm a regular tearaway, huh?"

"Relkin, this isn't the first time you've had serious charges against you. They know all about Trader Dook."

"Well, they didn't hang me for that one. And this one won't mean anything in the end. We'll get messages from our friends in Eigo. They'll back us up."

Eilsa squeezed his hands. "I know they will." She leaned forward and kissed him again, ignoring the snort of indignation behind her back.

"I love you, Relkin, no matter what they say."

Hollein looked studiously up at the ceiling.

At that moment, far away across the sea, the greatest witches met in a small chamber high in the Tower of Swallows, above Andiquant, the Imperial City.

Lessis was brooding, something she had done more frequently since the ambush of the Imperial Progress.

"He struck more quickly than I expected. He came very close to achieving his aim."

Ribela nodded. Lessis had been heavily bandaged for

weeks when she returned from the Argonath. She had been uncharacteristically subdued.

"Teress noted some interesting movements within the Imperial family at about the same time. Surveillance of certain persons has been stepped up."

"He has chosen *us* for his initial attack, not the Czardhans. This I didn't expect. They would be easier for his methods, I would have thought."

"He likes a challenge, I expect."

Lessis looked up. "Then, he's damn well going to get one."

Ribela turned professorial. "Waakzaam is of the world builders, but ever he was attracted to the subtle and the devious. He searches for the weaknesses in a society and then works to set civil wars burning in the holes. When chaos has weakened it enough, he appears on the field with an army and takes control. Every fiction is used to shield the truth of this process from the minds of the people. Usually it works because they are so inflamed with petty hatreds and war feelings that they cannot perceive the grander design."

"He failed in his first, brilliant stroke. He must be angry."

"The anger of Waakzaam the Great is not a thing to contemplate easily."

"He will want to be very sure of his second stroke."

Ribela fluttered her long fingers. "We cannot prevent every such stroke. There are political problems enough in the land to provide him with issues and sore places he can inflame."

"Oh, I know. Aubinas!" Lessis very rarely allowed her calm facade to crack, but now her anger was plain to see. "And Arneis! Arneis, which would have been devastated completely if the legions and the clansmen of the hills had not come down and stopped the great invasion in its tracks. Yet now there is no thought of what is owed, only the dream of great wealth from mercantilist trade with the rest of the Argonath."

"The greed of men is a fierce instinct. It will always test the limits of the Imperial system."

"Women are greedy too; it is not a vice restricted to men, Ribela."

Ribela sniffed. "Yes, perhaps this is true. But in Defwode we think that the greed of men is sharper, for it is entwined with the male need to dominate. This is a very deep urge. It is hard to keep men subdued enough so they forget it."

"The men of Defwode are great weavers and poets."

"They are gentle men and worthy of the respect of women."

"They are worthy indeed, sister, but they are not the greatest of warriors, perhaps."

Ribela sniffed again. "Perhaps not, but our men of Defwode are less greedy as well, and this makes them pleasant to live with. An important consideration, sister."

"I agree. The greed shown in Aubinas and Arneis is not pleasant to consider."

"Aubinas is very different from Defwode, that is certain. The grain merchants used their money and influence in Marneri to distort the markets, cornering certain grains at key times of the year. Money and corruption flowed from this to infect Marneri. The landowners fell into debt and were virtually displaced by the grain merchants who have become a class of petty tyrants, each ruling a township of the province."

"The greed of men, as I said. The women of Defwode are correct in fearing it."

"They certainly have a point, sister."

"And the men of Defwode more than make up for their relative absence in the ranks of the fighting men of the legion. They are the heart of the Engineer Corps, and as such they have won many battles for the empire."

"Indeed, sister, they have."

Ribela was mollified. "We have been lucky, but we cannot count on luck to last."

"You're right. We were terribly, terribly lucky that the Broketail dragon was on the trail that day. We were lucky that Relkin was able to come up with some unheard-of magical athleticism."

"A strange phenomenon. He has no knowledge of the secrets, and yet he has powers."

"That boy has changed, Ribela. He still has that spark that we noticed years ago, but now something new is developing within him. I feel something there, but I don't know what it is."

At the mere mention of Relkin's name, Ribela cringed inside. Embarrassment of a profound order rose in her heart. To her shame, she shared a disgustingly intimate secret with that particular dragonboy.

"Processes were taken during his duty in Eigo that may have affected his sanity," she remarked coolly. "Has this been considered?"

"Indeed. But he seemed very levelheaded about it all. I spoke to him. He's still confused about the gods and the role of the High Ones. He spent considerable time among the elf lords, yet he seems to have survived their evil designs."

"He saw things he should never have been exposed to. Cruel, terrible things that could affect anyone's heart."

Lessis heard the passion in Ribela's voice and raised an eyebrow.

"And still we face our greatest threat from this new player. The Dominator, they call him, for he rules twelve whole worlds. Billions of beings have died beneath his heel. The Padmasans are weaker since the loss of Heruta, and they will soon be twisted into knots within his schemes. No one has greater skill in deceit and manipulation."

"Let us try to anticipate his next move. If we put our heads together, perhaps we can prepare a noose with which to hang him."

Chapter Twenty-seven

A special ceremony began the Festival of Shoes, a season of dances and festivals in honor of the young women of the land. In every household new shoes were placed on the feet of the eldest daughter. The honor of placing these shoes went to her father, unless she were old enough to be married. In that case, her husband placed the new shoes on her feet and did up the straps.

In the receiving salon of the great apartment of the Tarcho family in the Tower of Guard, a great party watched and applauded as Hollein Kesepton tied the straps around his wife's ankles. Wine was passed around, and the fiddlers took up their instruments and began to reel out the lovely old dance tunes of Marneri, beginning, of course, with "A Fine Young Man of Marneri." Tommaso, the family patriarch, led the dancing with Lacustra, Lagdalen's mother. Lagdalen was dancing in Hollein's arms. And in the happy throng, Relkin, who'd been released only hours before, found Eilsa and swept her away from Aunt Kiri onto the dance floor. They touched their toes together and kicked out to the side and swung around arm-in-arm in the ancient way.

Faces flushed with excitement, they spun around and around while the fiddlers played on through "La Lilli La Loo" and even the "Kenor Song."

Then Lacustra Tarcho blew the first horn, a sharp piercing note that announced it was time to go in for dinner.

A long table had been set out with the traditional wooden plates that were used only for this festival. The servants brought out the traditional foods, Munkiore—a rissoto with fish and sea vegetables—mashed neeps, and a fish pie done in the old Cunfshon manner, deep and round. These were recipes that went back hundreds of years to the very beginnings of the Argonath revival.

Relkin led Eilsa to the table to sit opposite him, while Tommaso Tarcho, who was determined that Relkin should sit close to him, waved them to seats on either side of himself at the very head of the table. Older members of the family happily displaced themselves, while Aunt Kiri was left stranded far down the table among some country cousins from Seant.

Relkin had to admit, it was the finest Shoe Festival feast he'd ever attended. A plate piled high with Munkiore and mashed neeps was set before him, along with a mug of small beer. At Tommaso's call, silence fell down the length of the long table.

Tommaso said the grace, calling down the blessing of the Great Mother on their meal and their lives and giving their thanks for all they had in life.

"A toast." He raised his mug. Then inclined his face to Relkin and then across the table to Eilsa. "To our gallant young friend, Relkin of Quosh, and to his intended wife, the honorable Eilsa Ranardaughter of Wattel."

"A toast!" went up the cry, and the mugs were raised and drained and refilled. Flushed in the face, Relkin and Eilsa gazed into each other's eyes, and Eilsa smiled with simple happiness. Relkin's troubles with the law seemed far away and quite insignificant.

The meal resumed and conversation picked up. Tommaso wanted to hear all about the recent action in Quosh, which had so shocked the city folk in Marneri.

"Bandits, they said at first, but now I hear it was something else. There's a lot they're not saying."

Relkin glanced down to Lagdalen, but Lagdalen was no longer an associate of the witches and thus not part of "they." Still, he made sure to keep his tongue under control. Lessis had told him that the battle at Quosh had been a secret strike by Padmasa. Certain things were better not discussed.

"Well, there's always a good reason for secrecy in these things, Master Tommaso."

Tommaso nodded in understanding.

"The fighting was fierce, though? We heard that much of the village was destroyed."

"Very fierce fighting, but the villagers came out to save the town, and we were lucky that we had Bazil."

"An invasion, right in the heart of the Blue Stone country," broke in Uncle Iapetor. "You see, Tommaso, we need more frigates to patrol the inshore waters."

This was an old demand of ship captains, who lived in perpetual fear of piracy.

"Certainly," agreed Tommaso, more readily than he might have in the past. "Room will have to be found in the budget, somehow."

"And Aubinas will have to accept its place within the state."

"Ah, Aubinas," said Tommaso with a weary sigh.

"The Aubinans are saying they will fight for the right to be independent," said another man, sitting to Iapetor's right.

"So I hear, Cousin Marko, so I hear," Tommaso sounded sad.

"We cannot let them go. I do not think it is the Aubinan people who want it, only the grain magnates."

Iapetor grunted agreement. "Once the Aubinans wake up and find themselves at the mercy of that bunch of bloodsuckers, they will rue the day they cried for this so-called 'freedom' of theirs."

"Well, they won't be allowed to leave. I hear there are regiments on the march from Kenor, even as we speak."

Relkin was a little shocked to hear such a thing spoken of so openly. Tommaso frowned at Marko, and that dampened the conversation. Relkin wondered what regiments they would be.

Young Cousin Rozerto, who had grown since last Relkin had seen him and was wearing the uniform of an apprentice seaman, was sitting just a few places farther down. He took the opportunity of the silence to ask Relkin the question that had been burning in his brain.

"I have heard that there are beasts roaming the interior of Eigo that are so large they could eat dragons. Is that really true, Dragoneer Relkin?"

Relkin was glad to shift away from dangerous talk about the movements of regiments in these tense times.

"Yes, Rozerto, it is. There are many kinds of huge creatures there, and while the biggest do not eat other animals, they are still dangerous enough. Then, there are the meat eaters; there are lots of them, and some of them are three times the weight of a leatherback."

"Did they try and eat your dragon?"

Relkin chuckled. "They tried to eat me! We had a lot of trouble with them. They're the most dangerous animals in the world."

"Oh, how I wish I could see these animals. What were they like?"

All eyes were on Relkin.

"Well, the very biggest are called 'shmunga' by the Ardu people, who live in those ancient forests. Shmunga walk on four legs that look like pillars. They have long necks and very long tails, which they use to protect themselves."

"That doesn't sound so fearsome!" said Rozerto.

"Imagine a whip thirty feet long and as thick at the end as your forearm. With those tails they can smash the heads of the biggest meat eaters like they were eggshells."

Eyes had gone wide all around him.

"May the Mother preserve us," said Lacustra Tarcho.

"Did you have to fight with these things?" said Eilsa, wonder and concern mixed in her eyes.

"Fight them? No, there's no way to fight something that big. Baz and me made the mistake of trying to kill a young one once."

"Oh, my."

"We were starving, you see, but it came to nothing once its elders spotted us. We had to run for our lives."

"Well, well," said Iapetor. "Creatures that can make a battledragon take to its heels. Sounds like we should round some up for the legions!"

There was a genial murmur of laughter. Relkin smiled.

"I'm afraid they wouldn't really do. Their brains are tiny and they probably wouldn't cooperate too well."

"And if they're anything like dragons, they'd take a lot of feeding!" chuckled Tommaso.

They were interrupted by the arrival of the youngest children, with the nanny, come to say good night before going off to bed. Among these children was Laminna, daughter of Lagdalen and Hollein Kesepton. Now she was a proper little girl with excellent manners. She curtsied to Relkin and Eilsa, and bade them good night most precociously.

"Are you the dragonboy my mother told me about?"

"It's possible. I hope she told you good things."

"She said you were a rascal."

"Oh, well, then, she was right."

There was laughter all around them as Nanny swept the children away and off to the nursery.

Later there was more dancing and a round of singing over pots of mulled ale. Then at last the party came to an end. Relkin walked with Eilsa and her chaperon to the house on Foluran Hill where they were staying.

On the step they said their good-byes, all the while under the disapproving glare of Aunt Kiri just a few steps away.

"Good night, Relkin, that was such a lovely time."

"Good night, Eilsa, sleep well." Relkin ducked his head and kissed her lightly on the lips. Aunt Kiri gasped.

"Oh, Relkin, that will only cause trouble."

"Ah, yes, I know. One day, though, we'll be free to kiss as much as we like."

"I live for that day."

"I too."

He strolled back up Tower Street, made his way to the Dragon House, and tucked himself into his cot beside the great mass of the wyvern. As he was drifting off to sleep, he caught a large eye gleaming in the dark as it studied him.

"Good night, Baz."

"Boy smell of perfume and beer. Dream of fertilizing the eggs."

"Only dreams."

"That good thing. We don't need any hatchlings in the Dragon House."

Chapter Twenty-eight

Under the rain Marneri was a glistening warren of white stone, overhung by grey cloud. The gutters were filled with torrents of water, and on Tower Street they overflowed in several places and turned the street into a shallow stream.

Lanterns were lit inside the Tower of Guard, even though it was the middle of the day.

Relkin was back in the room with Bell and Selera.

"Tell us what you thought you were trying to do, again."

It was exasperating. He had told them a dozen times, perhaps more. He'd lost count.

"I thought that perhaps I could somehow reach out to them up in the camp and get them the message that we needed help pretty bad. You know, make them hurry. You see, the messenger we'd sent had been killed, and we didn't have much time left. There were just too many of the enemy."

"How exactly did you think you could reach out to them?"

"I don't know. I just found a way."

"Describe exactly the mental processes involved. What did you do to 'reach out'?"

Relkin tried, but it was so hard, especially since he didn't really know what he'd done in the first place. His explanations were never enough for them: they always wanted more. So he struggled to express the ineffable while the witches questioned him over and over about the same things.

At last they decided to call it a day, and he was released into the public area of the tower. He pulled on his freecoat and made his way through the downpour to the Dragon House.

Bazil was in the stall. Relkin hurried in, pulled off his dripping coat, and hung it to dry in the corner.

"Raining again," grunted the dragon. "It is raining a lot."

"Seems so. I think we could take the stitches out today. What do you think?"

"This dragon agrees. They itch. That usual sign that they should come out."

Relkin lit a second lamp and hung it over the dragon. Then he brought out his tool kit and set out small scissors, a sharp knife, and two pairs of tweezers, one with long tines and one with short.

The wound had healed quickly. There would be a scar, yet another on the leatherback's hide, which already had plenty of them, but there had been no infection or inflammation. Relkin bent to his task, snipping each section and then pulling them free with the tweezers. Piece by piece they came out and were laid aside for disposal until the job was done. He treated the wound with Old Sugustus once more, just in case, and packed up his kit.

Bazil got up and moved his limbs, stretching carefully.

"Feels good. Healed, I think."

"You heal well, Bazil, just like you always did."

"Thanks to boy, you help this dragon always."

"Sure."

Relkin's hand and a big talon gripped for a moment.

"This dragon go down to plunge pool." The leatherback went out, leaving Relkin to go over the kit and consider what further extras he might try to obtain for the arduous winter ahead in Axoxo.

Just then little Jak came running in.

"News, Relkin, the news!"

"What is it? We're to ship out?"

Everyone had been wondering if they were to embark on the white ship *Oat* that was sitting in Marneri harbor looking huge and beautiful.

"No, the trial. They brought in a verdict today. Glaves was found guilty."

"Oh, that. Again. I hope this will be an end of it. I'm tired of this trial."

"The Aubinans are demonstrating in the street outside the courthouse."

"In this rain? Let them."

"It's pretty serious. Curf says they sent the guard from the tower down there to protect the courthouse."

Relkin shrugged. "The guard will be glad of a chance to whack some heads. Nobody loves the Aubinans these days."

Swane and Rakama came in a moment later. The two bully boys of the 109th had become something like bosom buddies since the Battle of Quosh. Their rivalry, at least for the moment, was forgotten.

"Heard about the riot?" said Rakama.

"Yes."

"Guards are going down the hill. Gonna bust some heads."

"About time somebody knocked some sense into those Aubinans,'" said Swane.

"Well, Glaves is guilty. This time he's got to hang," commented Jak.

"I'll leave that up to the judge. She'll know best what his punishment should be."

"Hey, listen to the Quoshite, wants to leave it all to the judge."

"And you know better than the judge, right, Swane?"

Jak laughed loudly at this, and Swane shot him a fierce look.

"Anyway," said Rakama. "Someone's just delivered a monster great fish pie for the dragons."

"What's that, a subscription pie?" These were usually huge fish pies paid for by a group of merchants or a fraternal organization of tradesmen and donated to the Dragon House.

"Right."

"Who's it from this time?" The dragons had had a few of these gifts in the past weeks.

"It says 'The Independent Grain Traders Association, in gratitude for the prompt action that saved the village of Quosh and protected the life of the emperor.' "

"Never heard of them, but at least they're grateful."

"Gratitude is better than nothing."

"The dragons will like a pie."

"Right," said Swane. "Well, Rak and me was thinking that maybe we should all go in and buy them a barrel or two."

"By the Hand, that'll have them singing late," said Jak.

"That's a good idea," agreed Relkin. "I'm in."

"The brew master at the Curly Pig just released his Bock beer."

"It's a bit expensive."

"Worth it. Where we're going, there ain't gonna be much beer of any kind, let alone a Bock."

"How much do you think we can get?" wondered Rakama.

"Well, we need a full tun. We can't get our dragons beer and not get some for the resident wyverns too."

"And all their dragonboys," grumbled Swane.

"That don't matter," said Relkin. "They don't drink as much as one dragon anyway. But we need a full tun."

"Everyone has to dig deep in his reserves, then," said Jak.

"Right," said Relkin. "Only way, but maybe our only chance, so let's do it."

"We'll tell the others," said Rakama. "Everyone will chip in now that Relkin's in."

They all knew this to be the honest truth. Relkin was the unspoken leader of the dragonboys in the unit.

Not long afterward Swane, Rakama, and Jak made their way down to Brundle Street, on the edge of the Elf Quarter, where they negotiated a very good price for a full tun of the newly released Bock beer. A dray was loaded up with the big cask and pulled by four grey horses as it made its way up the street through the pouring rain and to the Dragon House.

Within the hour the dragons of the 109th were digging into the sea pie from the Grain Association while the tun was put in place, broached, and ale was trundled out to the wyverns in four-gallon buckets. The pie was pronounced delicious by all except the Purple Green, who still consumed every scrap that came his way. The Bock was a favorite brew with the wyverns, and they were soon well into the second pail when the singing was starting. The strange mind-set of the dragon choir took over, and their huge voices were in full song, threatening to lift the ceiling of the Dragon House.

The dragon voices could be heard all over the upper half of the city, echoing across the parade ground in front of the Tower of Guard and down Tower Street. In the cells in the Barbican, where former Commander Porteous Glaves paced, the song of the wyverns only increased the level of tension. Damned monstrous animals, why couldn't they shut up! Glaves had no love for the brutes. They ate the legions out of their pockets, and they sat around the Dragon Houses drinking ale. He was damned if he should have to pay for it.

Glaves, convicted and imprisoned at last for his mutiny in Ourdh, waited impatiently for the signal. The government had gone too far! This time Aubinas would rise. How he thirsted to pay them back, all of these noble bloods in Marneri. They thought they were so much better than the farmers and grain merchants down in Aubinas. Why, half of them wouldn't even receive someone like Porteous Glaves, and yet his family was just as old as theirs. They looked down on him, and they harried him with this awful case. Of course he was guilty, but there were extenuating circumstances. The entire campaign in Ourdh had been waged in a suicidal manner! The siege was close to lost, and everyone was doomed! It really looked like a case of every man for himself. Except these ridiculous people in Marneri thought their laws of the legion were meant to be taken seriously! It was all nonsense. In a situation like that, everyone just had to look out for themselves. But, of course, you couldn't admit to that in court in Marneri. Oh, no, all the proper facades had to be maintained.

That was it, he mused. The whole white city society was nothing but a facade. They made everyone obey these rules of theirs, which only benefited them, the ruling elite of Marneri. And behind the facade of propriety and order, they did whatever they pleased. Oh, he was sure of it. So they were hypocrites as well as fools! And they had no right to interfere with Aubinas' need for freedom.

Hell, there was a lot of money to be made.

A jingle at the window finally broke into his thoughts. The signal. Frantically he rushed to the narrow window and thrust his hand through with his handkerchief.

There came another jingle, and he pulled it back.

Now he began to sweat.

A few minutes later a party of men dressed as legion soldiers appeared in the Barbican cells. It happened that one of the guards had been called away just a few minutes before. The remaining guard stood to and challenged them, but he was quickly overwhelmed and slain. Soon the door to Glaves's cell swung open.

Outside the cells they turned toward the city wall, where lay the Barbican postern gate. Treachery by an officer in the gatehouse allowed them through. Outside the walls were swift horses, and in a few moments they were in the saddle and riding for the road to Lucule and Aubinas. Porteous Glaves was glad to be out of the treacherous white city, but he was unhappy about the prospect of riding on horseback all night. It was raining steadily, and it was cold. Why his rescuers hadn't at least seen fit to provide a coach, he just didn't understand.

What Porteous Glaves felt about such things was actually quite unimportant in the scale of things that night. Ahead of him and his rescuers, the lush province of Aubinas was already rising in rebellion. The Aubinan flag of independence was being raised in all the important towns. Torches were being carried by runners from Posila through Nellin.

In the morning it would be a fact, Aubinas would have declared independence from Marneri. A government of notable Aubinans was already prepared to take over the reins. The officials of the Marneri authorities would be rounded up and shipped down to Lucule, from where they could make their own way back to the precious "white city" on the Long Sound. Aubinas would be free!

Chapter Twenty-nine

In the Marneri Dragon House the peace of the night had descended at last. The wyverns had stopped singing and gone to their stalls and bedded down. The usual symphony of vast snores reverberated through the house. The Purple Green's extraordinary output provided the leading lines, as usual, while the brasshides snored in basso with very little tremolo. Alsebra expressed notes ranging into the lower edge of alto, often carrying considerable tremolo and variation. Dragonboys were used to it, of course. Dragon Leader Cuzo was getting used to it. He'd stopped using earplugs during the sojourn at Camp Cross Treys.

But a discerning ear soon picked up sour notes in the medley from the huge wild dragon in his double-size stall. He moaned and turned and rolled over, and then turned and rolled back.

Manuel was wide awake by then. He lit the lamp and examined the dragon from the safety of the floor near the door. When the Purple Green turned, he took up the whole stall sometimes. The snoring was definitely all wrong. Something was up. Carefully he moved in closer and put his hand on the inside of the folded-up wing. The Purple Green was hot.

And about to roll over again. Manuel beat a retreat.

He went outside to think this through. His lamp was joined after a few minutes by another. It was Rakama.

"Manuel," said the burly one. "The Purple Green is sick too?"

"He is. And Gryf?"

They were joined a few minutes later by Howt and Jak, then the rest. Relkin was among them. Bazil had awoken, complaining of a burning sensation in his stomach.

"Pretty clear there was something wrong with that sea pie," said Relkin. "We all can see that. Problem is we gotta get it out of them. Make them all vomit it up."

"Right," agreed Swane. "It's the only way."

"Old Macumber taught me way back that wyverns often have trouble with digesting things. One reason they like noodles so much. Macumber said the best thing to do when a dragon was sick to its stomach was to flush it out with a ton of water. He said pump 'em full."

"Let's do it," said Swane.

"We need a pump and some hose."

"There's hoses in the storehouse," said Curf. "There's the fire pipes, and there's water up in the roof tanks."

"Of course," said Relkin in elation. "The fire system! Use the hoses and the roof tanks!"

Boys ran to the fire hydrants and unscrewed the plates that held back the water, which was kept in case of a fire. Others hauled out the coiled-up fire hoses and ran to attach them to the hydrants. Then they hurried to the Purple Green's stall.

The wild dragon was awake and in considerable discomfort. He bellowed at the sight of a bunch of boys in the doorway to his stall.

"What you all want?"

They quailed a bit, but Manuel pressed on.

"We need to get a lot of water into you. Flush out the food you ate. That's what's making you sick."

"Bah! What do you know?"

Manuel stood his ground, though most sensible folk would have run for their lives as the Purple Green lowered his huge head down to the boy's level.

"I studied dragon lore for years. I think I know quite a bit now."

"Oh, do you?" The Purple Green broke off, consumed by a sudden wave of pains. The huge body rolled and contorted itself, tossing the hay pile into a cloud of fragments.

"Yes, I do!" shouted Manuel. Relkin and Swane pushed through the crowd with the first hose, already dripping water as the plate was loosened behind them.

"Here," shouted Relkin. "Take this." He and Swane passed the hosepipe up to the Purple Green as he sat up. Water was streaming from the pipe.

"Drink it down, drink as much as you possibly can, and

then drink more. It's the only way. We have to flush it all out of you."

The Purple Green looked down at them. His friend the Broketail dragon had warned him of things like this. The boys studied the dragons, and ended up knowing them better than they knew themselves.

He gave in. Without another word, he put the hose in his mouth and let the water run down his throat. He sat there for about ten gallons, took a rest, and then downed another ten gallons.

They watched with round eyes and awed expressions as the Purple Green began to gag and choke. He expelled the hosepipe and clutched his enormous belly with both front arms.

A roar-scream shook the Dragon House. More gagging and loud-barking sounds were followed by an awesome amount of vomit. The boys staggered back from it, out into the passage gasping in horror. Behind them they left Manuel, frantically trying to get pieces of dragon kit out of the way as the Purple Green let go again and again, and vomited up the huge meal he had eaten only a few hours before.

Thus did the night get truly underway for the dragonboys of the 109th. The same awful process had to be used on the wyverns next, all of them. The brasshides, for some reason, were really resistant and took several rounds of the hosepipe before they finally managed to cleanse themselves of the rest of the fish pie.

By then, of course, there was a search on for any uneaten parts of that pie. The fact that it was only the dragons of the 109th who were stricken was the clincher, since they had shared the beer, but not the pie. The other dragons in the Dragon House had eaten legion dinner. Unfortunately the giant pan had been emptied, washed up, and dried before anyone went to bed. Then a scrap was found on the floor of the refectory, where it had slipped from someone's plate. This was taken away in a glass jar by two mysterious witches who had quietly appeared in the Dragon House during the search.

The Dragon House doctors had shown up quite early in the proceedings, but they found that the dragonboys were already doing the only thing that was worth doing at that point. Until the dragons were emptied out, there was no point in giving them medicine.

At some point during the ordeal, with the Dragon House in complete uproar, someone brought in the news that Porteous Glaves had escaped from the cells in the Barbican. The city gates were being sealed, and a search of the city was underway.

Relkin heard this with a sinking heart. After all those trials, all that testimony, they still hadn't managed to punish Porteous Glaves. And he was sure that Glaves would no longer be in the city. Relkin spat in disgust, but he was too busy to worry about it for long because crisis after crisis racked the Dragon House.

First Alsebra seemed to be going into terminal shock. The vomiting had been so intense that she was struggling to breathe, as if affected by asthma. There was nothing they could do except watch her struggle for her life. Soon the crises of the brasshides drew the boys away as the struggle intensified to save big Chektor and young Churn.

Bazil was the seventh on the list. It turned out that the Broketail had one of the least difficult responses to the sea pie. He sweated some and moaned a bit and complained of nausea even before they began pumping the water into him. After about fifteen gallons went in, he turned aside and began to vomit right away.

By the fourth hour Alsebra's breathing became easier, and in time she began to recover. The brasshides were still very ill, however.

Of course the whole awful thing was a disgusting business. Huge volumes of watery vomit, half-digested fish, pastry, and beer were hurled to the floors of the dragon cells, mixing with straw, spattering everything in sight, and stinking the place to high heaven.

Dragon Leader Cuzo stalked around in a snappish fury, and dragonboys got to work with wheelbarrows and shovels, mops and brooms. At first Cuzo seemed to be more concerned about the image of the 109th Marneri Dragons than about their actual health. But as he realized the depth of the danger, his attitude changed visibly and he took up shovel and broom alongside the others.

The big brasshides suffered the worst cramps and pains, after the Purple Green, and they required more water to induce the endless vomiting that was the only way to clear the toxic food out of their systems. In fact, they had to endure the whole process several times before they finally joined the shivering, groaning wretches who were already beginning the process of recovering. By then the Purple Green was in a deep sleep, with just the gentlest of steady snores.

Tons of clean straw had to be brought down from the hayloft to replace the sodden muck that was being shoveled out of the stalls and sluiced away. This work was handled by the rest of the Dragon House crew, including the dragons who were still well, such as the resident champion Vastrox. With their muscle power in play, the brute work was done swiftly. Then the boys piled in with mops and rags. When the floors of the cells were clean and dried, fresh straw was piled high, and all the exhausted dragons were able to stretch out and fall into troubled sleep.

By dawn the crisis was past. Dragonboys labored on, and Cuzo still worked a huge broom with them. Dragonboys approved of that, and Cuzo's stock had suddenly soared among them.

By midmorning they'd finished, and the section was back to its usual near pristine state. The rain had stopped, and so they gathered outside to enjoy the unaccustomed sun. They were tired and filthy, and there was still a smell in the air, but they knew they'd saved their dragons. Now anger was building at whoever had tried to kill them.

Dragon Leader Cuzo came out to speak to them, almost as filthy as they were.

"A great effort, all of you, and in particular we should acknowledge that Relkin knew what to do and got us moving in the right direction from early on."

There was a modest cheer. Cuzo smiled, then left them to their own devices, and went in to clean up and get himself ready for the day. When he was out of earshot, Swane spoke up in a stage whisper.

"It's good that Cuzo's decided to be nice to us. Ain't we lucky!"

"He mucked in when we needed him. Cuzo's all right!"

Rakama was sitting next to Swane. Relkin thought to himself how strange it was sometimes. Here these two had been at each other's throats just weeks before, and now they were bosom buddies. What next? Were Gryf and Bazil going to be friends too? Somehow that seemed less likely.

"So where did this accursed fish pie come from?" said Manuel, who was squatting, hot and dusty along the wall.

"Independent Grain Traders Association. Who are they?" said Howt of Seant.

"Nobody's ever heard of them," commented Jak. "I already asked."

"I ever find out who they are I'll . . ." Rakama stopped, unsure just what he would do to whoever it was who'd tried to poison his beautiful green dragon.

"Looks like we should have checked more closely into who they were."

"Hey, who's ever wanted to poison a dragon squadron before?" Swane spread his big hands.

That was true. It was unheard of.

"By the Hand, but they dared much, whoever did this," said Manuel.

They were still there when Jomo, dragonboy to Tecaster, one of the grand old champions, came bounding in.

"It's all over the city!" he yelled as he ran down the line of sections toward the champions enclosure.

"What's all over the city?" said Swane.

"Hey, Jomo!" shouted Rakama. "What are you talking about."

Back came the ominous words. "Aubinas has declared independence!"

Chapter Thirty

The news of the rebellion spread like ripples in a pond. For the first time in the history of the Argonath, a province had declared itself independent and raised a rebel banner.

The trial of Glaves had obviously been an important point of crisis, but his escape from the Barbican had taken the authorities by surprise. Now an inquiry had begun into the treachery that had allowed Glaves's escape. A number of officers from the Marneri guard were sought, but they too had escaped the city and fled.

The news reached Andiquant through seaborne signals. From ship to ship, by signal flags, the word "Rising" followed by an "A" went bouncing down the shipping lanes between Kadein and Cunfshon. On any given day there were a hundred ships or more plying those routes, and in addition, there were the fishing fleets of both the Isles and the Argonath. Thus the signal went from mast to distant mast, and by the middle of that afternoon the word had been received in Cunfshon harbor and on the Tower of Swallows overlooking Andiquant.

The emperor summoned the Imperial Council. After that meeting he closeted himself with the Great Witches Lessis and Ribela for a private discussion.

The emperor sat in his favorite old navigator's chair, but he seemed shrunken, worn down by the woes of ruling his unique empire. In truth, he was still recovering from the wounds he'd suffered at Quosh.

"It has come at last," he said in a voice filled with sorrow. "And it has come in Aubinas, which is worse. They're a stubborn lot." Pascal had tried everything he could think of to keep this from happening, but the damned Aubinans could see a golden future for themselves as a grain-rich province surrounded by hungry customers, and they were determined to cash in.

The fact that but for the other provinces of the Argonath they'd be at the mercy of the most terrible enemy in history did not impress the Aubinans. They thought themselves completely safe, and able to fully exploit their captive markets. Their selfishness was singularly shortsighted.

"We predicted this would happen," said Ribela, still angry with the emperor. She had warned him about the Aubinans throughout her tenure as chief of the Office of Unusual Insight. She still felt that the emperor had failed to act decisively enough.

And, in truth, Pascal did blame himself to an extent. He'd thought to circumvent the rebellion by using that ill-fated Imperial Progress to reaffirm the Imperial "idea" among all the people of the Argonath.

In fact, the situation across the Empire of the Rose was close to optimal. They had weathered the worst the enemy could throw at them by defeating the grand invasion at Sprian's Ridge. They had eliminated the terrible threat posed by Heruta Skash Gzug's experiments in Eigo. Their allies in the far west were pressing the enemy hard, and they themselves were besieging his mighty fortress in the White Bones Mountains.

Meanwhile the economies of the nine cities were growing smoothly while the frontier lands of Kenor were returning quickly to the plow. Pascal had thought he could arouse the people's enthusiasm by his sudden appearance in all the nine cities. By showing himself, he'd hoped to focus everyone's attention on their successes. Alas his rash maneuver had ended in near total disaster. Not only had he nearly been killed, but the sudden end to his progress had spawned a thousand rumors, some of which contained part of the truth, that he'd been attacked and wounded by an enemy infiltration force.

"Is there a connection with our new enemy?" he said, turning to Lessis, trying to deflect the criticism he felt from Ribela. He knew she had a valid point. He had been in something of a state of shock during her tenure at the Office. The losses in Eigo were devastating, and that was all there was to say about them.

Lessis looked and sounded grave. "We do not know for

certain. Our resources in the ranks of the Aubinan rebels are scant. They have proved well able to avoid penetration."

"A very close-knit group," said Ribela. "All rich men, a club of them, who share harsh views of society and the poor. They have considerable wealth, and the power and sway that comes with it."

"Wexenne of Champery," said Lessis. "He is at the center of much of the discontent."

"Ah, Faltus Wexenne, yes, he has a thick file. An advocate of the importation of slaves to labor in the fields."

"A man of great financial acumen, driven by colossal greed and enormous egoism. A most dangerous opponent."

"Indeed, old friend," said Ribela. "We have not penetrated his circle."

"Wexenne, Porteous Glaves, Caleb Neth, and Salva Gann," Lessis recited the names dully, "these four are the heart of the thing. I thought we had Glaves disposed of at last, but treachery has been at work in the city of Marneri."

The emperor nodded and stroked his beard. "What can we do? What practical advice do you have for me?"

Lessis tented her fingers before her face, as if she wished to hide.

"We feel that it is bound to come to a fight. The Aubinans will use violence, even if we don't. Therefore we should strike first and try to dismantle the rebellion before it spreads."

"You're thinking of Arneis as the next likely rebellion?"

"Yes, but not exclusively. We have a similar problem in Arneis and in Kadein. All through the grain markets of Kadein, in fact, we have republican sentiments of increasing strength. They can see fabulous profits if they were to be allowed to rig the markets and bid up prices. Under Imperial controls this is denied them."

"Mmm. Have we perhaps controlled the markets too much?" said the emperor. "Have we created an artificiality in these markets? Is too much grain chasing too few customers? Are prices so low the farmers can't make a good living?"

"We do not think so, Your Majesty," said Lessis. "The farms across Aubinas and Arneis are prospering mightily. They fear the development of Kenor, of course, for they know it will break their control of the grain markets. But there will always be strong markets for barley and wheat, and the lands are very prosperous. The markets are regulated, it is true. We try to keep prices even from year to year, since we believe that stable food prices are a benefit to society. The Aubinans seek to make a killing by withholding grain to push up prices. They also intend to slow down or even prevent the development of Kenor. Some of their extremists have declared their intention of conquering Kenor and detaching it from the empire."

"How do they plan to do that? They do not have sufficient military strength."

"That has been the puzzle. Now we will see what strength they really have."

"How should we respond? What is your advice?"

"It's up to the military now. They have planned for this eventuality. They will move at once to crush the rebels."

"The Legion of the Red Rose will be mustered. Transports gathered at once. I think we can reinforce Marneri within one month."

"There are Marneri regiments in rest status in the Blue Hills and at Dashwood. Plus there's a couple of dragon squadrons: one in the city itself and another at Dashwood."

"Good point. I hadn't thought of it, but do the Aubinans have dragons?"

"Unlikely, Your Majesty. We'd have sniffed that out, I think. Not easy to raise and train wyverns for war without the secret getting out."

"They might have trolls. The Aubinan grain lords have bought trolls before," said Ribela.

"Mmm. And we don't know what our new enemy is doing, or do we? What do you think, Lady?" Pascal searched Lessis's face as he spoke. All he saw there was the almost inhuman calmness she projected at times of crisis.

"I think he will be involved, somehow. The Aubinan crisis has recently swelled in importance. I think that tells us something. The Dominator is among us, but working secretly. He knows how to bring down a world like ours. He knows that the methods of the Masters are somewhat self-defeating. He will be hidden deep in their plot somewhere."

"Then, we face a terrible test."

"We do, Your Majesty. That is the absolute truth."

Chapter Thirty-one

After morning inspection, a fierce-looking Cuzo called Relkin into his office. Relkin closed the door behind him a little nervously.

"Dragoneer Relkin, I have the sad duty to inform you that you are to stand trial in ten days' time. The case involves the theft of gold bullion from the natives of a far-off land."

Relkin shrugged inwardly. Lagdalen had warned him this would come. Aubinan money had been freely sloshed around in the higher ranks of the Marneri military apparatus. A court-martial was inevitable. So he and his advocate would appear and ask for a delay while testimony was sought from the far-off lands of Mirchaz and Og Bogon.

"From what I know of you, Dragoneer, I'm sure you took the gold." Cuzo's narrow forehead crinkled in a frown. "But I'm equally sure you probably deserved it." Cuzo was actually smiling.

Relkin was unused to smiling dragon leaders, so it took him a moment to respond in kind.

"Thank you, Dragon Leader."

"No, I want to thank you, Dragoneer. I confess that I was concerned when you returned from Eigo, alive when everyone thought you dead. I feared that you would be an unruly element in the unit. You have a long service record with any number of field decorations. You deserve promotion. Unfortunately you were away when the leadership of the 109th came open. They chose me, and that's put me in a difficult position now that you've come back."

Relkin kept his mouth firmly shut.

"Well, I can tell you this much, the next promotion to dragon leader in the Marneri Legions will go to you."

"And my dragon will accompany?"

"I don't think they will try and separate the Broketail dragon from his dragonboy. More fools they, if they even think of doing it."

Relkin nodded, he hoped so, though occasionally dragons were separated from their tenders by the process of promotion. Of course, it would be hard work taking the helm of another dragon squadron and keeping the leatherback in tip-top condition at the same time.

"But we will have to get along as we are until then. And with this damned rebellion in Aubinas, I think we will be busy before long."

Relkin jumped at this.

"You mean we won't be going to Axoxo?"

"Not this year, lad, they'll be sending us to Aubinas any day now. You may not even have to attend this court date next week if we're put on active duty as quick as I suspect. They'll shift the case to later in the year. The Aubinas matter will take precedence over everything."

"Suspected that might happen, sir, but we won't miss going to Axoxo. Miserable cold it is up there."

"Yes, Dragoneer, you're right about that. Instead of freezing our behinds off, we'll be hunting down rebels in Aubinas. Probably see some fighting."

"The 109th has never worried too much about that. As long as dinner is plentiful, this unit loves to fight."

"I've noticed," said Cuzo with a dry smile.

Relkin left Cuzo and went back to the stall. Bazil was down at the armorer's getting refitted for cuisse and greaves, since new styles of both pieces of armor had just been released. They were lighter and less cumbersome than the old, but just as protective. The steel plate was rippled in an accordion-like pattern, giving great strength to thinner plate.

He tried to clear his thoughts, torn between elation at the thought of missing the winter in Axoxo and concern about a campaign in Aubinas. It was bad to be fighting one's own people. Still, one thing was clear. If they were fighting in Aubinas, the food and beer would be fantastic. Aubinas was one of the richest provinces in the Argonath. Dragons would like that.

Relkin noticed that he had two knots tied in his handkerchief, meant to prompt his memory. He was so excited, however, that for the moment neither knot meant anything.

The idea of promotion was intoxicating. At last he'd be a dragon leader! And he'd stay with Bazil, though they'd be in a new unit. They'd miss their old friends in the 109th. Hell, they'd been together for longer than a lot of dragon squadrons lasted. Best of all, a promotion was one thing that would really help him with the Wattels. He would be a dragon leader, not just a dragonboy. They would respect that.

And even though there was to be a court-martial, maybe it wouldn't hurt. First off, it was likely to be postponed until after the Aubinan campaign. Secondly, if he was tried for having a bit of gold tucked away, that might actually help with the conservative old Wattels. They were a thrifty clan, but they hadn't seen much gold in their hills in a long, long time.

His good spirits continued. Even if they did have a court-martial, he thought that the testimonials from King Choulaput and whoever might be ruler in Mirchaz now would bail him out of trouble. Sure, he had brought home some gold, but the gold he'd brought from Mirchaz was taken from the fallen elf lords. He had paid the importation taxes on it and registered it, just as he had with the gifts from King Choulaput. Relkin had done everything nice and legal, except for that little sack of gold he had buried out on the road, and that was just in case they lost everything else.

Best of all, they weren't going to Axoxo. Like everyone else, he'd been dreading a year on the siege line at Axoxo. Even doubled freecoats and woolen face masks wouldn't be enough in deep winter up in those mountains. That was enough to make any dragonboy dance a jig.

And then the knots suddenly snapped into focus, and he remembered what they were for.

The first one was to remind him to investigate the state of the new scabbard that was being made for Ecator. The old one was literally falling to pieces after the wear and tear of the campaign in Eigo.

He could have had a legion issue scabbard, but Ecator was not a legion issue blade. It was longer and heavier and wouldn't fit well in a legion scabbard. Moreover Lessis had bidden him to remember that this scabbard would be housing her friend, the sprite Ecator, that haunted the blade.

Relkin had seen enough of the blade to believe that it was truly inhabited by a presence. Ecator would therefore need an elf-made scabbard, with the runes of his own kind inscribed on the inside.

Accordingly he had ordered a scabbard from a blacksmith in the Elf Quarter, over behind the imposing facade on the north side of Tower Street. He had made the knot to remind himself to get over to the smithy and check on their progress.

The second knot was to remind him to go to Lagdalen's office. There were scrolls to read, affidavits to witness, and lots of things to discuss with regard to the court-martial. By default, Lagdalen had become his attorney. Nothing else had even been considered. Lagdalen saw it as an outgrowth of the Glaves's case, and since the Glaves's case was technically over, she and her office had plenty of time and energy to put into Relkin's defense.

It was time to get moving. When the dragon came back from the armorers, there'd be the lunchtime boil. Huge amounts of noodles and akh, not to mention weak beer, would be rolled out to the wyverns. And after that there was the arduous task of hustling an extra ration of Old Sugustus skin toughener out of the pharmacy.

Relkin hurried out of the Dragon House and took himself down Tower Street for a couple of blocks, then turned up into the Elf Quarter on Half Moon Row. The streets grew narrow and twisty, and the whitewashed, brick houses had round front windows with narrow doorways. The folk in these streets were forest elves, with the tiny green marks in their skin that bespoke their strange and inhuman origin. They were related in some way to the high elves, but the relationship was lost in the sands of time.

He came to the blacksmith, Lukula Perri, a stoutly built elf with wide shoulders and a strongly hooked nose. He wore a red-and-white-striped cap that ended in a peak with gold tassles. Working for him were three young elves, all "rooted in the same grove," as Lukula put it. Indeed, they all looked very similar: slender youths with olive skin, fine features, and that distant look in the eyes so characteristic of elves.

"A strong greeting to you, Dragoneer," said the elf smith as he wiped his sweating brow and set aside long steel tongs and a sizzling piece of hot iron.

The younger elves went back to hammering.

"I return your greeting, Lukula. I hope the day finds you well."

The elf smith was plainly pleased at this old elf benediction.

"Truly, you are elf friend."

Relkin wondered what the Game Lords of Tetraan would say in reply to that.

The nearly finished scabbard was brought out. The runes were in place, which would comfort the fierce spirit of the blade. It was a nine-foot-long steel sheath wrapped in black leather, with a studded brass tip and a heavy brass reinforcement at the hilt rest. It was plain of ornament except for the single cat's-eye embossed at the hilt rest. But the heavy buckles were still to be welded on. A delay had been caused by slow delivery of the buckles, which had been ordered from the Cravath firm of bucklers down on Dock Street. Still, the work would be finished by the morrow.

Relkin walked smartly back to the Dragon House, checked at the armory. Bazil was still being measured for cuisses. The Purple Green was complaining about the greaves. They pinched behind the knee. Relkin left and went down Water Street to Lagdalen's office. The city was spread out below with the blue water of the sound filling the horizon. The rain had finally stopped, and the skies were clear.

At Lagdalen's office, the young lady at the reception room asked him to take a seat and wait. Lagdalen was closeted with an important visitor.

Ah, well. He relaxed and mulled over the good news. No Axoxo, winter spent here on the coast. Much more comfortable than even Kenor. As to what the rebellion might mean in terms of actual combat, Relkin was sanguine enough. The grain magnates would not be putting out an entire army of trolls, and he would never believe them capable of fielding battledragons—not until he saw it with his own eyes. So any fighting would be the guerrilla kind, and the dragons would not play much part. It would be a cavalryman's fight.

Lagdalen's offices were bustling. Two young women came down the stairs and exited after a short talk with the young lady at the desk. A man came in and deposited a bag of message scrolls, tipped his hat, and left. Moments later another man came in with a single large scroll that he left after the reception lady signed a chit for him. More messengers came, some of them took away piles of scrolls as well as leaving them. Every so often a boy of about twelve would come out of a door leading into the rear part of the ground floor carrying another mound of scrolls and message slips on a wooden tray. These he would set down by the reception lady.

Relkin was impressed. This was a veritable hive of industry. Time stretched out a bit, but Relkin waited patiently, mulling over the possibility of promotion and what it might mean to his life. And then he heard a familiar quiet voice coming down the stairs and immediately snapped out of his reverie. That voice was welcome, but it always meant danger. A few moments later the Lady Lessis appeared, with Lagdalen beside her. When Lessis saw Relkin, she broke into a big smile and held out her arms to him.

"Well, well, we meet again. This has to be a good omen, Relkin of Quosh. We survived the last meeting, eh? The patterns of destiny again, don't you think, child?"

Relkin got up to greet her. Lessis took his hand in one of hers and took Lagdalen's in the other. Her eyes were alight in a way he had never seen.

"You know, I have never had the chance to thank you both together for what the two of you did in Tummuz Orgmeen. That was the work of heroes, children."

The reception lady's eyes were bulging as she watched and listened. She knew perfectly well who the slight figure in the worn grey cloak was. And to see the Great Witch take this scruffy dragonboy's hand like that and say those things. Well, it took one's breath away.

The three remained like that, held together in Lessis's magical field. Then they relaxed, and Lessis turned to Lagdalen.

"Now that this young man is here, I can fulfill a second mission. Two partridges with the same arrow!"

Relkin felt a little tremor of apprehension. Relkin had had his fill of such missions as came in the wake of Lessis of Valmes.

"But first, before my manners forget me entirely, tell me how our great friend is? Has he recovered from the wounds taken at Quosh."

"Close. Another two weeks, and he'll be almost completely healed. Wyverns heal faster than men."

"Mmmm," Lady Lessis put a hand to her chin, absorbing

this information. Not for the first time the Grey Lady was learning something from the dragonboy.

"They are such fascinating great beasts, the wyverns. I was reading a paper published recently on the dissection of a wyvern brain."

At Relkin's furrowed eyebrows, she hurriedly went on:

"The dragon died of old age. She had agreed beforehand to give her body for research."

"What did they find?" said Lagdalen.

"That wyvern brains are more like the brains of crows than they are like our own. Different parts of the brain are much larger in each case. The animals of the land, and the whales, have brains similar in design to our own. There are various components, and a folded area all across the top, where we believe the processes of thought are formed and carried out. The dragon brain does not have much of that folded layer. Instead there is a large bulge at the front of the brain where another organ has grown, and apparently it is very similar to that which is found in the crows, the most intelligent of birds."

Relkin was excited by this information.

"That explains so much. They are so different in so many ways, the way they think, I mean."

"I should send you a copy of that report. In fact, you should see all the dissection research papers concerning the wyverns. I'm surprised this information wasn't made more widely available."

"I never heard of it. Tell the truth, I never imagined they'd do that to a wyvern, you know what I mean?"

"Ah, yes, well in Andiquant the Imperial science staff are investigating a wide range of topics in the biological world." Lessis paused a moment, it was so easy to get sidetracked.

"Still, I am glad to hear the good news about the Broketail dragon. Such a heroic fellow. I watched him fight in the street at Quosh, and I never saw such a terrifying sight. It's a wonder the enemy would even face him!"

"Bazil had a good fight there, and the wound was quick to heal—no rot set in."

"This is all very fine, my dear, but I must tell you that you have to answer more questions about Mirchaz and your own experiences there. Bell and Selera will be awaiting you tomorrow. I will join them."

Relkin's face fell. So he was the second partridge after all.

"The trouble is, Lady, I just don't know how to explain what happened."

"Yes, I have read the reports. But we won't go into that here." Lessis cast a glance over her shoulder to the reception woman.

"Tomorrow morning, right?"

"Yes, Lady."

He'd have to get Curf to sub for Bazil for the day. He hoped Curf would do a good job. That boy had his head stuck in the clouds most of the time.

Lessis had to leave. She had meetings in the Tower of Guard for the rest of the day. She pressed their hands once more and was gone.

Relkin accompanied Lagdalen past the awed reception woman and up the stairs to the second floor where her private office was.

Inside a room furnished with old chairs, tables, and wonky bookcases, they sat together and Lagdalen sent for a pot of tea. While they drank hot tea with honey, Lagdalen turned to something that had been troubling her.

"Relkin, this gold. There are a lot of questions we have to be ready for. Questions I have to ask. Now."

"I understand."

"I need your bank papers. The records from the Kadein Bank. You have them, right?"

"Of course." What did she take him for? He'd always kept records of all their money, his and Bazil's. They had saved a bit even before the trip to Eigo. Relkin knew his way around the market in public company stocks and consols.

"I'm sorry, I just have to know, is all." She looked down, sensing his rebuke. "Look, Relkin, the problem is that there's a fortune here. I've seen the list of amounts that they charge you with possessing, and it's enormous. Thousands of pieces of gold. Imperial gold weight, I'm talking about."

"Well, it's not all for just me and Baz. The king gave the rest for the fund for the dragons of the 109th. I've filled out all the papers. The fund is registered, and all taxes were paid."

"I know, Relkin. I know. But we're going to have trouble with a jury because this is a small fortune."

"I took some of it, I admit, but the king gave us a lot of it too. The gold chains, the medallions, all that came from Choulaput. Only the gold tabis are really loot. To tell the truth, I thought it was a payment well deserved for what we'd been through down there."

"Well, that's what we're going to have to convince a jury of. Unfortunately we can't tell them what happened in Mirchaz in too much detail. They won't believe it after a point. It will sound too fantastic to them."

"Well, I wasn't the only looter, and if you ask the folk running the city whether they mind if I keep the gold, I don't think they will. I broke the gates to the city and let the rebellion in. We both almost lost our lives in that fighting."

"Yes, I believe you did." Lagdalen took up a notebook and began to jot things down.

"Tell me more about the fighting and how you came to find the gold."

With a sigh, Relkin once again picked up the tale of Mirchaz and the fall of the elf lords of Tetraan.

Chapter Thirty-two

Hurrying back to the Dragon House the next day, Relkin saw a company of legionaries marching out of the city gate with a long line of supply wagons behind them. His question to a couple of men in the watching crowd brought a terse response.

"Heard it's part of the Fifth Regiment, First Legion."

Relkin nodded, understanding at once. The Fifth Regiment was mostly based in Blue Hills and was certain to be on the road to Aubinas. Relkin imagined that a lot of forces were in motion all over the Argonath and that several regiments would eventually be concentrated in Aubinas. Putting down a rebellion could be a difficult task.

"I hear that the Aubinans have put Posila under siege," said a fellow a little farther down the line.

"Damn them, it's those farmers in Nellin."

"Nellin and Belland, they'll be hot spots for the rebels. Too big for their britches, if you ask me," said a fat fellow with a soft green hat.

"Well, no one's going to, Ned Battock, so you can stow it," said the man standing beside him.

Relkin crossed the parade ground, dodging through the wagons, and went on to the Dragon House. Things were looking good on a number of fronts. The new scabbard would be delivered the next morning. Meanwhile he had gamed the Dragon House pharmacy system pretty well and would pick up a second handout of Old Sugustus skin toughener and liniment later in the day. That would give him enough to be sure of getting through at least two months in the field. Relkin thought that that was the most likely period of time they'd be in Aubinas on active duty.

General Cerius was in command of the operations

against the rebels. Cerius was old, but a good commander who'd fought against the Teetol and the forces of the Doom in Tummuz Orgmeen. Cerius had been stationed out at Fort Kenor until recently. Relkin wondered what other units would be drawn into this thing. Maybe they'd see old friends again.

The empire was flexing its muscles. Everything was in motion, and Relkin was sure the 109th would soon be leaving the city too. Dragons wouldn't be that important in a cavalry-dominated war of skirmishes and raids, but they would still be useful in gaining mastery of any field where serious battle was offered. Let the Aubinans dare to put foot soldiers on the ground against dragons!

He checked on the dragon and found him in the plunge pool after a morning of fittings and sword exercise, complaining already of a prodigious appetite. The wound was really healing well, a complete seal in the skin under a heavy scabbing. It couldn't have looked better, and the Dragon House Medico was pleased as punch with the case.

Nor had there been any aftereffects from the poison in that fish pie. Everyone had been really worried about that for the first day or so, but the dragons seemed unharmed, even the brasshides.

Soon came the bell for the lunchtime boil, and the dragonboys went down to the kitchens and wheeled away the big tubs of legion noodles, liberally soaked in good akh. The air became heavy with the aroma of akh, a compendium of spices, garlic, onions, peppers, and more peppers.

Swane had the latest news concerning the poison.

"It was tainted with Stibium, they say."

"What's that?' said Jak.

"Antimony," said Manuel. "It's real poisonous, some kind of metal."

"They never found out who the Grain Association was."

"Well, we know it was Aubinans," said Swane.

Relkin didn't say it, but he was wondering if it might not have been some revenge for the Battle of Quosh.

Bazil was soon happily at work on a solid lunch. Relkin brought him another tub, filled with the weak beer that was given for lunch. The dragon intended to eat, then sleep. Later in the day there would be an inspection, but after such a long workout with the sword, Bazil would be excused any further physical effort that day.

Relkin, in the meantime, would be back in that room with the witches. His interrogation was scheduled to resume that afternoon. He wasn't looking forward to it.

After the tubs were returned to the kitchens, Relkin made one final check on equipment. He was due at the pharmacy just before the evening boil. Until then he was booked in at the Office of Insight, officially. Unofficially he would be in the Offices of Unusual Insight. Relkin thought he would rather be almost anywhere else, even back in the forest of the Land of Terror, haunted by giant meat-eating pujish.

Sooner rather than later, Relkin found himself sitting in that musty room with Selera and Bell. Selera began the questioning and focused, as so often before, on the processes of thought that he'd gone through during the critical moments in the village of Quosh. He tried to explain. He knew deep down that what they were trying to do was very important.

"It was a long fight, a really desperate thing. I don't know if you've ever been in one, but fights are really tiring. And if they go on for more than a few minutes you get worn out, and you have a hard time thinking clearly, I never would have tried to send any thoughts to the camp at Cross Treys. I'm not a wizard, and I don't want to be one. I don't know how I did the things that happened in Mirchaz. In fact, most of the time I don't want to know. I'm afraid of being a freak, afraid I'll go mad. I don't like to even think about all this."

"But you must, Relkin. We must learn all we can from you. This may be a most critical juncture in history."

He sighed. "Oh, well, if you put it like that." The witches were very good at making you feel guilty if you weren't giving your absolute all for the cause.

So the questions went on, over and over the same ground, turning it for minute details of memory as Relkin strove to reconstruct the scene during those critical hours in the smoke and terror of the street in Quosh. Time passed, but Relkin could detect little progress.

He didn't notice the door open, but suddenly the Lady Lessis was there in the room. Bell and Selera had fallen silent. They bowed in their seats to the Grey Lady, and she nodded back to them.

"I thought it might be helpful if I joined you for these

discussions. I was at Quosh, and I know our friend here pretty well."

Relkin felt his spirits lift a little. Lessis was a dangerous person to know, but in these circumstances, she offered insight and enormous knowledge. If anyone could help him, it would be her.

"Welcome, Lady. We are most honored." Selera actually got up and brought a chair out for Lessis, who sat in the corner, away from the table, where she could watch both the witches and the dragonboy.

"You have been going over the events at Quosh, I take it."

"Yes, Lady," said Bell. "The moment when he produced the magical effect in Cross Treys."

"And he has little to tell, I'm sure."

"Correct, Lady."

Relkin spoke up. "I was telling them earlier that you get tired pretty quick when you're in a real fight. And that fight was a long one, or rather it was a long series of fights—I'm sure you remember."

"I do," she nodded. It had been an exhausting ordeal, a horror and a memory she wished she could blot out. Like so many.

"So I was desperate and kind of crazed. I just thought of Cross Treys: I visualized the camp and the Dragon House. Then I thought about the dragons, and tried real hard to see them clearly in my mind. It was like when you pray, which is what I told these ladies."

"Like a prayer?"

"Yeah, you give a prayer to the Goddess, or maybe to the old gods, and you try to see them as you say the prayer."

"Ah, Relkin, you still adhere to your faith in the old ones, do you?"

"Well, it's hard to know what to think sometimes. The old gods seem more real to me somehow; but then, there's times I think they can't be real. The elf lords in Mirchaz spoke of the gods too, but I couldn't tell if they were different gods. There seems to be a lot of gods, and then there's the Goddess too, so I don't know. I get confused. I've seen too much in the way of gods."

Lessis nodded to herself. This unlettered boy had been chosen by some combination of circumstance and the will of the High Ones to be tested again and again. What did they want with this child? Why him? Yet he had survived, along with his mighty wyvern. They wanted him for some great service, it was plain to her.

"Different gods, indeed, Relkin," she replied. "The Lords of Mirchaz were grown fell and evil. They had anointed themselves as gods. As with all of those who would rule and crush and destroy others, they thought themselves completely separate from the Mother of us all, who pervades everything."

"Why had they turned to evil, Lady?"

"The story of the Lords of Mirchaz is a long and sorry one, child, too long for me to tell it to you now. I will provide you with a book if you like, Dantone's history of Gelderen is what you need to begin with."

"They were strange folk, Lady. I spent a long time with the Lady Tschinn, who was a kind of princess among them. I would have died, but for her magical arts of healing. And then she sent me forth to destroy the power of her people."

"Child, they were once the noblest, fairest folk in the world. The first lords, secure in the glory of the highest estate. Perhaps she recalled that greatness and regretted their fall into such evil."

Lessis looked across to Bell and Selera, who she could see were reassessing their views of Relkin. As she'd expected, they had taken his unlettered exterior for the whole. They did not know all the details of his history; such matters were secret, even within the Office of Unusual Insight, and so they had seen a dragonboy and heard nothing but a dragonboy's answers to their questions. Even though they had been told something of his strange exploits in Mirchaz. Now they were realizing that he was much more than just a dragonboy. That Lessis was there to witness the interrogation had changed their minds. Bell and Selera needed more field experience, Lessis decided.

"I have an experiment that I wish to conduct with you, dear child." Lessis produced a small box from within the sleeve of her robe.

"I have placed an object in the box. I want you to try and imagine what it is."

Relkin looked at the box, then back to the Lady. He nodded. This at least made more sense than going over and over the same barren ground with Bell and Selera.

"Close your eyes, child, and try to visualize the object in the box. Give yourself plenty of time."

Relkin took a deep breath and tried to relax. He pushed all thought of the golden elf lords out of his mind. The box, the little box, what was in it?

It was no bigger than a snuffbox and made of unpolished wood from the look of it. Close the eyes. He did so. Lessis used no spell to help him relax. It was vital that Relkin do this all by himself. Any intervention could ruin the experiment.

Bell and Selera were watching with fascinated eyes.

Relkin found it hard to really relax. The chair was not the comfortable kind, and Bell and Selera were sitting behind their table still. He was wound up and nervous. After being under interrogation, it wasn't easy to just calm down instantly.

The box, the little box, what was in it?

A vision of his dragon came to him. Bazil was just waking up after a nice long nap. He was thinking of taking a nice long dip in the plunge pool. Tomorrow the scabbard would be delivered. Bazil looked forward to seeing Ecator properly housed once more. The old scabbard had really taken a beating; it was falling apart, in fact. The pool was waiting.

Relkin snapped out of it. A strange reverie, unusually strong. The box, what was in the box.

"Chess piece," he said. "A dragon."

Lessis's eyes grew more piercing than he had ever seen before. She opened the box and produced the little white wooden figure of the dragon, which played the position of rook or castle on an Argonath chessboard. Bell and Selera gaped.

"Child, what did you do just then? Think hard, and carefully."

Relkin stared at the chess piece. By the roll of Caymo's dice! Now he'd gotten himself right in it. He had no idea what he'd gone. He'd seen Bazil, and then he knew what was in the box. But how?

The witches were staring at him with a frightening intensity. He groaned inwardly.

Chapter Thirty-three

The 109th had finally been brought back to a full complement of ten dragons and ten dragonboys, plus trainee Curf. The newest additions were a leatherback named Gunter and his dragonboy Uri, plus the veteran Roquil, who had been absent since the Battle of Quosh with an infected chest wound. Gunter was a Blue Hills dragon, like Bazil, except he came from the western village of Querc. Uri was a solidly built, red-haired boy with a quiet demeanor. Roquil's Endi was his old self, glad to be back in the unit after weeks at the infirmary with a sick dragon.

As for young Curf, he was still a ways from being judged ready for a dragon of his own. Cuzo had decided that Curf would never get anywhere unless he kept up harsh pressure. Otherwise he'd simply daydream his life away.

Leatherback Gunter was young with a pleasant disposition and good sword moves. He soon became popular with the other wyverns. Even the Purple Green accepted the newcomer with little of his usual truculence. Meanwhile dragonboy Uri had showed himself to be a steady sort and no trouble to Cuzo.

As usual, the boys of the unit all came together in the early evening, while the dragons were finishing off their dinner. They had taken to sitting around on a long bench set outside the Purple Green's double stall. From the bench they had a good view along the line of stalls all the way down to Cuzo's office. His movements could thus be monitored quite easily, and as long as they didn't talk too loud, Cuzo couldn't hear what they were saying.

Mono and Manuel were sitting beside each other quietly discussing the technical difficulties of securing the new-style vambraces that had been issued for the dragons. The vambrace was a piece of steel plate that protected the forearm from wrist to elbow. Traditionally they had been secured by leather thongs tied to eyelets in the corners and down the sides, but the new pieces had chain fringes. The idea was that chain was harder to cut or break in the heat of battle, and thus the vambraces would be more securely held. Unfortunately the chains tended to chafe the delicate dragon skin of the inside of the forelimb, just below the elbow. Mono had made leather sleeves for these chains and that had cut down on the problem for big Chektor, the veteran brasshide. Manuel was keenly interested, since the Purple Green had complained loudly about the chafing from the first hour of wearing the new vambraces.

Meanwhile the rest of the group were busy with the matter of the mascot's ashes. Stripey, the little pygmy elephant, who they'd brought back from Eigo, had passed away from a sudden fever during the winter. Everyone, even Cuzo, had been saddened. Little Stripey had been a joyous creature, smarter than any dog and able to get into everything with that skillful trunk. However, while Stripey's spirit had gone to the Mother's Grace, his ashes were still in their possession. At the insistence of the Purple Green, Stripey had been cremated and his ashes placed in a small iron-lapped casket. The mascot's ashes had become the new mascot. This had satisfied everyone.

Unfortunately the little casket had become a focus for the attentions of the wagon-train master, one Captain Glif. The unit had far too much baggage. The dragonboys of the 109th had spent their stay in Marneri by acquiring as many duplicates of kit items as they possibly could. Thinking they were on their way to siege duty in Axoxo, they'd tried to think of everything they might need way out at the end of a long, fragile supply line in freezing, winter weather in the mountains. "Everything" became a descriptive term for their needs after a while, and stuff piled up outrageously in the Dragon House locker room.

Captain Glif had put pressure on Cuzo. The 109th baggage train was too long, filling nine wagons. They should only take five. Cuzo had begun a round of inspections, weeding out nonregulation items, and triplicates of things like joboquin straps. Frantic dragonboys had hidden spare helmets, breastplates, tail swords, joboquins, and blankets all over the Dragon House. Cuzo had led search-and-remove missions, scouring the gallery over the combat yard where several helmets were discovered, and taking a careful look through dragon lockers and the lockers in the plunge pool room. More armor and dozens of blankets were uncovered.

Now there was tension over the ashes. Cuzo had decreed that the casket containing the mascot's ashes would have to be left behind in Marneri. The casket was a nonregulation item that Cuzo could not bring himself to allow.

Needless to say, this was the last straw. The dragonboys were close to rebellion. It is one thing to never have a wealth of duplicate equipment. It is very much another to have a wealth of such equipment and then to lose it.

"I say we take the ashes, and we hide it really well and just let him try and find it." Swane was angry.

"Where would you hide it, then?" said Curf.

"I don't know exactly, we'd have to think it over carefully. Maybe we'd even move it around. It ain't big, doesn't take up much room. We can hide it easy, and to hell with Cuzo."

"All the dragons are well upset by this."

"By the Hand, Alsebra was ready to go and talk to Cuzo herself. And if she felt that way, I hate to think what the Purple Green would like to do."

"So we take the ashes away," said Howt, the other new boy, who tended big Churn.

"Right!" said Jak. "Hell with Cuzo."

Relkin tried to plead for calm. "Hold everything, before we get into going around him, let's try and reason with him. I'm telling you, Cuzo has gone out of his way to be honest with me. After Wiliger and Turrent, that's been a great relief."

"By the Hand, that Wiliger was a crazy!" muttered Jak. Swane chuckled. Wiliger was a legend in the legions now, the only officer who had ever transferred out of an infantry regiment into the dragon squadrons.

Relkin pressed on, since he had their attention. "Let's ask Cuzo first if we can't talk about this. He won't want the dragons all sulky. He's not stupid, he knows the dragons are the unit. They're the ones who do the important stuff."

Relkin's words seemed to ring true for the new boys. Howt and Uri nodded. So did Curf and Jak. Only Swane, obstreperous as ever, was still unconvinced. Relkin switched tacks after a while, feeling this was a good time to bring up the greater question of their gear.

"Anyway, the casket is a small thing. Cuzo will let us take it, I'm sure, once we talk it over with him. But we have to face the fact that we've got too much stuff. We're going to have to give some back. I mean, I'm not claiming to be innocent or anything, I've got three freecoats. Because I thought we'd be spending the winter at Axoxo."

Swane guffawed. "That Quoshite!"

"Yeah, well, how many have you got, Swane?"

Swane hemmed and hawed a moment or two. "Three," he admitted after the others hooted at him.

"Well, for an autumn campaign in Aubinas we'll only need one. And we can't hang on to all the blankets we acquired. We're going to have to give them back."

Faces around him reflected the war between good and evil as represented by the urge to keep all the stuff they'd winkled out of stores and the noble concept of giving it back.

Rakama came in the outer doors way down the broad passageway past the entrances to the plunge pool and the refectory. He came at a run.

"Something's up," said Jak.

Rakama skidded to a halt. He was in an excited state: his face was red, and his eyes were filled with a sort of shock, like one to whom the end of the world has been revealed.

"Did you hear yet?" Rakama said.

"No, what is it?"

"Battle in Nellin, they're saying the Fifth Regiment was defeated. General Cerius has been captured."

"Never!" Boys sprang to their feet, eyes wide in shock.

"What else are they saying?" said Relkin.

"Lots of casualties, hundreds."

They looked at each other, suddenly hot-eyed with anger. Up until now the Aubinan revolt had been a distant threat, something they'd only half believed in. Everyone had expected the legions to go in and clean it up in a month or so. Now there was bloodshed, and everything had changed. Now it was civil war.

The shock spread. By the following morning the details were trickling in. After relieving besieged Posila, the Fifth

Regiment had pushed out on a punitive mission to Redhill, the capital of Nellin County. On their way to Redhill, the Fifth were ambushed and took casualties. Angered by this, they had gone hard on the town, burning some of it down. The so-called "Sack of Redhill" had ignited the rebellion's tinder. Men who had resisted the call of the rebels thus far had been won over by the thousand. While Cerius stood to in the ruins of Redhill, an army of three and a half thousand gathered nearby. When Cerius pushed out from Redhill to engage the rebels, his force of one thousand was outmatched. In a cleverly staged ambush, Aubinan cavalry was able to break up the legion squares and slaughter many men. Meanwhile the Talion horsemen attached to Cerius's force were outwitted by the backwoods riders from Aubinas, who knew the country like the backs of their hands. In the complex terrain of hills, woodlots, and fields laced by sunken lanes, the Aubinans had set trap after trap for the legionaries and exacted a heavy toll. When it came to the crisis, the Talion horsemen were unable to aid Cerius's hard-pressed foot soldiers.

Now the remains of the Fifth Regiment were back inside the walls of Posila under siege from an army of rebels that was growing every day. All over Aubinas, and elsewhere in the Argonath, there was a wave of anti-Imperial sentiment. This kept the volunteers coming in to the Aubinan camp outside Posila. The rebel force was now more than five thousand strong, and quite a few of those were former legionaries who brought in shields, swords, and spears.

Not that there was much of a shortage of weaponry. Mysterious cases of swords, and other necessary elements, like helmets and shields, had appeared in the camp from early on. The rumor had it that the grain magnates, who had the most to gain from the rebellion if it was successful, had supplied the weapons and that they had plenty more in reserve.

An army of ten to fifteen thousand was now envisaged as possible. And in nearby Arneis, which bordered Aubinas in the south, along the Bel Awl Ridge, there was further rebellion brewing. If both of these powerful, grain-producing provinces rebelled together, they might force the decision against the Empire of the Rose.

Songs about the burning of Redhill were said to be spreading up and down the tradeways. "Imperial home burners," was a phrase said to be gaining in popularity. This despite the fact that the parts of Redhill that were burned were not the houses, but the new wooden palisade and gates that had been erected even before the rebellion was declared.

As the day wore on into evening, Relkin sent hourly messages to Eilsa. The city was in an uproar, and she was sitting tight with her chaperon in her quarters on Foluran Hill. He expected to be sent to Aubinas at any moment, probably in the next day or so.

The dragons were jumpy and ate less than usual. The Purple Green almost got into a fight with Gryf, and this time the wyverns took Gryf's side. Everyone bedded down in an irritable mood.

They had been asleep for perhaps two hours when the Dragon House was awoken by the battle gong. Men were running in the streets, and there was a fire beacon lit on the Tower of Guard.

Cuzo came running out of his room. Everyone, every unit in the city was to be out and on the road for Lucule at once. Posila had fallen through treachery. The survivors of the Fifth Regiment had been captured, and the Aubinan army was marching for Marneri.

So hurried was their departure that Relkin couldn't even pen a message to Eilsa.

Chapter Thirty-four

Rain clouds had returned and formed a dull gray ceiling over the city. The streets were running with streams of water, and in the harbor great trading ships rode at anchor, sails furled. Smaller vessels bobbed on the waves. On Tower Street the sidewalks were virtually empty, even at the corner with Foluran Hill, normally one of the busiest places in the city.

There were just a few souls abroad, hurrying along through the tempest. Behind shuttered windows, candles burned as the city of Marneri tried to come to grips with the incredible news from Aubinas.

The white city on the sound had faced many perils. Armies of the Demon Lord Mach Ingbok had besieged it and burned the hills for twenty miles in all directions, but it had never faced a siege by rebels from within the city-state. The rule of Marneri over its provinces had heretofore always been regarded as just. Taxation was raised even-handedly across the provinces. None were favored over the others, though more in taxes was expected from Aubinas and Seinster than from hilly places like Blue Stone and Seant simply because they produced far more wheat and barley, the so-called "gold" of the Argonath.

Now the city faced the prospect of civil war and of a rebel army ravaging the countryside around the walls. It was a disheartening prospect.

A slightly built woman, hidden within a gray cloak and rain bonnet, slipped out of the Tower of Guard and made her way across the open plaza of the parade ground. She headed south down Water Street, which zigzagged back and forth down the steep southwest slope of the hill below the Tower of Guard. Behind her, unobtrusively, came a pair of silent men, clad in equally colorless clothing, one in a brown cloak and leggings, the other in a dark grey cloak and hat. They followed the woman at a respectful one hundred paces, as steady as shadows.

Way down the hill in the Old Square section, the woman knocked at the door of a building with lights visible at several windows. The door opened, and the woman went inside. The men who were shadowing her went on quietly down the street, then turned and hid themselves while expertly scanning the street above to see if anyone had been following them. From their hiding places they exchanged a signal and then slipped back up the street to an alley set opposite the building that had received the woman.

"Nothing on our trail," said one of the men, whose face was flat and grim under black eyes that were hard and cold.

"Nothing we could see, but I feel something." The other man was thinner in the face, almost gaunt, and younger with piercing blue eyes and thin lips.

"So you said."

"Something has changed in this city. It wasn't here on our last visit, and it certainly wasn't following her. Now it is."

The first speaker grunted and looked up and down the street again. He was not a psychic sensitive, he was Mirk, and he was a killer. He was one of the most effective killers the Office of Unusual Insight had ever had, with one hundred assassinations to his name by the age of thirty-five. He was also one of the greatest bodyguards ever produced for the Office of Insight, possessing an uncanny ability to detect assassination attempts. Oddly enough, for this violent trade, he was a native of Defwode, the ultraconservative province of Cunfshon. Most of his kills had been of enemy agents, too sensitively entrenched within society in the Argonath and Cunfshon to be taken up for trial. Such men, and a few women, had to be dispatched with silence and stealth. That was Mirk's specialty.

Mirk scanned along the rooftops with his flat black eyes. At his left hip rested two throwing knives, nested together. On his right was a razor-sharp stabbing blade and a short sword.

He could see nothing. No one was following them on the street, or even on the roofs. But Wespern was there beside him because he was sensitive to such things. He had some sixth or seventh sense that detected hidden watchers, even when they were protected by magic screens. So despite the evidence of his own eyes, Mirk accepted that something was tailing them.

Mirk kept his eyes on the street. If it couldn't be killed, then it wasn't his affair. He could only kill what he could see. Besides, he thought with calm calculation, Wespern was sensitive in these things, but the person that they guarded was the Lady herself, and she had sensitivities beyond their understanding of such things. On those planes she could most surely look after herself.

Across the street, in Lagdalen's warm office, Lessis took off her cloak and hat and composed her thoughts. The room had a desk and a table, both covered in scrolls and books. Shelves lined one wall, and the carpeting was wearing out. It seemed typical of Lagdalen's crowded, busy life. She went to the window for a quick look at the view of the lower city and the harbor spread out to the west. Rain beat down endlessly over everything. It was raining beyond the Mother's patience. This was a record year for rainfall in the Argonath. It was already lowering harvests. She noted the two grey shapes in the alley opposite.

Mirk was there. She supposed that was a comfort, except that she always felt a chill from Mirk's presence. She had never met a colder man, and yet he worshiped at the Mother's knee and was a native of Defwode. Normally one thought of the men of Defwode for their weaving and their legendary subservience to their wives. Mirk was an exception to prove the rule, she supposed. No woman would marry him, not with the blood that was on his hands.

But whatever it was that shadowed her, and she could sense something out there, it wasn't corporeal enough for Mirk's weapons. But weapons could bite, even the greatest of witches could be bitten by them. She had only to recall the assassin that had struck her down in the gardens by the temple in this city, only a few short years before. She had almost died that time. She understood there had to be precautions. Mirk was necessary. So was Wespern.

The door opened, and Lagdalen tumbled in, with Eilsa Ranardaughter behind her. The two had been meeting privately before Lessis's unexpected arrival. They seemed a little breathless, their faces fresh with the bloom of youth.

At the sight of Lagdalen, now grown to womanhood, a

mother and an advocate for the crown, Lessis felt an almost maternal sense of pride. At the same time she reflected that she had risked this girl's life a dozen times and so should really be thinking thoughts of the miraculous and of repentance.

We must serve with what we have . . .

"Lady, how wonderful to see you," gushed Lagdalen.

Lessis embraced both of them and held Eilsa by the arms while she took a long, careful look. The girl was beautiful, with that long jaw and distinctive cheekbone, a prize for young Relkin.

"It is good to meet you again, Eilsa of Wattel. My memories of Sprian's Ridge will always be dominated by the work in the hospitals afterward. You were a stalwart in both aspects of the battle."

"I thank you, Lady, these are kind words. Those were grim days, and will never be forgotten in Clan Wattel."

"Troubled times, it is our fate to have to live through them. We are in the middle of a long war. Our enemy is pitiless and very strong. They have recently been reinforced and reinvigorated."

The young women met her gaze. She sensed their concern.

"I have just returned to the city. I heard the news just a few minutes ago."

"We have never had such a thing before, rebels rising against the city, defying the empire and killing legion soldiers." Lagdalen's anger was sharp . . .

"Ah, yes," Lessis pressed her hands together and rested her chin on the tips of her fingers. "Even worse, Relkin of Quosh has been sent off to what may be a nasty battle. That child is much too valuable to be risked like this ever again."

Both younger women's eyebrows rose. Lessis realized she must choose her words very carefully.

"This is information that must not go beyond these walls, you understand, but I know I can trust both of you. And, indeed, you both should be privy to this knowledge for it concerns our mutual friend Relkin." Their concern grew. "We tested Relkin, and we found that he has been changed by his experiences during the last two years. In his long sojourn in Eigo, he was introduced to power far beyond his own experience. Unexpectedly these influences have opened something in him. He is no longer just a dragonboy."

"Oh, my Lady, how, how was he tested?" said Eilsa.

Lessis heard the sudden fear in the girl's voice and thought, She loves him, there can be no doubt about it. If he lives, he may end up a very lucky man.

"He was not harmed. All I did was to hold a small object in a box. Relkin sat in the same room. He was asked to tell me what the hidden object was. He did so."

"But how?"

"That we do not know. Suddenly he saw an image, and that image told him what was in the box."

"Oh, my," Lagdalen put a hand to her mouth. "By the Hand, poor Relkin." Lessis caught the implication of Lagdalen's concern. They would never leave Relkin alone now, not until they had understood what it was that allowed him to perform this way.

"Indeed, Lady, this is news I wished I had not heard," said Eilsa, reaching the same conclusion.

"Alas, child, he has been chosen for some great purpose. Again and again he has been thrown into the crucible. An unusual man has been forged within that dragonboy's hide."

"He has gone to war," said Eilsa, a little blankly.

"I regret it."

Eilsa heard the pain in Lessis's voice. The Lady had seen too much bloodshed, too much slaughter. Indeed she had retired as a consequence of the horror she'd lived through in Eigo, but still the struggle remained. Their enemy still held the field, and they must fight or accept the rule of the nightmare tyranny of Padmasa.

"This war is the work of the Aubinan Grain magnates, Lady," Lagdalen said.

"Yes, of course. Though I think there are powers beyond the Aubinans that are at work here. It is as I told you before. Padmasa has allied itself with a foe of dreadful proportions. Those fools in Padmasa do not understand their peril. Heruta would never have allowed this infiltration by the Dominator. He would have understood the truth. But Heruta is no more, and now the Dominator is here, at work behind the Aubinans, somehow."

"But the Aubinans, Lady, they are marching to the coast even as we speak."

"Yes, dear Lagdalen. I know. He attempts another swift, knockout blow. We understand such strategy."

Lagdalen nodded. This was exactly what the witches had done to Heruta Skash Gzug in Eigo.

"A new enemy?" said Eilsa, unsure in the presence of such talk. She had no experience of the Office of Unusual Insight and its ways except what Relkin had told her.

"Yes, my dear. Our enemies in Padmasa have formed an alliance with a power for great evil. Although he came from our world in the beginning, he has been in exile for many aeons. In that time he has become very powerful. He bends the very fabric of the Sphereboard of Destiny."

"What is this enemy?"

"I believe you have a strong heart and a sound mind, Eilsa of Wattel. So I think I can tell you and not fear that it will drive you mad with fear."

Eilsa tightened her jaw, looked as if she were measuring Lessis for a sword stroke. They were fierce, those people of the fells of Wattel.

"This enemy is a relic from the dawn of the world. A fell and evil spirit, one of a class of great beings that were designed to serve in the creation of the world. They were meant to have short lives, and in their passing they were to give the land and the seas their strength to make the world ready for ourselves. They were seven in number. Six long ago surrendered their lives. This one did not. He rebelled and took the path of long life and endless cruel oppression. He pursues boundless power and has erected empire upon empire. Billions of lives has he crushed in his pursuit of these ends. He will take our entire world if we do not stop him right here in the Argonath."

"What is he called?"

"His name we do not use. Some say that his strength grows with every repetition of his name."

"In that case, tell me not, and I shall never speak it willingly."

Fire returned to Eilsa Ranardaughter's eyes.

"This rebellion in Aubinas is just the opening move," said Lessis.

"Then, before it is over, I deem we shall all have our chance to smite this foe."

Lessis was impressed. She hoped such courage would last

through the coming time of darkness. Lessis knew that they would be sorely tested.

"I am afraid that you will be proved correct on that point, child."

Lessis squeezed their hands.

"Now, I have to speak alone with Lagdalen. It is an urgent matter, but it will not take long to complete our business. I would very much like to talk further with you, Eilsa of Wattel."

"Then, I will happily wait here. My chaperon is downstairs."

"Good."

Lessis and Lagdalen withdrew to a smaller room, where Lagdalen occasionally took naps, or where Laminna would sleep in her cradle.

Lagdalen was dreading what the Lady would say.

"My dear, I hate to have to ask this of you. I have only just returned from Andiquant. The empire faces a grave crisis. Lagdalen, dear, I need your help. I am alone, with no trained assistant. You are all I have."

Lagdalen heard the words with her heart thudding in her chest. They had promised to leave her alone. She had given them the best years of her life. It was supposed to be over. And now they came after her again. You could never be free of them.

"I know what you are thinking, dear. And let me say that I think you're right. It is outrageous to ask this of you, but we must. We have nobody else, and the rebellion must be defeated."

Lagdalen slumped into a chair with a heavy sigh. There was no way out.

"Yes, Lady, of course I will serve."

Chapter Thirty-five

The 109th Marneri Dragons marched through pouring rain up the great Wheat Road into Lucule. Behind them, a full day's march, lay the small city of Sesquila, a place where panic reigned. Ahead of them, somewhere between their present position and Posila, fifty miles away, was the Aubinan army, estimated at five thousand men.

Accompanying the 109th were two companies from the Marneri Fourth Regiment, First Legion, known as the "Four-Ones," and two companies from the Bea Fifth Regiment. In addition, there was a mixed company scraped together of men from Pennar and Vusk. Altogether this gave a force of just under a thousand foot soldiers.

Spread out in the wet fields and woods ahead was a force of seventy volunteer horsemen from Marneri, joined at the last moment by two hundred troopers from Talion, who had ridden down the moment they'd had word of the disaster. The Marneri riders were mostly the younger sons of some of the best families in the city, young men who owned their own horses and could afford to outfit themselves for a campaign in the field. The Talion men were a detachment under the command of Subadar Calex. Fortunately Calex was good at small-troop tactics. His small cavalry force was engaged in a complex game of wits with a much larger force of Aubinan cavalry, and had so far stymied the enemy.

For their part the Aubinans had already proved themselves quite capable. They had obviously trained for the day. Allied to their natural skill in the saddle and their intimate knowledge of the ground, this gave them an advantage.

The Aubinans' greatest problem was the split in their own ranks between the riders from the up-country counties of Aubinas such as Auxey, Muissy, and Biscuit-Barley, and the riders from the down-country counties of Belland and Nellin. The Nellin men were the most eager to attack Marneri itself. The up-country men were concerned only in stopping an invasion of Aubinas. This split greatly diluted the effectiveness of the rebel force, which had been the decisive element in the defeat of the Marneri Fifth Regiment at Redhill.

Some of these things were known and understood by Commander Urmin, who was the commanding officer of the legion force.

The Wheat Road ran virtually straight across the flat plain of Lucule, whose fields of grain stretched to the horizon, broken here and there by dark patches of forest. The road was made of brown bricks and was well sited and drained. Indeed, it was built to Imperial specifications, twenty feet wide with drains every twenty yards. Along the road were villages set every few miles. As they marched, they heard temple bells ringing through the rain, calling the faithful to prayer even with an invasion on their doorstep. Perhaps even more remarkable than the attachment to normal routine was the fact that the country folk responded to the summons and went to worship. They felt quite secure within the blanket of the power of the empire and more particularly of the power of the city of Marneri. Fortunately they had no idea that the small force marching down the pike was all the empire had on hand to cope with the oncoming invasion from Aubinas. If they had, then perhaps they might have panicked like the folk of Sesquila.

Commander Urmin felt the weight of his responsibility. He was a veteran officer who had served in the Teetol campaigns, but he had been deskbound for a decade now. When General Kesepton had asked him if he was sure he could handle this command, Urmin had almost said no. Quite often he wished he had. The Aubinan forces were several times larger than his own. They'd broken General Cerius and had taken him captive. A greater humiliation did not exist. Commander Urmin prayed he didn't end his career in such a sad manner.

He looked back down the line of the marching column, the men huddled against the rain, the horses slick and wet, and down there the moving masses of the great dragons. He prayed to the Goddess that he would find the strength to keep his force intact and protect the white city.

The dragons covered the ground easily enough. Down in Blue Stone they'd taken a lot of route marches. Cuzo had been determined not to let the unit get soft under his command, so everyone was kept at a peak of fitness. Now this was paying off. Even those that had been wounded at Quosh were almost completely recovered. Dragon metabolism was fast-healing, especially when diet was at optimum, and even Bazil was back to full condition. They marched on, content enough, but looking forward to dinner. The rain was monotonous, but it was cooling on big dragon hides. Wyverns liked to get wet, after all. Even the Purple Green had yet to complain. They swung along the road with their shields and swords over their shoulders, great metal hilts and bosses glinting amid the downpour. Far less sanguine, the dragonboys marched alongside, under their own packs, with freecoats and rain hats keeping off the worst.

They stopped in the village of Treeves for a quick boil and a round of stirabout for the dragons. The villagers were happy to contribute cheese, akh, and fresh onions by the hundredweight. A little ale was served up too, and then the legionaries got to their feet, the cornets shrieked, and they marched out of the village. Soon afterward they entered a wooded stretch. Here was a section several miles long and three wide that was covered in woodlots, since the soils were not suited to grain. On the maps it was called "Treeves Wood."

Commander Urmin was nervous about entering this wooded country, so perfectly suited for ambushes. He wished the Marneri horsemen would understand that their role was to keep him informed, not to play games in the woods with the Aubinan riders. Despite his lectures on this point, the young bucks from Marneri hadn't done a good job of feeding him information. As for Subadar Calex, Urmin hadn't seen him all day. The Mother alone knew where the Talion riders were.

After careful perusal of the situation and some scouting of the immediate way ahead, Urmin ordered an advance, and they took up the march once more. They had gone perhaps a mile when a group of Marneri men came galloping down the Wheat Road flat out. They thundered up to Urmin, and after hurried salutes, announced that the Aubinan army was approaching at a fast walk and was only a mile or two down the road.

In an icy tone Urmin inquired as to why he was getting this information only now, when the enemy was two miles away. The Marneri scouts could give no answer. It had been their orders, they said. Urmin looked to the heavens and dismissed them for the moment.

At once the commands went out and the column halted. The 109th fell out and the dragons took a rest, hauling up under the eaves of some old oak trees along the roadside. Dragonboys went over their charges with careful eyes, applying blister sherbet where necessary, and checking bandages and overall condition.

At the head of the line, the Marneri men abruptly turned and galloped off into the woods, while the officers rode down the line and grouped with the company captains and Dragon Leader Cuzo.

Watching this little grouping, the dragonboys gathered together, lips pursed carefully as they stared through the rain at the cluster of officers.

"Wish it would stop raining," said Howt.

"Wishing won't make it happen," grumbled big Swane.

"What d'ya think all that's about," Rakama asked, nodding in the direction of the officers.

"How should I know, you big ape!"

"Who's an ape? You're an ape!" Rakama shoved Swane good-naturedly. They laughed together, caught up in an ongoing joke. Cuzo had been unwise to call them a "pair of apes" after they'd both failed a snap inspection. They'd been joking about it ever since.

"Aubinans are out there, I'll bet," said Curf.

"Well, we know that," said Swane.

"Question is what are we going to do about it?" said Manuel.

"Yeah," Relkin agreed. "That's the real question."

The terrain around them was flat, but covered in woodlots, areas of one to five acres covered in trees at various stages of growth. It was good country for ambushes, which the Aubinans had shown themselves to be good at.

But dragons could be deployed effectively in ambush settings too. The veterans in the unit had set quite a few in their time, particularly in the long fight up the Bur River back in the invasion year.

Suddenly the conference among the officers broke up. Hooves clattered on the road as lieutenants rode past at a gallop to their units. Behind them at a more leisurely pace came the captains and Cuzo.

The 109th were ordered to take up hiding positions among a screen of mature oaks set back about fifty paces from the road. A low stone wall marked off these mature trees from a field of stumps with saplings growing among them. The dragons were told to hide themselves, which they promptly proceeded to do. They were exceedingly good at this, and even the Purple Green managed to make himself virtually invisible among the tree roots and blueberry bushes.

They waited. Soon there came a thunder of hooves, and another group of Marneri riders came galloping up, whipping on tired mounts. They gathered around Commander Urmin. More orders were sent along the line of hidden men in the woodlots. Meanwhile the Marneri riders rode into the rear to rest and water their horses.

More messengers rode through the woods, pausing to talk briefly with the officers. Cuzo called the dragonboys together and passed on the news.

The Aubinan army was coming straight down the pike, along the Wheat Road to Sesquila, and it was coming blind. The Marneri men were convinced that the Aubinan cavalry had been lured away by the Talion troopers and was temporarily out of range. The Aubinans were coming on without caution. Clearly they didn't know that a second small Marneri army had been put together to oppose them.

The dragons were to hold their positions in the woods until the cornet blew. Then they were to move out and attack the Aubinan column. If the Aubinans detected the ambush, fresh orders would be sent out and the dragons would remain hidden.

Of course, it was clear that the Aubinans had to strike a knockout blow very quickly. Given time, the empire would bring greater forces to bear, and the rebellion would be smothered. So they were in haste to reach Sesquila and could not wait for their calvary to return from chasing the Talion troopers.

This, at least, was how Commander Urmin read the situation. Carefully he positioned his force along both sides of the road with the dragons on the left side. When the head of the Aubinan column came in range, he would send his force right at them in a headlong charge and do his best to knock the whole column into a panic. Urmin knew it could be done; he'd seen it work on Teetol war parties several times. The trick was to let the enemy get up close enough and then pitch into him with everything you had. Get the front ranks turned around and running, and you could often panic the rest.

They waited. Time passed slowly as rain dripped from the trees. The clouds lessened just a little as the afternoon wore on. The rain had stopped again.

"Here they come," whispered Jak, who had the keenest sight in the unit.

Bazil confirmed Jak's observation in the next moment.

"Boy right."

A distant flash way up the road, and again, and then a solid mass of marching men was visible up ahead on the road between the trees. At the head of this column came a small group of riders, horses moving at a steady walk. The enemy gave no sign of caution or concern.

On they came while the men and dragons in the woodlots kept absolutely still. This was the critical time. The leading riders were less than a hundred yards from the ambush line. Urmin watched with bated breath. The enemy column kept coming over the rise; they were just marching into it. This was his best chance to snatch victory from the defeat at Redhill, to beat them at the very first contact before the Aubinans had had a chance to measure his strength.

And yet he dared not be too rash, for if this small force were lost, there would be nothing but the citizenry to defend the walls of Marneri.

The Aubinans marched forward, the riders passed through the invisible ambush line. The leading rank of foot soldiers came up to it, and Urmin gave the order. A cornet squealed, and with a roar the Marneri and Bea men came storming out of the woods.

Whistles shrieked among the Aubinans, and they turned and ran back up the road, not putting up the slightest resistance. They even dropped weapons in the road and just ran for their lives.

It was a wonderful moment for Commander Urmin. He ordered the men forward in pursuit. Now to just roll them up and send the whole lot running back to Aubinas in disorder. Urmin could almost taste the victory.

The Aubinans ran back up the road, giving every indication of being panicked. The legionaries followed, more slowly, but at a steady trot. The dragons had emerged and were following, with dragonboys at their sides.

Still, there were those who smelled a rat. Among them was Relkin, uneasy about the swiftness with which the Aubinans had stopped, turned around, and retreated. It had looked almost rehearsed. He confided these suspicions to Cuzo, who thought about it for a while and shrugged as they jogged along.

"I think Commander Urmin will have taken all of that into account, don't you?"

Relkin didn't think Commander Urmin had, in fact, taken such things into account. Relkin had a less generous view of the capability of commanding officers than did Cuzo, who had simply seen far less of the sharp, messy end of war than Relkin. Relkin knew that in the crucible of battle, commanders often let themselves see what they wanted to see rather than what was actually in front of them.

Alas, Relkin was only a dragoneer first class. Cuzo was the dragon leader.

They continued to pad along behind the foot soldiers, up the Wheat Road to a point where the woods on either side grew down close to the road.

Relkin could sense that that was the enemy's ambush line. He could feel the enemy there, waiting in a line on either side of the road, ready to engulf the legionaries and trap them.

Cuzo wouldn't hear of it.

Relkin looked up and down the trotting column with a growing sense that disaster loomed. Way up the road were the Aubinans, legging it back to Aubinas it seemed. Then almost miraculously he saw Commander Urmin riding up with some other officers aorund him.

Urmin studied the ground ahead where the trees came close to the road. Urmin's own sense of soldierly suspicion had been awakened. There had been perhaps a thousand Aubinans on the road and they were running, but the intelligence he'd received had said there were five or six thousand in the Aubinan army. The set of those trees was perfect for an ambush.

Urmin looked over to the column of legion soldiers. His eye rested for a moment on the dragons, carrying their shields and swords, and then he saw Relkin, just another dragonboy, but one who was staring at him with a most determined expression.

For some reason Urmin wanted to talk to that young man. It was the strangest feeling, but he knew he had to speak to him, and that it was very important.

"Excuse me a moment," he said to his staff, and flicked his horse to move her over to the marching dragons.

"You, the dragoneer," he said pointing to Relkin. "Come here a moment."

Relkin trotted over, aware of Cuzo's astonished gaze on his back.

"Yes, sir!" he saluted. His eyes still resting on Urmin's.

"What do you make of that line of trees up ahead?"

"Sir, it's an ambush. I can feel it."

"Mmmm. You have a propensity for these things?"

"I don't know, sir, but I just feel certain that the enemy will be lined up in those woods."

Urmin accepted the young man's salute, then turned his mare and rode back to the officers.

"Deploy into line, gentlemen. The enemy is waiting for us in those woods. Dragons will hold the road. We will move forward on the cornet. They're in the wood. Let's catch them there and turn their numbers against them."

Commander Urmin looked over to where the dragons were deploying, hauling shields off their shoulders and strapping them to their arms. What had that been, that strangely powerful thought? He just knew that the dragonboy was correct. He'd had his own suspicions, but the boy was so certain, so absolutely sure.

Urmin shook his head. There was a battle to be fought. Later he could think about this strange little episode.

Chapter Thirty-six

Deployed in the skirmishing line with flank guards and the dragons in the center, the legionaries trotted forward. The Aubinans had not prepared fully for this, expecting the legion general to fall into their trap. It had worked before at Redhill, why shouldn't it work here? As the legion soldiers approached, a shower of arrows came out of the woods, but it was ill-coordinated and ineffective. Legion archers immediately replied, and their crossbows were far more deadly.

Then the troops were in among the Aubinans under the trees. The dragons broke up the middle and encountered almost no resistance. The Aubinan force was cut in half, and both halves were taking a beating from the highly trained legion forces that were engaging along their fronts. It was hard to beat legion men at this kind of thing. They fought in triads in such conditions, and worked to coordinate their efforts by having a spear and shield man rush the enemy and distract several untrained men, allowing two swordsmen to confront a single opponent. The Aubinans were not well versed in such techniques, except for the few old legionaries in their ranks, and they suffered accordingly.

Within five minutes or so the Aubinans had lost a hundred or more men and were moving backward through the trees, bunching up in knots that became helpless as the legionaries compressed them to the point where men found it hard to raise an arm or drive a sword thrust. Such globs of men were ripe for slaughter, and the Aubinan casualties mounted.

Meanwhile the dragons pushed up the road with little opposition. They fanned out into the trees and met the retreating Aubinan foot soldiers in the glades and on the open road. The Aubinans were forced to bunch at the places between the dragons, and that meant they had to scramble through deep thickets. The legionaries coming up behind exacted more casualties on them as a result.

For Commander Urmin there remained only one important question—where was the Aubinan cavalry? According to the young men from Marneri, the Aubinan horse had been decoyed away by the Talion troopers under Calex. Urmin wondered if that could be true. Certainly the Talion riders were not nearby, no trace of them had been seen for hours. Urmin listened to reports from the front, watched with his spy glass, and sent scouts out on either flank. The Marneri riders were ordered to form up, and more scouts were dispatched. Urmin didn't intend to be caught by a surprise flank assault by a mass of Aubinan horsemen.

In the woods the fighting became a haphazard affair, with the Aubinans retreating as quickly as they dared while the legion soldiers chased them, with dragons now spread out among them.

The woodlot checkerboard pattern allowed the dragons a bit of room, and whenever they could catch men in the open, they would charge and send them running. The Aubinans weren't intoxicated with the black drink, and they knew the sheer impossibility of men taking on dragons in the open field. They did not try and make a stand in such situations.

In the thickets and dense groves it was harder work, and dragons and dragonboys had to work together carefully there. Some brave souls would hide themselves in the brush and hope to emerge in the rear of a dragon and run a spear into the wyvern's back.

Dragonboys were there to cope with that.

Under a fallen pine tree, in a lane between two woodlots, Relkin cut his arrow free from the chest of a fallen man. Briefly he looked into the other's face. A young man, not much older than himself, with a brown beard covering a wide face that in death had gone slack, but which had once been alive with smiles and frowns. Relkin felt no sense of victory. This was just a waste of a man's life. Relkin wondered if the man had left a wife and young children behind. Children that would now grow up without a father. Who would hate Marneri and the empire because it had taken their father.

The arrow came free, and he cleaned it and slotted it back into the quiver. He moved on, covering their position and looking for usable arrows. The fighting was over for now. The Aubinans had finally managed to break contact by running away across the first open fields they'd come to.

The legion troops had halted at the edge of the woods; the dragons had been pulled back to the road in the center of the position.

Bazil was crouched behind a group of small pine saplings that marked the end of the woodlot. His shield had arrows in it, but he'd suffered no wounds except some scratches from thorns in the dense thickets. Ecator needed cleaning, however. A couple of unwary men had come too close in one of the fights in the clearings.

The clouds had continued to thin out, and now there were a few visible patches of late afternoon sky. Bazil stared across the open field that lay before them where the Aubinans had run in headlong flight. It was distasteful to the dragons to fight like this. They wished only to fight the true enemies, the Masters and their trolls.

Relkin approached and crouched down beside the dragon.

"Can you see anything?" he said.

"This dragon wonders why we didn't try and keep up with them and chase them all the way back to Aubinas."

"They have a big cavalry force, Baz. All of this might have been a ruse to get us out into that open space. There's only a thousand men here, plus ten dragons, not enough for Commander Urmin to feel comfortable taking that kind of risk."

Bazil clacked his jaws slowly, turning this over in his mind. It was a cautious approach. He realized it might well be the best.

"Take no chances."

"Well, this is the only force there is standing between the rebels and Marneri. Urmin has to keep that in mind. He could lose the city with a false move in this campaign."

"Ah, dragonboy see the strategy clearly. Dragonboy should be commander, eh?"

"You said that, not me."

Cuzo came by to inquire what exactly it was that Commander Urmin had spoken to him about.

"He asked me if I thought there was an ambush in the trees, sir. I told him I was certain of it."

"Do you know the commander, then?"

"No, sir."

"Mmm." Cuzo gave Relkin a puzzled look and then went on his way along the position.

Time passed, and the weary Talion troopers rode in an hour before sunset. Subadar Calex passed on the unwelcome news that the Aubinans had given him the slip hours before, and he had no idea where they were. Worse, the rebel horses had also been reinforced, and he now estimated they had at least twelve hundred horsemen.

This made Commander Urmin uncomfortable. He had scouts out on either flank, but had heard nothing from them. He sent the Talions to refresh their horses, and considered the map.

This part of Lucule was dominated by wheat fields, strips and patches of woods breaking up the monotony of grain. The land was almost flat, but there were long gentle slopes, so the view in any direction was not clear to the horizon. A thousand horsemen could approach quite closely, especially if they came at a walk.

Urmin set out pickets in the woods on either flank. He told the men at the horse watering station back close to Treeves to keep their wits about them. He ordered a boil and a feed for the dragons and everyone else. Some beer was to be brought up from Treeves, and a wagon went rattling back for it. The fires were soon blazing, and the cauldrons were set up on their tripods.

Dragons gathered to partake of the rough-cooked stirabout, liberally stirred with akh. Their big spoons made short work of the biggest cauldrons.

"No beer?" said the Purple Green as he finished his share and more.

"Not usually get beer when we are on march," commented Vlok with his usual insight.

"This is not march in the woods!"

"It isn't? How can this be? We are here, these are woods, we have marched."

"Correction, we have fought. This was a fight in the woods."

"By the fiery breath, it was a pretty pitiful fight."

"By our standards it wasn't much, but it was a fight. So there should be beer."

"Mmm, you seem to be right." Vlok sounded puzzled by this discovery.

"Fight not over, that's why they cannot give beer," said Alsebra with a sharp hiss.

"How do you know that?" The Purple Green swelled. She always seemed to know everything, it was almost as bad as talking to a dragonboy.

"Because I feel approaching vibrations in the ground. I expect these are made by horsemen."

Dragons looked at one another.

Just then there came a distant squall of cornets and some shouting. Then they all heard it, the rumble on the ground of hundreds of horses coming toward them.

"The Aubinans!" went up the shout.

The legionaries ran to form up in defensive positions along the edge of the forest on the left side of the road. The dragons hid in the center of the line, spaced out twenty feet apart, lurking in the dark shadows.

The wagons were whipped up and went trundling past to get them to safety up the road. With them rode a small party of Talion troopers.

Meanwhile the thunder of hooves grew much louder, and soon they could see a great mass of horsemen galloping up the road from Treeves. The Aubinans had swung around in a wide hook and were coming in on the rear of the legion force. If the Aubinan ambush had worked, they would have been able to pile in on the rear of a confused force and drive it into rout.

Urmin spurred his mount into the woods, and the legionaries prepared themselves. Orders went out quickly. They were to stay on the defensive and let the horsemen fill up the road, if they were that incautious. Then the dragons would attack, and the infantry would assist them. Men were to be careful when fighting in proximity to dragons. They were reminded that dragonsword was lethal to both foe and friend, and that dragons could not always control the backward sweep of those great blades.

The Aubinan horsemen came loping up with plenty of scouts out front. The men and dragons hidden in the woods kept perfectly still. The dragons were practically invisible so well were they dug into the ground, wedged into dense thickets, hidden behind thick oak trees. And yet ten pairs of huge eyes watched the oncoming horsemen, and calculated the chances of getting to grips with them.

The Aubinans had slowed a little. They had expected to catch the legionaries in the woods close to Treeves. Now it looked like the legionaries had chased off the Aubinan foot without much trouble and made more progress than expected. Worse, the legion commander was warned of the cavalry thrust into his rear.

The Aubinan commander was Caleb Neth, one of the famous Neths of Nellin. He was starting to feel that something was wrong here. There was nothing ahead on the road except a few riders and a bunch of wagons. Where were the legion troops?

They had to be hiding in the woods, in ambush.

He raised his arm to summon the front riders back. He would send out more scouts before advancing any farther.

Just as he did so, the legion cornets blasted from the woods on either side. The vegetation shook as ten great battledragons burst from hiding and scrambled toward the horsemen.

Horses milled, screaming, riders toppled, a horse or two went down in the confusion, and then the dragons reached them. Those huge swords whirred through men and mounts together, and after a few moments of dreadful violence, the Aubinans were in flight, leaving a dozen or more dead on the ground. The dragons withdrew into the woods, arrows flew from both sides, and Neth ordered his force back out of range.

He studied the position.

The legion force had taken the woods. The Aubinan foot was somewhere way up the road. Neth needed to make contact and work out a new strategy. He turned the Aubinan cavalry back and retreated toward Treeves. The fighting was over for the day.

Chapter Thirty-seven

The dragons sat quietly under the trees as the daylight waned. Dragonboys left them to gather around Relkin and Swane, who were standing near the road, watching the officers grouped around Commander Urmin about a hundred paces away.

"What's up?" said Rakama.

"Well, the light's starting to fail. Looks like we'll be spending the night here," replied Swane.

"Could be worse, we've got cover under the trees."

"Yeah, but the enemy is on both sides of us."

"You could also say we've split his army in two."

"Shut it, you two," said Endi. "What's Relkin think?"

"Oh, right," chortled Swane. "What does the Quoshite think?"

In fact, all the other boys were very interested in what Relkin thought, and they indicated so with a chorus of "sshhh!"

"Yeah, Swane quiet down."

"I'll get you, Endi."

"Hey, you owe me twelve silver pieces, remember?"

The muscular Swane had still not figured out that he was never going to get the better of Endi at cards.

"You shut it, Endi!" growled Rakama.

"By the Hand," groaned Endi. The two beefs had become so friendly that they defended one another like brothers.

"What's going on, Relkin?" said Curf speaking for the rest.

Relkin turned back from studying the knot of lieutenants and captains.

"Well, looks like they're all a bit excited down there.

That makes me think we're not just going to sit here on the defensive. Commander Urmin wants to take the initiative."

"Good thing to do when you're heavily outnumbered, right?" said Swane, forgetting all about sitting tight where they were.

"Well, of course," said Manuel, a little impatiently. Manuel was already worrying about the difficulties of maneuvering at night in the forest.

"Going to be hard to keep together if we hike off this road in the dark."

"Right," agreed Relkin.

"Going to make a mess of the equipment," said the new boy Howt.

"Cuzo won't like that," groused Rakama.

"Hey, did anyone see Cuzo in the fight?" said Endi.

"By the Hand, he was smiting them," said Jak.

"Well, it's good to know we've got a fighter for a dragon leader, just as long as he knows what not to do."

"Remember Wiliger at Koubha?" said Swane.

The veterans of the Eigo campaign groaned in unison.

"Cuzo's not like Wiliger," said Endi.

"By the breath, let's hope not!"

"Cuzo ain't like Wiliger, that's certain," said Relkin, confirming the unit's impression of its new leader.

Behind them, a hundred feet back under the trees, the huge bodies of several wyverns had clumped together in a tight group as they kept an eye on their dragonboys.

"I still think we should have waited a little longer before we attack," said Vlok.

"We have heard this before," responded the Purple Green.

"We didn't get enough of them," said Vlok, patiently.

"Doesn't matter now," said Alsebra. "We're between the two parts of the enemy army. They outnumber us. Something will happen tonight."

"What are boys doing?" said Chektor.

"They are talking and watching the officers."

"What are officers doing?"

"They are also talking. Commander Urmin is there."

Chektor subsided into silence. The big old veteran was not a talky dragon.

Bazil shifted his weight behind the tree.

"This dragon thinks we'll be marching tonight. Better get

dragonboy to tie everything down tight. marching through woods in the dark can be tough on equipment."

The others sighed at the thought of a nighttime march through dense thickets while carrying full pack and armor. Wading through mires, forcing a path through alders and hemlocks, having the sword and shield get caught in these tangles, having to hack them free with a tail sword. It would be hard going.

"Makes this dragon wish he had the flame of the ancestors!" grumbled Bazil.

Meanwhile, at the center of all this remote attention, Commander Urmin looked at the map spread out on the little fold-up table and pondered the imponderable.

"The Aubinan horse are lead by Caleb Neth, an able commander," said Commander Task of the Bea Fifth regiment as he indicated the woods behind them on the map. "He'll try something before long."

Commander Fellows of the Pennar Third and Subadar Calex nodded together grimly.

"An able officer and a suspicious one," grumbled Urmin. He scratched at the three-day-old fuzz on his chin. Neth had pulled his men back before they could be seriously damaged by the dragons. They'd taken a rebuff, not a slaughter. It was a pity, but one couldn't expect every trap to work perfectly. The Aubinans had tried to set an ambush as well, but that boy in the dragon squadron with the peculiarly bright eyes had confirmed his own suspicions. Then the dragons had been too much for the Aubinans to face. After that experience they would take measures to be more effective against dragons. Dragons were vulnerable to well-thrown spears, for instance.

Urmin had already decided not to sit still on the defensive. The Aubinans had to be hit hard and often to keep them off balance. Urmin now chose from the options they had examined.

"Neth is a canny leader, but his force is new to war. He'll be inclined to caution. We will hook around their infantry's left flank. We go south to the Old Turnpike, which was the Posila Road before they built the Wheat Road that made Aubinas rich."

Fellows and Calex nodded vigorously. The wealth of Aubinas was resented in much of the rest of the Argonath.

"The old road passes close to Avery, but it's screened from the village by a rise in the ground and Avery heath."

Indeed the approach route would be well masked by that low ridgeline and its forest cover.

"Calex, I want you to cover our rear. Neth will have some men on the Old Turnpike. Make sure he doesn't get in on our rear while we're marching."

"Sir!" Calex saluted.

Urmin looked to Fellows.

"I want everybody up and moving as soon as possible. We've got a long way to go if we're going to be in position by tomorrow morning."

Three miles of it would be through woodlots. They would have to march like magicians to get through the thickets in the dark. If they were quick enough, thought Urmin, they might catch the Aubinan foot napping.

Officers were thundering away into the dusk. Orders were bellowed into the trees. Immediately there was a jingle of equipment and the sounds of men, horses, and dragons coming to life.

"Move out!" came the order. Within minutes the small army of Marneri was on the move, heading south into the woodlots.

Torches were used to guide them through the worst parts, but Urmin had ordered that lights be kept to a minimum. He had left a few souls to build big fires near the road in their old position to fool the enemy into thinking he was standing pat on the defensive.

Standard military procedure would have advised that he do exactly that. With his force so much smaller than the combined Aubinan forces, he had little margin for any failures. However, Urmin was worried about the quality of the Aubinan cavalry. It had already shown itself able and deadly. The destruction of General Cerius's army was the result of the Aubinan cavalry striking home at the perfect moment. Urmin hoped to drive the Aubinan foot soldiers even farther away from the cavalry, and in the process hurt their formations. If Urmin could keep them apart, he could continue to inflict damage on the foot army and stop the invasion. Soon, in a week or two, there would be reinforcements, and after that the Aubinans would be doomed as far as mounting an effective invasion of Marneri.

Progress was slow at first, but then the Marneri riders

brought in a local man who said he could lead them to a logging trail that would take them right through the wood-lots to the southern road.

Fresh orders went out. Within a short time the men and dragons were moving down a reasonably straight, if hardly well cleared, logging trail. They wound through the worst bogs and avoided the dense, unmanageable thickets. There were still some tricky places, and the trail was never much wider than four feet, which wasn't exactly enough for a dragon. Equipment got caught in branches and had to be cut free again and again.

Still, their progress was much swifter than they had expected, and within a couple of hours they were all out upon the Old Turnpike. Urmin breathed a big sigh of relief. Now they turned west and set their faces toward Posila. They soon picked up the pace while the last few stray branches and bits of vine fell off the dragons' gear. The road stretched ahead, visible only dimly under the faint starlight. The trees thinned out and were left behind. The handful of wagons they'd managed to drag down the logging trail rumbled on the paved highway, which remained in good repair.

The rumbling was the only thing that could betray their passage, swift and dangerous, heading for the edge of their enemy's flank.

Chapter Thirty-eight

Avery Woods rustled with the quiet progress of men, dragons, and horses. Urmin's luck had held. The Aubinans' inexperience had betrayed them. They had set out only a few sentries in a line at the edge of the woods. By neutralizing half a dozen of these men, the door was opened to the Aubinans' camp. The legion force crept through the woods, and where the trees thinned, they found scattered Aubinan men, relieving themselves as dawn intensified in the east. These men were slain quietly, and now the legion troops and the dragons of the 109th were standing right at the edge of the Aubinans' temporary camp, a hodgepodge of tents, shelters, and stacks of equipment with men sleeping in, under, and around them.

Urmin put half of his legionaries in line with the dragons in the center. The wyverns were set to attack on a three-hundred-foot front. The other half of the men were held back as a reserve and as archers. Meanwhile the Talion horsemen were working to slow any advance of the Aubinan cavalry down the Old Turnpike. The enemy were probing, but coming on very slowly. It was beginning to look as if Caleb Neth had been surprised by Urmin's nighttime maneuver. Indeed, the Aubinans were still scouting for the legion troops in the area along the Wheat Road and had yet to wake up to the fact that they had absconded and were now miles away to the south and west.

The dragons drew sword at the whispered command. Great blades appeared from their scabbards and long, pale gleams of deadly steel shone in the dawning light. Dragonboys pressed up behind the wyverns, checked equipment, and whispered encouragement to each other.

"Good luck, Relkin," said young Howt, who was visibly

nervous. These were his first battles. His dragon had done well, but the adrenaline and terror of battle were at work on him. His voice sounded tight.

"Let Caymo throw the dice," muttered Relkin as he clasped hands with the younger boy.

Bazil gave him a sardonic glance. Ecator rested on the wyvern's shoulder for a moment longer.

The cornet blast shattered the quiet. A high shrill shriek presaging slaughter. The legion force moved out and swept down into the tents and shelters. Caught in the drowsy moments of early dawn, the men were easily panicked. Here and there some made an attempt at resistance. A bunch of thirty or forty would make a stand against the general rout, but the legionaries would back off, move around them, and continue to press the ones who were running, leaving the standing groups to the dragons, who made short work of them.

The Purple Green was particularly effective. He used his shield to sweep aside spears and lances and then hacked at the men with his ugly legion issue sword. It lacked soul, but it was still a huge piece of deadly steel, and men were sundered and cut into fragments whenever they placed themselves within range.

Bazil, Alsebra, and some of the others were less eager to kill men. The sacred bond between dragons and men was strong in wyverns raised among people and tended all their lives by dragonboys. The Purple Green's cheerful lust for slaughter was absent from their hearts in this fight.

Still, grim work was done on those fields, and by the time it was over, several hundred Aubinan men were left slain among the grain stubble. The rest were in headlong flight, heading north and west, running for the Wheat Road and the quickest way to Posila.

The dragons were not used for pursuit once the panic really got underway. They were kept back and grouped with two hundred men to form a force to keep the Aubinan cavalry at bay when it finally put in an appearance. Urmin judged that the Aubinan foot would not re-form before reaching Posila. These were only partially trained troops, and their disorganization was almost total.

Over in the woods to the north and east, Caleb Neth finally understood what was going on at about the time that the fight in Avery Woods ended. He sent his force hard for the Old Turnpike, and they finally drove the Talion troops into flight and began to push up the road. Neth urged haste, deadly afraid of what might have happened in the first light of morning.

But Neth was not sure where the Aubinan foot had camped. They'd retreated in disorder the previous day and communications in the night had been poor. He came into the margins of Avery Woods at last, and the dragons, with an hour of rest under their belts emerged into the open to oppose. There were quite a few legionaries too, though their numbers were disguised because they hid in the woods and scrub. The Talion troopers were also ready to engage in combat once again.

Neth studied the situation. The Old Turnpike passed through Avery Woods. To go around the woods would take him a couple of miles south, which would waste precious time. To go through on the road meant charging the dragons.

Caleb Neth was a wheat-farming horseman from the heart of Nellin. He had a prejudice against dragons, who ate way too much out of the public purse and kept the cavalry arm of the legions from becoming dominant. He accepted the challenge.

The men of Nellin surged up to form the vanguard of the attack, dropping their lances and heavy spears into place.

The order was given with a shriek, and they went away with a thundering roll of hooves, galloping up the road straight toward the line of wyverns, which was backed by a double line of infantry. As the horsemen came in, they aimed their lances at the dragons, but they were met by those massive shields and the lance heads were turned away or snapped clean off the shaft. By then it didn't matter anyway, since the dragonsword would have swung around in a gleaming arc and taken the rider. There were close moments, especially for slower wyverns like old Chektor, but not a single Aubinan lance head went home. Dragonswords flashed like razors over the corn, and heads were lopped all around them.

The horsemen staggered to a stop, and when their impetus was gone, the legionaries surged forward through the gaps between the dragons, and attacked the now milling horsemen. Horses were hamstrung and brought down, and spearmen finished off those men who resisted further. When the Aubinan cavalry finally managed to lurch away from the contact, hundreds of men were down, and half of those were dead.

With bitter curses streaming from his lips, Caleb Neth pulled his force back and drove farther south, aiming to get around Avery Wood. The Talions then charged from the cover of the woods and fought a fierce fight in Miller's field. They were too heavily outnumbered, however, to prevent Neth's movement, and the decimated Aubinan horsemen eventually rounded the wood and moved south to regain the Old Turnpike and place itself between Urmin's small army and Posila.

The battle at Avery Woods was over. The Aubinan invasion had been stopped cold. Commander Urmin had bought time for the Empire of the Rose to concentrate forces to combat the rebellion.

Chapter Thirty-nine

In the heart of Aubinas ran the Running Deer River, and on its green bank stood the splendid mansion known as Deer Lodge. Crowned with green roof tiles, the house was equipped at each corner with a tower surmounted by false machicolations. Long lawns ran away into lush shrubberies on all sides. Above, on the far side of the river, loomed the Sunberg, the chisel-shaped mountain famous in song and legend for centuries.

Deer Lodge was the primary residence of Faltus Wexenne of Champery, the greatest of the grain magnates of Aubinas. In this splendid house had been hatched most of the plots that had shaken Aubinas into rebellion over the past five years.

The picturesque valley, the forest of Nellin, the distant Sunberg, these places were the heart and soul of the rebellion, at least to hear Wexenne tell it. On this particular evening the house seemed to brood beneath its dark roof. Clouds had obscured the Sunberg all day. It had already been a very wet season, and now it threatened to rain again.

In the dining hall there was a celebratory dinner in progress. A dozen magnates were gathered to mark the release of Porteous Glaves. However, a strange field of tension overlay the celebrants, like the shadow of the darkling Sunberg across the valley. The early news from Posila had been most encouraging. The army of free Aubinas had moved on past Posila and directly into Lucule on the Wheat Road. The legion commanders in Marneri had scraped up a small army and set it to bar their path. General Neth had maneuvered his cavalry with his accustomed skill and was getting into a position from which to do fatal damage to the legion force. After that, Marneri itself would be open. Then the news had stopped. There had been no word all day, and the celebrants were increasingly uneasy as a result.

At the table they talked of nothing but the war, which in their minds had already become a cause for the entire world to take up: The struggle of a small oppressed people rising against the greatest power in the world and fighting for freedom.

"We shall light a torch for freedom that all men shall hail!" said Faltus Wexenne. For the occasion he wore a suit of dark red velvet. His shoes, fashioned from fine Kadein leather, bore fat golden buckles shaped like hunting dogs. With his height and mass, he made an imposing sight.

"Let me second that proud thought!" bellowed Porteous Glaves, rising to his feet and lifting his mug. Porteous had been seconding things for a while now, ever since the third pot of ale, so only a handful of his cronies cheered and raised their mugs.

Faltus Wexenne ostentatiously applauded Glaves.

"I give you, sirs, our hero, Porteous Glaves!"

Another slightly more enthusiastic round of applause.

Glaves held forth in a drunken discourse that consisted of little more than slogans pasted together with imprecations against Marneri and the Imperial system of regulations.

Paying no attention were Melkert Vanler and Darnay Degault, two powerful men from Belland, across the river.

"Damned fool," muttered Melkert. Darnay nodded.

"Doesn't signify. He served as the figurehead for the cause."

"Ah, yes, the cause!" Melkert's cynicism dripped from his words.

Darnay chuckled mirthlessly. "It serves its purpose."

"Yes, but what about the other purposes here? We both know that there is more going on here in this house than Wexenne will admit."

"We've heard all sorts of stories. Something's in the cellar here, right?"

"A demon, I've heard. A floating demiurge." Melkert fluttered his fingers by his goblet.

"Well, whatever it is, it's unholy, and Wexenne is keeping quiet about it."

"Doesn't want the witches to find out. They have an uncanny knack for finding and killing demons."

"Damned witches, damn them and the entire army of women in this land. Nothing but trouble with their rights and their property!" Darnay voiced a common sentiment among the powerful men of Nellin.

"Onward our glorious warriors for a free Aubinas!" said Melkert loudly, breaking into Glaves's droning on about the wickedness of Marneri. Heads inclined toward him and then followed with a polite round of applause for his patriotic spirit. Mostly they did it to try and keep their own spirits up.

Melkert caught Wexenne's eye across the table. Faltus smiled, nodded to him politely, and then returned his attention to Baron Hurd, who sat beside him.

Wexenne could sense the growing wariness in the hall. His colleagues were ridden by their fears. He, Wexenne, was not. He had mastered fear. Victory was theirs for the taking, and the fools were worrying themselves to a tatter. He ordered another round of ale to be served at once. Clearly it was necessary to keep their spirits afloat!

"What can be happening?" said Baron Hurd, a tall, angular man with singularly pale skin and dark beard, neatly clipped and pointed.

"War has its uncertainties," Wexenne replied.

"But we have had no news for a long time now, what can it be?"

"I have no idea," sniffed Wexenne, "but I'm sure that General Neth has done his job and cleared the way to Marneri. To believe anything else is to deny the reality of our success."

"Indeed," said Salva Gann, across the table from Hurd. Gann at least was still in control of himself, Wexenne noted with relief. They weren't all turning into frightened rabbits!

"Yes, yes," said the baron. "But think, man, what can have kept the messengers?"

Faltus Wexenne glowered down at the pot of ale in his hand.

"Anything can happen to a rider. He might have fallen off his horse, for all I know. There'll be word, but we'll just have to wait."

Hurd grunted unhappily and sat back.

Gann leaned forward, filling the space. "The way I see

it, once Neth has crushed this last legion force, there's nothing to stop us rolling all the way to Pennar."

"We must take Marneri," said Wexenne.

"We will waste our impetus trying to take the white city. We can roll all the way to the ocean. Take Bea and Pennar, those are far less well defended than Marneri."

Faltus Wexenne shook his head and stabbed his finger into the tabletop. "Marneri will give us a crushing victory. It might be enough to end the war in a single stroke."

"But we will have to take the city. Not even Mach Ingbok and his demon hordes could do that!"

"Mach Ingbok did not have good men inside the walls who were ready to rise and deliver the city to him! We do."

Baron Hurd grunted.

Just then there came a sound of voices in the courtyard. One voice over all could be heard bellowing, "Make way for the messenger."

Shortly afterward a man, disheveled and begrimed from a long ride in the saddle, was ushered into the dining hall. He stepped up to the head of the table.

"Sirs, I bring word from the field, from General Neth."

Every eye in the room was fixed on him.

"Victory, I take it," said Wexenne.

"Ah, no, lord. Not really."

"Not?" Wexenne's puzzlement was genuine and strong. He stared at the messenger while his knuckles whitened around his goblet.

"Out with it, man."

Gann had a look of horrified amazement on his face. The messenger came to attention, and gave them the rest.

"General Neth says to tell you that despite some hard fighting, the enemy has failed to destroy our glorious army of free Aubinas. Following two inconclusive engagements, our infantry forces have regrouped at Posila."

"Posila!" exclaimed Baron Hurd. "But that's far behind our positions; how can this be?"

"If these engagements were inconclusive, then why are we so far back from our starting position?"

"General Neth believes that these maneuvers will soon enable him to take complete control of the area around Posila."

"But we don't want Posila!" snarled Gann. "Onward,

man, onward to the sea!" Gann was staggering onto his feet and waving an imaginary sword.

"What you're saying is we've been defeated!" said a voice.

Bedlam broke out.

"What?"

"Defeated!"

A dozen voices spoke at once.

"The legionaries will be here in a matter of hours then. We're doomed."

"My horse!"

"Mine too. We can reach the gap by morning if we move quickly."

There was a stir. Men were on their feet, eyes wild with sudden apprehension.

"Hold!" roared Wexenne. "Are ye mice or men? Hold, damn you all! Hold! This is the time when we must prove ourselves. There has been a check; it may be serious, but it cannot yet be a deathblow. We still have their measure. Now, hold on, get a grip on yourselves. We have work to do!"

They moved uneasily. A few argued. Baron Voss actually did leave, but when he saw that nobody else was following, he came back and was welcomed with loud acclamation. They pounded on the table and roared.

They retook their seats and toasted Faltus Wexenne, and then Porteous Glaves. More ale was brought out. Faltus Wexenne had taken hold of the situation. Wexenne had shown himself to be in charge. All were suddenly aware that the great landraut of Champery was also becoming the leader of the rebellion.

Subtle recastings of alliance were already taking place as others in the Aubinan hierarchy reacted to Faltus Wexenne's elevation. Porteous Glaves, for instance, felt it very acutely. His own position had diminished considerably since his imprisonment in Marneri. Much of his own property had been sequestered by the crown. Some had been sold to pay creditors from his previous campaigns. Porteous had once been in the running for leadership. Now he was reduced to the role of a bit player. His star was fading now that he was no longer rotting in a Marneri jail cell.

"Tell me the rest of your story," Wexenne bid the messenger. Wexenne was struggling with the urge to scream from frustration. How could they have been defeated when they so outnumbered the Marneri forces?

"Well, sir, it is not as bad as all that. We took some losses. They surprised us with an overnight march, and the dragons exacted a toll."

"Dragons! Damnable worms!"

Aubinas had not been dragon friendly in a long time. The magnates preferred to send their corn to market rather than to feed it to ungainly great dragons with appetites beyond restraint.

"Where's the heavy cavalry now that we need them?"

"That's it, send in a charge with the lance; that'll take care of dragons."

The messenger looked around at them and noted that none of these well-fed men looked askance at these words. Did they understand what they were asking for?

Wexenne finally turned back to the messenger.

"Well, did they stop them with the charge?"

"No, sir. The cavalry was out of contact all night. They attacked later, but they did not get through, so I don't know what happened. Later they rode into Posila. General Neth took overall command."

"Posila!" snarled Gann. "We should be carving our way into the Marneri peninsula by now!"

With a glare at Gann, Faltus Wexenne moved quickly to emphasize the positive.

"We can hold Posila. Even against the dragons."

Inside, Faltus Wexenne was boiling with rage. These damned generals couldn't organize a drunken brawl in a tavern full of farmers. If you wanted anything done, you had to do it yourself! Setting his shoulders, he got down to working the group's emotions and boosting their morale. At the same time he announced new measures they should take. They needed to raise more men and prepare for a longer war.

Faltus Wexenne had already given up on the thought of the knockout blow and early, easy victory.

Melkert heard Wexenne speak and marveled at how cool the big man seemed. He also wondered just how well their improvised cavalry force under General Neth would handle trained battledragons.

"How many?" he said at last.

"How many what?" said Faltus Wexenne.

"How many dragons?"

They turned to the messenger. He shrugged.

"There are different stories. Some say many, others around ten."

"One squadron! That's all they have?" Melkert felt his confidence return.

Faltus Wexenne was nodding to himself.

"If they have only a single squadron, they could be overwhelmed."

"A sudden attack by overwhelming force!" said Gann, his spirits suddenly revived.

"Absolutely," said Melkert.

"Use poison spears; that will do the trick!"

They fed eagerly on this crumb of consolation.

Faltus Wexenne adjourned the meeting and withdrew to his private office with just Glaves and Salva Gann.

Unavoidably somber, they took seats around the table.

Faltus Wexenne refused to be downcast.

"We face a grave situation, my friends, but it is not unmanageable."

"Indeed," Glaves broke in. "We shall lure them on and then destroy them in the heart of Nellin."

"The heart of Nellin?" exclaimed Gann. "We cannot allow that. The looting of Nellin would be a tragedy." Gann's own lands were in the central parts of Nellin.

"I'm sorry, old friend," said Glaves. "But the enemy will be sure to invade our lands. We shall have to see great sacrifices. Some of us have already given everything for the cause."

Knowing the truth about Porteous's sacrifices, Gann sputtered at this.

Wexenne drove his fist into his palm.

"Glaves is right. We will draw the enemy on—let them get deep into Nellin. Meanwhile we shall try a thrust of a different sort. Not every stroke need be on the field of battle, am I right?"

"Of course," said Glaves, who was sobering up by this point.

"But Nellin? Must we sacrifice Nellin?"

"Not by choice, dear Salva, not by choice. But wherever the enemy decides to aim his blow, that's where we shall trap him, all right?"

Gann nodded, reluctant still.

"Good. We have special work to do. You know what I keep in the cellar here, do you not? I shall want you two to accompany me tonight when I visit our great friend."

Both Gann and Glaves looked up with sudden hard looks. Both had heard the tantalizing stories concerning this mysterious "great friend" of Aubinas. He was of some ancient elvish kind, they said, and glowed all over with a mysterious blue light. Some had even likened him to the Demon Lord Mach Ingbok.

"I have heard that he is a great wizard," said Gann, trying to impress Wexenne with the extent of his information.

"He is no wizard, my friend. Do not mistake this lord for some mannish sorcerer, for he is not of that limited breed. He is a being with a boundless sense of what is best for the world, and he is determined to bring it about. Aubinas is his chosen cause."

They were visibly torn by indecision. Fear competed with desire to see this "lord," so described.

The fear was especially strong in Porteous's eyes.

Wexenne felt little but contempt. Porteous had always been a vain, timid soul. It had taken a great deal of goading to drive him into the military service. Porteous had failed as a soldier, but in the process had re-created himself as the martyr of Aubinas and so had been useful to the cause, after all. Still, Faltus Wexenne judged that Porteous would not be missed overmuch.

"Come on," he snorted. "You two are such great lions for our rebellion, such captains of war, don't tell me you're afraid of meeting our guest?"

Salva Gann and Porteous harrumphed together.

"I have no fear of the supernatural," said Glaves. "We saw enough of that in Ourdh."

"And I have yet to see anything that I would mistake as the supernatural," sniffed Gann. "It's all bunkum. I'll be glad to show you how the tricks are done!"

"Good. Then, let us take up a lamp and visit him."

Show you how the tricks are done! Faltus Wexenne looked forward to seeing that!

They used a servants' stairway to descend to the kitchen level. The light here was dim, and it took a while for their eyes to adjust to the sepulchral gloom. They turned toward the center of the house, passing storerooms and wine cellars. Then they passed through a heavy door and down some steps to another door, which opened with the key carried by Faltus Wexenne. They stepped into an even murkier space. A strange, sour smell pervaded the dead air. The space was very large.

"Where are we going?" said Glaves nervously.

"Do not make any sudden movements," said Faltus Wexenne.

They were not alone. Even as the door closed behind them, huge shapes shifted out of the darkness and approached. Glaves felt the breath solidify in his throat. They were as tall as trolls, and carried swords and shields.

"What are these things?" said a trembling Gann.

"Bewks, of course. Have you never met a bewk?" Wexenne toyed with them. He had removed a gem from his purse and raised it so that its glitter winked off the big, lucent eyes of the pig-faced monsters. They slid back into the shadows.

"Splendid creatures. Our guest bred them up from pigs. They're quite intelligent 'tis said, and can wield sword."

Glaves was dry-mouthed. To think that troll-like monsters were living right underneath Deer Lodge was somehow earthshaking. It was the last thing he would have expected. His heart was beating rather more strongly than he would have liked. There were at least five of the things, and they seemed almost as big as dragons.

"Come, my friends. Let us proceed."

They stepped past the lurking monsters and went down another passageway to a heavy, iron door. Porteous was glad to have left the brutes behind. Wexenne knocked loudly. They waited in silence for half a minute, and then the door opened with a loud squeal. A pair of human guards, grim-faced men in steel helmets, regarded them with a level gaze. Faltus Wexenne lofted the gem once more and let its glitter be seen. The men nodded gravely and stood back. Wexenne entered and encouraged the others to follow.

Past these men was a final passage and then an open door. A soft green light bathed the passage and filled the room beyond. Tables, cabinets, tall-backed chairs, the green lamp hanging from the ceiling, all these things were glimpsed.

Then a tall figure, glowing at its extremities, arose from behind a huge desk that was covered in small cabinets, retorts, and other scientific equipment. As it stood up, the elvish features seemed to dissolve and refix themselves in more manlike fashion. Gone were the long skin folds that marked the eyes of elves and made them seem slanted. Gone were the long ears and the thin-lipped, perfect mouth. Instead they were met by a man, a tall, powerfully built man with pale silver hair, level features, a straight nose and a hard, square jaw.

This figure wore a simple black tunic and slippers of gold cloth. On its fingers glowed rings of power, two on each hand. The eyes met theirs, and each of them felt the power in that stern gaze. They were in the presence of a being of great strength, a person of vast importance.

"Welcome," said the guest in a deep, powerful voice. "I'm afraid these are cramped quarters. You must take seats where you find them." He gestured to the scattered chairs, set at different tables. Each table hosted a special experiment in its cabinets.

They found chairs while their host in this strange lair resumed his seat at the main desk. He was occupied with inscribing results on a scroll.

"I beg your pardon, dear friends, but I must just finish here. It won't take but a moment."

His quill scratched upon the parchment while Wexenne, Gann, and Glaves found chairs and turned them to face the desk. The green light gave the room an eerie appearance and turned the faces of Faltus and Salva into grey masks. Oddly the flesh of the guest did not turn grey under this light, but instead radiated a brighter hue altogether.

Porteous examined the room, and his eye lit on a cabinet nearby. The glass door revealed a pale, monkeylike animal inside, clearly starving. Its ribs stood out, the face was sunken. Then with a nearly physical shock, Glaves realized that the creature was actually a boy, perhaps no more than ten years old, but now very close to death.

With a slight shudder he shifted his gaze. There was a pig in another cage, covered in enormous red boils. He shuddered again. What strange pursuits were these?

He looked back to the first cabinet. The boy's eyes were vacant. He was already too far gone. Porteous decided there was no profit in making a fuss about this. He glanced over at Faltus. He didn't seem to be bothered.

Porteous was suddenly stricken by another thought.

There were a dozen cabinets in the room of that size, and several more that were smaller. His gaze flicked here and there around the room. He could only see into a few of them, but he spotted another child. A young girl, who sat helplessly on a stool, her head held to the back of the cabinet by a chain around her neck.

Porteous Glaves felt the hair lift along the back of his own neck. In his inner heart he knew himself to be a useless, work-shy fraud, but he had never done anything truly evil; indeed, he had never imagined evil such as this. He had mutinied, and they had killed innocent men and women when they took over the *Nutbrown*, but that was just murder. This was something else again.

He glanced at Gann, but Salva Gann seemed oblivious of anything except the massive man, or shape shifter, or elf, or whatever it was that sat at the desk writing with a short-cut quill on parchment sheets stacked inches deep before him.

The scratching ceased. The parchment was added to the stack. A book was closed, and the quill placed in a holder.

"And now, dear sirs." The great head inclined to them, and they felt the interest in those powerful eyes fall full on them. They were lined up like schoolboys before the headmaster. Glaves felt the room fill with overtones of dominance, and wriggled uncomfortably. The great one held them all for a moment in his grip, and then he relaxed the field.

"So, Faltus Wexenne, what can I do for you?"

Wexenne was the least affected. He had met with the Dominator before, and he was one of that rare group of men who were able to resist his spells and intimidations.

"Ah, yes, the purpose of our visit!" Wexenne rubbed his hands together. "Well, in fact, great one, I should ask you what it is I could do for you. You do us enormous honor with your mere presence here in my humble manse. As it is, I wish I could provide you with more spacious accommodations, but you insisted on absolute secrecy."

"Yes, secrecy, a sore subject, Faltus, a very sore subject."

Secrecy had not lasted long. Servants' whispers had spread to the village.

"I apologize my friend, but to keep such as yourself a complete secret is beyond the abilities of mortal men. Tongues will wag, unless I cut them all out."

"Yes, perhaps that's what should have been done."

Faltus shifted uncomfortably. "Surely you jest?"

"Mmmm."

The big head turned, and the eyes fell full on Porteous Glaves, who quivered visibly as their eyes locked.

"This is the newly released Porteous Glaves," said Wexenne, gesturing proudly. "A man in search of his mission!"

Porteous was fighting to keep his composure under that merciless gaze. The eyes seemed to bore through one, to see into one's heart until all one's faults and weaknesses became quite visible and open.

"Ah, yes, the hero of Aubinas," the tall figure smiled sardonically "Welcome to my temporary abode."

"Honored to meet you, uh."

"You may call me Lapsor."

"Lapsor?"

"Yes."

"Honored." Glaves trembled, feeling that great intellect bearing down on him. It was as if he were an insect being put on a pin. Glaves had witnessed sorcery, but not at this proximity. For a brief, frightening moment he sensed the other's mind, all huge and greedy with a lust for knowledge and control, over everything! This greed was so hungry, so enormous that it terrified him. He shrank back from it and hid like a rabbit confronted with a leopard.

Glaves dropped his eyes like a bashful child.

What did it want from him? Why did it stare so hard?

The deep voice grew velvety. "And your mission, what is that to be?"

Glaves looked back stupidly. "My mission?" Faltus had been going on about this mission too. "What are you talking about?"

The guest known as Lapsor smiled for a moment.

"Come, great Porteous. We must light a beacon to arouse our forces. Give them something to fight for! A visible sign of the freedom we desire for Aubinas!"

"Yes, yes, but . . ."

"There can be no 'buts' Porteous. We who are chosen to lead must give our all for the cause."

"Well, if anyone's given to the cause, it's been me. I've lost everything."

"No man that still has his health and his body can say that. Come, Porteous, think of the cause!"

Salva Gann had said nothing. He was still staring, thunderstruck at the tall, powerful figure seated at the main desk. Gann's beliefs regarding the powers of sorcerers appeared to be undergoing some revision.

"Well, of course," Porteous said wearily. "I live for the cause."

"Yes. So if I were to aid you in that endeavor, you would approve, would you not?"

"Aid me?"

"Yes. I will give you the strength you need, and it is plain that your own reserves are low. You have given much during your years of troubles. The flames have burned down, your fires are banked, but not all is lost. I can reawaken your strength and your anger!"

Glaves felt more than ever like a rabbit in the presence of a rabbit-eating predator of inordinate speed and ferocity.

"Well, that sounds wonderful. I wonder . . ."

"Yes, of course, you agree." The figure arose and seemed to tower over them. It moved out from behind the desk toward Porteous, who wanted to run, but could not.

Lapsor had raised his hands, which were larger than those of a normal man, with very long fingers. He seemed to cradle Porteous Glaves's face in a mesh of these giant fingers, which elongated like huge pink worms and formed a basket surrounding Glaves's head.

The giant shuddered and moaned, and his face began to glow with a greenish fire. Then green light glowed softly within his hands and intensified momentarily until a white flash burst there for a moment and was gone. The giant withdrew.

Porteous Glaves slumped back, mouth slack, eyes vacant. A few horrified seconds went by, and then Glaves shook himself and seemed to come around. He sat up and looked at them, and his face was transformed. The lines of worry and concern were gone. His cheeks were hard, his eyes merciless. A sneer of arrogance and command had appeared in place of the rabbit-faced fear. The others looked at each other. Gann was shaking visibly. Faltus Wexenne raised an eyebrow.

So, Salva, it's all bunk, he wanted to say. You were going to show us how the tricks are done, eh?

Chapter Forty

Porteous said nothing, just stared about himself and sneered, his eyes empty of intelligence. Salva Gann still shook silently in his place. Wexenne smiled with barely concealed contempt. The huge figure of Lapsor had returned to its seat. It looked up after a moment and saw them staring at Glaves.

"Have no fear, my friends. He has not been harmed in any way. He has been, shall we say, invigorated."

Hearing this, Salva Gann made a silent recommendation to himself. As soon as he was able to, he was going to ride away from this place—and never return.

"And now," said Lapsor. "What is the news? What has happened on the battlefield?"

"Ah," Wexenne became a little crestfallen now. "We have undergone a reversal. The enemy has bamboozled our poorly trained troops in the scrub beyond our border with Lucule. Our men have fallen back to Posila."

"Fallen back, and so soon? How humiliating."

Wexenne shrugged and smiled. "We were perhaps a little overconfident before. Our forces are but recently mustered. They lack experience. Against good legion troops they are perhaps overmatched."

"Yes, perhaps." Lapsor sat back and rested his massive chin on tented fingertips.

"Well, that is why we need your aid, great Lapsor. You have other resources, do you not?"

"Mmmm, perhaps."

"Well, this might be a good time to think about using them. We need to regain the initiative, get our momentum back. We were driving on Marneri. Remember we achieved an historic victory last week right here in Nellin."

"True, we were all impressed."

"And now we've run up against something that has bedeviled other armies when facing legion forces."

"Discipline?"

"Well, there is that, but there are also dragons."

A glitter appeared in the eyes of the tall elf man. His jaw ground for a moment.

"Ah, yes, the famous fighting dragons of Argonath. I have heard much of these beasts. They have put in an appearance against you, at last?"

"They appear to have held off our heavy cavalry charge, which is our best weapon. I think it will be hard for our forces to hold a battle line if they come up against legion troops equipped with dragons."

"So you come to me, because you know I have bewks."

Wexenne nodded, quite submissively. Lapsor sat up and rubbed his huge hands together. "The bewks you shall have," he said with a slight smile. "However, I shall want some say in how they are to be used in any battle. I will not allow them to be wasted. I have only a few at the moment. They take time to generate. Later we will have as many as we might need, but it will take time to achieve that. So for now we must husband them carefully."

"Yes, of course," agreed, Faltus. "And casualties were high in that fighting down in Blue Stone, were they not?" Wexenne had waited for the right moment to launch that shaft. We have information too, great lord of the ancient elves!

The great face hardened, and the eyes burned slightly with green fire. Lapsor made no reference to the embarrassment in Blue Stone, however.

"This absurd empire of theirs has some surprising vulnerabilities. These witches for example, they are clearly the force behind the throne. We should strike at them immediately."

"Strike at the witches?" Wexenne felt a frisson of fear. Like most of his kind, he wanted nothing to do with the ancient hags. They were dangerous creatures. No one could be quite sure what to make of the stories told about them. By the breath, they might even be true! And that meant you had to be careful where witches were concerned.

"Yes," Lapsor spoke precisely.

Salva Gann wished he were somewhere else, anywhere else.

"This may not be so easy to do," said Wexenne.

"In Marneri I have followed the activities of one of these witches. She has the most interesting disguise. She wears grey rags, assumes a meek appearance with no hint of power or mystique. She could be a charwoman. And yet she wears a ring with a stone of power upon it, and her aura fairly pulses with hidden strength."

Wexenne swallowed. "That is the War Bird, the emperor's Storm Crow. They call her Lessis. She has a most evil reputation."

"Yes, I can imagine. A most active creature. I have followed her for several days, since she abruptly appeared in the city."

Wexenne was left to wonder how Lapsor could detect such things. Lapsor was here, under Deer Lodge. And yet he claimed to know what was happening in distant Marneri. Preposterous on the face of it, but this elf king was gifted with enormous powers.

A part of Wexenne wished he hadn't pressed Lapsor for his help. To beg for the attentions of the War Bird seemed a foolish move. That hag had many legends attached to her name. Her powers were considerable.

"We shall trap her," said Lapsor with gloating confidence. "Right here. I know just the right lure that will bring her unerringly to her doom."

"Here?" Wexenne's discomfort crept into his voice.

"Yes."

"Is that absolutely necessary?"

Lapsor snorted with amusement.

"Come, my friend, tell me this. If you do not fear to stand here in my presence, knowing as you do who I am, why in all the names of hell would you fear this silly old witch?"

Wexenne spread his hands helplessly.

"No, my friend," the great face twitched to friendliness. "Have no fear. I shall deal with this creature. Witches, shamans, mage-lords, I have met her ilk many, many times and ground all of them into the dust."

Salva Gann renewed his internal pledge to flee the moment it became possible.

"No mortal being can match my power."

"Ah, yes," agreed Wexenne, "of course." And let's just hope that you're right about that, great lord, else it'll be twenty-five years hard labor on the Guano Islands, he thought.

"I have a plan, so listen carefully."

"But what about Porteous?" said Wexenne. "He has a peculiar sneer on his face, but has said not a word since you, uh . . ."

"Invigorated him?"

"Yes, that."

"I thought it best that he not hear what you were about to tell me about your depressing lack of military success. I can awaken him at any moment. Would you care for me to do it now?"

"Ah, no. Hold off a little longer." Wexenne's mind was whirring. Salva Gann took another look at Glaves. Porteous was wide awake and looking about himself with eyes devoid of intelligence.

Lapsor resumed the recitation of his plan.

"There is a young person much loved by this witch. She visits her often. The witch herself is guarded, but this young person is not. We shall abduct her and remove her to these quarters. I need a young, but mature female subject to experiment on anyway. We shall leave a clue or two to draw the witch on, and when she comes we will destroy her."

"Why will she come?"

"Because this young woman is either her friend or perhaps her lover. Sometimes these ancient hags take very young women as lovers, did you not know that?"

Wexenne tried not to think about it.

"No, I hadn't, but of course it's possible."

"Whether lover or friend, the young woman is very important to the witch. She visits with her regularly. She does not provide any protection, however The young woman frequently walks the streets alone. Such foolishness can be exploited."

The Lord Lapsor favored them with a chilling smile.

Chapter Forty-one

In the woods just to the east of Posila, the 109th Marneri Dragons were camped out in rough shelters, thrown up from branches cut from the trees. A boil-up had produced some cauldrons of stirabout, and dragonboys had brought out emergency supplies of concentrated akh. It wasn't exactly filling, but it was something, and it would make it easier for exhausted dragons to sleep and wake refreshed.

Oddly the wyverns didn't complain much. They understood that in the chaos of a fight like this, marching for hours, fighting for a few minutes, then more marching, good eating was going to be rare.

While they settled to sleep, the air was full of the sounds of the cavalry reinforcements going by, three hundred riders from Talion moving at a trot under torchlight. A dozen supply wagons were also passing up the road with the creak of wooden wheels and the crack of drovers' whips. These sounds were encouraging. By morning there might be more than just a boil-up of stirabout to look forward to.

Commander Urmin stopped by to speak with the unit and to praise their efforts of the day.

"Our victory this morning was largely to your credit. You handled that cavalry thrust with great skill. You have earned another battle star for your illustrious reputation."

The dragons clacked their jaws in appreciation. By their lights Urmin had done a creditable job. He had taken a big risk, but a well-calculated one. By finding that track through the woods to the road, they had gotten a jump on the enemy, and that had been enough to knock his army to pieces.

"I wish I could say otherwise, but I'm afraid there's no beer tonight."

The dragons slumped a little in their places. They had not expected any, but to hear it put like that was depressing confirmation of their worst suspicions.

"But as soon as possible, I'm going to fund a good sing around the fire on some strong ale."

Now, that sounded better. Sleepy dragon heads perked up momentarily and a murmur of deep-throated appreciation went up. Urmin was visibly pleased by this when he stepped away. Then after a final word to Cuzo, he rode off with his escort of two troopers. Cuzo was left beaming with pride.

While dragons slept, dragonboys toiled by the firelight to make emergency mends and patches to joboquins, vambrace harnesses, and the like. When multiton dragons were in prolonged motion, they played havoc with the web of leather straps, belts, and thongs that held their equipment in place.

Around the fire Relkin worked on Bazil's joboquin, where the weakest chest strap had given way again. Little Jak had a problem with the chin strap on Alsebra's helmet. Swane was vainly trying to sew together a belt that had split, and Manuel was struggling with the mess left from the thonging of the Purple Green's vambrace harness. The harness holding these forearm protectors in place was a weak spot in the standard equipment. The thonging was too lightweight for the job. Dragonboys spent a lot of time making emergency repairs, and the Purple Green had not taken to the newest style of vambrace with chains instead of thongs because the chains had chafed his skin.

The conversation was desultory until young Howt finally gave voice to something that had been troubling him for days.

"Why are we fighting these poor Aubinas boys?" he said suddenly.

Eyes blinked, everyone looked up from their tasks. Wasn't it obvious?

"What's his problem?" whispered Rakama.

"Who knows, maybe got the wits knocked out of him," replied Swane.

"No, really," protested Howt at this inhospitable response. "Maybe it's because I'm just a hill-bred orphan, but I don't understand what we're fighting about. There's hundreds of them laying out dead back there, killed by us. Why are we killing them? It seems like such a bloody waste."

"Well, young Howt, see it's like nobody really understands why," said Swane, who tended to speak up first for the group. "But it's them Aubinan boys that wants this fight. Look at what they've done. Attacked Fifth Regiment, cut them up really bad, killed a lot of men. Then they attacked Posila and invaded Lucule. It's not as if we wanted any of this."

"Look, the Aubinans think they're better than everyone else. 'Cos they grow so much grain." Little Jak voiced a commonly felt perception.

"Grain is what it's all about," agreed Manuel. "This whole thing was stirred up by the grain magnates. If Aubinas were independent, they could withhold part of their crop to keep grain prices high. Because they're in the empire, they can't do that."

"But if it's just the grain magnates," protested Howt, "then, why are all these other boys fighting for them? We killed plenty of men today, and I don't think too many of them were grain magnates."

"They're payin' them," said Endi. "Stands to reason."

"They can't be payin' all of them; there's too many."

"Well, how rich are these grain magnates, anyway?"

"Rich but not that rich," said Manuel. "They use their money to stir up the people. Any small grievance can be turned into a cause of some kind. Then they spread rumors and twist it so it helps them push their agenda."

"What's that?" said Howt . . .

"Boy, you really are from the hills, Howt."

"Ho ho, listen to ol' Manuel there. The college boy!" said Swane.

Manuel gave no sign of being embarrassed by Swane's epithet. He was a scholar from the small academy that had been set up to train older boys to be dragoneers. Such as he were still pretty rare in the ranks, however. The vast majority of dragonboys remained orphans that no one would miss.

"Look"—Manuel shrugged off Swane's mocking grin—"an agenda is like a sort of list of things they want to do. And what they want most is to be independent, so they can jack up the price of grain. They produce one third of all the good wheat and barley grown in the Argonath. They've got the best soil in the world."

"Hooray, now we know all about it," grumped Swane, who was plainly a little angry at being shown up by the "college boy."

Howt was unappeased, however. "But I still don't see why the Aubinas boys fight for the magnates. Don't they see that the magnates ain't risking their own lives?"

"They got 'em all whipped up with this trash about how Aubinas has a bad deal and pays too much taxes," said Endi with a snort of contempt. "It's like they're all gonna be rich once they're independent." Endi clearly didn't care for the Aubinans much.

"Yeah," agreed Jak, "except that only the grain magnates are gonna get rich." Little Jak already understood the ways of the world too well.

"And everyone else would pay a lot more for bread."

"And everything else," said Manuel. "You raise the cost of something as basic as bread, and the price of everything will go up with it. That would hurt the poor really hard."

"But the magnates already make plenty. Don't they have great palaces and armies of servants?"

Everyone asserted that they did; it was well-known. To be "as rich as a farming Aubinan" was a popular saying, after all.

"How come the Aubinan boys don't see through all this?"

"That I don't know. Maybe we should ask Relkin," said Swane. "That Quoshite's been real quiet tonight."

"What do you think, Relkin?"

Relkin had been brooding.

"I don't know why they're fighting, and it's not my job to find out. But if they fight us, then they'll die. We all saw it today. Men cannot stand in battle against dragons. It's just a slaughter when they do that."

"The Purple Green seemed to enjoy it."

"He still wants revenge. Not a day goes by when he doesn't lament the loss of his wings."

There were nods at this.

"So do you think that's it?" Endi wondered. "No more fighting? They'll give up and go home."

Relkin shook his head. If only it could be that easy.

"We beat them, but we didn't crush them. I don't think this thing is over. There's going to be a battle soon."

"Real battle?" said Little Jak, who heard that prophetic certainty in Relkin's voice. Little Jak had learned to trust Relkin's visionary moments.

"Yes, I can sense it. Real battle, not too long now."

As if cued for dramatic effect, there was a faint, but unmistakable rumble of thunder. Another storm was blowing in from the Bright Sea.

"By the Hand, more rain?" grumbled Swane.

"Streams are already overflowing their banks."

"Better make sure everything's stored under cover. Cuzo will want to flay anyone with a wet joboquin on their dragon."

They broke up and began to make preparations for a wet night.

Chapter Forty-two

Rain splashed in the gutters; it thrummed on rooves and windows. A fierce wind whipped through the streets of the city of Marneri. As a result few people were out. It was an hour or so before dark, and already the light was dim because of the heavy cloud cover.

Down Tower Street the shopkeepers were shutting up early. Shop boys were battening down awnings and fastening the shutters. The lamplighter was making an early start on his chores, and not having an easy time of it either with the wind so fierce.

On Water Street, one purposeful figure was walking uphill, her waxed rain cape and hat shedding water as she dodged the puddles on the sidewalk. The wind kept trying to pluck her hat away, but it was firmly tied on under her chin.

Lagdalen of the Tarcho was hurrying home to be with her daughter Laminna, who would be waiting for her evening lesson. That night it would be a reading from the great *Geographia,* which had descriptions brought back by sea captains from the white fleet. Laminna loved these stories of far corners of the world.

She crossed the street where it bent back on itself as it zigged up the steepest part of the slope. Here the gutters had overflowed, and a brown stream was surging down over the pavement. There would be more flooding down by the Watergate, and along Fish Row the shops would be awash. Lagdalen couldn't recall ever seeing this much rain at this time of the year.

She consoled herself with the thought that at least the day was over at her office. Ten hours solid of frantic work had just about cleared the backlog of paperwork. Letitia and Rose and the other girls would keep things running without her. Lagdalen had great anxieties about this, but there was nothing to do except trust everyone. They would have to keep the cases going. Which meant meeting with their court advocates, preparing evidence, hunting for witnesses. There was always a lot to do in the service of the crown of Marneri, and for a while Lagdalen wouldn't be there. She would be, well, almost anywhere, because she would once more be in the service of the Lady Lessis . . . a prospect that filled her with mixed feelings, very mixed. She had served Lessis for some years and felt extremely lucky to have survived.

And yet all her anger at being torn away from her work and her little girl was countered at times by an almost inexplicable thrill at the thought of working with the older woman again. It was exciting, she had to admit, to just be in Lessis's company. That ancient mind, so wise, so understanding, so farseeing. It broadened one to be that close to her. Then there was the intoxicating effect of being close to the center of the empire's nexus of power. Lessis was privy to the greatest secrets, and spoke regularly with the emperor himself. Lagdalen had seen enough in her service with the Lady to understand some of the deeper flows in the deadly game they played with the enemy. She could grasp the international picture fairly well too, having been exposed to so much during her service in Ourdh and Eigo.

Lagdalen chided herself for even thinking these things, but that excitement did not go away. Then she realized that really she was the only person in the world who could adequately serve Lessis as an assistant. There was no one else who had seen the other side of the curtain for herself, who had been there where the witches fought Padmasa's cruel tooth and claw with their wits and their magic. The things she'd seen. The things she'd been!

Lagdalen still had nightmares on that score.

But there was no escaping this duty. Laminna would have to get Nanny to read to her in the evenings. Nanny would read lots of nice stories, which Laminna even preferred to the *Geographia*, really. Lagdalen understood the limits of the appeal of information about the world. But how would Lagdalen feel about not being there to read to her daughter? How would her mother's heart take that blow?

There was a bitter taste to this kind of service.

Her motherly anger put an extra kick into her step, and she increased her pace up the hill. Laminna, poor child, had finally grown used to having her mother around this past year. In the girl's earliest years, Lagdalen had often been absent. But since Lagdalen's return from Eigo, she and her daughter had been together every day. Now they'd be separated for who knew how long. It might be a few days; it might be years. It might be forever.

And then there was her husband, Hollein. When he'd heard about Lessis's request, his face had just sagged. He knew the terrors that Lessis fought. He knew the risk. Then his anger came to the surface. As far as he was concerned, she'd given more than her share for the cause. Hollein Kesepton loved Lagdalen with all his heart and soul. He could not abide her being put at risk. The thought of losing her drove him to distraction.

But this was part of her service to the city, and no one else could do it.

Poor Hollein, she gave an inward sigh. But then he too was on his way into danger. Riding the Wheat Road to join the army in Aubinas. There was fresh fighting around Posila, and they needed every man who could ride. Reinforcements had been landing in Marneri all week. Several detachments of Kadeini reserve infantry had arrived and headed west at once. With them had gone more riders, mustered from the wealthy classes of the city, who had responded strongly to the call.

The bankers and merchants of the city had also raised one hundred thousand pieces of gold for supplies. It was their recognition of the severity of the need. Lagdalen had not been surprised at this news. She had expected it from the Marneri merchants, who weren't at all like the Aubinan magnates. In Marneri there was little ostentatious display by the wealthy. Plain cloth and pewter was preferred to silk and gold for the most part. Marneri's wealthiest men were also the city's most charitable, although this too was done quietly. The white city on the sound shone for the brilliance of its soldiers and sailors, and for its extraordinary efforts in every area of the Imperial enterprise. Which was why it was the recognized heart of the Argonath, even though it was scarcely a third the size of great Kadein.

Lagdalen was at the switchback on Water Street, where it zigzagged up the steepest part of the hill, when two other figures appeared, coming up the street behind her. They spotted her and increased their pace. Lagdalen, too absorbed in her own thoughts, while at the same time dodging the puddles, never saw them. She skipped over the deepest part of the stream and started up the next section. Here the sidewalk ran beside a four-foot-high retaining wall. As she stepped up the walk, four men emerged abruptly from the shadows, where they had been crouching, watching her approach.

Lagdalen saw them for barely a moment before one had an arm around her throat. She let out a yell and bit his arm. He struck her head, but she bit harder and kicked backward into his knee. Another man had her arms. She tried to kick him, but a third was wrapped around her legs, and they were tying her ankles together. The one she was biting hit her much harder, and she lost her grip. She felt her arms pulled behind her back by overwhelming strength. Rope was looped around her wrists. It was done in a moment, and she was trussed. A gag was forced into her mouth, and a sack was slipped over her. Then she was picked up and carried away.

The two figures who were coming up from the lower part of the street heard Lagdalen's scream. They started running, calling out. As they came they soon separated, since Eilsa Ranardaughter was twenty years younger than her chaperon Aunt Kiri.

Eilsa sprang up the road, turned at the zigzag, and saw four men briefly at the top of the zag. Then they disappeared between houses. Eilsa looked back. Aunt Kiri was far behind, calling her name. Eilsa ran on, keeping quiet now, regretting her earlier shouts. The men would know that someone was coming. She carried a long knife, and she knew how to use such a weapon. She was the daughter of Clan Chief Ranard of Wattel, after all! But she was alone.

At the top of the zag, the street bent back toward the east and climbed to the edge of the plateau on which sat the Tower of Guard, the Dragon House, and the parade ground.

The men had gone down a side street. She ducked along, listening carefully. There, was that a click of steel? She peered down Feather Lane, but saw nothing. On she went to the next, Meal Lane. She looked east down the narrow little street, and saw three men standing outside an open door no more than ten feet away. By ill chance one of them looked up just then, and saw her.

"Get her!" said someone in a harsh voice.

Eilsa turned up the street and ran, calling for the watch as loudly as she could manage. Unfortunately there were few inhabitants on that stretch of the street, which was filled with warehouses and workshops. Before she'd gone sixty feet, they were on her. A hand caught her cloak. She whirled to face them, her knife ready.

The first man was overconfident. In a moment he gave a gasp as Eilsa's knife found his belly. He doubled up and went down.

The others attacked together. A club just missed her head, and she ducked, but a net was cast over her and this proved her undoing. Her knife hand was trapped. The club struck the back of her legs, and she went down.

"Little bitch! She's done for Etrap."

"His own fault, should've seen that knife."

The club struck her a few times as she struggled to rise, and one of them dropped on her, bearing her to the ground with his weight. Her knife was wrested from her hand, and she was gagged and bound and carried around into Meal Lane.

Meanwhile the noise had aroused a few lights, and some voices were calling for the watch.

Eilsa continued to struggle until she was struck with the club a few times and sagged semiconscious in their arms. They dragged her through a door into an ill-smelling passage.

"Damned bitch brought the watch. I saw 'em," growled a harsh voice.

"She's killed Etrap too."

"Got to move now!" said another.

They moved down the passage. Another door opened, and they were outside in a court. A sack was passed over her head, and then she felt herself swung up onto a cart. There was a whip crack, and the cart was in motion.

She could hear men running alongside. Harsh whispers rose among them to keep their eyes open. The watch never found them. Instead a twenty-minute trot down side streets took them past the temple, across Broad Street, and down to the docks just above the fish market. The streets here were an inch or two underwater, as usually happened when it rained like this.

The cart was driven through the floods and straight out onto the docks. A small light showed in a waiting bark. The horse pulled up, men hauled the two sacks across to the bark and stowed them below. A few minutes later the bark slipped its moorings and began poling out as the sails were lowered.

There was a stiff offshore wind that soon filled the mainsail, and the bark moved out into the Long Sound.

Chapter Forty-three

In the crypt beneath the great Temple of Marneri were ceremonial rooms, storage rooms, and a secret place where met the Committee of Insight. One entered through a closet in the senior priestess's vestry. Within was a square room filled with a round table on which sat a great copy of the Weal of Cunfshon. On this wet and windy night, the committee had gathered to meet with Lessis of Valmes, who was acting emissary from the emperor in Andiquant.

Lessis felt a special tension in the air from the beginning. She traced it to Chamberlain Axnuld, who seemed uneasy in his place. And well he should be, considering what he faced. The situation was still very dangerous. Defeat at Redhill had magnified the rebellion. They were singing of it up and down the Argonath. Most recently the little battle at Avery Woods had turned the tables. But the rebel army was much larger than the legion force, for the moment, and remained a threat.

Time was precious, so Lessis pressed on with a report on the emperor's health and what actions he had taken most recently. Reinforcement was being rushed to Lucule from all over the Empire of the Rose. A force of ten thousand would be assembled within a month. The emperor had fully recovered from his battle wounds. He was in full command of all Imperial forces, and everyone should understand that the Imperial response to the rebellion would soon be felt.

Axnuld listened abstractedly, nervously chewing his lip. He kept looking across to Ewilra, High Priestess of Marneri. Ewilra's face was stony. Whatever it was Axnuld sought, it would not be discerned there.

Something was bothering the chamberlain. Could it be

he was at last ashamed of his friendship with Wexenne of Champery and the other Aubrinan hotheads?

The table also held Merchant Slimwyn and Banker Wiliger, representing the prosperous folk of the city, plus the Warden of Watch Glanwys, and General Hanth, and General Tregor. These last two were in a state of excitement, but it was of a different quality from that which possessed Axnuld the royal chamberlain.

Then Lessis realized that Axnuld was afraid she would discover something about Besita, Queen of the Marneri city-state. An awkward job sometimes, being chamberlain under a queen like Besita. She wondered what the queen had done now.

Later, after hearing a fulsome report on the state of the city's security from Glanwys and then some inconsequential remarks from Axnuld, Lessis seized the bull by the horns. Tossing subtlety aside, she asked poor Axnuld directly how Besita was coping with the emotional stress of the crisis.

Axnuld sucked in a breath. A haunted look came into his eyes. He had discovered that it was not easy to be chamberlain to a weak-willed monarch. When he had first been raised to the post after Burly's retirement, he had enjoyed dominating Besita and ruling through her. She had been pliant enough, willing to let him take over the grueling work of ruling a busy city-state. He had taken the opportunity to reward his friends in Aubinas very well.

And how had they repaid him? "Imperial Home Burners" they were singing while they torched the farms of Lucule! It was no more than a kick in the teeth. The rebellion cast him in a most unfavorable light. He had befriended Wexenne of Champery. Now Wexenne was one of the chief rebels. Axnuld felt intensely vulnerable. The agreement he'd had with them had been that they would threaten rebellion, but not actually step over the line and proclaim independence!

Meanwhile Besita had taken the weakling's way out of her situation. She had never wanted to be queen. Her brother's untimely death had thrust her into the role. She rebelled, and she drank too much. She took lovers, often unwisely chosen. She hated giving royal audiences. She hated paperwork. This led to many sulks and fits of depression. Axnuld had long since lost any enjoyment of his position.

"She is indisposed at this moment, Lady. I would inform you, just between ourselves, for we all know the queen and respect her, uh, difficulties of character, that she began the crisis very well."

Lessis warmed slightly to the man. She respected loyalty.

Axnuld went on.

"She even managed to find her courage after the defeat of General Cerius. But then her little dogs disappeared, and she was heartbroken, for she loved the little dogs. And then her lover, Jadon of the Guard, was killed in mysterious circumstances. That sent her over the edge. She found the period leading up to Commander Urmin's victory at Avery Woods too much for her nerves."

"I see," said Lessis. "And when will the queen return to active duty, do you think, Lord Chamberlain?"

He looked around as if desperate for escape.

"At this point it is hard to say. The shock of the rebellion struck her hard, but she did well for a while, as I said. Just lately, however, things have been less, ur, smooth. She needed a rest. Two weeks at her manse in Cheverny was required."

No wonder Axnuld was tense.

"Two weeks?"

"Ah, urm, yes, well, you see . . ."

"I do, Lord Chamberlain. Believe me, I do." Lessis wore a slight frown for a moment as she considered the royal family of Marneri. Things had gone well for the city, despite them, but the last three rulers had each been difficult. Great King Wauk had been a great warrior, but an amoral monster in his personal life. His son Sanker had ruined himself with drink and rich living. Sanker's daughter, the current queen, was spoiled and lazy.

Was it time for the witches to engineer a change in dynasty here in Marneri? They hated to do this work, but sometimes it became necessary. It had been hoped that by pruning away the vicious brother Erald, they would be able to keep the monarchy moving smoothly along. Unfortunately, in a time of national crisis, Besita was failing the people. She had a duty to be in the city, to be visible and to provide a focal point for the spirit of the people. Instead she shrank away to her country house.

Besita was just a weak reed, and there it was.

Lessis was angry at this dereliction of duty and resolved

to ride to Cheverny at daybreak. The queen would have to be persuaded to resume her duties and lead her people.

She turned to General Tregor with an angry shake of the head. Axnuld was left trembling. The Grey Witch was visibly angered. Besita would have the coals heaped upon her head before too long. Axnuld knew the stories they told about Erald's death. He could only wonder how long he would have a queen to serve.

Lessis had turned away from him, eager for other news.

"General, what word from you? I can see you're bursting with something!"

Tregor was indeed a happier story.

"I have twelve hundred men on the Argo Road to Posila. They should make contact with Commander Urmin in two days."

"Excellent news." Lessis chided herself for her previous display of emotion.

Merchant Slimwyn tried to keep the good cheer going. "There are nearly one hundred more volunteer horsemen prepared to leave tomorrow."

"Very good. It sounds as if Urmin's force will be more than doubled in size. General Tregor, you will be taking over command?"

"I will. I have orders from Dalhousie, written by General Dameo. General Hanth has seen them."

Lessis nodded to Hanth, who obviously had some news of his own to tell. Maybe he had raised some money. That might be why this banker was here. As she flicked a glance at the banker she realized who he was. This was the very father of Delwild Wiliger, the former dragon leader of the 109th Marneri.

She studied him more carefully. He seemed a perfectly sober member of his profession with none of the madness that infected his son. Nor did the banker give off any emanation of ill will. Delwild's fate had not made his father a traitor to the state. Lessis was encouraged. The high citizens of Marneri were still capable of making the great sacrifices that were needed.

She turned to Tregor.

"Well, General Tregor, if we can double the force in front of Posila, then we can be certain of keeping the Aubinans penned up. Meanwhile the Red Rose Legion is on the ocean as we speak. Of course, at this time of year the winds are unfavorable, so it will be weeks before they get here. Until then we must keep the cock in the bottle down there in Lucule."

Lessis exchanged a look with the high priestess.

"The enemy must know all this too," said Ewilra with a slightly raised eyebrow. Ewilra had read Lessis's private report, and knew that they faced something more than just the Aubinans in this war.

"Oh, yes, he does," said Lessis, allowing the conversation to work on two levels at once. "This next week or two will be crucial. We can expect another thrust from him very soon."

Tregor and the others were slightly puzzled by this, but Ewilra understood.

Lessis now turned to Hanth, who had waited patiently to give his news. Normally a stolid man, Hanth was obviously excited.

"First, let me say that I have word that a force of two hundred horsemen has been raised in Bea and Pennar, and is on the road to Posila as we speak. Ryotwa has also raised a company, more than one hundred young men, all with horses. They too are on the road."

"Excellent! The greatest problem Commander Urmin faces is that he is heavily outnumbered in horsemen. The Aubinans have a powerful cavalry division."

"Secondly, the Merchants' Association of Marneri has raised ten thousand pieces of gold for supply. We have already sent out the first wagon train, forty wagons full, on the route to Posila. A second train will leave within a day. The men at the front will soon be properly supplied."

"Well, it's true what they say," said Lessis. "An army marches on its stomach. Men, dragons, and horses all need to be strong, fit, and well fed."

She turned back to the banker. "Thank you, Master Wiliger. I know your influence in the city must have been vital to secure such a prompt and generous donation to the supply of the campaign."

Wiliger was plainly pleased.

"And, by the way, tell me, how is your son? You know I was privileged to serve with that brave young man in Eigo. The things he did!"

The banker nodded ruefully. Delwild had earned himself

a somewhat mixed reputation in the legion. Lessis sought to soften any ill feeling.

"He was not meant for command of dragons, perhaps, but that boy was there at the end when we needed him the most, and served with great courage."

Wiliger flushed with pride at these words. "Our family is honored to serve, ma'am. Delwild recovers. Sometimes he is almost his old self again."

"Such gallantry will be remembered. It will always be said that when Heruta was broken, Delwild Wiliger was there."

Banker Wiliger's blush deepened.

Through this exchange with the banker, Lessis had subtly laid a spell on the group: nothing directed or specific, just a general elevator of spirit. They all felt it, even such a seasoned hand as Ewilra. She marveled to herself at the subtlety of the spell, for that was what she surmised the sudden boost of élan to have come from. She had never felt a glimmer of the sorcery involved. Even poor Axnuld had recovered a little of his normal poise.

"General," said Lessis, turning to Hanth. "What is the most recent news from Posila?"

"Commander Urmin has Posila in sight, but he is avoiding contact with the enemy. To attack Posila is inconceivable with only a thousand men. The Aubinans even have enough catapults that it would be extremely dangerous to use dragons."

Lessis nodded. They could not afford to waste dragons, especially when they only had ten at the front.

"How long before we can reinforce our dragons down there?"

"Well, that's still a bit of an unknown. There's a half squadron, the 120th, which is on its way from Dalhousie. Also there's the 155th, which is resting up at the Blue Hills. A message has been sent to get them on the road."

"We must get more dragons into that force. Our enemy has many resources."

"Indeed, but for now, Commander Urmin must husband his force and demonstrate outside Posila while avoiding battle."

"Unfortunately that also means we give up the initiative."

"Just for the next few days. Once my men have joined Urmin's, the situation will be much improved."

Lessis had to be satisfied with this. Things were moving in the right direction at least. Commander Urmin's maneuvering at Avery Woods had bought them a little time. Once Tregor reinforced Urmin, the legion force would be just about big enough to handle the Aubinans on the open field. More dragons would help tip the balance.

After a discussion of supply problems and solutions, the meeting came to an end. Ewilra said a blessing and closed the great book. They rose and filed out through the vestry into the dusty hall that led up to the steps.

The generals went ahead, wrapped in their cloaks. Axnuld and Ewilra followed, leaving Lessis and Glanwys to bring up the rear. Upstairs, in the main rotunda of the temple, the soft singing from the chapel brought balm to the spirit.

It did not last long, however. A man in the brown uniform of the watch stepped up to Glanwys and presented a message scroll.

Glanwys read the scroll and took Lessis by the elbow. Wordlessly she handed it across. Lagadalen had been attacked in the street and abducted along with Eilsa Ranardaughter, heir of Clan Wattel.

Lessis felt her heart skip a beat while a cold shiver passed down her spine.

This was his work. She had sensed that ghostly presence, watching her, ever since she had returned to the city through the Black Mirror. Her visits to Lagdalen had been observed.

She cursed herself for an inexcusable lapse in security methods. She should have taken much greater caution in contacting her young friend. Lessis had to wonder if she was still up to the demands of the job. Maybe she was just too old.

And, of course, the enemy knew that Lessis would follow the trail they would leave for her. And at the end of it, they would be waiting. Ribela had warned her. Neither Mach Ingbok nor Heruta the Great were a threat as great as this one, and already he had shown them why.

Chapter Forty-four

There was no rain in Aubinas that night, although the rest of Marneri was soaking. In the forest of the Running Deer, across the river from Wexenne's great house, there was a gathering around a bonfire. A mound had been thrown up behind the blaze. Armed men ringed it, and kept the onlookers gathered in a crowd in front of the fire.

The sky was threatening, with massive clouds in the east, but overhead the stars shone brightly.

Wexenne arrived deliberately late, and made his way through the crowd of Aubinan notables to the edge of the line of guards. He noticed, with a slight thrill of unease, that these guards were clad in legion uniform and wore legion issue weapons. They were, in fact, prisoners from General Cerius's command that had been captured at Redhill.

Their faces were set like stone, their eyes blank. After what he'd seen the Great One do to Porteous, Wexenne understood that to the Lord Lapsor, men were as plastic as clay.

Wexenne noticed a single, massive figure, brooding at the rear of the mound, hidden in shadow. Wexenne tried to catch the attention of the brooding one, but his wave was not acknowledged, and the guards did not respond to his attempts to speak to them. To make a fuss was only to risk much greater humiliation.

Chewing his lip thoughtfully Wexenne shifted his weight and turned back into the crowd. Lapsor had asked him to set up this ceremony. This was to be the coming out of the Great One in public. He would introduce himself to one hundred picked men of Aubinas. Wexenne had invited all the top families and many had responded. Not just from

Nellin, either, for there were men here from Belland and even from the uphill counties. After this, the legend of Lapsor would be firmly established in Aubinas.

Wexenne knew what was coming, for he had seen it before when the Great One had first come to him. Wexenne had thought him a djinn, or a demon at first. Only gradually had he learned more.

From the beginning Wexenne's fear of this sorcerous creature had been balanced by his raging greed. Such a djinn might be most useful in the struggle with Marneri. And so it had proved, except that the djinn, or demon, or whatever it was, was showing itself to be quite unruly. Wexenne was starting to wonder just who was using whom.

He almost bumped into Porteous Glaves, who seized him by the elbow.

"Ah, Wexenne, this is a most propitious night, don't you think?"

There was a mad glare of fanaticism in Porteous's eyes.

"Most propitious. I think we are going to witness great events."

"Yes, Wexenne, I think you are right about that. The Great One will reveal himself. Our struggle can only take on new strength."

"Indeed," Wexenne mused on the difference between the new dynamic Porteous and the old one. His friend had changed from a frightened old rascal to a bellicose bore.

Porteous had seen someone behind his back. Wexenne turned and found the Baron of Nellin himself, Curmilious of Paukh, with his retinue around him.

"Baron," said Wexenne, with a well-executed courtier's bow.

"Wexenne. They promised us fireworks, that's why most of them are here."

"Well, old friend, I think I can safely say you won't be disappointed on that score."

"What, fireworks?"

"Indeed. It will be spectacular."

Curmilious was a fleshy fellow in his forties now. He wore his grey hair long around his shoulders and dressed in costume more befitting a youth of half his age. Still, he was far from stupid.

"So what is this wight you've been keeping in your cellar? I have heard the most outrageous stories."

"He is far more than some common wight or pixie. You will be surprised, I think, dear Baron."

"Is it true, though?"

"Is what true?"

What outlandish rumors had ridden out of the house now?

"That he buggers children and drinks their blood."

There had been a number of missing children in Nellin, and several of them had died unpleasant deaths in that chamber underneath Deer Lodge. Wexenne had accepted it. He didn't like it, but the demon demanded a few children to experiment upon, and if it was necessary to secure the monster's service to the cause, then so be it. A few young martyrs to the cause would have to be created.

"He has no sexual interests, Baron, and I don't think he drinks their blood."

Curmilious's eyes popped.

"What, no sexual interest? A capon!"

"Hardly that, but the question can not be answered in such simple terms."

The second part of Wexenne's original answer had now filtered through, and Curmilious gave a gasp and took another long look at Wexenne.

"What does he do with them, then?"

"Don't ask, you would not like to know." Wexenne clapped Curmilious on the shoulder. "Don't worry, much will become clear to you very shortly."

There came a sudden hush. Wexenne looked up and saw the tall figure of Lapsor on the top of the mound, lit up from below by the bonfire. He stood there unmoving, a tall, massively built figure of a man, with inhuman features on a face shaped like a shovel.

They stood there in silence. A voice spoke up, Graams of Belland, trying to be jocular.

"Hullo! What's your name, then?"

The figure ignored him and continued to stand there staring down at them. Graams fell silent. Nobody else spoke.

After a full minute of silence the figure raised its hands and spread out its arms.

"Aah wahn, aah wahn, gasht thrankulu kunj . . ." he cried in a huge voice that seemed to echo off the sky itself and crackle in their ears.

The hair on their heads rose. A wind blew up that rattled the trees.

"By the Hand, Wexenne, this is very good. You've got something here!" Curmilious Paukh was enjoying the show.

The guards began throwing more wood and bundles of rushes onto the fire. Quickly it blazed up high. The figure atop the mound became hard to see in the smoke and flame.

More guards marched a naked man to the top of the mound. His arms were bound tightly behind him. They thrust him forward until he stood beside Lapsor. Compared to the lord, the man seemed a mere stripling.

Lapsor spread his arms wide once again.

"Welcome my friends. I am to be known among you as the Lord Lapsor." His voice was huge and smooth, warm and rich. "Lapsor is a name that invokes a mighty river. I would like to be a mighty river for you. I will raise such a torrent that we will drown your enemies in our flood. I will help you to achieve your great dream. Aubinas shall be independent! Free Aubinas!"

From their throats it came unbidden, "Free Aubinas!"

"Free Aubinas!" his single shout seemed almost as loud as their combined cry. They responded with a roar. "Free Aubinas!"

The fire was piled high, the blaze grew fierce. The heat at the top of the mound was considerable. The tall figure did not flinch. When the man beside it tried to step back, Lapsor seized him with one great hand and held him still.

The other hand was raised high, and the great voice bellowed more words of ancient sorcery. Then with a suddenness that shocked them, Lapsor reached down and lifted the man off the ground, swung him up over his shoulders and held him, wriggling, high above.

"Tshagga avrot!"

He dropped the man into the center of the roaring fire.

The man's screams of agony were almost lost in the roar of shock and disbelief among the Aubinans.

Then their cries subsided to horrified hisses, while the man in the fire screamed and struggled to escape the flames. He had fallen into the center of the blaze and was instantly burned over most of his skin. His legs had sunk deep into the coals, and one foot was caught there. He thrashed. His piteous shrieks failed. He flung one leg up and fell back, and was consumed.

And then came an enormous flash of light that seemed to implode the center of the fire. With a gigantic sucking sound, the blaze went out. A cold wind blew over their shoulders and tore the ashes and cinders into a cloud that blew back over the mound. A thin whistling shriek ripped through the air and was gone.

They looked up. The figure on the mound raised its hands to the sky.

He had sacrificed a man right before them, and not one of them had lifted a finger to save him. Curmilious Paukh turned to Wexenne with astonished eyes, but voices were raised in the crowd. Men pointed upward.

Black clouds, huge and ominous, had ridden in from the east. The figure on the mound emitted a great cry and raised a clenched fist to the sky.

Now came a green flash that enveloped him, and a bright spark shot from his fist straight up into the leading edge of the cloud. The cloud flickered for a moment and then came on, floating overhead and blotting out the stars. Vast and black and spread to the horizon, it crept up until all the stars were gone.

Abruptly lightning erupted from the cloud and struck down to the mound with jagged ferocity while the thunderclap drove men almost to their knees. Gaping in awe, their ears ringing, they stared through slitted eyes at the fierce blue glow that shone from the figure on the mound. He was lit up, as if he was on fire within, and burning with energies never seen before.

Curmilious Paukh could barely see for the spots before his eyes, but he could see enough to know that the figure on the mound had absorbed that lightning bolt and still stood there, unharmed. Except that he glowed. It was truly an amazing show of fireworks. Wexenne had been correct on that score.

Lapsor raised a hand, and the light grew brighter still, until an orb of light slowly formed in the air above his hand. When it had reached the size of a man's head, it floated away to hover over the men, suspended like a pearl lit up with lightning fire. Stark shadows were thrown back to the trees at the edge of the clearing.

Curmilious Paukh found Wexenne grinning at him.

"Quite a show, I think you'll agree."

"Astonishing."

And then the clouds spoke, or seemed to. They looked up in wonder as they heard "Free Aubinas!" bellowed from the sky. The voice echoed like that of a God from horizon to horizon, as loud as the mightiest thunder.

The echoes faded away. The ball of light had vanished. Stunned, eyes watering, ears ringing, the assembled notables of Aubinas stared up at the figure on the mound. The fire blazed up again, refreshed by the guards, and red flames mounted quickly into the air. He turned, came down from the mound, and walked among them, exchanging handclasps here and there, allowing them to pay him homage.

"Free Aubinas!" he shouted, and they shouted it back in their joy and amazement.

Somehow Wexenne found himself gathered into the small group allowed to walk close with Lapsor. The meeting had turned into a coronation of sorts. Lapsor was filled with this great energy of attraction. The men had met their master.

Lapsor paused to bid the greater group farewell from the edge of the clearing, then he turned into the trees and told Wexenne and several others:

"Come, I have something you must see."

They followed him through the trees, and across the stream at the old stone bridge. Beyond and across the meadows lay Deer Lodge. However, long before they reached the big house, they turned into a gully hidden in a copse. There at the bottom was an astonishing sight. A cut in the ground had been made, and huge gates stood open in front of a tunnel forty feet across. It was guarded by six of the captured legionaries.

Lapsor indicated that they would enter the tunnel.

Wexenne gaped. The tunnel was twenty feet high and opened into the bank on which stood his house. The gates were of solid timber. Above the tunnel were lintel stones and a grating covering a smaller passage. How such an enormous undertaking had been completed so quickly and with such secrecy was beyond his comprehension. Anger boiled over.

"Who dug this without my permission?" he snapped.

Lapsor smiled indulgently. "I found that I needed my own entrance to the little cellar you have provided for me.

You aren't suggesting that I need ask your permission every time I have to go in or out? Every time I wish to stand in the light of the moon, most sacred of all lights to me, I must come and ask permission of you?"

Wexenne felt his position slipping badly. This was not quite the way he had imagined things would be arranged.

"I need to be informed of all such modifications of the house and surroundings."

"Well, now you have been, so take note. Now, come."

There was nothing to do but obey while wondering how in the world Lapsor had managed to dig this thing. It represented the labor of hundreds of men, day and night for weeks.

Glowing coals, emitting a reddish light, were affixed to the wall every twenty yards. They never seemed to burn out. Wexenne wondered what magic had been used to create them. His respect for the abilities of his strange visitor was growing rapidly.

Lapsor turned to him.

"By the way, I notice that Salva Gann is not with us. Where is he?"

Miles away, thought Wexenne.

"Oh, Salva? Well, it seems he had urgent business at home. He made a hurried departure just hours ago."

"Mmmm."

Lapsor did not speak again as they strode on for another hundred yards beneath the ground until they reached a portal, guarded by another half dozen former legionaries with blank eyes.

Past the guards they entered the realm of rooms that lay beneath the great house. The rooms had grown in number, Wexenne was certain of it. Lapsor was hollowing out the ground under his house; he was driving huge tunnels out beneath the back lawn; he had converted the legion captives they'd given him into a private guard force. Wexenne's misgivings about this venture were growing rapidly into the beginnings of panic. What could he do to change any of this? To halt Lapsor by physical means seemed beyond his capability. There were these guards, and there were the bewks, which were almost as terrifying as battledragons or trolls. Wexenne didn't have anything like enough men to stop this sorcerer he had unwittingly allowed to run loose.

A humiliating thought ran through his head. Would he be forced to flee ignominously from his own house, in the steps of Salva Gann? He recalled Salva's words.

"Get out now, Wexenne, before it takes you like it took Porteous."

When Salva said this, Faltus Wexenne had waxed indignant. Now he knew he had been denying what was already plain before him. He had caught an angry dragon by the tail.

They passed through a set of heavy doors and entered a chamber at least one hundred feet long and fifty wide. Four tables occupied the room. On the tables were set glass-fronted cabinets. In the cabinets were dark, contorted shapes. Wexenne averted his eyes, not wanting to see more horrors from the sorcerer's experimentation.

In one corner they passed some odd little folk, dog-men it seemed they were, for they had the faces of animals and wore leather aprons across furred stomachs. The effect was marred by their enormous turtlelike eyes. They were engaged in removing some matted material from within a cabinet, and placing it in a box. Wexenne had never seen them before. He certainly hadn't been notified that they were to be imported into the cellars beneath his home. They went back to their work even before he'd passed. He blinked angrily for a moment.

"What are they?" he demanded.

Lapsor halted, glanced back.

"They are Neild."

"Where did they come from?"

"Another world, far away. Do not concern yourself with Neild. They are very useful creatures; that is all you need to know. Come."

They passed through another large chamber filled with tables and cabinets. More Neild were working in here, where most of the cabinets were empty. One by the door was not, unfortunately, and Wexenne caught a glimpse of a terrified young woman with terrible lesions across her face and neck. Her eyes were filled with fear, and she was chained to the back wall of the cabinet. He moved on. There was nothing he could do. Nothing he could do for any of these poor folk, most of whom he assumed were from the surrounding lands. Such a terror he had brought them, he, Wexenne, the fool, the idiot, the emasculated oaf.

He who was supposed to guard them and keep them from harm had instead delivered them into the hands of this human spider or whatever it was.

"Free Aubinas!" they cried, but Wexenne was wondering if instead they would all wind up as Lapsor's slaves.

They entered another room, this one smaller than the others. Three seven-foot-tall, manlike creatures were chained to the walls. Their eyes were bright, a sign of intelligence, he thought, but their massive build and the tusks projecting from their lower jaws were clearly inhuman. As he looked more closely, he saw that they had the faces of bewks, that same rough, piglike countenance. They seemed perfectly peaceable, yet they were chained closely to the wall.

"What are these things?" said Wexenne in a shaky voice. The sorcerer was producing new creatures at an alarming rate.

"These are my bewkmen. Magnificent aren't they?"

"How?" was all Wexenne could splutter.

"There is usually a way if we look hard enough for it. Of course, it took considerable experimental work. We tried at first with some females of your kind. They proved insufficiently vigorous, and the issue failed to come to term."

Wexenne blanched.

"Since then it has been tried with pigs, deer, and horses. It worked well on horses. These three for instance were produced in a matter of hours from the horses in your stable."

Wexenne stared in horror.

"My horses?" Prize mounts, his beautiful stallion, Runner!

"At least half survived the first birth. They have been reimpregnated of course. The yield is much better than with any other animal tested so far."

"But I only had a few mares."

"Oh, that doesn't matter. We do not require the full reproductive apparatus to generate the bewkseed."

"All the horses?" Wexenne was shaking with horror. "But surely cattle would have sufficed?"

"Yes, cattle will do, though the bewkmen from cattle were not as quick and lively as the ones from your horses."

My horses. Oh, by the Hand. Wexenne wanted to vomit. Those beautiful animals had been his pride and joy.

"I must protest. I think you should at least have asked me before doing this to my horses. Those are prize animals."

Lapsor grew cold. Frost coated his words.

"Of course, of course, there are always those who carp and complain. Don't you see that it had to be done at once. We need to generate some infantry capable of holding their ground in battle. Otherwise our bid to free Aubinas will die here in the mud."

Wexenne shuddered, how neatly he had been taken. Like a trout to the fly! Lapsor already spoke to him as if he were little more than a servant. And with these monsters Lapsor would soon assume control of the Aubinan army, and then?

Lapsor seemed to be reading his mind.

"I see you are just awaking to your true position. It will be hard for a while, but you must understand that you will fail without me."

Wexenne gasped for air. Lapsor leaned close.

"The point is, my friend, that we need to gather a lot of horses and some cattle, and then we need to gather food for them. We could have several thousand bewkmen within a few days."

Wexenne brought himself under control somehow.

"Why do you keep them chained up?" he said with as much determination as he could muster.

"Oh, we must test them, of course. We are determining how much food they need for different levels of effort. All have undergone intelligence tests and reaction times have been noted."

"And the results?"

"They are less intelligent than men, of course. But they are twice as strong and almost equally agile. They are not so good at distance running. In fact, endurance is their weak point. We have begun to test them with weapons. They are a little slow, but they are very strong, and I think they will be able to break the legion lines."

Wexenne stared at the brutes. If they could produce a few thousand of these and put them in with the rest of the Aubinan army, they could well destroy the legion force advancing on Posila.

But, if they won, would it be the victory of Aubinas or this dark mage-lord who had sprung himself on them?

"Great Lord Lapsor," said one of the others, Dirfling of

Nellin. "May I ask why you have those people confined in the cabinets?"

"Ah, the cabinets." Lapsor sounded weary and sorrowful, as if bringing them bad news of a personal nature. "It is sad to look at, I know. Believe me, it is hard work to do, because of the sensitivities of your kind. I commend it, I do. Such qualities lift you out of the ruck of the lower orders of life. But we have to research the susceptibilities of men in case we must act against the general populations."

"Act against the people?" Wexenne was puzzled. Dirfling of Nellin was not.

"You mean you will loose plagues?"

"For the swift removal of large populations of your kind, such things can be necessary."

"We only seek to establish Aubinas as a free nation," said Dirfling.

"Of course, dear Master Dirfling, but we face a most determined foe. To capture the city of Marneri may be beyond our strength. In that case, after giving them a chance to surrender first, of course, we would begin a campaign to launch a pestilence among them."

Wexenne heard this with a shiver. What had he hatched here in the darkness beneath Deer Lodge?

Chapter Forty-five

Lessis tracked Lagdalen into the west. Actually Wespern did the tracking, riding ahead with Mirk while his fantastic sensitivities were kept focused on the faintest of trails. Lessis stayed back with their string of horses. They each had three mounts, with supplies of enriched oats, all to allow them to move around the clock at a good pace. Rain, hail, gusty winds, all were ignored as they rode on with a ground-devouring trot.

They changed horses again at the one-hundred-mile marker. While the horses ate small amounts of the oats and malt mixture, since too much would give them indigestion, the witch and her companions ate salted cod and pickles, washed down with water from the roadside fountain.

Remounted, they went on. Lessis now rode Felicity, an ordinary-looking little black mare, who turned out to be an exceptional horse to ride. She was strong, lithe like the best fillies, and blessed with an endurance far beyond that of most horses. She gave the impression that she would run with you to the ends of the world. Best of all, Felicity was both good-hearted and quite intelligent in her horsey way.

The pair of big roan geldings that were her other mounts were strong and able, but not very bright and not nearly as much fun to ride. Indeed, she recalled clearly that when Banker Wiliger had given her Felicity, he had mentioned that she was a champion ride.

It was cold enough that she was very grateful for the cut-down Kenor freecoat she was wearing under her waxed rain poncho.

The two big roans were running side by side in the string. They were wet and steaming, but seemed to be moving well, no sign of tiredness.

By the Breath she wished this rain would stop. Since she'd arrived in Marneri, it had rained almost continually. She had begun to suspect that it was the work of great sorcery. The magic of the First Aeon was beyond that of all subsequent times. That was when Gelderen glittered on its hill and the lamps of Salula shone across the world.

During the day they had seen thunderclouds moving south and west, and at times the dull boom of distant thunder was more or less continuous. All the wheat along this stretch of the road had been left too long and was now soaked and beaten down in places. The harvest would be poor this season.

The wind picked up and hurled the cold rain into their faces. Lessis hunched over, letting her hat brim take the worst of it. Felicity shook her head determinedly and plowed along, hooves splashing in the puddles. Lessis thought for a moment of the delights of spending such a horrible day working indoors, in a warm room with a fire going and some books of spellsay and artful rumor. She might be working on any of a dozen projects that she had dreamed of doing for years. And there would be hot tea whenever she wanted it, and time for meditation. Ah, the delights of such a life. Alas, it did not seem to be for her. Retirement now was just a memory.

Near Posila they paused. Wespern detected a break in the trail. The psychic echoes of Lagdalen and Eilsa that he was tracing were gone. They had to backtrack a half mile and then work forward again slowly until Wespern picked up a faint thread of the essence he followed.

They turned off the paved highway onto a muddy path that wound southward into the plain of Posila. It was evident that the abductors knew that the western approaches to Posila would bring them into contact with Commander Urmin's force. They were going southwest, heading for Lake Torenz. After that they'd be in Nellin, where they could be sure to get fresh horses. Then their pace would pick up, and it would be even harder to catch them before they got into the very heart of rebel Nellin.

Wespern drew up to a gate leading into a field that stretched off south. Farther fields were dimly visible beyond, hedged by darker masses of woodlots.

"They left the road here, and they went across these fields."

Lessis simply nodded. She was sure he was right. Wespern was uncanny, his sensitivities beyond the simply human. Mirk dismounted and opened the gate. When he was back on his horse, Lessis briefly exchanged a look with him. Such a drab, ordinary-looking man, if it wasn't for those eyes, you would never imagine what his career was made of.

She knew that Mirk was wondering where this pursuit would take them. He had heard the legends of Lessis, the death crow, who had taken regiments to their deaths out in the steppes of the Hazog. She knew he was probably wondering if he was about to join those lost souls. She also knew that Mirk could be trusted to the bitter end.

"Lead the way, Master Mirk," she said. They rode into the fields.

It was as she'd feared. The kidnap party had taken a loop south past Posila through Riverstrand, then through Bluebell Gap to Lake Torenz. They'd soon be in the river lands of the Running Deer, the very heart of the rebellion. In those rich little towns like Chavanne and Champery, where the landowners had grown wealthy on abundant harvests of grain, that was where the enemy would be.

He would also be well hidden, she imagined. He would have taken precautions against discovery. But she was certain that He himself was present in Aubinas, ever since that great light had shone down on them at the ambush and the bewks had appeared in the battle in the village of Quosh. He was physically here among them, working to destroy the Empire of the Rose. He had missed on his first blow, his sudden strike at the emperor. Now he bolstered the Aubinan revolt and aimed a blow directly at her, the Queen of Birds.

Lessis understood better now who this enemy really was. After the ambush she had conferred with Ribela and then studied the lore of the First Aeon and the Celadon Aeon, long, long ago at the very dawn of the world.

This creature was a rebel from that very beginning. One of the seven great spirits sent to infuse the world with life, and the only one who had failed in his duty. He had long since succumbed to bottomless evil and had destroyed world after world, ravishing them in his insane quest for ultimate power. Billions had died as a result of his cruelties. If he succeeded here he would enslave the entire world.

Such tyranny would be unleashed as would make the very stones weep.

And with this enemy to face, Lessis had let her guard slip. What had she been thinking of? She cursed her stupidity. Retirement was all she was fit for! She should never have visited Lagdalen openly. She should have had the girl under full-time security cover, with Mirk on hand. Instead she'd allowed this terrible foe to make Lagdalen a perfect pawn.

Now she was walking into a well-laid trap, for Lagdalen was bait that the enemy knew Lessis could not resist.

By the Hand! How blind she'd been! Lessis tried to drive away the self-defeating guilt that threatened to overwhelm her at times. She must not succumb to it. If she had to, she would match wits with this Dominator of Worlds. She would make up for her mistake. She had slipped, but she would recover, she swore it.

Mirk rode ahead, straight into the stubbled field where the grain had been harvested. Wespern followed, his head bowed as he considered the trail. Lessis urged Felicity forward with the slightest nudge with her knees. It was getting dark, they'd have to camp in the wet forest for the night. It promised to be uncomfortable and cold. Making a fire would be inadvisable since Aubinan cavalry was abroad. Still, at the least they had food and remained mostly dry under their waxed ponchos and rain hats.

She ate in silence, absorbed in reflection. Mirk finished, rolled himself in a blanket, and dropped off quickly. Lessis noted Mirk's famous stolidity. He could sleep anywhere, at any time. She doubted that she would sleep for months.

A few hours ahead, Lagdalen and Eilsa were indeed on the southward trail tied to the pommels of their saddles, their horses lead by horsemen in black, mercenary troopers from Padmasa.

Well-paid killers all, they rode their own string of horses hard, determined to reach the lake before stopping for the night. At the lake there'd be warm beds and hot meals among friends. They would be in Aubinas after that. There'd be fresh horses, and they might make it to the Running Deer by evening if things went well. Well paid, they were, but they were also conscious of who they worked for. They had seen his methods. They knew that the penalty for failure would be more than unpleasant and that speed in the execution of their orders would be noticed too. The Lord was harsh in his rulings, but he was also fair and rewarded success.

Lagdalen looked back over her shoulder. Eilsa was riding with her head down; there was just her hat to see.

The Highland girl had taken it well so far; she seemed immune to discomfort at times. Up on Wattel Bek she had lived an outdoor life where the climate was changeable and often stormy. When it came to strength and endurance, Lagdalen was more worried about her own abilities. A year of soft living in the city had not been the right preparation for this.

She forced herself to try and think straight. The future, while it did not look bright still had to be thought about. She had had time to analyze the situation. There had to be some way to escape.

There were five of these men, and they had the look of seasoned fighters. She knew the type, for hundreds, perhaps thousands of them served the Masters in Padmasa. They were not likely to make many mistakes in handling two female prisoners.

She confronted the reality. She was bait, she knew that. Eilsa had been taken only because she was there. It was Lagdalen of the Tarcho they had wanted because it would draw Lessis. Lagdalen did not quail in her heart. The enemy was very terrible, but so was the Lady Lessis. No one knew this better than Lagdalen herself.

They broke through some trees and found a wide vista before them. They were atop a bluff and could see out across the lake. The wind had whipped up whitecaps on the water, and low clouds obscured the hills on the far side.

Aubinas.

The trail doubled back along the steep slope, and they saw the lights of the village stretched along the bottom of the bluff, facing the lake.

Another ten minutes brought them to the first houses, which were large and well built, with blue stone facings and large white shutters. The roads were paved, another sign of affluence. The men paused at the gates of a large, white-washed building near the center of the place. Doors opened at once, and they were ushered within.

They left the horses to grooms in the stables. Lagdalen

tried to be observant. How many other horses were there here? How good was the security?

They were hustled into the house and taken up a back staircase to a small room furnished with a pallet and a straw mattress. The gags and bonds were removed. Two men stepped back, the rest crowded out of the room.

"You will sleep here. Some food is being brought," said the leader.

"What is your name?" said Eilsa.

The man colored. "That does not matter. You not talk to me. Forbidden."

"Seems a shame," said Eilsa quite innocently.

The man frowned at her while a couple of old women in plain grey tunics entered with bowls of oatmeal laced with honey.

"Eat, then sleep!" said the man closing the door. The only light in the room came from an opening above the door, covered with a metal grille.

They looked at each other, then fell on the oatmeal, for they were very hungry.

"I could eat a lot more of that," said Eilsa with a sigh. "They don't seem to be concerned about what we'd like, do they?"

"Insensitive thugs, all of them."

"Do you know where we are?" said Eilsa.

"I'm pretty sure this is Lake Torenz. That means we're in Aubinas now."

"I was afraid of that." She sighed and then squared her shoulders. "What do you think is happening in the city?"

"Well, they're following us, you can be sure of that. Maybe even the Lady herself."

"I was afraid of that also. They meant to take you as a bait to trap her."

"I think so."

"And she might take up that bait?"

Lagdalen shrugged. "The Lady is a strange person, you understand that. She is hundreds of years old and steeped in witch lore, yet she is still human. In this situation that could be her undoing. What we've got to do is try and get some weapons. These men are good, they are practiced at keeping captives from escaping. We have to improve our chances in case we ever do get an opportunity."

"Sounds like a good plan."

"Doesn't seem too promising in here."

"True."

After a little while they found they were too tired for talk, so they laid their heads down on the straw and went to sleep. One thing they could be sure of, they would not be molested in the night. On the first night, while they were camped out in a barn, they heard the men discuss raping them. They were still bound at wrist and ankle. Lagdalen and Eilsa had steeled themselves to face the ordeal.

When the men showed themselves in the main part of the barn, nerving themselves for the attack, Lagdalen prayed for strength from the Mother. Then, quite suddenly, the men were shaken when a hot white bead of light flared in the air above their heads.

A heavy sibilant voice had spoken.

"This is forbidden. Do not speak of such things again."

The men looked at each other and went their separate ways. There was no further thought given to raping the young women.

Chapter Forty-six

In the woods outside Posila, Commander Urmin was allowing optimism to shine through the clouds of anxiety that had hung over him for days. The enemy's cavalry had become a persistent presence on his flanks, but on the bright side, the enemy's infantry remained shut up inside Posila, and Urmin had received reinforcements, mostly volunteer horsemen. Among them, Captain Hollein Kesepton had ridden in with a hundred men from Marneri and Bea, riding their own mounts. There had also been a forty-wagon supply train. That made a great difference to morale.

There was a boil-up going on right then. The cauldrons were astir, and the hungry mouths were being fed.

All in all, these were grounds for cautious optimism. Urmin had confided as much to Hollein Kesepton when he reported in, soaked and weary from a long period in the saddle shepherding a second supply train down the road.

"Hail, Captain Kesepton, glad to see you. How goes it out on the road?"

By the flickering light of a torch, Hollein could see the deep lines of worry and concern that had developed on Urmin's face. What a difference a few days of command could make!

"The wagons are stopped at Glevert, a hamlet twelve miles back. Captain Takise has his troopers screening them off. The Aubinans are close, but we have led them a merry dance today, and they still don't know exactly where the wagons are."

"Welldone, excellent work. We must hold on for just a few more days, and then I think the situation will change. I have word of further reinforcements, approaching from the north."

Kesepton already knew that General Tregor was approaching from that direction with a few hundred more men. That would indeed improve their situation, heavily outnumbered as they were and stretched thin in their positions outside Posila. If the enemy tried, he might bludgeon them off the field simply by force of numbers. Tregor's reinforcements were desperately needed. Still, it was only a few hundred men—not enough to end the crisis. That would not happen until the Legion of the Red Rose arrived in a few weeks. After that the picture would change quickly and positively.

"I have a suggestion, sir. Might we try running the wagons in tonight? The road is straight and well paved. With minimal light we could lead the wagons all the way here."

"Twelve miles in the dark?"

"You have forty teams of oxen already here that came with the first wagon train. Let me take those back with me. We'll add them to the oxen we already have. Together they should have those wagons here by dawn or soon after."

"That sounds too optimistic."

"We can do it, I'm sure. The train made very good progress today, all on nice flat roads. Thanks be given for the flat plains of Lucule. The oxen at Glevert are feeding now, but they can be whipped up again in a few hours. We'll start them rolling and perform the changeover when we meet up with them on the road. Give me twelve hours for the entire thing."

Urmin frowned for a long moment as he weighed the various risks.

"That puts all our oxen at risk." He mused a moment more and then sighed. "But the Aubinans could bring us to battle for the wagons tomorrow, and I cannot risk pulling out from my positions here. They're well defensible against any sorties from Posila, but if we were pulled away from them to protect the wagons, then this line might be attacked and overwhelmed."

He struck his palm with his fist.

"So, all in all, I think it might be better to risk our oxen rather than risk fighting for the wagons tomorrow."

Kesepton saluted crisply.

"Sir. We can leave the Aubinans an empty road to attack tomorrow."

"And we're going to need those supplies. Dragons have

to eat, so do men and horses, even oxen. Plus we're about to be reinforced, and those men will be hungry. Go with the Mother's Grace around you and bring me back those wagons."

"Sir, may I take Hunzutter's troop with me to cover the wagons?"

Urmin pressed his hands together and stroked his chin. Of course they would need some covering cavalry, just in case an Aubinan patrol ran into them. However, without Hunzutter, he would be down to just fifty horsemen at Posila. Unfortunately he couldn't keep Hunzutter and have the oxen adequately protected.

"Well, damn it. In for a penny, in for a silver crown," he rasped. "Take Hunzutter, Captain, but be sure to get those wagons here. I don't want to have to face General Tregor without supplies if you don't."

"Yes, sir."

Kesepton rode away, and Urmin looked back to the map on the lectern. The Aubinan forces were new, they could not respond with the same efficiency as legion troops. During the day Caleb Neth's cavalry force had been mixed up and scattered by the efforts of Kesepton and the other Marneri captains. Caleb Neth would have as a priority the need to hold his forces together. He would be desperately reconcentrating, and at night, under clouds and in the wet woods, it would be a slow task. With luck, that would give Kesepton's night moves the room they would need. It was a finely tuned gamble, but Urmin was convinced that it was better to risk this than to risk facing two fronts the next day with insufficient forces to fight on even one.

The question was, when would General Tregor put in an appearance? Urmin was looking forward to his arrival. Then he could hand over the crushing burden of his responsibility and go back to taking orders rather than giving them. The fear of making a mistake at this level of command was awful. One slip and he could lose everything and put the city itself at risk.

Hurry on, General, he thought, and hurry on Captain Kesepton. The world hangs in the balance, and I can only handle this strain for a little while longer.

In the woods not far from Urmin's command post, the 109th were resting up under the wet trees. They were full of stirabout and akh, which was good, but they were feeling the damp after daylong rain that was bad. Dragons didn't mind being wet all day, but they were finicky about being dry when they slept. Dragonboys were working hard at spreading ground sheets to make tents of a sort, but it was hard to keep things dry in the conditions, and everything was faintly damp if it wasn't already wet through.

A cold, miserable night was in prospect.

When shelters were finished, they gathered around Cuzo to report. He checked off the dragons. All were down and either asleep or heading that way. All were fed, and all had functioning equipment.

Cuzo warned them to check joboquins. It had been a busy day, with much marching up and down the line. Leather thongs would have felt the strain. Then he dismissed them. They drifted back to the line.

"It'd be bad if we hadn't had that boil-up," said Rakama as they were walking back together.

"Dragons were right edgy," agreed Swane. "Way too long without a good feed."

"And all that marching," grumbled Little Jak.

"Urmin's trying to make them think he's got more dragons than he has. Making ten do for thirty," said Swane.

Relkin was too tired to talk much. It had been a long, exhausting day. He was looking forward to finding a corner under the ground sheet and putting it all behind him.

They split up at the lines. In the first row were Alsebra, Vlok, and Bazil, each reposing under a pair of ground sheets strung up as a tent. Relkin found that Bazil was sound asleep and that the ground sheets had kept the wyvern out of the rain. There was just all the wet that had existed before underneath, so everything was damp. Nevertheless, to Relkin it was warm and almost dry. He curled up next to the dragon's side and was fast asleep in moments.

He dreamed of Eilsa, but not the usual pleasant images. It was a strange, troubling dream in which he saw Eilsa at the rail of a passing ship. She was going east, and he was going west. She waved sadly to him across the growing gulf between their ships. Even if he dove after her, he would never catch her ship, which was plowing on before the wind. Nor could he, a mere dragonboy, stop the ship he was on and send it in pursuit of the other.

The sails on Eilsa's ship had turned black. The sun was setting, and as it set it was turning into a face: the face of the dead Elf Lord Mot Pulk. Relkin moaned in his sleep.

Chapter Forty-seven

In the dim light just before walking, Relkin saw Eilsa's face frozen in his thoughts. She was caught in a trap of some kind, but more than that he could not clearly remember. He shook his head to try and clear it. Then he realized somebody was actually shaking him by the shoulder. He focused, and finally woke up completely.

"Manuel, what is it?"

"The Purple Green says he smells something bad in the woods. It's coming up from the south side."

"Something bad?"

"Like the new trolls we fought at Quosh."

Relkin scrambled to his feet.

"He's sure of this?"

"He says so."

"Tell Cuzo. There must be an attack coming. Sound the alarm."

Manuel ran off to the dragon leader's position, and Relkin ran up and down the lines shouting for everyone to wake up. Bleary voices shouted back at him, but bleary or not, their owners were awake.

The Purple Green was already on his feet and stamping his huge legs, driving his ground sheets into the mud, hissing angrily like some enormously overgrown snake.

Cuzo ran up, still struggling to clear sleep from his mind.

"What do you smell?" he shouted to the Purple Green.

The great wild dragon flared his huge eyes wide. "Same things we fight in Quosh."

All around them the woods were alive now with great dragons fumbling for equipment and swords. Dragonboys bustled to help while they also took up their bows and made sure they had dry strings ready.

"From the south, sir!" said Manuel.

"Move out on the double," said Cuzo. If it was a false alarm, then it was a false alarm; but if it wasn't, then they dared not waste a second.

"Curf, take a message to Commander Urmin. Tell him we're concentrating at the south end of our position and that the Purple Green has caught the smell of the enemy trying for a surprise attack on our flank."

Curf saluted and sprang away.

Dragons hefted their shields. Dragonboys tried to attach armor. Helmets went on. Ready or not they were in motion, heading south. There wasn't much light, and they needed to move carefully because the ground was cut up with gullies and holes.

Bazil fell in beside the great wild dragon, who just smashed his way through the trees.

"You are sure of this smell? Since this dragon doesn't smell anything, but wet wood and mud."

"Bah, wyvern dragons have weak noses. I smell those things again."

He hated to admit it, but Bazil knew that the Purple Green had the strongest sense of smell of any of them, nor was the wild dragon inclined to easy panic. If he smelled the enemy, then he damned well smelled them. Bazil said no more and concentrated on not putting a foot down a rabbit hole in the dark.

After a hundred yards they halted along the edge of a deeper gully, where a small stream had cut its way. This was the southern or left flank of Urmin's position in front of the town of Posila. Across the gully in the uncertain darkness, lay more trees, scrub oaks, white ash, gnarled little pines for the most part. The darkness there was thick, almost palpable.

The Purple Green sniffed.

"They are there, coming closer."

The other dragons were starting to smell it too.

"Same thing we smell at Quosh," said Vlok.

Then Bazil's nostrils twitched, and he caught it too, a stench like pig excrement, foul and thick. He tensed, eyes scanning the woods ahead.

"By the fire, what is that?" snapped Alsebra's voice off to his left.

A strange deepening of the shadow seemed to fill in the

trees opposite, across the gully. The trees had hardly been visible before. Now they were gone, and the world was caught up in a dark sack. All light had been sucked from the scene. And yet something stole upon them, something sly and merciless. They could feel it coming.

Relkin felt an odd tug in his mind. A sense of the eldritch made his skin crawl and the hair on the back of his head stand up.

He looked up and met Bazil's eyes. Even in the pitch-darkness, Relkin could sense the wyvern's unease.

"Strange feeling, something is wrong. Must be magic."

"Magic it is, Bazil, but there's that smell too. We can all smell it now."

"Stink like pigs," muttered the wyvern who drew Ecator.

There were loud creaks and cracks in the trees across the gully, but still nothing could be seen.

Relkin shuddered at the sudden feeling of having dozens of busy flies running over the skin, tiny feet skittering at the edge of sensation.

Swords were unsheathed quietly among the trees. Huge bodies tensed themselves even though they could see nothing.

The dense shadow paused at the edge of the gully. The dragons remained crouched in the undergrowth, swords held low to the ground. For a long moment the wall of shadow hung there on the opposite bank; then it moved down into the gully and up the other side. They watched with distinct unease as the front of the shadow approached, sliding up the gravel to the top of their side and forward into the trees. Then it was right on top of them. They readied themselves, for they knew not what, but as the dark terminating line passed over them, they were abruptly stunned by a harsh green light that blazed from a point source on the far side of the gully. Outlined in front of them was an army, fronted by dozens of great, hog-faced bewks with swords and shields.

Behind them were men and things that were taller than men and had the same hunched shoulders as the bewks. Spears and axes were borne in their hands.

Relkin heard a movement at his side. Cuzo had pushed up close to see this. He winced at the glare.

"By the Hand," Cuzo drew his sword.

"Duck!" Relkin shoved the dragon leader aside. Bazil

had risen, his tail had shot out and would have caught Cuzo across the back of the head.

"Got to watch those tails, sir!" Relkin had sprung up behind Bazil. The tail came back hard as Bazil set himself to wield the sword; Relkin ducked without even seeming to see the tail.

Ecator met a bewk blade a moment later with the first great ringing blow. Moments later the clangor up and down the position grew fierce, along with the roaring of the dragons and the shrieks and moans of bewks, men, and the new beasts.

Through that greenish light a man in black uniform tumbled toward him. Relkin had always associated that uniform with Padmasa. Without any regret he put his arrow in the man's chest. Behind the first came a second. But it was no man, the weird piglike face told him that in an instant. It was massively built, more bewk than man and carried a woodsman's ax. Relkin was briefly puzzled over that. It wasn't even a battle ax.

Then he ducked as Ecator flew low overhead and clipped the piglike brute's head from its shoulders. The dragon backed toward him, crushing a tree, and Relkin had to move. A second pig-faced brute was lunging at Bazil's right leg with a spear, but then Relkin's arrow stood out from its mouth and it twisted away and went down on its knees.

Whatever they were, they were killable. Relkin dodged and ducked and aimed his Cunfshon bow. Another man, another shaft, and the man was down.

A towering bewkman was cleft by Vlok's sword and the upper half fell back into the gully, blood spraying over the host of men massed there.

A bewk thrust at Bazil and was parried. Bazil noted again how unpleasantly quick these new trolls were. The bewk grew more confident, fatally so. It swung overhand, a clumsy effort, and Bazil took the blow on the shield and turned the weapon while he ran the bewk through with Ecator.

Bazil vented a roar as he thrust up his foot and shoved the bewk's corpse back onto the mass of smaller enemies coming up behind. Men with round shields, levies from the Aubinan peasantry. They screamed as they took the brunt of the fall of the great bewk.

A man halted at the crest with a dragonboy's arrow projecting suddenly from his face. He toppled back, arms milling, and sank through the spears of the oncoming.

Another bewk hove up through the ruck, its sword in motion. Bazil, forced to backhand away several more men edging in with spears, was wrong-footed. He could only evade with a clumsy sideways stumble. A bewkman was there, his spear lunged and scraped along the greave, barely missing flesh. Before he could pull back for another effort, he was knocked down by the dragon's foot. Relkin leaned across and applied the sword to the exposed throat.

"Sometimes boy like an extra hand . . ." purred the leatherback wyvern.

Bazil regained his balance, and Ecator swung once more.

But there were too many, and the bewk was still hewing at Bazil, who defended consistently, but was forced to worry too much about the men with the spears. Arrows and javelins already decorated his shield, and Bazil had several minor wounds. Worse, there were men and these other things getting past them. The woods were filled with enemies. The damned bewks were too effective to leave the dragons sufficient time to keep their front clear of smaller fry.

He had to retreat. The other dragons were doing the same. It was difficult to clear away the smaller foes among the trees and undergrowth; dragonboys were overwhelmed by the numbers.

The dragons retreated slowly, too slowly in some cases. Big Churn was the first to fall. Speared again and again, he lost the use of his legs and was slowly pulled down on the mountain of dead that he created in front of himself. A bewk finally took his head. Young Howt died with his dragon.

Gunter was next to be speared by a bewkman who got in too close. Gryf killed the bewkman, but more were coming and big Gunter was in trouble.

Rakama's shouts for help were heard, however. A few moments later Alsebra cut her way through to Gryf's side, and her active blade soon cut down the bewkmen and drove the survivors back.

Gunter was staggering. Alsebra turned and roared for the Purple Green. He came within moments, exploding through the vegetation to reach them.

"Help Gryf carry Gunter," said Alsebra.

The Purple Green exchanged a momentary glare with Gryf, and then heaved the wounded Gunter off the ground by himself and carried him at a staggering kind of lope back through the tunnel of broken trees.

It was an astonishing effort. Even Alsebra had to admit she was impressed by the brute strength of the Purple Green as she backed through in the wild dragon's wake, where trees were knocked over wholesale. The bewkmen were slow to follow up against her and Gryf. Jak and Rakama covered the retreat from the side, arrows flicking out to take down imps and men who ventured too close.

Elsewhere the fighting continued to rage in the wet thickets.

Bazil danced out of the way of a spear point and smashed the man behind it with his elbow. The bewk on the other side hewed at him, and he caught the sword on his shield. This bewk was too quick to catch with the shield trick, however, and Bazil had to ward off a second blow from the bewk. Again the brute was too quick for him and left no opening for a riposte. The bewk circled, another was closing in. A spear stuck momentarily in his tail, but before it could do much damage, it caught in a thicket of alders and broke free.

Men ran in at him. Relkin engaged one, Bazil got another, but the third vaulted onto his chest and stabbed home with sword above the chest plate. All that saved Bazil was the joboquin, the sword glancing off a stud and sliding away along the wyvern's ribs.

With a convulsive heave, Bazil dislodged the man and sent him tumbling. Before he could rise again, Bazil kicked him into the thickets. Relkin had slain another, but there were more, and in these trees it was hard to stop them all. Hard to even see them until they were too close.

Ecator swept aside another thrust from the bewk, and this time Bazil was able to whip the tail mace into the bewk's face. It staggered back into the trees, then bounced forward and Bazil hammered it with the shield and knocked it cold.

The other bewk was caught up in a thorn tree. While it struggled to extricate itself, Bazil spun away and slipped down a bank. A man scrambled out of his way, then tried to cut him from behind. Relkin hurled a rock that spoiled the man's stroke. The man recovered his balance, turned to face Relkin, and the tail swept up and brained him from behind.

Relkin lunged past the body, skidding down into the deep darkness that pooled at the bottom of a shallow gully. They saw Alsebra lit up brightly atop the slope, moving back in retreat, a pack of men at her heels. Gryf broke out of the shadows and scattered the men, then both green dragons disappeared into cover.

The cornets were blowing, but it was a little too late. The 109th had been overwhelmed and driven from its position. Two dragons were down, and cohesion was gone.

In a moment Bazil and Relkin found themselves virtually alone. They heard the fight, still raging in the woods to one side, but they had lost sight of it. The green light glared over their heads, coming from the south, though Relkin had lost all sense of where he was. The small trees, difficult scrub, all dark and wet and filled with enemies, had left him confused, even lost.

"Let's move up this streambed, stay in the shadow, come in on the fight from their rear."

In response, the dragon hefted his shield and crouched down low. They moved forward with maximum stealth. For a moment Relkin was transported back to those dangerous days when they'd traveled in the forest of the ancient monsters, in the heart of the dark continent.

They clambered over the wet rocks and fallen trees and edged up into a district of taller pines. There were clearings visible not much farther on. A moment later the green light became much brighter, and in a few more they glimpsed its source.

Out of the woods on the south side came four bewkmen, armed with swords and crude shields. Behind them strode another quality of life altogether. A heroic figure, manlike, but more than seven feet tall, wearing gleaming steel-plate armor. It strode forward with a silvery staff in both hands. At the top of the staff blazed a coruscating star of green fire.

Suddenly they were aware of a faint glow emanating from Ecator's steely surface.

Bazil and Relkin exchanged a look.

"Sword is hungry."

Relkin whispered. "The Lady mentioned a bright light when the emperor was ambushed in Blue Stone."

"Who is this, then?"

"I don't know, exactly, but he's a sorcerer, that's plain enough."

"Doesn't see us."

Relkin made sure of the string on his bow and reloaded. He had only the four shafts left. He would have to use them carefully.

There were more cornet calls in the woods. Urmin had gotten a stronger force into action. The sound of the fighting had intensified considerably.

The bearer of the green fire was barely fifty feet away now. He would pass within thirty or so when he had to go around a huge pine with three separate trunks.

The bewkmen bunched at the same place. Relkin sighted on one of them. Behind them came the figure, walking with a purposeful stride. He wore a flat-topped helmet, bearing no device. His mantle was white with a gold blaze on the chest. A long sword, a two-handed blade, was borne over his shoulders.

The light flooded their hiding place in the hollow.

"Now!" said Relkin, and they burst out of the thicket and charged.

Bazil swept forward with Ecator in hand, and his big claws digging hard into the soft ground. Something hummed past his ear, and one of the bewkmen fell back with an arrow in the eye. The others were still bunched too close to be effective. Ecator swept a sword aside and hammered them. Only one survived to scramble back.

The imperious figure bearing the staff and the light had thrust the staff into the ground and drawn its own sword, which glittered with a deadly shine that screamed at the edge of blue vision.

Relkin glimpsed the face beneath the square-topped helmet. He shivered, for there he saw the same visage as that of the dreaded Elf Lords of Mirchaz. That same pitiless beauty, the perfect mouth, chiseled nose, pale blue eyes with gold in their centers; all that was missing was the silver curls, which were hidden beneath the helmet.

Relkin also sensed the enormous presence in the tall figure. It was like one of the Lords of Mirchaz, and yet it was greater, denser, more powerful.

On every score it raised his hackles.

He aimed carefully and sent his quarrel straight for the

elf lord face. Incredibly the helmet dipped, and the arrow bounced away harmlessly. The helmet was a magical device of some kind, for at this range he should not have missed.

Bazil closed, towering over the tall sorcerer. Ecator gave off an intense sparkle. Ecator knew this enemy from long, long ago. None could be more satisfying to kill for the fierce little spirit that inhabited the great sword. Bazil swung, and the sorcerer brought up his own fell blade to parry, and there was a tremendous flash and Ecator was parried. A tiny wail of rage rose above the noise.

Bazil was just as surprised at the strength in the other. The sorcerer was taller than a man but nowhere near as massive as a troll, or even one of these new pig-faced trolls. Still, the stroke was strong, and swift. There was no time to contemplate. Bazil took the return stroke on the shield and felt again the strength of the tall elf-faced figure.

Bazil had come to hate faces like that. They were impervious souls, immune to the sufferings of others, suffering that they inflicted.

They clashed again. The enemy sword blazed with dark fire, while Ecator was virtually alive with hate and fury, trembling in his hand. Not even when they'd fought the great Heruta had the sword been this affected.

"Aha!" roared the giant. "I sense an old enemy here!" He spoke in the ancient tongue Intharion, and both dragon and boy heard his words as if in their own languages.

"Oh, yes, I feel you, ancient one, and I feel your hate!"

The tall figure in gleaming steel launched an assault on the dragon, his strokes coming fast and furious. They possessed such strength that not even a wyvern dragon could discount them. He was forced to parry and deflect, unable to regain the initiative. Bazil was forced back a step, then another. The shield was taking a beating, a stud flew, bindings cracked.

Somewhere in the distance cornets were shrieking over the rumble of battle, but Bazil never heard them, so intent was he on surviving.

Roused by the anger that those elfin faces resurrected, the wyvern dug deep and raised his response rate. He parried, turned his opponent, riposted, and had his thrust almost go home. With inhuman rapidity the armored figure dodged, and Ecator slid by harmlessly.

The sorcerer came back onto the offensive at once, and

Bazil had to parry and step back, while the shield received even more punishment. Never had he fought an opponent with such a mixture of strength and speed. It was as if he fought a green wyvern, with the strength of a brasshide, but all compressed into a relatively tiny form.

Relkin had two shafts left, and was keeping a wary eye on the surviving bewkman, which had stopped running, turned about, and stood there gazing in awe at the sight of the two giants fighting under the harsh green light. Relkin looked for an opening, but dared not waste a shaft. He might need both to slow the sorcerer.

A clang followed, the shield took another blow, and a fragment flew off and bounced away. Time was running out. Relkin bobbed to one side, crouched, and aimed.

His arrow bounced away, even at a range of fifteen feet. He had to duck as Ecator swung by at a lethal height.

When he regained his feet, he saw the bewkman coming. He left his bow, drew his sword, and put himself in the way.

The bewkman was barely able to focus on him, so eager was the beast to get at the dragon's back. Relkin dodged the clumsy swipe from the creature, stepped inside, and drove his own blade home. The bewkman gave a hideous shriek and pulled back, freeing Relkin's sword and letting a stream of dark red blood fountain out.

The bewkman was not discouraged in the slightest. It launched itself at him, and Relkin would have been crushed beneath its weight if he hadn't anticipated the move and shifted out of the way. It landed with a massive thud, and he drove his sword down into the hollow at the back of its skull, above the spine.

The thrust was clean, and went right through. The brute ceased to move. Relkin leaped for his bow.

Unfortunately he'd lost track of the dragon's tail, and it caught him in midair with a solid thwack, on a par with getting kicked in the belly. He bounced, rolled, doubled over. The bow was out of range. He sucked for breath.

The armored elven sorcerer swung over. Relkin knew death was coming and somehow pushed himself up and tottered away. Ecator hummed overhead just a few inches from his spine. Another great clang rang out just behind him as he fell and slid to where he could reach the bow.

He was still trying to get a breath; it was hard to move.

Bazil was being outfought. The silvery figure was too

quick for the dragon, and he was still as strong as at the beginning of the fight. His arm never tired.

Relkin sat up, brought up the bow, and aimed. The dragon slipped while stepping back, and Ecator was turned. The sorcerer stepped up to take the dragon's life, but Relkin released, and his arrow struck home beneath the silver gorget and above the breast plate.

The enemy staggered, then vented a shriek of hate as his thrust was ruined and his sword caromed off Bazil's breastplate.

The dragon punched him in the face with the shield and knocked him away, spinning him around. He tore the arrow free with a scream of pain and rage that made Relkin's heart shiver from the terrible hate that suffused it.

Blood gushed down, staining the white mantle, dripping on the silvery armor.

The sorcerer pointed a long finger at Relkin.

"Thou shalt pay for this agony that you have caused me," it hissed. But before it could do more than threaten, Bazil moved in to resume the contest.

The sorcerer lurched back out of range, then reached up to the silver staff. The green light went out, and they were plunged into utter darkness once again.

For a few seconds they could see nothing. Then, as their eyes adjusted, they peered about themselves, but saw no sign of their opponent. There were only the corpses of the bewkmen.

"He's gone," said Relkin. "Whatever he was."

"Strong, too quick for this dragon. Boy save worthless dragon's life."

"After all the times you've saved my skin, it was the least I could do."

Cornets shrieked nearby in the woods. They headed for the fighting.

When they reached it, they found the 109th had regrouped and fought off the bewks, killing three. Urmin's men had barely held off the bewkmen, and the fight had been savage and terrifying in the dark woods, but in the end, with the aid of the dragons, Urmin was able to break the enemy up and send them back in disorder. Then the green light that had flooded the position had gone out quite suddenly, and the contact with the enemy was lost. Urmin was sending out scouts.

A sense of muted elation permeated the small army. A deadly surprise attack had been met and repulsed, but it had cost them. One dragon dead, and one with a bad spear wound. Then there were twelve men dead, and little Howt who'd died with his dragon. Beyond that there were dozens of wounded.

Still, Urmin was able to get most of his men back into his lines in front of Posila before the morning was too far advanced. Fires were lit for a boil.

About the same time Hollein Kesepton and his men brought in the surviving thirty-nine wagons of the second train. They'd lost one wagon to a broken wheel, but most of its cargo had been redistributed. They had all the oxen.

The cooks boiled noodles by the hundredweight. By then the clouds were breaking up. The sun came out in mid-morning, and the land began to dry.

Around noon a scout came in with word that General Tregor would reach their position by nightfall. With twelve hundred more men, two hundred of them horse, the position would be much more secure and their chances of holding out until the arrival of the Red Rose Legion vastly improved.

Hollein saw that his horse was watered and fed, and then he took himself to the cooking fire and sought out some food for himself. Noodles with dried cod broth was on offer, and he took a healthy helping and ate it by the fire.

He'd finished and was walking toward Commander Urmin's command post when a figure glided up from the night. He whirled and almost drew his knife.

It was a witch, a woman wearing the plain robes of her order.

"Captain Kesepton, I believe."

"Yes, Lady."

"I have a message for you." She adopted a conspiratorial smile. "It was brought to me by an owl. I think you understand."

Hollein shivered a little. The breath of sorcery again. How he wished that were behind them now that Heruta was dead. Alas, the war went on.

"Yes," he whispered. "I understand." When the Queen of Birds reached out, it was never good news.

"Does she expect an answer?"

"Perhaps. The bird is still where it was."

He opened the scroll, read its contents, and gave a groan

of despair. His heart turned to ashes. Lagdalen had been snatched right off the streets of the city. Along with her had gone Eilsa Ranardaughter, the striking girl from the Wattel country.

He put a hand to his forehead for a moment. Lagdalen abducted, Eilsa Ranardaughter too, and taken into the west. Right past Urmin's little army. Right past Hollein. And he was unwitting and unable to do a thing.

Chapter Forty-eight

The next day was an improvement. The sky cleared, and the waterlogged land began to drain. Lagdalen and Eilsa were riding on fresh ponies, with another meal of oats and butter in their stomachs. Despite their uncertain futures and status as captives, they could not help have their spirits lift a little. The scenery was beautiful. The hills around the lake were lovely, and in the afternoon they rode down the long avenues that traversed the beautiful Forest of Nellin.

Eventually they entered a picturesque valley, where seven round hills framed the view. The river wound smoothly through the scene. Ahead in the distance loomed a larger mountain with a sharply defined upper crest, jutting up like a chisel's blade. Lagdalen had never seen it before, but she knew at once that this was the famous Sunberg.

"The valley of the Running Deer River," she said quietly. Eilsa nodded. This was an area that was famous for its natural beauty—and its rebellious inhabitants.

Nellin Forest ended with a long meadow that led up to a sweeping lawn and a massively built house with a green-tiled roof. As they got closer, they could see the towers at each corner of the great house and their false machicolations.

To their right towered the Sunberg, its upper surface glowing in the sun's light. Ahead loomed the house. They passed a perimeter wall set beside a sunken lane, then a gate of white stone where they were admitted to the inner yard. There they were pulled off the ponies and conducted directly into the house. Armed guards were evident at the doors.

Inside, Lagdalen's first impressions were of immense wealth. There were paintings by Aupose and Ieff Hilarde, fabulously expensive beauty. The floors of the halls were carpeted thickly, so the entire place held a deep hush. Even the boots of their captors were reduced to quiet thudding.

They entered a long corridor with pale blue walls and dark blue ceiling. They were ushered into a long room, with gilt-framed mirrors on the walls. A man in black uniform was arguing with a much fatter man clad in an expensive-looking brown suit of worsted. Lagdalen recognized him after a moment or two, it was Wexenne of Champery. One of the worst hotheads in the original Aubinan cabal.

At the entrance of the two young women and their captors, the argument stopped for a moment while the men looked them over. The fellow in the hated uniform of Padmasa turned back to the other with fury.

"My Lord Lapsor will not accept this sort of interference."

"My dear Kosoke, this is my house, and I will retain the right to interview whoever is a guest here, thank you very much."

Kosoke looked as if he wanted to draw his big knife and set it athwart the fat man's throat. With a visible effort he restrained himself, bowed, and left the room with a last glance in Lagdalen's direction. His face had a strange, vacant look that chilled her.

They were left with the fat man in the brown suit. Lagdalen could almost hear her father's cough of disapproval at his expensive shoes and yellow silk socks. Tommaso Tarcho was of the old school and believed that wealth should never be flaunted. Rich and poor should wear the same clothing, good stout sandals or boots, warm but sober clothes and sensible hats. Excessive display was in poor taste.

"Flashy softie, that one!" she could hear Tommaso's derision in her head.

"Ah," said the man, "let me welcome you to Running Deer House. Please be seated." He extended his hands toward the comfortable-looking lounge chairs. "I will send for hot kalut. I am sure you would welcome it after your ride."

This was unexpected, but after an exchange of looks of surprise, they did as they were bid and waited to hear more. Their wrists were still bound together, yet they were waiting to be served a nice hot cup of kalut. As if they were simply on a social visit!

The well-dressed fellow seemed to understand the incongruity of this, nonetheless he strove to extend his own illusions.

"Well," he said with a sad shrug, "this is not quite the way I would have wished to welcome you, Lagdalen of the Tarcho, to my house here on the Running Deer, but now that you're here, I shall endeavor to make your visit as comfortable as possible."

This veneer of hospitality struck Lagdalen as being very strange. Still she decided to go along with it. Until her wrists were cut loose, there wasn't a whole lot she could do about getting free.

"Then, we thank you, Wexenne of Champery, Lord of Nellin." She kept her voice as neutral as possible.

"Nellin is a proud place, Lady! As proud as Marneri." He thrust out a lip, as if challenging her to contradict him.

"So I have heard, Master Wexenne. Alas, now I understand that the pride of Nellin lies in the dust as a result of this rebellion against the rule of justice and law."

"Infamous law, madame, infamous! Laws that prevent us from realizing the proper level of profit from our hard work."

Lagdalen looked around her and then back to him.

"You seem to have done well enough, Lord Wexenne. You live more graciously than anyone in Marneri. Not even the bankers can match this."

Wexenne fluttered his eyes, he was plainly pleased by the comparison. Lagdalen was disgusted. As a Tarcho, she was of the highest level of society, and though her horizons had been broadened in the service of Lessis, still she retained some of the aristocrat's disdain for social climbers. Compared to the Tarcho or any of the great clans of Marneri, this wealthy grain magnate was a jumped-up nobody. His wealth and his pretensions were both unpleasant.

Fortunately he was oblivious to her unspoken contempt.

"This house is a marvel, isn't it? I have spent my life building Running Deer House, and I think it suits the valley very well. A crown jewel for the helm of Aubinas."

"I see." Lagdalen's eye took in the magnificent painting on the far-end wall. A pastoral scene, undoubtedly it was another Aupose. "Certainly it makes a fine place to hang the works of Honoriste Aupose."

Wexenne beamed. To sit in this parlor with a young attractive scion of the aristocracy of Marneri and hear such praise of his creation, this was wonderful. It helped to take the sting away from much of what had happened lately. That fool Kosoke! And the demands of the Lord Lapsor! It was getting to be insupportable.

At least well-bred young ladies from Marneri knew who the great Aupose was. Unlike some of these Aubinan oafs, who were ignorant of everything beyond their fields and the hunt.

"Thank you, Lady."

Wexenne now turned to Eilsa.

"I regret that we have not had the pleasure of a proper introduction. Please accept my apologies for this situation. I am Wexenne of Champery."

"I am Eilsa of Wattel."

"Wattel! Great heavens, you're a long way from home." Wexenne seemed to think this was an amusing thought. Eilsa did not.

"I am not here of my own free will, Master Wexenne."

"No, of course not. I regret it, young lady, I truly do. It's all in the name of the cause, you see. But, never mind, it'll be over soon, we'll be free, and we'll bury the hatchet. Perhaps you will come again in the future, as a guest."

Lagdalen and Eilsa exchanged a glance. This assumption of future friendship was bizarre.

"Why have I been brought here now? What do you want from us?"

"I? I want nothing of you, young Mistress Wattel. It is not I that sent for you. Oh, no, it was Him."

"Who is that?"

Wexenne pursed his lips and seemed to weigh his words carefully.

"He is a most remarkable being, an ancient lord of extraordinary power. His mind is very deep. He has knowledge beyond anything known to ourselves."

"Indeed. What do you call this person?"

"He terms himself 'Lapsor.' I suspect that he has many names."

Lagdalen found her patience had eroded. The smug stupidity of these Aubinans had grated on her for years during the case of Porteous Glaves.

"Yes, Master Wexenne, we have heard of this person. It takes many names and is an enemy to all living beings. A true, deadly servant of the darkness, a thing with no more compassion than a stone, perhaps even less. It will use you and spit you out with no more thought than if you were a cherry."

Wexenne stared at her for a moment. "What?" he began, then changed his expression with an effort.

"No! Do not malign him, young lady. Please restrain your opinions. The Lord Lapsor has been of incalculable benefit to our rebellion."

"They say this is how he always begins, by fomenting rebellion and civil wars. Later he hews down his friends as well as his enemies, and piles them together in a common grave."

Wexenne fluttered his hands.

"You cannot make omelettes without first breaking a few eggs."

"That means you ride roughshod over the rights of others, even to the point of taking lives. How many men have been killed now because of your rebellion?"

"We fight for the principle of freedom!"

Lagdalen's accumulated resentment of the Aubinan gentry surfaced.

"Freedom from what? The freedom to use your present situation to enrich yourselves and impoverish the rest of the Argonath! Without unity the nine cities will fall, just as Veronath fell long ago!"

"Oh, do not speak of ancient history to me! Why should we not take advantage of our fertile lands?"

"You have been well blessed. I see no poverty here. And these fertile lands would not be yours if others had not fought for them and cleared them of the enemy."

"Enough! You are quite the imperious young witch, are you not? Well, he will soon take that out of you."

There was a silence.

"I see," said Lagdalen in icy tones. "Your 'welcome' does not include safety."

There was a knock at the door.

"What is it?" said Wexenne.

The door opened and another overly well-dressed man entered, Porteous Glaves himself. Lagdalen got over the shock in a few moments. After all, where else would she expect to find Glaves?

"Porteous," said Wexenne. "This is a surprise. You are back from the front already?"

"Didn't actually go there, Faltus, old friend. I was ordered to keep a watch on the home base."

"Oh, really, I had thought you would be longing to be at the front of the battle line, leading the charge for Aubinas!"

"Well, of course, old friend, of course. But one must follow orders, don't you know."

"No, actually I've never been very good at taking orders, Porteous. I'm better at giving them. I'm sure you understand."

"Well, I suppose so, but things have changed, old friend. The cause has moved to a higher plane. We're at war now, and so everything must be laid on the line. And that means taking orders when they're necessary."

"Mmmm, well."

"Anyway, old friend, I'm here because Kosoke asked me to come and talk to you. He told me something ridiculous, that you had refused to hand over the prisoners and were holding them yourself. So I thought I'd better run up and see what's what."

Wexenne stared at Porteous. How had Lapsor done this to his old friend?

"No," he said.

"No?" Porteous's eyebrows furrowed as if he could not comprehend this concept.

"I am not keeping our guests myself. I am meeting them, that is all. I retain the right to meet anyone who is invited into my house."

"Ah, yes, well, very good, then. But now, don't you see, it's time they were conducted to their cells. They should be there in case the Lord Lapsor returns and wishes to see them himself."

Wexenne's nostrils flared. How dare they? This was his house, and it was his rebellion, and here they were acting as if he was a nothing! As if they could do whatever they wanted in his house without even asking his permission!

"They will be released to Lapsor in good time. For now they will remain here while I interview them myself. You forget, Porteous, that I am a commander of the Aubinan army."

Porteous's puzzlement showed on his simple, fat face.

"But the Lord Lapsor ordered that they be confined to

the cells. He was most eager to begin work on them at once."

Lagdalen felt her heart freeze. "Work?" she said in a soft voice.

Porteous glanced at her, but did not seem to recognize her. He had changed dramatically. He had lost a lot of weight. There was also a slightly vacant look in his eyes, like that of a newborn calf. He looked back to Wexenne, who continued smoothly.

"That may be, Porteous, but I have not yet completed my interviews. When they are done, these young women will be available to see Lapsor."

"Faltus, think carefully here. You will anger the lord and disturb his work. He will be unhappy."

"Alas, dear Porteous, sometimes things like that can happen. The Lord Lapsor will understand."

Porteous could scarcely comprehend Wexenne's refusal.

A further knock at the door brought a maid bearing a tray with hot kalut. She served them, though her eyebrows rose at the sight of their bonds. Lagdalen and Eilsa eagerly drank it down anyway. Porteous muttered for a while to himself and then abruptly left the room.

"I must apologize for my friend Porteous's behavior. He just hasn't been himself lately."

Lagdalen sipped the kalut and eyed Wexenne. She thought she understood the situation. Wexenne had caught a tiger by the tail in this Lord Lapsor. Now his own position was endangered, even in his own magnificent house.

"So the Lord Lapsor is your guest here, Wexenne?"

Wexenne stifled his first retort while a rather insincere smile spread across his face.

"Ah, yes. Extraordinary fellow. Taken over the cellars, you see. Down there with an army of things, you know. Quite amazing what he's done in just a few short weeks."

"And what will he be doing with us in this 'work' of his that was mentioned?"

Wexenne blanched. His hand wobbled, and his cup clinked in the saucer. Nightmarish images rose up to haunt him.

"Ah, let us not, no, let us not . . . discuss such things. Come, I think you might enjoy a walk in the orangery. Yes, that would be a good thing. You mentioned the great Aupose. I have several fine examples of his early work. On our way to the orangery, I can show you his first painting of the Sunberg. Aupose will always be associated with the beauties of Nellin, as you know, and he was particularly fond of the country around here."

Refreshed by the kalut, they rose and accompanied Wexenne on a walk through the fabulous halls of his grand house. Two guards followed them at a discreet distance. At one point they stood beneath an enormous canvas, covered in the writhing masses of war beneath lowering clouds and darkness.

"Ieff Hilarde's 'Tanagos.' Has there ever been anything that could match it for its fury and passion?"

Lagdalen had to agree. Hilarde made the battle of Tanagos almost come to life before them. On white horses the knights of Aubinas were charging into the foreground, about to shatter the line of the demon lord's forces. Men, imps, and trolls wrestled and writhed across the midground. Civilization swayed in the balance under the dark masses of cloud.

Once, she recalled, Aubinas had indeed been a proud name, and the home of great warriors in the cause of the Argonath. Over the generations, though, they had lost that loyalty and had grown contemptuous of their fellow men.

In a well-lit hallway, they stopped to admire Honoriste Aupose's great first painting of the Sunberg.

"In his lifetime, the great Honoriste painted the Sunberg forty-one times. The paintings are all different. Each is unique in its angle of view and the weather it depicts. The Sunberg has many moods."

Eilsa Ranardaughter had been progressively impressed by the wealth and beauty of the great house. They had ancient lineages in the Wattel Hills, but being sheep farmers they had never amassed riches. The age-old houses of the clan were bare of luxuries. And though she had heard of the famous paintings of Honoriste Aupose and the others of his school, she had only seen one, in a banker's house in Marneri. Here they hung everywhere, along with canvases by the immortal Hilarde and Desley of Vo.

"Your collection of paintings is uncommonly lovely, Master Wexenne. I wish I could indeed see them without having my arms bound."

Wexenne struggled with his internal conflict. He felt dishonored by having to keep these noble ladies cuffed at the wrists. Yet Lapsor had ordered this, and he did not dare to unbind them. Just how much should he fear Lapsor? He recalled those hands stretching out to Porteous's face and trembled slightly.

"And so do I, Madam Wattel. Come, the orangery awaits."

It was a charming gallery space facing south, almost a belvedere, with a glass ceiling and an array of long windows to let in as much light as possible. On the long wall there were orange trees, trained on trellises against the walls. They were in a recessed court open only to the south. Through the glass could be glimpsed the surrounding walls of the house. Lagdalen noticed that there were drainpipes running down from the glass roof in the corners of the room.

Wexenne was obviously proud of the place. He rubbed his hands, thrust out his arms, and turned on the spot.

"No matter how cold it gets outside, we always keep this part of the house good and warm."

They moved closer to the south-facing windows. They overlooked a thirty-foot drop, to the paved path in front of the house.

Lagdalen was wondering if she could break the glass in the door and cut her wrists free before Wexenne could summon the guards that undoubtedly waited just beyond the door. She decided it was very unlikely.

Wexenne gestured to the grand view.

"Here is where the great Honoriste sat to paint the 'Running Deer' series. I made sure of that before I began building the house."

Lagdalen nodded. "I have heard that the great Aupose lived in this valley for most of his life, and the majority of his paintings were done here. Yet in Marneri we treasure his paintings of the sea and the coast."

"Yes, yes, Honoriste traveled widely. He made his two great sea voyages. Great paintings resulted. I have his *Gates of Cunfshon* hanging in the great hall."

Even Lagdalen was impressed. Lagdalen had grown up surrounded by the art treasures of the Tower of Guard and knew that *Gates of Cunfshon* was one of the greatest paintings in the canon of civilization.

"Are you not concerned that your unruly guest may threaten your collection?"

Wexenne paled. The thought had never occurred to him. Now it struck him like a hammer.

"He would not dare; no one would damage such priceless beauty."

"If I were you, Master Wexenne, I would hide my favorites. This Lord Lapsor will use them to control you. Mark my words."

Wexenne blinked furiously. His fear of Lapsor had taken on a new dimension.

Abruptly the doors opened behind them. A servant approached. Wexenne turned away from them to listen to the servant.

"The Lord Baron of Nellin, master."

"Curmilious? What's he want? I thought he'd gone home already." He turned back to Lagdalen and Eilsa.

"Ladies, please excuse me. I must attend to this matter for a moment." He started for the door and then turned back once more. "For the sake of dignity, I must inform you that there are guards at every exit. Escape is impossible."

Wexenne left them.

Eilsa was out of her seat in a moment. They met by the door, which swung open at the touch. The guards were waiting right outside. Back inside they examined the windows and the drop to the pavement below.

"He has left us just like this?"

The windows were not locked. There were no obvious ways to climb. Eilsa, a good climber in the fells of Wattel, thought it could be done, but with difficulty, under normal conditions. Bound at the wrists it was impossible.

"So it seems."

Eilsa was looking up. The orange trees grew staked to the wall. An easy climb, if their hands weren't bound together. And at the top the glass was laid in two-foot panels. Perhaps they could be pushed out.

Lagdalen pointed and whispered.

"The pipes?"

They found that, even bound at the wrists, they could get their hands around the pipes. There was just enough room for slender fingers at the back. The ornamental stonework in the corners offered plenty of footholds.

"Race you to the top," said Lagdalen.

"You're on."

It wasn't easy. Their arms grew weary, but they kept

climbing and reached the top almost together, Eilsa ahead by a few seconds.

They found it hard to keep their balance at the top while they examined the ceiling glass. It was set in ornamental panels.

Eilsa tried hers with the top of her head. It gave quite easily. She pushed some more and felt it rise.

"This one's loose," she whispered.

"Good, because this one isn't."

Eilsa pushed up as far as she was able with her head and lifted the pane of glass out of its frame. She was able to raise it and move the pane. There was a confluence of drainpipes right there, which gave just enough handholds to allow her to get her shoulders up through the opening. From there she was able to draw herself up onto the glass roof of the orangery. A catwalk passed across the center. She moved toward it, stepping on the frame joints, which she thought must be the strongest parts of the structure. There was an occasional ominous sag as she went, but she kept moving quickly and reached the catwalk safely.

The walk allowed her access to doors on either end. One door was open. Inside was a room filled with carpenter's wood, planks cut to various sizes. Beyond was a room filled with tools. Her heart leaped. There was no one in sight. She listened carefully, but detected no sound of anyone working nearby. She slipped inside and found a long bench set up for maintenance and repair work. Saws, pliers, drills, tools of a dozen kinds were set along the wall. Nothing to cut her bonds with, however. Then she saw it, in a rack with seven of its kind, a small chisel with a sharp edge!

The difficulty was in holding it and cutting her wrists free at the same time. She cut herself while trying this with it between her teeth. Then she saw the vise bolted to the bench and realized after a moment what it was. After a few moments' fumbling, she got the chisel solidly in place and then cut through the thongs around her wrist. One, two, three, and they gave, and she was pulling off the rest.

Taking a softwood mallet and a spike, she ran back to the roof of the orangery. Wexenne had still not returned. Eilsa had to laugh at how well Lagdalen had played him. He was undoubtedly overseeing the removal of his most treasured paintings. There were a lot of them, so he should be busy for a while.

Moving very carefully across the creaking roof of glass, she made her way to the corner where Lagdalen was crouched, still clinging to the drainpipe. Eilsa motioned to Lagdalen to crouch back out of the way. Then she used the softwood mallet to break the glass. One well-delivered blow produced a small hole and a radiating mass of cracks.

They waited anxiously for a moment to see if the guards reacted, but the single sharp crack was not enough, it seemed, to stir a response. Eilsa worked with the spike to knock small pieces loose. They fell past Lagdalen down to the dirt at the base of the trees and made very little sound. Bigger pieces she pried up and laid on top of the roof. Within a few minutes she had removed enough glass for Lagdalen to climb through. Eilsa assisted Lagdalen up the last inch, and for a few moments they lay there on the glass roof, gasping from the exertion.

Recovering, they tiptoed across the delicate roof to the catwalk. In the workshop they cut Lagdalen's bonds and armed themselves with hammers and gimlets.

Outside the workshop they discovered a narrow hall. Plain wooden doors lined it. The floor was bare. Clearly this was part of the servants' quarters. At the end of the long passage was a stairway leading up. They tiptoed warily down the hall. The only sign of life, however, was some snoring from behind one door.

They climbed up the stairs and discovered a warren of workrooms, dormitories, and later, attics, into which they disappeared.

Chapter Forty-nine

Outside Posila, Bazil and Relkin were relieved from duty in the afternoon and allowed to head for the 109th's bivouac. Relkin was tired, but there was work to be attended to first. Bazil needed treatment.

First there was a long scrape on the right side of the tail that required cleaning and a rubdown with Old Sugustus's medicinal. Then there were several bad cuts and a deep bruise on the left side of the rib cage, where Bazil had fallen over a dead tree in the fight. Finally he turned to the minor cuts and bruises, then checked the scar over the recently healed wound received at Quosh. Despite the furious exertion of the fighting during the night, that wound showed no sign of reopening. Relkin breathed a sigh of relief. Some wounds reopened with exertion, even weeks after healing. They could be the bane of a dragonboy's life, and a direct threat to his dragon.

While the sun shone in the breaks between clouds, he worked with needle and thread and applied Old Sugustus liberally. A few places needed poultice and bandage, and that took a little more time, but at last he was done.

Bazil had hissed a few times with displeasure during all this, but as usual he met the pain with stoicism that was actually pretty common among wyverns. It was Manuel you had to feel for on that score, tending the Purple Green, who was far more sensitive. Bazil had concentrated his thoughts on a nice snack, to take them away from the Old Sugustus bubbling in his cuts. So, as soon as he'd finished clearing up, Relkin went down to the cook fires and used up a few favors to get a big pot of soup and a dozen loaves of bread.

On his way there, he checked at the medical section,

where the leatherback Gunter was bandaged and sleeping. It appeared that he would recover. His dragonboy, Uri, was sitting there doing mindless work on a leather strap.

Swane and Rakama sat with him and did their best to keep his spirits up.

On everyone's mind was the thought that Gunter might be lamed by the spearing. That would end his legion career.

"The dragon will live," said Relkin. "Good news."

"You pray to those old gods of yours, Relkin. Gunter's going to come back. You'll see."

"I bet he will, too."

"Shame about the young brass, and Howt," said Rakama.

"Everyone's real cut up about Howt," said Swane. "Just a kid, damn it. Churn was a good sort too. Nobody ever said anything bad about old Churn."

How many young men had they left behind, slain on the field, alongside their dragons? Relkin and Swane clasped hands. Rakama added his, and then so did Uri.

"We will avenge them."

"You bet," said big Swane. "They'll be remembering the 109th Marneri, I reckon."

They parted, and Relkin went on to the cook fires. Although his faith had suffered in the past year or so, he still made himself whisper a prayer for Gunter to the old gods. Who could say for certain whether they were in the heavens or not? And Swane was right, the leatherback was going to need every bit of help he could get.

One thing in their favor was the strange passivity of the Aubinans in Posila. Like everyone else, Relkin had expected an attack to follow up the night assault. But hour after hour the lines in front of Posila were quiet. The enemy content to sit inside the town walls and play it safe.

Relkin took grim encouragement. They had less than a thousand men and nine dragons, and the Aubinans were loath to attack. Meanwhile, each precious hour brought General Tregor closer, hurrying down the Argo Road.

When he got back to their bivouac, he passed on the news while the dragon devoured the snack. Relkin polished off half a loaf himself, along with several cups of soup. The food spread a warm, comfortable sensation through his body.

Bazil was soon snoring, lost in deep, dreamless sleep.

Relkin felt the warm comfortable feeling soak into his

tired bones, pulled his blanket out, and wrapped himself in it as he lay back against a tree. There would be no inspections on this day. Cuzo knew it would be pointless. Relkin was glad to find that Cuzo was catching on quickly. He was going to be a good dragon leader. And now they'd been blooded together in two hard fights with these new enemies. There would be a good spirit in the 109th again, even though they'd all miss big Churn and little Howt.

Still it felt good to have a dragon leader you could count on. Cuzo was definitely an improvement.

He settled himself and drifted off to sleep. His snores were soon combining with those of the dragon. The lull continued.

Throughout the wet woods the situation remained quiet. Urmin kept saying his prayers every few minutes. The Aubinans remained quiet. The Aubinan horse was still out on the Wheat Road, but there was no sign of an attack from that quarter either. The Aubinan foot inside Posila still made no effort to take the offensive, although after the fighting in the woods during the night, Urmin's small force was licking its wounds.

The hours crawled by through that afternoon. The sky remained clear, and the sun warmed the ground and dried out the shallow puddles. The Aubinan foot in Posila ignored the commands from Nellin that they attack. They'd seen those dragons out there; they weren't going to throw men up against them. You had to have troll and imps to take down dragons. Everybody knew that. The grandees down in Nellin would have to come up with something that could hold off those beasts before they'd waste their lives trying the impossible.

As a result, the dragons got in a sound sleep and so did their dragonboys.

Unfortunately for Relkin, sleep was soon punctured by a return to the strange dreaming that had disturbed him before. Again he had that sensation of feeling close to Eilsa, but of not being able to either see or touch her. She was in danger, of that he was certain. There were many dangers abroad; indeed, there was some ancient thing filled with malevolence that was trying to get at Relkin himself, tearing through a thousand sheets of cobweb with steel-clawed fingers to reach him. The eyes burned like points of red fire.

Then the dream changed to a dark landscape. Eilsa was at the edge of a precipice, and Relkin staggered on a muddy rock.

Something like a gigantic steel-legged insect was emerging from a scrub of black brush. Long pincers snapped toward Eilsa. She ran across a flat lawn that writhed in the warm evil wind. The thing behind them was giggling. Relkin ran, the evil wind stank of corruption and death. A huge house rose up ahead.

He stirred, shaken awake by the dragon. For a moment he stared into Bazil's huge eyes.

"Boy not happy in sleep."

The evil dream was gone.

"You can say that again."

Wearily he moved to sit up and take stock. This time the dream was etched on his memory. Even the way the thing had moved, so swift and fluid a motion, like a snake made of water.

"What wrong?"

"I keep having this dream about Eilsa."

The wyvern clacked his jaws a couple of times. Amused.

"That not unusual. Boy dream of fertilizing the eggs of Eilsa all the time."

"No, not like that. She's in danger. Something weird, some magic, I think."

The way Relkin said this, Bazil knew that he was no longer joking.

"This dragon not like to hear that word. We suffer every time."

"Too right, but something's happening, and I keep feeling these strange flashes when I see things. I don't know, Baz, I hope I'm not losing my mind. You know what happened in Mirchaz and everything."

Bazil studied him carefully. He understood something of what Relkin had gone through. It had reinforced his innate dislike of human magic. Boy had done well to stand up to it.

Of course, Bazil also remembered that strange, magical force that had brought him back from death. He was grateful to that being, whatever it was that had stood there so still and watchful.

"You seem the same Relkin, but who can see mind of dragonboy?"

"Who indeed? Not even this boy."

Relkin found sleep impossible now, so he pulled himself to his feet and wandered down the line to the latrines. On his way back he passed the thunderous snoring of the Purple Green, who had also been relieved from duty to catch up on sleep. Manuel wasn't around, probably at the cook fires.

He saw Curf running somewhere carrying a pack. Cuzo was still riding Curf pretty hard, trying to see if he would shake off that dreaminess. So far the boy had shown himself able to take it. Whether he could ever handle a dragon was another matter, though.

Then Relkin saw a familiar figure in officer's dress coming toward him. Captain Kesepton it was, and his face was set in a frown. Long before Kesepton reached him, Relkin had prepared himself for the worst.

"Relkin, I have bad news for you."

"What is it, sir?"

"The Lady sent me word. Eilsa Ranardaughter has been abducted and taken to Nellin."

Relkin shook his head. The dream! Hollein put a hand out to steady him.

"Nellin?"

"Yes. Lagdalen too. Snatched off Water Street in a rainstorm. It was Lagdalen they were after, but Eilsa tried to stop them and was taken too."

Relkin understood. Eilsa Ranardaughter would have been bound to throw herself into any fight that involved Lagdalen of the Tarcho.

"Why? Why would they want Lagdalen? Why Nellin?"

"Lagdalen kept the case against Porteous Glaves alive through to his conviction. That made her many enemies in Aubinas, particularly among the wealthy farmers of Nellin."

"What can they do to her?"

"That we don't know. They are gentlemen, so presumably they will not harm either of them. Eilsa is noble-born, the Wattels are an ancient clan. One can only hope that they will offer them nothing but respect."

But Relkin couldn't forget his dream.

"The new enemy, the one we aren't supposed to name, he is in Nellin, isn't he?"

"I do not know. You fought him it seems, or some demon that he employs."

"It was a demon all right, so strong and so fast. Stretched the dragon to his limits."

Hollein nodded, sobered by the thought.

"This enemy is foul, I sensed that last night very strongly," said Relkin in a quiet voice.

Hollein nodded with a thoughtful glance at the younger man.

Relkin pawed the ground with his foot feeling angry, but afraid. He thought of that elf-lord face and its soul-searing hate. He prayed that Eilsa would not end up in the hands of that enemy.

After a few uncomfortable moments, Hollein made his excuses and left. Relkin squatted down beside the softly snoring wyvern. The Purple Green's snores warbled from nearby, but Relkin didn't hear them.

Eilsa in the grip of that monster! He couldn't allow it. Her darling face framed in her wild, corn-gold hair floated in front of his mind's eye.

He sat there, leaning against the warm mass of the dragon and wondered what to do. Where were the gods now that he needed them? Was old Caymo paying attention?

He was still there when General Tregor came marching in just before dusk, raising a ragged cheer from the men in the woods. They were saved!

Behind the general came a thousand foot soldiers, two hundred horsemen, and a welcome surprise in the seven dragons of the 155th Marneri. This was a unit that had seen hard service recently at Axoxo. They were stationed in the Blue Hills for recuperation, but at the first news of the rebellion, their dragon leader, Yufa Dayn, had put them on the road for Posila. Tregor and his men had caught up to the dragons about forty miles north of Posila, coming down the Argon Road.

Tregor's men joined in the cheering, and the 155th dragons roared and woke up the sleeping members of the 109th who roared back, leaving the men in Posila in no doubt that their decision not to attack had been most wise. There were far more dragons out there than they'd seen before. It was a damned good thing they'd refused the demands from Nellin that they attack that day. The great night attack hadn't succeeded. Why did anyone think a day attack would do any better?

Urmin happily surrendered command to General Tregor, who listened to the descriptions of the night attack with widening eyes. Lessis had briefed him about a sorcerer that had taken up residence in Nellin, but he hadn't worried about it too much. Whatever it was, if it stayed in Nellin, then he needn't concern himself overmuch about it. The report about the swarm of bewks and the even newer things that they were calling "bewkmen" changed his mind.

Tregor and Urmin talked for a while, then Urmin went off to get some much needed sleep. Tregor studied the maps in the failing light and went over the scouting reports. The crushing weight of preserving the Argonath now rested on his shoulders. He could not afford to make any mistakes.

Commander Urmin, on the other hand, slept well for the first time in weeks.

In the lines, the two dragon units met up with much bellowing and slamming of bodies and tails in cheerful greeting. Among the older dragons there were friendships built up through previous campaigns. Younger dragons were soon welcomed into the circle. Then they sat down to eat, and a big boil-up was soon being rolled across to them, with everything lathered in akh.

As they ate, they discussed the situation: the march that had just been completed and the likelihood of more fighting. The loss of big Churn was mourned, and revenge was spoken of.

Later when every scrap of food was gone, the dragons broke up and headed for individual bivouacs. Bazil found the little glade he and Relkin were temporarily calling home. Relkin was just tying on his sandals. He was wearing a freecoat and had a pack waiting beside him.

Relkin was not the type to seek out extra duty.

"Boy volunteer for night watch?"

"No. Look, I have to tell you something. Hard news."

Bazil sat back on his huge haunches and listened while Relkin told him what had happened to Eilsa.

"So I have to go. It's wrong, I know it, but I can't leave her to that monster. Nobody else should do this, but I have to."

"And what happens to this dragon? You leave me behind?"

"It's up to you, what you do."

"This dragon comes with you, of course. Lagdalen dragonfriend, Eilsa dragonfriend, I not leave them."

"This is desertion, Baz. We'll be drummed out of the legions for this, no matter what happens."

"We take early retirement, then."

Relkin took heart from the dragon's cheerful acceptance of the hard road ahead of them.

Later, when big snores were shattering the peaceful night all around them, Bazil and Relkin rose silently and crept out of the lines. The southern flank was still resting on that deeply cut little valley, but there were more men there now. So they had to work their way back through the small army's position to the rear. Then they moved off to the south, across the upper part of that rocky little valley and into the woods beyond.

Chapter Fifty

Through the great house in the valley of the Running Deer went Faltus Wexenne, his voice a symphony of anxiety as he ordered, cajoled, and wheedled his servants to make them hurry. Haste was vital. The paintings had to be taken down and hidden. Later he would smuggle them away to one of his other properties elsewhere in Aubinas. For now let them be hidden carefully in the hayloft. It was dry, recently reroofed, and repaired throughout. It was away from the main house, and it was quite insignificant-looking. The monster would never notice it.

Wexenne fought off the formless dread that kept threatening to well up and paralyze him. It was essential to keep going, to stay active, and to retain the initiative. Still, there was this pit of dread in his stomach. He did not know how he was going to finesse this situation. Things had gotten badly out of hand. This ancient lord that he had allowed to penetrate Aubinas was no mere remnant of another time. Wexenne feared for his very life. This brought on such craven speculations as to whether he could successfully bargain for his own freedom, by handing over the young women.

The loss of his honor as a landed lord in Aubinas would be total, but if he was still alive and far away from Nellin, what would be lost? In the great scheme of things, what was the need to live down here in the countryside? His money was banked in Kadein. So what would he really lose?

His identity, said his conscience. He was Aubinas; Aubinas was he. How could he abandon the cause he had championed so long? He would have to live under cover, hidden by a new identity, afraid of discovery at any time, unless he forsook the Argonath and headed away to some far part of the world.

But then a vision of Porteous would rise up before him. He had only to think of Porteous to start to plan a departure to Kadein. And from Kadein to the ends of the world if necessary, anywhere that was out of the reach of this monster he had let into his life.

How gulled he'd been. He cursed himself for a fool. "Our master will bring you the assistance you need to make your dream of free Aubinas come true," they'd said, those greasy emissaries of the lord. And he'd bought it, especially after the incident in Blue Stone. They said the emperor had come within a hair's whisker of death. The door to Aubinas was then opened wide by an awestruck Wexenne. He now realized with a dreadful shock of self-realization that his hatred for the empire had made him stupid.

On the landings of the first floor, in the rooms facing west, were a series of charming pastoral scenes painted by Aupose in his early years. There were six of them, all painted in the Running Deer Valley, and each was valued at ten thousand gold pieces. They were taken down and packed up in thin crates, ferried out to the stables, and spirited up into the hayloft. Secrecy was the watchword. The servants of the house, loyalists all to the cause of Aubinas, took this to heart.

In the bedroom of the grand south apartment suite, there were two more major works by Ieff Hilarde, great battle scenes from Spargota and Jelm. They had to be carefully taken out and packed in hurriedly knocked-up crates. There were also some lovely minor works by such as Dowdly and Kenor Cherdaden. Everywhere Wexenne's eyes were cast, he saw more beauty, more jewels in his truly extensive collection of great art.

Then came the dreadful news that the young women had vanished. None dared say the word "escaped," but it hung there in the air. Fear and anger produced a shriek of anguish from Wexenne, who ran through the halls, pushing servants out of the way. In the orangery he stood, bewildered. The young women had climbed the drainpipes and broken through the glass roof. Wexenne, portly throughout life, couldn't imagine young ladies doing something like this. The ceiling was twenty feet high. The young women had even been bound at the wrist.

Now they were loose somewhere in the house. The house would be searched. They must be found, at once!

Wexenne staggered away. Found that Honoriste Aupose's *Sunberg* had still not been packed up because the case had been built six inches too short, and began screaming. Carpenters and hangers dropped everything and ran to attend him.

There were more than a dozen there when there came a grim interruption. A pair of Lapsor's brutal-looking creatures, the bewkmen, appeared from a lower floor. They wore black armor and carried swords and spears. Behind them came Kosoke, Lapsor's lackey.

"May I have a word with you, Wexenne?"

Faltus Wexenne stared at him, trembling a little, fighting down the urge to flee.

"Of course."

He stepped away from the huddle of craftsmen.

Kosoke murmured in his ear.

"The Lord Lapsor has returned, and wishes to interview the young women that were brought here for him."

"Ah, yes, well, please tell Lord Lapsor that I must review this situation most carefully. The laws of Aubinas do not allow for the wanton murder of young ladies of noble blood."

Kosoke gave no sign of being prepared to go away with such instructions.

"The Lord Lapsor insists that the young women be brought to him at once. His agents secured them in the first place; they are his."

Wexenne disliked Kosoke, and he particularly disliked this contempt for all men that was expressed over and over by these men who served Lapsor.

"Look, my friend, this is my house. The Lord Lapsor will have to wait while the Aubinan Council makes a decision."

Kosoke gave him a flat stare.

"The Lord Lapsor does not accept such replies."

"I'm afraid that he must, in this case."

"The Lord Lapsor has given me my orders," said Kosoke.

To Wexenne's horror, Kosoke turned to the huge pig-faced brutes and said something in a harsh-sounding language.

They pounced on Faltus Wexenne and lifted him off the ground with huge hands tucked under his arms and bore him away, as if he were no more than a young shoat. He saw the horrified looks on the faces of the workmen, and then he was out of the entrance and being lugged down the passageway to the main stairs, his feet barely touching the floor. The grip of the huge brutes was indescribably painful, and Wexenne was barely able to breathe. His thoughts were a whirl of panicky fears. This adventure was taking on a nightmarish aspect.

Down the stairs he went, too fast to even think of calling for help, with Kosoke trotting along behind. Wexenne contemplated pleading with Kosoke, and decided he would achieve nothing by it.

Then they passed through the entrance to the catacombs below, and those enormous bewk things loomed out of the dark. Wexenne realized at last just what an utter fool he had been.

The realization came a little late. He was whisked on into the bowels of the new kingdom here, the realm of the Lord Lapsor.

There were several rooms now, filled with the ghastly experiments on children that were so important to the elf mage. Wexenne tried not to look at the little faces in the glass booths. The sores and the lesions, the boils and pustules that covered their little pink skins.

Doors opened, and he was swung into the presence of the Lord Lapsor. The brutes released him, and he stumbled and went down on hands and knees. Painfully he regained his footing.

Not ten feet away Lapsor, heavily bandaged around the throat, was lying back on a raised couch covered in gold cloth. Wexenne recognized the couch at once, for it came from the front drawing room of Deer Lodge. Cold fury filled his veins. They were even daring to move the furniture around in his house without his permission!

For some reason this thought made him angrier than ever. For the moment his terror was forgotten.

"What is the meaning of this outrage!" he snapped as if he were addressing just another Aubinan magnate.

"Indeed," purred the wounded Lord Lapsor. "What is the meaning of your outrageous conduct, Wexenne? I took the trouble to secure a couple of young women for my work, and you have sequestered them from me! How dare you interfere in my study program!"

"You cannot use young noble women in this way. I cannot allow it. Nor can I allow your creatures the free run of my house. This outrageous seizure of my person is absolutely unacceptable."

"Oh, yes, so you think."

Lapsor nodded to Kosoke, who snarled something horrid to the creatures.

Huge hands were laid on Wexenne. He struck at them and received a lazy slap that almost knocked him headlong. His clothes were unceremoniously torn off his body, just ripped right off him, and he was thrust down on the floor and struck three times with a heavy whip.

His screams echoed in the room. Shocked, gasping, terrified, he stared up at the elf mage.

"You have brought this on yourself. Now, send me the young women as I demand."

Wexenne paled and shivered. There was a problem with that, unfortunately.

"I'm afraid I can't. They, um, escaped custody and are at large."

"What?" The anger that blazed from the elf lord eyes made Faltus Wexenne quail.

"They somehow escaped from the gallery, where they'd been confined. They will be found shortly. They can't have left the house."

"You had them, and you let them get away?" Lapsor raised himself onto one elbow, and gave him a look of such malice that Wexenne almost swooned.

Lapsor snapped his fingers and said something to Kosoke. Kosoke left and returned a few moments later with a group of men, naked, marked by the lash, and wearing new brass collars on their necks. The men, former servants of Wexenne, were carrying the great painting by Aupose, *Gates of Cunfshon*.

Faltus Wexenne felt the blood drain from his face.

The ancient lord spoke in a soft, velvety whisper now.

"This daub is your most treasured piece, yes? You will bring the young women to me by daybreak, or I will burn this thing to ashes."

Chapter Fifty-one

The absence of Bazil Broketail and Relkin was discovered in the middle of the night at the change of watch. Cuzo was informed after a few minutes of debate among the dragonboys. He took it quietly, though his eyes registered enormous shock. Then he sent Curf hotfoot with a message for General Tregor. Very shortly there came a visit to the 109th's lines by a group of junior officers. Then General Tregor himself roared up to see them in person.

No one had any idea why the famous pair had absconded. Tregor was left baffled and furious.

Meanwhile Hollein Kesepton was unable to sleep. Indeed, he'd been contemplating slipping away himself and heading into Nellin to find his wife. It would be the end of his career, but Lagdalen was down there somewhere and in danger. It was impossible to think of anything else. Moodily he poked at the embers of a small fire with the point of his knife.

Then he heard the news, which was electrifying, even if he'd half expected it, from the moment he'd passed the word to Relkin. Hollein was ordered to present himself at the command post. He found Tregor staring at a map under a dark lantern.

Hollein had heard pretty much all the story from the messenger. Relkin had clearly cracked under the pressure. Hell, Kesepton was close to cracking too. It was damnably hard to think of duty when the woman he loved more than anything in the world was a captive being taken further into danger every moment.

Tregor greeted him with a sharp denunciation of the absconded pair.

"Sir," Hollein drew himself up. "I wish to volunteer at

once to go after them and bring them back. I know them well, sir. We fought together at Tummuz Orgmeen."

That dread name floated there quietly for a moment.

"Ahem, yes, that is well-known to me, Captain. That's why I sent for you, in fact. I think they might listen to you. So take a couple of good men and go out and bring them in."

Just like that? Bring in a two-and-a-half-ton battledragon, who just happened to be the reigning champion with the sword?

"Yes, sir."

"We have the barest minimum force to do this job, Captain." Tregor was now grimly aware of all the problems that had worried poor Urmin to the bone. "To lose even a single dragon risks disaster."

"I'm certain there must be some very compelling reason for this dereliction of duty, sir."

"Sure there is, but still this is unacceptable. Those two have been in trouble again and again. I was one of those who doubted the boy's word in that killing up on the Argo a few years back. They absconded over that, if I recall correctly."

Hollein was tempted to blame the Purple Green, but thought better of it.

"They stood trial, sir. They were found innocent of murder."

"On the evidence of dragons, Captain. It did not sit well with the public."

"Yes, sir."

"They were involved in some other scandal quite recently, were they not? Something to do with gold they'd looted on the southern continent. Peculation and plundering, we can't have it."

"Yes, sir."

"Now this, absconding from duty. There'll have to be a court-martial, you understand."

"Sir."

"I know this is a famous dragon, but now we have a direct challenge to the chain of command. If every dragon behaved like this, we'd have no dragon force worthy of the name."

"Yes, sir."

Tregor vented his anger for a while longer, and then

Hollein was set free. He rode out at once with two troopers from the Talion 64th, Dricanter and Tegmann.

The dragon's tracks had already been followed down to the wash on the southern flank of the position. There they appeared to double back and work eastward to the rear of Tregor's force. Then they headed south again.

Hollein realized that the Broketail dragon wasn't trying to hide his tracks in the damp, soft ground, and it was easy to follow the trail on muddy lanes through the early dawn. The three horsemen traveled spread out, but within spyglass range, carefully working through the landscape ahead. There were enemy patrols around; they'd seen plenty of tracks earlier.

The dragon had gone on four feet, as they often did on a march, always heading southward. Through fields, down lanes, even on a logging trail through a woodlot filled with young trees. The fugitives had been moving fast as well. Hollein felt sure they wouldn't catch up before nightfall at the earliest.

The hours wore on, and Hollein struggled with himself. By now he was finding it hard to deny the thought of joining Relkin and Bazil and going on to find Lagdalen. His sense of duty to the army was part of the core of his being, but Lagdalen was the girl that had bewitched him, whom he loved more than any other, who was the mother of the baby girl he adored. Hollein Kesepton's inner core was made of rock, but that rock was taking a terrific pounding all that day as he rode southward through the lush lands of Lucule, with Nellin growing closer all the time.

While Captain Kesepton rode south, a heated conference was in progress in the lines of the 109th. Vlok, Alsebra, and the Purple Green, with Manuel, Jak, and Swane, were discussing the Purple Green's proposal that they all follow the Broketail and help him with whatever it was he had to do. The Broketail was in some kind of fix, that was obvious. The dragons of the 109th had better go and take care of this problem, before it got any worse. You could never tell what that Broketail dragon was going to get into.

The Purple Green's notions of obedience to legion rules and regulations were rudimentary, but Alsebra, and especially Vlok, had the innate conservatism of the wyvern dragon that had spent its life in the legion system. They found it hard to imagine taking off without permission and going outside the walls of discipline that had bound them all their lives.

"Purple Green is right when he say this enemy is evil," rumbled Vlok. "But can we leave position without weakening it?"

"They have 155th here."

"This dragon thinks the fighting here is over for now," said Alsebra.

"What is this enemy?"

"Same thing we fight in Quosh. Evil elf of some kind. I sense him, and I sense that we will be needed to destroy him."

Vlok and the others stared at Alsebra.

"Dragon sense?"

"Deep feeling, like when the red stars are high in sky."

"That settle it for this dragon," growled the Purple Green. "We go. Find the Broketail and kill this enemy."

Manuel, of course, was against the idea. Swane was for it, and Jak was not sure. Jak had been in a heap of trouble at various times in the past, and he wasn't sure he wanted more of that. On the other hand, Relkin was his friend, and the Broketail was a legend. The Purple Green was adamant in his usual vast, implacable way.

"We go south, like Captain Kesepton. The Broketail went south."

"That leads to Nellin," said Manuel. "Right into the heart of rebel country."

"If we're going to go, we'd better go soon. They already have a long lead on us."

When Alsebra said this, Jak looked up and found that he was ready to go. He'd already made his own decision. If Relkin needed help, then Jak would be there for him.

"They'll court-martial us, for sure, but we gotta go help them."

Jak was right about that, and everyone knew it.

Swane was ready, of course.

Alsebra had obviously made her decision. Vlok shook his head, deeply troubled.

"Not good to leave. Break rules."

"Yes. This hurts this dragon too." Alsebra clenched a huge green forehand into a clawed fist and waved it menacingly for a moment.

But it was the Broketail who needed their help. Their

decision was foreordained. The Purple Green even had a plan, such as it was.

"We will all be on first watch together. We leave then."

"There'll be no watch at all."

"We leave Curf to watch."

Alsebra hissed at this thought.

"That boy doesn't have even one-half brain."

"True," said the Purple Green, "but this is an emergency. Curf can raise the alarm if anything attacks."

"There's been one night attack. We only just beat them off that time."

"Even without us, there will be almost as many dragons as there were before the fight."

"It's wrong to do this," said Manuel, still troubled. The Purple Green grew snappish.

"Boy always say it is wrong. This time it is not. Listen to this dragon who has flown many skies and eaten prey on every mountain in the north."

Manuel was well used to the ways of the Purple Green, he was not intimidated.

"They will court-martial us, and we'll all end up in military prison."

"They not dare, we are 'Fighting 109th.' "

"Oh, of course," Manuel threw up his hands. His career was about to be destroyed, and there was nothing he could see to do to stop it. He groaned and sagged a little.

"Whatever those two are doing, it's bound to be trouble, big trouble. It always is."

"Very likely," said Alsebra.

"But it is them, isn't it, and we couldn't do anything but go," concluded Manuel.

That evening, after a big feed, the three dragons stood the first watch, spaced out sixty feet apart down the front of the position. The fires were dimmed, snores arose from the lines, the dragons became invisible in the great murk. At Jak's whistle they moved. Slipping quietly away, fading southward, climbing down into the streambed and up the other side, and moving on with the sometimes startling silence of which their kind was capable. All metal had been previously wrapped and tied down tight to avoid clinking and clanking. They were gone, and no one was aware of it.

Their disappearance wasn't noticed until hours later when Cuzo came through the lines and found nothing but

Curf, at the front position. Curf, who'd been humming out a tune and trying to come up with the best chords, had noticed nothing. He didn't even know the dragons were gone.

Cuzo nearly went berserk. He controlled himself, but he was clearly under a great strain. The urge to box Curf's ears was strong. Instead Curf was sent running with a fresh message for General Tregor.

Chapter Fifty-two

The roof of the great house of the Running Deer River was a world unto itself. The tiled parts faced outward, but in the center was a hidden plateau of copper plates that had rusted to a rich green.

Moving quickly, Lagdalen and Eilsa explored this fantastic landscape of gables and chimneys. They needed a hiding place and an escape route.

"How are we going to get out of here?" was Eilsa's first thought.

"Find a way down that won't be guarded. Sneak out in the dark."

"Hide until dark?"

"I suppose."

"They know we came up here."

The search would begin on the roof, no doubt.

"Then, we don't have much time."

They ran lightly across the roof scape, ducked through a canyon between six paired chimneys, and emerged onto a space lined with four water cisterns. From the tanks, pipes ran down into the house via sets of conduits and air shafts. Each tank was twenty feet long and six feet wide. At each corner pipes sank down air shafts and disappeared into the darkness. Lagdalen peered over and studied the nearest air shaft.

A man's shout brought her head up. Eilsa rose onto the balls of her feet.

"Back between the tanks," Lagdalen pointed down the width of green copper. They crouched there in the dark, ears keen for the slightest sound.

Soon they heard footsteps. Voices called back and forth.

Steps came closer. A man wearing riding clothes and boots in black leather came around the corner.

As he did, Lagdalen rose up and brought her mallet down on his head, and he flopped back into Eilsa's arms like a sack of grain. They laid him alongside the cistern and listened tensely, nerves taut, for a long half minute. Silence continued. The other man had gone on. They took the fallen man's short sword, a Padmasan-style blade, plus a long knife that he kept in his boot top. The knife had a poison runnel that zigzagged down one side of the blade. Lagdalen shuddered slightly and was very glad to find the poison cache, hidden in the pommel, empty.

They returned to the top of the nearest air shaft. It was no more than six feet square, and copper conduit and piping snaked down the walls, disappearing into complete darkness. There were no windows or lights from below.

"There must be some access, though, perhaps at the bottom, to allow for maintenance work," said Lagdalen.

"Down!" said Eilsa swinging a leg over.

Lagdalen nodded, there wasn't much choice. She climbed over and began the descent.

In fact, it was not that difficult a climb. There were handholds and footholds aplenty. But farther down the shaft, the air was dank and moldy, the pipes and conduits were clammy and slippery, and the dark was absolute. They had to make their way by touch and feel, which slowed them considerably.

Fortunately the pipes conformed to repetitive patterns. Brackets held them at every bend and junction, and offered regular footholds. They developed a technique, with Eilsa leading the way like the crag climber she was.

The top of the air shaft became no more than a patch of light high above, and then, at last, they stood on a flat surface once more at the bottom. In the dim light they could just make out a ventilation grille set into the wall. It was loose. Lagdalen pried it open, and they pulled it free and climbed through.

Inside, in total darkness, they followed a curved passage around a ninety-degree turn and then squeezed themselves through a narrow stretch. They came to a place where it widened again and dropped straight down for an unknowable depth. Lagdalen could feel her feet kicking over the empty space. There was warm air coming up.

Eilsa lay on her stomach and put her hand down to examine the wall of the chute. It was smooth, more copper plates welded perfectly together. Then on the other side she found a set of steps attached to the wall.

"Probably to let them clean it out if it ever got blocked," said Lagdalen.

Again they descended into darkness an unknown depth, but now the light from above was almost nonexistent. Still, the steps went on, one after the other. Lagdalen felt herself lost in some troubling dream, as if she were actually climbing down into hell.

At last Eilsa touched down on a hard surface. They had exited the air duct and climbed down to the floor of a narrow room, dimly lit by a red button on one wall. There was an unlocked door that they went through, and found themselves in a larger room, lit by another of the red buttons. The next door was locked, but not strongly, and Eilsa broke the lock with the sword and pried the door open.

They emerged into a much larger space. There was greenish light here that emanated from a farther passage, and though it was weak, it was enough to show them that the huge room was filled with long tables on which sat dozens of large, rectangular boxes. Odd little sounds, suckings, coughings, an occasional soft sigh, came from the boxes.

Lagdalen felt the hair on the back of her head rise. She kept the long knife extended in front of her as they made their way through the room.

What was this place?

Eilsa was leading the way on tiptoes, the sword held ready. The tables were built on a giant scale, coming up to their shoulders. The things on the tables were either cages or glass-fronted cabinets. Lagdalen couldn't see anything inside them, but there was a smell of urine and excrement, covered over with a sharp, stinging odor of chemicals.

They came to a doorway leading out into a dark passage. More dim green light came from its farther end about fifty feet away. After a nervous glance around them, they moved through it with quiet strides. At the far end was another chamber, like the first, only there was a brighter light at the far end. The structure doubled back on itself, the passage heading back the way they'd come through a parallel series of rooms, much like the others, filled with long tables, stacked with cabinets and pervaded by the disturbing smell.

The light in the next room was bright enough to pierce the gloom. The cabinet had something inside that moved weakly. Lagdalen shook at the sight of a face. It was a little girl, covered in pustules. She seemed to stare out of the glass with dull eyes, but gave no sign of seeing Lagdalen.

She was the same age as Laminna! Lagdalen's heart almost stopped.

There were children in these cabinets, dozens of them. Some were distorted horribly, tortured in the foulest ways. Others were merely dull-eyed, staring back at Lagdalen and Eilsa with no change of expression.

In the cages there were women, living like animals on straw and feeding from a bucket. These women were slack-jawed: unable to speak or make any response to their urgent questions. Most were pregnant.

Eilsa's face filled with anger.

"What is this devil's work?"

"This is the work of that enemy the Lady spoke of. These are the ways of the darkness. I have seen it before."

They grimaced in horror together.

Then Eilsa spun and pulled her down below the table.

"Ssh, someone comes."

They waited, and then after a few seconds Lagdalen heard a heavy tread. The double doors crashed open. They crouched low while four bewks entered the chamber carrying a bier upon their shoulders. They walked in step, slowly and solemnly. Lagdalen thought they had to be seven feet tall. And their faces were those of enormous pigs. She shuddered—here was a fresh horror to be unleashed on the world of Ryetelth.

The four huge brutes never looked aside from their path. They bore the long bier down the passage to a smaller room, standing by itself behind a massive door.

Impelled by unquenchable curiosity, the girls followed, hiding in the recessed doorways, and then slinking quickly to the next.

The door ahead swung open at the approach of the beast men. Green light flooded out of the room, throwing harsh shadows down the passage.

After their eyes adjusted, Lagdalen and Eilsa saw the four giants bear their burden into the room of light. A heavy sarcophagus stood in the center of the room. The brutes put down the bier and then lifted off the top of sarcophagus. Even for these brutes, this was a heavy burden. They then placed the bier within the sarcophagus. Then they replaced the heavy lid.

Two of the brutes then went to stand in front of the sarcophagus and stood there, watchful and awake. The other two moved back to the wall.

Lagdalen and Eilsa found a door that opened to a push and gave access to another corridor. They slipped away down this passage into the darkness.

Chapter Fifty-three

Relkin and Bazil saw that Nellin was a prosperous land as they moved westward through rich farm valleys, checkered with wheat fields. Whitewashed wooden houses were set back from the streams, usually under elms of considerable girth and antiquity. Barns were in good repair, as were the fences.

Seeing all this prosperity only made Relkin hungrier. He didn't want to think how hungry his dragon was, though Bazil was being heroic and quite uncomplaining. Relkin wondered how he was doing it. A famished wyvern was not normally a quiet presence.

After dark, Relkin decided, he would raid a chicken coop. These long whitewashed structures were everywhere. The flavorful chickens of Nellin were a famous part of the local diet, after all. Three or four plump pullets would stave off the worst hunger for the dragon, and provide a dragonboy with something too.

There was a risk, of course, but Relkin was confident of his abilities in this area. At dusk they crept toward an isolated farm, set well away from the nearest village. A pair of long chicken coops straddled the slope. The house was beyond a stone wall, so there was cover almost all the way to the coops.

They pitched up on a little rise under some poplars.

To their surprise, a young man appeared out of the shadows carrying a brace of rabbits over his shoulder. He gave a startled cry and jumped back, dropping his bow and quiver.

Relkin stepped forward instantly to reach the younger boy's side. The youth was in dragon-freeze. Relkin pinched his cheek and shook him to wake him out of it.

"That's an Imperial battledragon," said the boy in awe-struck tones.

Bazil loomed there in the darkness, huge and menacing.

"You're right," said Relkin.

"Golly, I never seen one before. They don't grow 'em around here. In Nellin, we grow wheat. Kind of boring."

"Pretty country."

"Yeah."

"What's your name?"

"I'm Garrel, what's yours?"

"I'm Relkin, this is Bazil."

"What are you doing around here?" said the boy, as if suddenly thunderstruck by the thought of just what he was talking to. Enemy troops, of the most dangerous kind, right here in Nellin!

"They've got my girl, some men from downriver of here. We're going to get her back."

"Oh, yeah, men from the Running Deer?"

"I think so."

"Yeah, they're hotheads down there. So you're going to go down there and get her?"

"Something like that, but we have a problem."

"Let me guess," said the kid with a grin. "You're hungry."

"Right first time."

"I heard that dragons are awful big eaters. That's why no one will grow one around here."

"Yeah, we're pretty hungry."

"And I bet you were looking at Uncle Silas's chicken coops when I come through here."

"How'd you guess?"

"Uncle Silas has two good dogs watching those coops. You'd never have stood a chance."

"Damn. What can we do about this, Garrel?"

"Hell, I'll get you some food. Have to be from the feed bins, though. Think you can manage on some oats? Maybe some syrup with it? I might be able to get you something better later, but not enough for the dragon."

Relkin put a finger to his lips.

"Not so loud . . ." No point in telling the wyvern more bad news than he had to know.

"Sorry." The boy sneaked a glance at the dragon, and found Bazil examining him with one big, intelligent eye.

Dragon-freeze almost came back, but Garrel swallowed, and it went away. "I'll do my best, see what I can find."

"Garrel, I want you to know that we will pay for everything we eat. After this is all over, I'll make sure of it. I swear by the old gods."

"The old gods? What are you, some kind of barbarian? No one goes by the old gods anymore."

"Some folks still honor them over in Blue Stone."

"Blue Stone? Is that where you're from? We have some relatives who live down that way. In Querc. I hear it's beautiful country."

"Sure is, but not as rich as Nellin."

"Well, not many places are. Soil here is just the best; everyone knows that."

Relkin was still a little unsure of the boy in this situation. This was rebel Nellin, perhaps this kid was just acting like this to get them to let him go unharmed. Soon as he was out of range, he'd be hollering that there was an enemy dragon out back.

"You know, one thing." Garrel was troubled by something. "I don't think my dad should know about this. He ain't too much in favor of the empire these days. They got him all excited with the rebellion."

Relkin felt a certain encouragement, the way Garrel said this.

"But not you, eh?"

"Nor my brother, 'cept they made him join the army and fight. He took our three best horses and rode off. We buried him about a week later."

"I'm sorry."

"Yeah, but it weren't any battle or anything. His horse bucked him. Got bit by a fly, and he broke his neck when he fell."

Relkin shook his head sadly. He'd seen far more than his share of deaths both glorious and banal. Both kinds had the same end result.

"Anyway," the kid went on, "I don't carry no grudge against the empire for the death of Ulmer. Lots of folk around here, they ain't so keen on this rebellion. Looks to us like it's all just so the big landowners can make a killing."

Relkin nodded, this kid had his head in the right place.

"Thanks to the Goddess then for letting us run into you, Garrel, and not your father."

"Heh, heh, yeah. Look, you wait here, and I'll go see what I can find for you. Why don't you give these rabbits to the dragon as a start."

"Many thanks, Garrel."

The boy slipped away up the lane to the house. Relkin and Bazil waited, tense and hungry, in the poplars. Could Garrel be trusted? Relkin prayed so. They didn't dare go any closer, for fear of arousing the dogs that guarded those tempting chicken coops.

Bazil hissed slowly through his teeth. He was beyond hungry, close to that uncomfortable frame of mind when he would start regarding everything as a potential meal, including youths, and even dragonboys. Relkin cleaned the rabbits and handed them to Bazil, who ate them in a couple of bites. They weren't much, but they were something.

They waited, wracked by their different demons. In the evening air they heard the comfortable sounds of the farm. A cow was calling from another field. A voice called out something, and there was a distant slam of a door. Relkin chewed his lip and listened very carefully.

Someone had started a fire; he smelled smoke. Must be getting ready to cook an evening meal. He imagined the farm family sitting down to a fine big dinner. Piles of pancakes, sausages, and roast chicken, washed down with kalut or thin beer. Relkin was salivating, just at the thought of it.

Out of the gathering dusk came Garrel, pushing a barrow loaded down with a pailful of oats stirred into boiling water. There was a jug filled with molasses.

"Here's a start," said the youth.

"Hey, this is great," said Relkin, scooping some hot oats up in his hand. They were barely cooked, but they were chewable, and the molasses was sweet and strong. Bazil gave a vast grunt, then went to work on the oats, leaving aside a small portion for Relkin.

It was only a few mouthfuls, but it was solid food, and the molasses spiked it well with sugar. Bazil chewed the stuff as well as dragons could with their predator dentition, a perennial problem for wyverns living within civilization.

Garrel reappeared ten minutes later with an armful of long, fresh loaves of bread, six in all.

"Some of these are a bit stale, I'm afraid."

Bazil ate them in a couple of minutes. Relkin grabbed half of one of the fresher loaves and enjoyed it enormously.

Garrel came back a third time, with some apples, some hard biscuits, and a shoulder of smoked pork.

"Thanks, Garrel. You've really done us a great service. I'll be back to pay you soon as I can, once this fighting is done."

"When you can, and be careful down there in the Running Deer. Folks down there are all hot keen on the rebellion. They'll surely turn you in."

Chapter Fifty-four

Ooutside Deer Lodge, in the rhododendron glade at the bottom of the long lawn stood the implacable, silent figure of Mirk. About fifty feet to his left was Wespern. Behind him, just a few feet, the Lady made magic.

Mirk, normally so impassive he seemed to lack emotions, was distinctly unhappy. It was the birds again. She had dozens of them back there, all with this weird look in their eyes. There were starlings, sparrows, thrushes, and even a shrike, all perched around her, watching and listening carefully. She was talking to a thrush in a language that sounded as if it belonged in the mouths of cats.

Mirk knew you had to expect this kind of thing from witches, but this was weirder than anything he'd been through before. The bird on her wrist was actually answering, chirping back in a decidedly conversational manner. The assassin shivered a little.

The sky was lightening from the east. The pall of clouds that had covered them for weeks was lifting. Mirk felt a sudden release from the sense of oppression that had hung over him almost as tangibly as the clouds above. Something had gone away, some strange force of nature that had lowered their spirits with every step they'd taken.

Wespern appeared out of the dark.

"Yes?" said the Lady.

"He has gone."

"Yes. But where?"

"I do not know."

The fact remained that he was gone, perhaps to some other realm. He was the Lord of Twelve Worlds, after all. Perhaps to sleep. Whatever it was, Lessis knew there would be no better opportunity to find the girls and get them out of this place.

She selected another bird, this time a wood thrush that had been hunting for snails along a nearby ditch. Thrushes were smart birds with considerable agility. She held the thrush gently in her hand and stroked its head while the bright eyes gazed helplessly back.

Lessis sang the quiet, but deadly, little magic of the language of cats, which was the key tongue for the capture of birds—though it was useful in many other areas as well. Perched here and there all around her were her gathering flock of spies-to-be. They watched the Queen of Birds with rapt attention.

Wespern and Mirk exchanged a look. Wespern was sensitive, but he knew no more of witchcraft than did Mirk.

"You tell me what you think she's up to," he muttered to the assassin.

Mirk shrugged.

Mirk wished he could move farther away himself. The little yowling noises had odd, but powerful, effects on one. Your skin crawled one moment, and then you felt this cold chill run through you as the hair rose on your neck. Mirk, however, would not move any farther away. He was her protection. He would stay within a knife throw of her at all times.

The cisterns were searched on the second pass over the roof, and the unconscious body of Bilgus was found. Faltus Wexenne questioned Bilgus himself when he'd been brought around. The search was intensified on the roof of the house and in the high floors. Still, no sign of the missing women had been found, and the hours were ticking by remorselessly.

There was an interruption when a group of black-uniformed riders thundered into the main yard. They brought Salva Gann, his face bloodied and his arms bound to his saddle pommel. Wexenne watched helplessly as a terrified Salva Gann was handed over to four of the huge bewkmen who marched him away into the house.

Dreadful screams had echoed hauntingly up from the catacombs for a while after that. Eventually silence fell. Wexenne and his servants returned to the task of finding those girls. They scrambled through every nook and cranny on the roofs and the upper floors.

There were sixty-four rooms in the main house, set up on three floors. Below that were three more levels: a basement, a subbasement, and cellars. The search moved down through the house methodically. Meanwhile trackers were working the grounds around the house, looking for any sign of flight.

And then quite suddenly they felt the presence lifted. That great oppressive power that had loomed over them was turned off. The air itself seemed lightened and refreshed.

Wexenne hurried down to the parlor to see what was left of Salva Gann. He found his erstwhile friend trussed up like a chicken, hanging upside down in a cage. The marks of the whip were all over him. Salva could not speak, his eyes were vacant, unseeing. Faltus Wexenne was left to tremble in his shoes. He'd been considering escape, just taking a string of good horses and riding out for freedom. He could reach Kadein in a week if he kept a good pace. Now he felt his heart flutter at the mere thought. Salva had tried to run, and they'd brought him back. For all Wexenne knew, poor Salva was destined to be dinner for the bewks.

And there were the paintings to consider. If Wexenne fled, there would be no one here to protect them. The monster might destroy them all, an irreparable desecration of art.

That threat to burn the *Gates of Cunfshon,* the masterpiece of masterpieces, had almost unhinged him. Such a threat was a blow to the wellspring of civilization itself, and something that could not be borne!

But then Wexenne's cup of bitterness already overflowed. Such galling humiliation, such pain and horror had been inflicted on him, Faltus Wexenne, Magnate of Champery, that it was almost beyond imagination! Things like being whipped like a dog were not supposed to happen to Faltus Wexenne, Magnate of Champery and leader of Aubinas!

He remembered the ignominy of those three terrible strokes of the whip. Never had he suffered pain like that. Never had anyone dared strike Faltus Wexenne since he'd left school, long ago. He shivered. He had been utterly helpless. Those brutes had simply torn his clothes off and beaten him. Lapsor had made him see his true position.

This knowledge was bad enough, then came the threat to the *Gates of Cunfshon.* Wexenne tottered on the precipice above insanity now. He could never allow the works of Aupose to be burned. He would have to do everything he possibly could to preserve them.

The girls must be found, for the painting had to be saved from destruction. But the house was huge, and the gardens extensive. The search would take time—and there wasn't much time. If those two young devils weren't captured soon, the monster would burn the *Gates of Cunfshon.* Wexenne felt his head close to bursting.

He glanced out the window. A thrush went bouncing by down the balcony. It looked back at him. It came back, sat up on the balustrade, and looked in the window at him. Then it hopped away again.

Wexenne shook his head. Everything was getting very strange. Now even the birds were looking at him like he'd gone mad. Maybe he had. Maybe this was just some terrible, terrible dream, and soon he'd wake up and be leading the glorious rebellion of Aubinas again. He would be in charge of his destiny, free, proud, and wealthy—a man destined for greatness. Anything but the terrified worm he had become.

Chapter Fifty-five

Birds in the service of the Queen of Birds were usually quick. Within twenty minutes Lessis had received a general picture of the house and its occupants. There were parties of men doing something to the walls in some rooms. Birds couldn't describe what it was exactly. Birds could only go so far in deciphering the things they saw in the world of men. Other men were busy on the roof. Some were letting down a rope into a narrow shaft.

Then came a finch, wings scissoring the air. It flew straight to Lessis and perched on her shoulder. It sang of the courtyards and the rooftops, then it sang of young women crouched down in a room filled with vegetables.

Lessis was certain the girls had been seen finally. Her hopes rose at the descriptive note added by the finch. One young woman had hair the color of ripe wheat, the other much darker.

And, by the sound of it, they were hiding in a scullery behind the main kitchens.

In the rest of the house it seemed, there were roaming parties of men. Lanterns were lit everywhere, and the place was like a huge anthill disturbed by the plow.

Lessis wasted no time. She sank down into a lotus position and placed herself in deep trance. There she concocted a spell of invisibility that would cover herself, Mirk, and Wespern. Such a spell would deceive any but the most discerning eye. In such magic there was perhaps no person alive with the skill of Lessis of Valmes. She finished the work within an astonishing thirty minutes. The effort was enormous, but the spell was first-rate. She came out of the trance drenched in sweat, and she felt a little unsteady as she got to her feet.

She told the finch to lead her back to this scullery—at once. Then she signaled to the others and uttered a few swift volumes. They heard something like the song of the whales or the howls of distant coyotes, and felt a sudden, short gust of wind that left them with a shiver.

Lessis urged them forward. The evening light was fading into dusk, and lights were coming on in the house.

"Now, into the house and find these girls. Then let's get out of here. We don't know how long we'll have before the enemy awakes, and we don't want to be here when he does."

Under the umbrella of witch magic, they moved out across the lawn. Mirk led the way, walking crouched over, eyes scanning the lawn and house as they approached. The witch said no one would see them, but Mirk found he didn't trust witch magic that far. He kept a hand near his throwing knives as he went, trying to present as small a target as possible.

The shout of alarm Mirk half expected never came, and then they were in among some ornamental shrubs and an herb garden that were set close by the house.

Lights moved constantly in the windows of the big house. Men shouted down from the rooftops. Others were lowering a lamp on a line down the outer wall at a spot where several gutters came together and the pipes ran down to the ground.

Lessis paused a moment there to examine the scene. The main house had entrances on three sides, but the northern side was hidden by a screen of poplars. Here the main kitchens, storehouses, and a stable projected across the grounds. The finch was waiting by the trees.

They slid through the poplars and went on down a straight gravel path to the courtyard behind the main kitchens. The two men guarding the entrance to the courtyard were engaged in an animated conversation and never looked up as Mirk, Lessis, and Wespern slipped quietly past them.

Mirk's appreciation of witch magic slid up another notch.

Inside, windows overlooked them on all sides. Washing was hanging here to dry.

A maid walked out with a pail of slops, which she tossed onto a midden piled up on a cobbled floor. The maid never noticed Mirk, though he was just twenty feet away and visible in the light from the kitchen windows.

The assassin grew more comfortable with the witch magic. That girl had looked right at him and saw nothing.

An old black dog woke up and then struggled to his feet with a coughing bark.

Lessis went straight up to the dog, took his head in her hands, and silenced him with a spell that turned dogs back into puppies, at least in their thoughts.

The old dog began to chase its tail, in somewhat arthritic fashion, and had no further thought for the three of them. The finch had come to rest above a low roof, where the sculleries projected out of the back of the main kitchen.

Lessis pointed to a door that offered easy access to the house.

Mirk went through, knife drawn, and found no one around, although they could hear voices calling somewhere farther in. A moment later they found the sacks of beets and the pile of turnips. Unfortunately the girls weren't there any longer.

Lessis sighed. Things were going to get more complicated.

Back among the rhododendrons, at the bottom of the long lawn, there was movement, very cautious movement made by something big. The careful eye could soon detect a huge bulk hunkered down among the bushes, a deeper shade among the shadows. Bazil Broketail came from a long line of predatory hunters, he could hide with the best of them.

Relkin crouched down beside the wyvern.

"Something's going on, that's for sure," said Relkin with a nod to the lights in the house and the men on the roof.

"Whatever men do, we in time to join the party."

Relkin looked at the dragon, who stared back with wyvern seriousness.

"Well, yes, I think you're right."

Voices suddenly echoed from their left. Men were searching the rhododendrons.

"Move!" And Relkin was in motion, cutting back into the bushes and away to the right. The wyvern followed, shifting his huge bulk with remarkably little noise.

The big house was abuzz. Relkin wondered what the hell was going on and if Eilsa and Lagdalen were involved. Somehow he felt sure that they were.

Chapter Fifty-six

At that moment, on the far side of the great house, up on the third floor, Lagdalen and Eilsa were running for their lives. Discovered during their disastrous attempt to sneak away from the house, they had been chased back inside. Now a group of imps, backed up by a pair of the enormous bewkmen, was on their heels.

Down a wide passage they went, ignoring the tasteful painting of lilies done by Aupose's great pupil Semere, their feet thudding on the parquet floor. Behind them came the pack.

At the end of the passage, they skidded into the end wall. Lagdalen cranked open a door, and they slipped through and slammed it shut just as the first imp arrived. The door shuddered under repeated blows as Eilsa reached up and shot a bolt home at the top.

They danced back from the door while they examined the room. It was a lavishly decorated salon. Heavy couches and wonderful rugs of a vibrant red were set out at one end. Windows looked out on an interior courtyard, one of the many such courts that broke up the interior of the huge house.

The door shook as one of the huge brutes slammed into it. It shook, but held.

"The window!" Eilsa ran to it.

They looked out. The courtyard was dark. There was ivy growing on the walls, climbing down would not be that difficult.

The door shook and shivered some more as huge bodies thudded into it.

"It's not going to keep them out for long."

Eilsa climbed over and started down, and Lagdalen quickly followed.

The door exploded inward in a cloud of dust. Two huge bewkmen struggled to get through at the same time. Immense limbs strained, and thick grunts came from their throats before they sorted themselves out and charged the open window.

Lagdalen was ten feet down and going strong by then. Eilsa was almost at the bottom.

There came a hoarse cry of rage. Lagdalen looked up. The pig-faced brutes were glaring over the edge at her. They screamed with hate and vanished. She redoubled her efforts.

Eilsa was down. Lagdalen jumped the last few feet and landed heavily. Sprawling on hands and knees, she sobbed for breath. From here they had to find a way out of the house. They had to get away from this mad place.

And then the doors to the courtyard burst open, and a dozen men with torches ran in. They gave a shout and sprang toward them.

Eilsa turned to fight. Lagdalen got to her feet, and readied the mallet in her right hand and the knife in her left.

The men rushed them, but one fellow reeled back from a mallet blow to the forehead. Another took a slash across chest and arm. A third squealed in pain as Eilsa cut him with the sword. Bemused, they stood back a moment.

Faltus Wexenne pushed through to face Lagdalen.

"Young ladies, I beg you to cease this unmannerly display. You must surrender. You have no choice in the matter. You have been selected, and therefore you must go. Otherwise he will burn the Aupose."

"Made you his lackey, has he?" hissed Lagdalen. "Sent you out to fetch him his victims?"

Wexenne threw up his hands.

"I don't have the time to be polite." He signaled to the men.

The men made play with ax handles and brooms. Lagdalen evaded for a minute or so, but then an ax handle took her legs out from under her, and those brooms came down and kept thudding into her as she rolled into a ball. Eilsa kept them off with the sword for a while but eventually was felled from behind by a baton across the back of the head. The one with the baton wanted to beat them further, but Wexenne forbade it.

"Enough!" snapped Wexenne. "Bring them, quickly!"

Wexenne gestured down a corridor. A door opened and closed behind them, just before the imps and bewkmen thundered past on their way to the courtyard.

Another door opened, and they entered the servants' stairwell. Quickly they descended to the butler's apartment, which was at the back of the house on the first floor. More doors were shut and bolted.

Lagdalen and Eilsa were shoved behind a table in the big kitchen. Wexenne sat on a wooden chair and sighed to himself. This was not the way things were supposed to be. As much as he felt the urge to gloat, the situation remained quite terrifying. Once he gave Lapsor these young women, what power could he continue to hold over the demon he'd let loose? With Lapsor he had no more power than a mouse with a cat.

"Believe me, I regret this most dreadfully, but I must save the painting."

"Which painting?"

"The *Gates of Cunfshon* itself. The monster will destroy it if I don't give you to him."

"And what will he do with us?"

"Ah, what indeed?" Wexenne scratched behind his ear. "This is something that it is best not to think about. I would advise that you try to live moment by moment."

Lagdalen saw that Wexenne understood his fate already. The proud cock-rebel of Aubinas was laid low. His honor and reputation were destroyed. Soon he would be nothing but a slave for the monster he had helped unleash.

"You know that you are doomed, Wexenne. You cannot save your painting collection; you cannot save your own life. What you have let loose will devour you from within until you are but a husk."

He flinched and threw up a hand.

"He will use you," she hissed, "and when he is done with you, he will cut your throat and toss you away."

With a sob in his throat, Wexenne nodded. He knew his fate was sealed. He'd known it since the moment he'd seen Salva Gann brought back. But somewhere in the process, he had found a new purpose for his own existence.

"I must save the paintings. I know the truth of what you

say, but my course is set. In the end they will kill me. I have seen it in my dreams. But I must save the works of Aupose. They must not be lost to the world."

She marveled a moment at the odd contradictions in Wexenne of Champery. Here he wished to serve nobly in the cause of great art, but to do it, he would trade two lives to save the jewel of his collection. It made her laugh bitterly to herself. Were they worth so much, she and Eilsa? Were they worthy of this honorable fate?

Was any painting worth a life? Or should it be read the other way around?

The door opened behind her. Lagdalen felt a familiar presence.

No! How? It was impossible.

A cool breeze seemed to blow through the room for a moment. It was almost as if a cloud had suddenly obscured the sun. A change had occurred. Wexenne had gone slack-faced. His eyes stared vacantly at nothing. His men were in a similar state of vacuity.

Then, with startling suddenness, Lessis and a pair of fierce men seemed to pop out of nowhere. Wexenne and his servants moved nary a muscle.

Lagdalen shook her head with disbelief.

"Come, children, we must leave quickly. My spell of invisibility is broken now."

Lagdalen took Eilsa's hand. The Highland girl was stunned into silence, but she responded quickly enough to Lagdalen's pull. They skipped quickly behind Lessis. The tall man with the pale hair ran ahead, and the other took up the rear.

They paused by the outer door. A handful of sentries were on duty, but that was all.

Lagdalen had to speak.

"Lady, we saw this enemy you speak of."

Lessis swung around.

"Saw him, child? How?"

The witch's calm grey eyes seemed to peer into her. Lagdalen suddenly felt the power of the Queen of Birds.

"There are extensive cellars below the house. They put him in a thing like a stone coffin, only very large."

"A sarcophagus?"

"It took four of those huge beasts to lift the lid off it."

"Yes? Go on."

"And they put him inside it and put the lid back on."

"When was this?"

"Not long ago. We had to hide for a while. Then we tried to get out of the house. That's when they spotted us."

"Could you find your way back there?"

"I think so. We took the servants' stairs to get out of the cellars."

"Describe this place and how it is guarded."

A desperate plan had blossomed suddenly in Lessis's thoughts.

Chapter Fifty-seven

The rhododendron grove grew in a fat crescent around the end of the long lawn. From one horn of the rhododendron crescent, there extended a series of shrubberies that ended with the tiered shrub-garden beside the house.

Bazil and Relkin crept through these shrubberies with all the stealth they could muster. Bazil hugged the ground, Relkin covered him with his bow, and they slithered close to the house.

They came up short at the end of the shrubberies. A flower bed and then a gravel walk about fifty feet wide lay between them and the western entrance. A pair of guards stood by the door talking to each other in animated tones and looked up toward the roof from which could be heard shouts and imprecations as the search parties continued their labors.

It seemed unlikely they could surprise these men. And once they were inside the house, the dragon would be vulnerable due to the confined space. Relkin didn't like it at all.

Shouts from farther up the gravel walk announced the arrival of a group of ten men, bearing torches and spears.

"Back," whispered Relkin.

The dragon was already in motion, slipping back beneath some ornamental pines. Relkin heard the approaching men shout to the guards at the door, "They've caught the women!"

The guards whistled and shouted. The men came up, and the group conversed in loud voices. Everyone was very much excited by the events of the night.

Relkin knew these women could be no one but Eilsa and Lagdalen.

"We have to do something fast," he said to the dragon. Bazil nodded.

"True. Question is, what?"

Relkin hushed him. There was a sound off to their left, not far at all. They waited, ears straining. There it came again, a muted clink.

Cautiously Relkin stole forward. Past an ancient poplar, the ground fell away into a defile that led to a gaping entrance dug into the ground. Heavy wooden gates were propped open in front. This tunnel was on a much larger scale than the doors to the house. It also led directly toward the house.

"More our sort of size, anyway. What do you think?"

"Dragon could wield sword in that."

"Well, in that case." They stood up and moved down into the pit that led to the tunnel mouth.

Two bewkmen were there to guard the entrance. At the sight of their grotesque features, Relkin was moved to feelings of disgust and something almost like pity. These creatures of the enemy, made so abundantly and so horribly, were given no choice in the matter. Once brought into existence, they were set to the work of evil.

The huge men turned at the sound of Bazil approaching downslope. With grunts of surprise, they took up enormous spears and readied themselves to meet the dragon. Relkin, running on swift feet from farther up the slope of the defile, was in position before they noticed him. His arrow was sticking straight through the cheeks of one of the brutes a moment later. It shrieked and pulled the arrow through with a rough jerk. Relkin readied another as Bazil drew Ecator.

An imp, which had been napping behind one of the propped-open gates, jumped up with a squeak of alarm and ran into the tunnel and out of sight.

The bewkmen lunged at Bazil with their long spears. He tried to knock the points aside with Ecator, but the bewkmen were quick enough to evade. Bazil retired a step, defending with Ecator, but forced into awkward maneuvers by the speed of the bewkmen's thrusts.

Relkin threw himself to the ground as the great sword whistled low. The bewkmen dodged back and then thrust forward again. Bazil attacked, and they withdrew a step, but lunged forward at him as he came to the end of his stroke. A spear grazed his chest.

Relkin's heart was in his mouth. His aim steadied, and he planted his arrow in the eye of the bewkman he had already wounded. It staggered back, still not dead, still trying to fight. Relkin was stunned at such brute persistence of life. Bazil took the opportunity, though, and Ecator cut the wounded one down a few moments later.

The remaining bewkman tried to throw his long spear, but before he could get his arm all the way back, Relkin spoiled his aim with an arrow that sank into his hoglike nose. Bazil knocked the spear up and ran its wielder through in the next moment.

The witch blade gave a soft gleam against the black of the tunnel.

Relkin had run ahead, hoping to nail that imp. He reached the tunnel mouth, knelt, and took aim. The imp was going hard. He released, but the shaft bounced off the imp's shoulder plate. He tried again, but missed completely. It was just too far.

"Imp is getting away!" said Bazil.

"Looks like it. Come on! We'll just have to arrive on its heels."

"What is this place?" groused Bazil, shifting into mode for running, bent over with the tail outstretched, sword held back on the shoulder.

"Don't know, but it goes toward the house. Must connect with the cellars."

They headed down the tunnel, moving at a lope. Ecator was still glowing slightly. Bazil felt the excitement in the blade. Their enemy was here, that much was certain.

Chapter Fifty-eight

Lagdalen and Eilsa led them to the laboratories. Lessis heard the soft cries and coughs of the dying children, and gave a sorrowful sigh. Such callous evil appalled her, but the enemy displayed this malice to all living things. The only thing she could do was to destroy him utterly, as quickly as possible. Lessis's jaw set hard while into her eyes came a pale fire.

They moved through the nightmarish rooms with their tables and cabinets of death. Even Mirk found tears in his eyes by the time they were halfway through these chambers of horror.

They emerged in the passage that led to the sarcophagus chamber. At the far end stood the two bewks that guarded the doors.

"Come," said Lessis, moving out into the passage. "These brutes will not see us."

Mirk glanced down the passage. He hoped she was correct. The brutes in question were formidable indeed.

"These are the things that Thorn spoke of?"

"Yes."

"Bewks?" It sounded like the noise given by a poisoned ox or something. Mirk hoped fervently that Lessis's magic would restrain them, since the creatures were almost the size of trolls, and apparently a lot smarter.

They moved down the wide passage, past the doors to the hellish chambers of torture, each one filled with a different class of victim. The bewks continued to ignore them until they came within twenty feet, then the brutes lifted their weapons and took up a defensive stance. Intelligent malevolence shone from their hoggish eyes.

Lessis calmly approached and stood right in front of

them, producing a swift spell that would freeze them in place. Slightly astonished, Mirk opened the immense doors to the chamber and pushed them open.

The two bewks inside responded at once, looming out of the dark at the rear of the chamber. Lessis planted herself in front of them, a slender reed set against these behemoths of muscle. She repeated her spell and threw it in their faces. As with the first pair, they stopped in mid-stride and remained frozen in place.

Lessis almost skipped on the spot. These things had one weakness: they were considerably easier to control than trolls. Trolls were resistant to witch magic.

Now they approached the massive stone sarcophagus. Lessis marveled at the size of this coffin for a giant, sculpted from white marble. Where had this thing come from? How had they smuggled it into the Argonath? Its simple, harsh design had the look of the work of Padmasa.

Perhaps it had come off the same ship that had brought these monstrous bewks and the army of imps that had almost assassinated the emperor. Lessis had to admit that the coasts were not as secure as they should be.

"The lid must weigh a ton or more," said Mirk.

"The four monsters lifted it off together," said Lagdalen.

"Ah, yes, let us see if we can get them to repeat that trick." Lessis turned back to the bewks, frozen in place by the door.

This would take a great effort of control, but it was the only way.

Lessis composed herself, dug deep for reserves of strength, and quickly recited the opening phrases of her spell. She ran off spellsay, formed volumes, and took the declension to its fullest. The work was swift and demanding. Sweat ran off her temples at the height of the spellsay. When she stopped, the bewks came out of the freeze and turned to regard her with those bright eyes. Captivated.

She had their full attention. She spoke the phrases of hypnosis and gentled them down smoothly, straight into a hypnotic coma. When she stopped and clapped her hands, they straightened up and then strode over to the sarcophagus and took hold of the lid. With a grunt of effort they lifted it off, carried it away, and set it down on the floor.

They stood up to the edge of the sarcophagus and looked within.

Lessis turned to Mirk.

"Now, Mirk, please slay our enemy."

Mirk sucked in a breath. Immediately one could see that this was not a mortal man. The form was manlike, but the body was seven feet tall. The frame was massive, but the flesh was that of a withered mummy, dried like wood. Silken garments lay loose around the seemingly dead thing.

Cradled in skeletal arms was a great sword, sheathed in a heavy scabbard, decorated in runes of death.

Even Mirk's skin was set to crawl by this fell sight. Lessis, however, felt her spirits soar. She could sense that there was no mind within the hulk. But it was not dead, not yet. The great enemy was absent, away on some fantastic mission of astral projection. His hulk was vulnerable.

"It lives, but it should not. Put your sword through its heart." Lessis pointed to the mummy's chest.

Mirk swung his leg over the edge of the sarcophagus.

At once Wespern yelped in pain and then shouted a warning.

"A trigger! He comes!"

Lessis whirled, her voice in a shriek.

"Slay him, Mirk!"

Mirk jumped into the sarcophagus. His sword was raised.

And the eyes in the withered head snapped open. Mirk felt, more than heard, the scream of rage and fear that exploded from the mummified head.

The assassin staggered, knocked back by the sheer power of the hate that welled up from those open eyes. In that moment Waakzaam the Great came back to life with an audible snap. His flesh took on vigor, and he rose up out of the sarcophagus.

By then Mirk had shaken off that disabling blast of hate. He swung his blade, but the massive scabbarded sword was flicked up in time to smack him sideways into the side of the sarcophagus. He dodged a punch that rocked the massive stone coffin. Waakzaam howled, and glass shattered in some of the rooms beyond.

Lessis's grip on the bewks was gone. The situation was lost. Mirk sprang headfirst out of the sarcophagus. The bewks came to life with sudden snarls, and their hands went to their sword hilts.

Lessis shouted, "Run!" as she threw a disabling spell into the face of the Dominator.

It was enough to buy them a moment.

Mirk barely evaded a bewk sword as he scrambled to his feet. A second swung at him, and he came even closer to losing his head.

He ducked, threw himself into a forward roll, and came up behind the bewks.

Wespern gave a choking cry as a bewk cut him in half with its big sword.

Mirk leapt on the back of the nearest bewk, seized the thick hair on its head, and sawed his sword across its throat, leaving it to collapse in a fountain of its own gore. Lessis and the young women were out the door and running swiftly down the passage, with Mirk close behind.

The remaining bewks were after them, shambling with surprising speed.

Lessis ran with her mind in a whirl. Disaster! But she had had to make the attempt. Not to try and kill the monster would have been reprehensible. It was just that he had rigged his sarcophagus to warn him in the event of someone entering it. That was something she should have anticipated. Perhaps Mirk should have thrust down with a spear.

They ran down the line of laboratory rooms and turned into a larger passage.

More bewks blocked their way, and from the other direction came a squad of six of the bewkmen with their strange piglike faces.

Lessis faced the unthinkable.

Chapter Fifty-nine

Relkin marveled at the scale of these underground tunnels in this strange subterranean realm. Huge rooms filled with tables and cabinets lined a long, straight passage that was at least fifty feet wide and high. His nose wrinkled at the acrid odor of human wastes. He looked around with a lot of questions forming in his mind, but there wasn't time to investigate these rooms, or the odd little noises he kept hearing.

They had drifted through two of the long rooms when they heard the distant clash of steel, then shouts and a deep roaring that Bazil and Relkin had only heard once before, at the Battle of Quosh. It was the sound of bewks.

More shouts, a woman's voice, high and frightened, followed by the sounds of heavy feet thundering toward them.

Double doors burst open up ahead, and Lagdalen, Eilsa, Lessis, and a man in dark costume came through with bewkmen and then actual bewks in pursuit.

More bewkmen emerged from another door. Lagdalen fell down as she stopped herself. Eilsa tripped over her and almost went down too. The bewkmen lurched forward.

Relkin knelt, aimed, and released in neat, fluid motion. A bewkman stumbled, hands clutching at his throat.

Bazil stormed past and slammed into the enemy, which uttered astonished snarls and shrieks. Bazil didn't give them much time to recover. Full tilt he crashed into them, Ecator's mass cleaving the space in front of him. Bewks ducked back, swords flailing. Bewkmen threw themselves flat. One who was too slow was cut in half.

Lessis, meanwhile, had bounced off the wall and darted past the bewks. She was, if anything, as astonished as the bewkmen.

Lagdalen and Eilsa were still backed against the wall by a ring of enemies. Mirk sprang in to distract them. Swords were raised against him as he tried to break the ring and free the girls.

Lessis, struggling to control her breathing, cast a crude spell of distraction. It came with a "pop" directly into the minds of everyone standing in the passage as if the air pressure had suddenly dropped in half. Chills and shivers ran up and down their spines. The spell was shoddy work: it took hold, but only for a moment.

In that moment Mirk had reached in, grabbed the young women, and started them running. They were out of the ring of enemies in a second, and Mirk danced backward in their wake, putting his blade between them and the foe.

The bewkmen came back to life with grunts of dismay. They shook their heads, raised their weapons, and sprang after them.

"Back, Baz!" yelled Relkin, dropping one more bewkman before taking to his heels. He was running low on arrows; there were just too many foes. Bazil was running to avoid getting speared.

Mirk killed an imp that got too close and drove back the bewkmen for a moment with the fury of his assault, but then he ran too.

A spear caromed off the wall near the dragon, then another.

Doors were thrown open ahead by Eilsa. Inside, Lessis was trying to ready another spell.

An arrow sank into Bazil's back, near the shoulder blade. He grunted and kept moving. Arrows were pinpricks. Spears were the deadly weapon for a wyvern without armor and shield.

But the thrice-damned imps were gaining, and the bewkmen weren't far behind. If he was speared, then the bewks would catch up and attack from all sides.

Desperation was taking hold in the dragon's heart, when there came a brilliant flash of bright green light. Suddenly the passage resounded to the thunder of hooves, and a great white horse clattered up. It bore a tall knight in shining armor. Imps scattered out of the way. The bewks and bewkmen stood back. The knight brought the horse to a halt and threw up his helm. Revealed was the steely perfection of features that marked the elven lords of antiquity.

Relkin noted that the huge horse had unpleasantly red eyes that seemed to glow like hot coals.

Bazil had turned to face the knight, but now the steel-clad figure raised a hand and uttered words of power that froze his minions in their places. From the greatest to the smallest, they stood there just like statues.

He spoke in a great voice, in the magical tongue Intharion, which was understood by all who heard it, no matter what they spoke themselves.

"Never can revenge have been so timely and so sweet." He drew his great sword, and it emitted a chill green glow.

"To arms, great worm! I, humble Waakzaam, I will take up the challenge. Will you fight me, one more time?"

Bazil motioned with the sword, Ecator was glowing hot, fairly singing with hatred.

"This dragon ready."

Relkin had only two shafts left. He took careful aim.

"No!" said the witch in a clear, sharp voice that cut through the space like a knife. She stepped forward to stand close to the dragon and raised her arms high and began to conjure, weaving slow movements of power, tracing the great signs.

"No?" boomed the armored elf knight. "No? Who is this that would stand between Waakzaam the humble and his prey?"

Lessis motioned to the air again, called out in the language of cats, and threw volumes in declension.

Instantly the sorcerer spat out a word of power and summoned blue fire that smote Lessis to the ground. A harsh chemical stench filled the air. Lessis's spell was shattered. She was pinned to the ground by an invisible hand.

Bazil moved quickly, a lunging stroke for the knight on his tall mount. The sorcerer pulled back, his mount screaming in rage. Ecator whistled forward and back, but the sorcerer retreated, the huge horse leaping under him. Now he raised his own sword.

"That witch won't bother us now. Prepare to taste my steel."

Bazil paid no attention.

But Waakzaam had noticed a movement in the corner of his eye. Relkin shifting silently into position off to one side, taking aim with that deadly little bow.

Relkin had learned from experience that sorcerers could be put off their stride by a well-placed arrow.

So had this sorcerer.

"You!" boomed the voice. "You again! Don't think I haven't noticed you, you little devil. I'll have you now." Relkin felt an immense pressure tighten around his mind. It closed like a fist seeking to wring his will out of him. He dug in his heels and resisted successfully. The pressure was pushed away.

There was a momentary shock, followed by disbelief, and then a furious renewal of the assault.

Relkin stood his ground, eyes staring, fighting for control of his mind. Forming a barrier to the clenching mental fingers of the enemy.

Bazil's roar-scream ended the test of strength as he went in with Ecator two-handed and broke the sorcerer's concentration, and then some. Ecator was giving off that fiery false glow again.

Waakzaam laughed madly at the sight of it.

"And you too, ancient one, you are here as well. Oh, how you hate me!"

Great blades clashed. Bazil, swinging two-handed, overpowered the sorcerer's arm and drove him to fall back, turning his huge mount so nimbly, you'd have thought it was a pony and not a warhorse of twenty hands. Bazil pivoted onto the back stroke and came back quickly enough to force further retreat. Waakzaam looked down on them with raging, almost insane eyes.

Lessis had regained her feet. Her voice was icy. "Hate you? Yes, we hate you. As do all who know you, Deceiver Waakzaam, Betrayer Waakzaam, Thief of Worlds. Wound to the Mother's side."

The armored super-knight retreated again. Bazil paused, not wishing to get any closer to the spear-wielding bewkmen just behind the foe.

"Who calls me by these feeble slurs? Some hag witch, impressed with her powers of plants and nursery? Some old scarecrow obsessed with the rights of humble things to live! Be careful, old witch, in my presence, lest I shrivel ye to dust. What do you know of Waakzaam's destiny? What did humble Waakzaam do to deserve the fate that was prescribed for him? To build the world, to make it lovely to walk upon, and then to die? How can this be called just?"

"It was your duty."

"Do not talk to me of duty, witch. I built the worlds. I embody the forces of the very matter of the universe. I have performed my duty. If I hadn't, this world would not exist."

"You were gifted as one of Seven Great Spirits. The others did their work and became as one with the world. You alone betrayed the great design. Worse, you then entered the design and ruined it for your own vanity."

"Vanity? Don't you understand that we're trapped in these shallow worlds? There are other planes of existence, the planes of magnificence and the abysmal. But there is no way to reach them. They are kept for the selfish few. We must find the way to escape from these petty low-level worlds. We shall ascend to the higher planes and enter unto the magnificence. It is not vanity to dream of this."

"How many lives have you sacrificed for your schemes? Billions, entire worlds, all for your selfish dreams."

"Bah, you understand nothing. Your little empire, your religious ecstasies, all of this is meaningless."

"Many people have been very happy under that system."

"Sheep. You must learn to smash through the deceits of this plane. It is nothing but illusion, don't you see? If you penetrate the illusion, you glimpse the higher planes at once."

"This I have done. I have seen the glorious planes of the High Ones. But I accept my place. This world is beautiful enough for Lessis born in Valmes."

"You have seen the glories?" Waakzaam was astounded.

"We are not unskilled in the arcane arts in my order."

"And you wish to remain a snail within this shell of a world?"

"I do. That is the Mother's purpose."

"Rubbish! You surrender to their game. You make yourself into the mud that pervades these dreary worlds. I shall transcend and take my rightful place. I am close now. My researches have led me to some interesting areas lately. Soon I shall break through and join them on the other side of the magical mirror."

"And how will they greet you, the great Sorcerer of Twelve Worlds?"

"It shall soon be thirteen, witch."

"How shall they greet you, Dominator of Thirteen Worlds, when they contemplate the little children that you murder so casually and so cruelly in these rooms all around us?"

"Bah, you allow raw sentiment to cloud your vision. The race of men has grown too numerous, can't you see? It is time their numbers were reduced. I am in the midst of great research. When I'm ready, we shall have a fine plague, or perhaps two. That will whittle them down quickly enough."

Lessis listened with horror. Plague! Not even the dreaded Enthraans of the Padmasan school of sorcery had ever contemplated this.

Relkin, on the other hand, had heard this callousness before, in ancient Mirchaz.

"I have seen your kind before," he growled, bringing up his bow. "And I have seen them taken out and burned alive in the streets by their former slaves. Beware, great lord, whoever you are, such a fate is not beyond you."

The knight pointed at Relkin with the sword in his hand.

"You! With your little arrow who made such torment for me. You shall be crushed first!"

Again the mental fingers descended around him and tried to squeeze him out of existence. It was almost as if a giant hand was actually pressing on his skull from both sides. Relkin had endured different styles of this torment before. He had learned ways to block. The best way seemed to raise a strength inside himself to counter the pressure. He barely held off the next thrust, but it ebbed at the last, and he pushed it away. The force tightened around him again for a few more seconds, but he still resisted, and finally he shrugged it off. It slipped, missing its grip. He was free of it. He took aim.

Waakzaam screamed with rage and frustration, then unleased another bolt of the blue fire. Relkin was knocked aside, and his shaft flew wide. Waakzaam urged his mount into a sudden charge at the dragon. Their swords rang together as Bazil moved to parry the first thrust. They came together again with a fiery clash of steel, until Bazil beat the knight by a split second and sent him flying from the back of his evil steed.

Relkin was shocked the next moment when the knight hit the ground and then bounced up unharmed. He realized that the knight's armor was imbued with magical power. Ecator's strike had been held.

Still, the Dominator was struggling to breathe after the shock of that blow. He called harshly to his fell horse.

The red-eyed steed charged, turned, and lashed at the

dragon with its hooves until Bazil smacked it hard with the tail, sending it staggering sideways.

Ecator was emitting a cry of triumph, high and tinny and only just audible to the dragon. Bazil grunted for silence. Triumph was far from assured in this situation, and in the meantime his right shoulder and hip were sore where that damned horse, or whatever it was, had kicked him. Bazil hoped that the Purple Green ate this particular horse someday.

Now on foot the tall knight came forward, eager to engage. Their swords rang together. In the first fight Bazil had fought with sword and shield. Now he had just the sword, but the two-handed grip gave him extra speed. Now he got in a full stroke that rocked Waakzaam back three paces. Bazil dipped and swung low on the backhand and forced the knight into a clumsy backward leap.

Out of range for the moment, Waakzaam regained his poise. Sword at the ready, he circled, looking for an opening against his giant opponent. He had noticed an unpleasant increase in the dragon's speed since their first encounter.

Relkin came back to full consciousness, rolled over, and crawled away. The dragon's tail hurtled low overhead, just as he'd expected. He stayed low, and the great sword flashed above just a moment later.

Then he jumped to his feet and sprinted back a few yards, where he spun around, ducked down on one knee, and took aim. He had one arrow left.

The tall knight was dodging back and forth in front of Bazil, looking for a way past the mighty sword. As Relkin came to his feet, Waakzaam gave a shout and lunged, Ecator parried his thrust, and the dragon lashed at the sorcerer with a foot tipped with claws.

Waakzaam used the magical shield of Granite just in time to stymie the smashing blow. But still, it rocked him back ten feet. Even he, the Dominator of Twelve Worlds, was impressed.

These great dragons were worthy foes of the mighty! That had been a test of the shield. With his laugh rolling before him and his malice filling the air, Waakzaam went in again. The swords met again in a flash of energies, and Waakzaam summoned the strength of the ground itself into him and tested his power against that of a full-grown battledragon.

For a moment they rocked there, irresistible force blocked by immovable object, then Baz smacked the knight over the head with his crooked old tail tip. The helmet spun around, and the sorcerer lost his grip and was thrust backward. Ecator came down in the overhand, but struck only the stone-flagged floor as the knight rolled away.

Bazil was off balance and had to dip away. He flashed his tail at the knight to distract him and then turned by the doors.

Waakzaam came at him again, and they checked and parried each other for a while there and neither could find an opening. Bazil tried kicks, but the magic shield deflected them. He tried tail slaps, but the knight was aware of them now.

Then Waakzaam sought to test his strength again. He locked swords and strove to bend the dragon back.

Bazil had the mass to absorb the sorcerer's pressure and then to overwhelm him. Waakzaam was forced back, almost folded to the ground, and recovered just in time to receive a hefty tail slap that knocked his helmet off his head.

The silver curls of the elven lords were exposed. Waakzaam was enraged, even afraid. He scrambled as Bazil swung the dragonsword and almost took his head. Waakzaam screamed the command to release his minions from their state of suspended animation.

With an audible hiss, they came alive. Spears were cast, but Bazil had dodged through the doors, which were slammed shut by Mirk and Lagdalen right in the faces of the bewkmen.

When they were shut, Lessis's spell of fundament took hold, and the doors took on the strength of steel. The bewkmen hurled themselves at them, but to no effect.

Inside the chamber of horrors, the small group got their breath back and began to ask questions.

"How?"

"Why?" and "What do we do now?" followed.

"Long story," said Relkin. "Now we've got to find a way out."

"How did you get in?" said Mirk.

"Big passage, with a gate out in the gardens."

"Where is this passage?"

"Out there. On the other side of these doors."

Chapter Sixty

Bazil found it hard to trust witch magic. Weird sounds and uncanny sensations to one's scale tips and talons were one thing. Doors were another. Doors were solid material things that could be shut and could be smashed open. He had to admit that the doors were holding, despite receiving a tremendous pounding by the enemy. Still, he wanted to shore them up further by shoving the long tables against the door lengthwise and propping them in place. There were eight tables, far more than necessary. He started clearing the cabinets from one table to another.

At which point he realized that the soft, sad sounds he'd been hearing ever since they'd entered this subterranean warren were coming from these cabinets. Since he'd already found them to be the source of the acrid stench, he examined the next cabinet more closely. Inside, to his surprise, was a little girl, wide-eyed, but silent, crouched in a corner on dirty straw.

Farther along the table he peered down into a cage and saw a pack of little boys. They squirmed like puppies and stared back at him with dull little eyes.

"What is this?"

Lessis stood beside him.

"Our foe does experiments on the children. He seeks to make a deadly plague that will annihilate the population of the world."

Bazil's big eyes dilated.

"By the fiery breath," he hissed. "This is one who deserve to die!"

The doors were suddenly shaken by a heavy blow. After a couple of seconds it was renewed.

"That's a ram," said Mirk, stating the obvious.

"Will the spell hold?"

Lessis spread her hands. "I don't know, dear Lagdalen. The enemy has greater powers than I, as he demonstrated so forcefully just now."

"Lady, are you all right? I feared for you."

"Just a little shaken, dear. As are we all." She smiled. "And yet we still live, and we have even secured your freedom. Let's look on the bright side."

"A good idea, Lady." Lagdalen was glad of her freedom, even if it looked as if it might be a temporary thing.

"And now, dears, we have to get these children out of this place."

They looked around them at the cabinets. There were so many.

"Right."

Eilsa pulled open a cabinet and helped out a girl of perhaps five years. The girl cried softly, but continuously from some mixture of relief and fear. Eilsa tried to comfort the little girl, but she was unable to make real contact. The little girl was tractable, but her mind was severely damaged.

The horror of the place bit into them more deeply than ever as they opened the cages and cabinets and liberated dozens more children. Soon they had a group of thirty. The children were not noisy. They were half-starved, and this kept them quiet and apathetic. Still, they did make little soft cries, some sobbing, some mumbling nonsense words to comfort themselves. The plagues tested on them had long burned out, but their suffering remained.

They gathered the children together in a group in the center of the room. The ram renewed its thudding at the door.

Speaking softly, but with her bright eyes peering deep into them, Lessis laid a spell across them that would boost their spirits and make them ready for an adventure. The children perked up. Lessis's personal magic was very effective with children. She informed them that they were going to take a journey now, away from this bad place.

That was enough for the children. They were ready to go.

Bazil piled up tables by the door.

At the far end of the experimental chambers, Eilsa and Mirk pried off the grille covering the air vent.

"This is the only way out now," explained Mirk.

"Some of the children will need help to climb the first

part," said Lagdalen. "But after that it's mostly level-going, and most of them will be able to walk upright."

"Better get started, then." Lessis started sorting the children out by how healthy they seemed to her in the dim light. The healthiest went first with Eilsa to explore the ventilation system and find a way to the outside world.

Behind them the doors shook at a regular beat. The ram was still at work.

Lagdalen led the next group, who were stupefied by hunger and mistreatment, but could walk and crawl. They began to climb into the air vent. The dull pounding continued.

Lessis went to the door, put her hands on it, and felt for her spell. Her mind softened and relaxed, and she let her field of perception flow outward. After a few moments she detected it, burning bright within the matrix of the door. It still held firm, although she could sense that it had been picked at, scratched, and torn by some other magic, intent on ripping it apart. Lessis's work was always neat, and this spell was tucked down tight with nary a gap that might be exploited. Still, all her work had a certain patina, a quality that marked it as hers. That gleam was badly eroded here. She withdrew.

This enemy had enormous powers in some areas, but was less omnipotent in others. That blue fire he employed like a club was a terrifying thing, but it was a matter of brute power. The art of unhinging a spell such as Lessis's on the door was a finer, subtler thing, and here he was deficient. Still, she knew he would not give up. Nor was this just another Enthraan of the Death Force, like the Masters in Padmasa. This was one of the Seven, closer to a god that a mere mortal.

In time the children were all lifted into the vent and moved up the shaft. Then they were led down the wider air passages by Eilsa. It was a pitch-dark world that had to be navigated by sound. The children, kept in near darkness for so long, took to this very easily.

When Mirk had carried and pushed the last few into the vent and helped the littler ones to climb to the ceiling level, Lessis turned to Relkin.

"We must go," she said softly.

"I will stay with the dragon."

Lessis looked into his eyes, and for a moment felt her spirit touched by something she saw there. He would never leave the dragon, any more than the dragon would ever leave him. A scapegrace in many ways, this brave young man. Always in trouble with the law for something or other. By the Hand, the first time she'd clapped eyes on him, he'd been stealing orchids from her neighbor's balcony on the tower in Marneri. Of course, even then he'd been doing it for his dragon.

And yet there was a pure and mysterious energy about him. The High Ones had selected him for their purposes. As a result, she had come to know him well and watched him grow, miraculously, from a scruffy youngster to the calm-eyed soldier before her. She remembered the box and the dragon chess piece.

What had he become? What had he been on his way to becoming?

And now, it would all be for naught. He would die beside his dragon.

"Don't let Eilsa come back," he said to her before turning back to the door, where the dragon was sprawled behind the stacked-up tables.

"By the fiery breath," Bazil muttered. "This dragon very hungry."

"Yeah, so is this dragonboy. Unfortunately we forgot to bring a hamper."

Lessis climbed the vent, with tears welling in her ancient eyes.

At the top of the first steep slope, she found level space. Mirk and the weakest children were just a little farther ahead. She raised her ring, and the stone illuminated the space with a faint light.

They went on into the air passages. The ventilation system lay directly above the network of big tunnels that had been driven into the green bank beneath Deer Lodge. By following the system they came to the trunk passage and thence to the spot, right above the gates, where the ventilation tunnel reached the outer sir. The passage was sealed with a barred grille. Beyond the bars was the slightly damp air of the night. The moon had risen, and the sky had cleared of clouds.

Mirk examined the bars.

"These are solidly set. We need the dragon's strength."

"Which we do not have," said Lessis.

Eilsa was examining the vent covering, and it was she who discovered the way out.

"It opens from the outside. There's a lock here."

Lessis put her hand out to the lock.

"It can be opened, but it will take time."

Mirk reached and examined it with his hands.

"Perhaps we can break it."

He went to work and found a way to put his sword into the lock and then get some leverage on its hasp. He heaved until sweat stood out on his forehead, and then at last the lock broke with a snap and the vent burst open and he fell out, clinging to the bars of the grating. For a moment he swung suspended over the drop past the great gates, which were firmly shut now that the lord was back in control of his lair.

Mirk scrambled back onto the stone ledge that ran across the top of the gates. They waited for a long, tense moment to see if the enemy would investigate. The gates remained shut. Their escape had kicked the great anthill into life. All the doors were now locked and watched. The air vent was the only way they could have gotten out, and no one seemed aware of it.

They emerged onto a narrow ledge that ran across right above the gate. Mirk explored the trees on the slope beyond. He came back and whistled softly. Now the children crawled across to him. He boosted them off into the bushes, where they were to lie low and be quiet.

This part of the gardens was given over to shrubs and ornamental rock gardens. There was plenty of good cover, even for a hundred or so children. At the end, getting the weakest children across went slowly, since they had to be carried. But at last it was done, the vent was replaced, and Eilsa crawled across.

She crouched beside Lessis and Lagdalen.

"Relkin didn't come. I have to go back."

"No, dear," whispered Lessis, with no pretense at sorcery. "You can't do that. He will stay with the dragon to the last. He is a dragoneer. You understand, I'm sure. Besides, we need you to help us save these children."

Eilsa looked into Lessis's eyes and felt her heart break.

"They will die in there."

"We must get these children to safety."

Eilsa fought for self-control. "Yes, of course," she managed after a moment or two.

Chapter Sixty-one

Across the dark lawns the children passed, some scampering, some hobbling, a few being carried. Lessis had a small boy on her back whose legs had been amputated. Lagdalen supported a girl, starved to emaciation. Mirk carried two boys, too weak to walk this fast themselves. Lessis's anger was like white-hot lava when she recalled the children they'd been forced to leave because they were too far gone. Lessis swore that this monster would pay. Somehow she would bring him down.

But it would not come from a frontal attack. Her brush with him had shown her that. He had powers that he sucked from the world itself. That blue flash had been a form of lightning, and thus she knew that this was the true lightning lord, and indeed one of the Seven.

They came to the edge of the rhododendron crescent. From behind them they could hear a bugle blowing in the house. Confused shouting followed.

"Time to be off," whispered Mirk.

Lessis nodded. "Absolutely."

Mirk led them along the edge of the rhododendron thicket and then across a short patch of lawn into a grove of ornamental pines. Beyond the pines lay a shrubbery. Cotoneasters were trained on trellises between hedges of yew and box. The box had been cut into the shape of hens and trees and the like. Now the fanciful creations of topiary made a fantastic background to a scene out of a nightmare, as the child slaves of the Dominator fled through it under the pale moonlight.

They came to another expanse of lawn. On the far side trees beckoned them to shelter. The gardens were coming to an end, and the woods were beginning. They made a quick head count and found that some of the children, seven in all, were missing.

"I'll go back," said Eilsa.

"No, child," Lessis began, but then realized that she needed Mirk to protect the children.

"It must be me, Lady." Their eyes met for a moment.

"We cannot wait here for long," said Lessis. The noise from the house had subsided, but torches had been briefly visible on a distant lawn. The hunt was definitely up for them.

Eilsa slipped away through the dappled moon shade and was gone.

Lessis kept her senses loose, relaxed, but alert. Mirk had explored the terrain on both sides of their position in the shrubs. Lagdalen stood there, as if she'd been carved in stone, her arms around two little boys that had been surgically connected at the hip. They were in great pain, but they had managed to keep up nevertheless.

Lessis prayed that Eilsa would be quick. Time wasted here was exceedingly precious. There were more parties of torchbearers leaving the big house. She dared to imagine that they might yet escape, but it would not be easy.

Moreover, she realized that is was essential that she survive to warn Ribela and the emperor about their foe. Ribela was correct in her identification of the threat. The empire's resources would have to be mobilized and kept ready. The Office of Unusual Insight would have to be strengthened. They faced a dreadful challenge, and they had to rise to it and win or else the world would become his, a wasteland crushed to dust by his urge to force his way into heaven.

How had Lord Waakzaam succumbed to this pitiless evil? In the beginning he had been great, but fair, most beautiful of mind and body, a giant in spirit, designed to infuse that spirit into the worlds and give them life. Instead he had withheld it to himself and refused his duty. He was not meant to dwell on this world. He was supposed to be a part of it.

So life had struggled into existence on its own and soon surrounded him in his solitary majesty. Standing amid the lesser beings of the worlds, he had inevitably taken to rulership. Absolute power had corrupted him, and he had descended into absolute vileness.

What thread had come loose in the tyrant's brain that he would stoop to the torture of children? For, while the children were not of his own rank in the world, they were its most precious fruit.

Her thoughts were shattered by a burst of noise from their right. Torchlight tinged the farthest shrubs with scarlet. Dark shapes were in motion there.

"We must leave," said Mirk, who had reappeared out of the shadows. They got the children to their feet and struck out across the lawn. They had to cross to the trees before they were seen. It would be a desperately close thing.

The sound of excited hounds arose. Then the harsh caws of imp soldiery.

"Dogs," said Lagdalen in dismay.

"Hurry!" said Mirk.

They spurred the children to make their best effort. Lagdalen carried three, two on her back clinging like monkeys, another in her arms. She knew that there were horses not too far away now. They could put the weaker children on the horses, and that would be a great help.

But there was no sign of Eilsa. Lessis shook her head with regret. First the dragon and Relkin, and now Eilsa Ranardaughter. These were heavy losses to a certain witch in her sixth century of existence.

She lingered in the shrubs long enough to cast a spell of confusion over the immediate area of their trail. By then the dogs were getting close. Then she followed the others, catching up to a little girl who was running out of breath halfway to the trees. Lessis picked up the girl without breaking stride and kept up her trot. It felt as if her heart were going to explode, but she kept up the pace. Lagdalen was just ahead, bent over under the two children on her back.

Behind them they could hear the hounds coming closer with terrifying rapidity. The little children could never outrun the hounds.

But at the edge of the shrubbery, the hounds ran into the spell. They went wild and circled, baying in ecstacy, as they took up the scent of the great rabbit from the sky.

Mirk and Lagdalen were helping the last children over the ditch and into the woods when the imps started screaming abuse at the dogs on the far side of the lawn. They looked back. Were they seen? The imps milled around in the dark. It seemed they had not been spotted.

Within the safety of the darkness beneath the trees, they let the children rest for a few minutes. They had a long way to go yet, before they could even begin to think they were safe.

Back across the lawn, men were now bellowing in deeper voices and striking the imps with heavy quirts to improve their performance.

"We must go on," said Mirk. "This would be a good time to gain a little ground."

"Right." If they were going to have any chance of escaping, they had to reach the horses. Eilsa had not returned, she was trapped over there somewhere with seven lost children. She would have to make her own way out. Lessis left a prayer for her.

They went on through the woods. It was hard to keep the children moving, but with Lessis's help they kept up a walking pace. Soon they had traversed this band of forest and were confronted by a road and fields beyond. A farmhouse stood on the nearest rise, stark white under the moon. For a few moments they examined this scene, plotting their course across the fields.

Just as they were preparing to cross the road, something flew down it, five feet off the ground, huge insectal eyes scanning its surroundings. It shot past them, and Lessis glimpsed a creature like a dog, with wings and the eyes of a huge insect. She shivered. It was nothing she had ever seen on Ryetelth. Some further monstrosity from the laboratories of the Dominator.

It flew by and disappeared while everyone lay flat, scarcely daring to breathe. Then to their horror, it swung around and came back. It had seen something, flew back up the road on leathery wings, and circled above them, uttering a triumphant cry that echoed across the fields.

Lessis reached out with a spell to try and disable it. It dropped from the air and crashed to the road, where it thrashed a few times, then bounced up and flapped away with a harsh squeal, streaking back up the lane. Lessis tried again, but it was too late, the creature was too swift. Lessis knew immediately that they were going to regret her failure.

Across the road and into the field they went. The horses

were tethered on the far side of the field, a distance of perhaps a third of a mile. The field had been left fallow that year. The furrows were gentle. They kept up the walking pace, though some of the children were lagging. Their slender reserves of strength were almost spent.

And there came shouts from behind them. Riders were in the lane, and more hounds were baying too.

Lessis turned and tried to set another spell of confusion, but the excited shouts among the riders confirmed that they had spotted the children.

Imps were coming at the run, with the hounds before them. There wasn't time for sorcery.

"Run, children, run for your lives," she said, and turned her powers to the children, kicking them into a mad dash for the trees.

The children responded with a crazed, desperate effort. Even on broken limbs, they ran flat out while Lessis, Mirk, and Lagdalen dropped back a little to put themselves between them and the oncoming riders.

An arrow flicked past, well wide. Behind the riders, imps were flooding out onto the field, a dozen torches flared. Dogs were streaming toward them across the furrows.

Lessis felt defeat approaching. They could never reach the trees in time. They could not protect the children from the dogs.

Another arrow flicked past. The riders were getting into range.

The first dogs were passing the riders. Lessis couldn't conjure swiftly enough to stop them now, and the dogs had the children in sight. Their barking grew high and excited, and then the baying began in earnest with the roaring and high yipping of the imps coming in behind. Mirk stopped and threw stones with a punishing accuracy. He struck his first dog in the chest, his second on the head, knocking it cold, and his third in the chest. The rest sheared off, looping around the fugitives.

Lessis stopped to throw a confusion spell, but even as she began, she knew she would not have time to finish it. The riders were bearing down. An imp with a lance was approaching, and behind it came more.

And then there came a high sharp cornet cry from the trees. An Argonath cornet, silvery and bright. Their heads whipped around.

Under the trees huge bulky shapes suddenly moved out of concealment. A wooden fence splintered under huge feet, and then moonlight glinted off big helmets and shields.

Lessis gaped. Battledragons, an entire squadron from the look of it!

The enemy riders had pulled up, amazed at these terrifying apparitions that were marching out of the trees. They called out to each other in consternation. One of them began blowing a horn.

That provoked a great roar-scream from one of the advancing monsters, and Lessis realized it had to be the wild dragon, the Purple Green himself. She wanted to laugh and cry at the same time. The 109th Marneri were there!

The riders pulled back, the imps came up in a dense mass. The hounds were running around like berserk things, but after one or two came too close to the dragons and perished, the rest steered clear.

Dragonboys advanced behind the dragons, bows ready to give covering fire.

The imps were not under the influence of the black drink. They stood there irresolute for a few moments, but as the dragons came closer, the riders rode back through the imps and formed a line behind them. The imps were between the riders and the dragons. The imps started to move back at once.

The men cursed the imps and struck them with their heavy quirts, but the imps ran anyway. Soon the men were forced to turn their terrified mounts and run ahead of the imps while the dragons came on behind them.

A dragonboy appeared out of the dark, flushed and breathing hard.

"Lady! I am Manuel of the 109th Marneri. We recognized you, and the Lady Lagdalen."

"And I recognize you, Manuel. I just saw the Purple Green with my own eyes. What a sight! We thank you, for you have saved all our lives. Your unit is making this a habit!"

"It was the dragons, Lady. They insisted we come here. They've been tracking the Broketail all the way. They just knew to come here."

"Ah." Lessis nodded. The mysteries of the dragon mind were exposed again.

"Captain Kesepton is here too."

"What?" said Lagdalen.

The next moment Hollein was there, and Lagdalen leapt into his arms with a glad cry.

"Lady?" said Manuel.

"Yes, child."

"Have you seen the Broketail dragon, by any chance?"

Lessis sighed unhappily.

"Yes. They saved us from certain capture and death. Alas, they are trapped in the labyrinth beneath the big house."

"Can you show us how to reach them?"

Lessis stared at the youth. Was he serious? Then she reflected, with the 109th Fighting Marneri at your side, you could go almost anywhere.

"Yes, I can."

Her eyes fell on a hobbling child.

"But first we must hide these children. They were captives of the enemy. We must try and get them to safety."

Manuel and Kesepton whistled to the others. Soon the children were placed among the trees and told to huddle together for warmth. Lagdalen and Hollein remained with them, along with the two Talion men, Dricanter and Tegmann. Lessis and Mirk accompanied Manuel and headed off in the wake of the wyverns.

They came across the remains of a few men, horses, and imps at a point where the lane narrowed between two banks of trees, and the dragons had caught up with the riders.

Then they retraced their steps over the lawns and shrubberies to the big house, which was still ablaze with lights. At the entrance to the underground lair of the Dominator, they found the gates closed and a sense of watchfulness in the air.

The dragons were hidden just out of sight of the gates when Lessis and Mirk arrived. The gates were stoutly built. They would not fall easily, even to a squadron of battledragons.

"How are we going to get in?" said Mirk.

"The Purple Green thinks he has the answer," responded Manuel.

A few moments later the big dragon reappeared, a vast dark mass moving on two legs. He carried over his shoulder a marble statue of Faltus Wexenne. It was an imposing piece, twice life-size and carved in the finest marble. It showed Wexenne as the great thinker, sitting on a tall chair. It was the work of Chatook, the leading sculptor of Aubinas.

The dragon set the heavy statue down with a deep groan of effort.

"What are you going to do with that?" said his dragonboy.

"By the fiery breath, what do you think? Break gates."

Chapter Sixty-two

Bazil was the first to notice the change. The ram had ceased.

"Ram!"

Relkin looked up from his efforts to repair an arrow.

"Stopped."

There was a strange tension in the air. Relkin sensed magical powers at work. Icy fingers scraped down distant walls of glass, he felt his eyes tearing for no reason.

"He's out there; I can feel him."

The tension built slowly, as if a thunderstorm were gathering. Relkin felt increasingly oppressed as it ratcheted up a hidden scale. Both he and Bazil were standing now, watching the doors intently.

There began a hum, and a vibration built up in the room that rattled their teeth and seemed to shake right through their skulls. The hum continued, getting louder if anything. A light gleamed beneath the door, then flashed up through the center and spread across at the top. It vanished with a sharp crack, and they were left with a harsh chemical smell.

The hum returned, grew loud, and continued. Now the material of the door itself began to glow softly while the tension in the air grew. When it was quite unbearable, there was a rupture of some kind and a flash of brilliant green light.

Relkin knew at once that the doors were no longer protected by Lessis's powerful spell of fundament.

There was a harsh cry on the far side of the doors, and the ram began again. The doors shook, and a panel split from side to side. A triumphant guttural roar broke out. On the next stroke the ram burst that panel inward. Axes and picks were at work, widening the gap, tearing out the centerpiece. Imps were thrusting themselves through, their eyes blazing with the black drink. The bewkmen behind them were baying like dogs.

Bazil stepped forward and swung a bench two-handed to swat the imps that got through. Relkin found a bow and a quiver full of arrows on one swatted imp's body. Staying low, he scuttled back while the huge bench went whirling by just inches overhead and slapped a pair of bewkmen back through the hole in the doors.

Imp arrows had to be cut down to fit his Cunfshon bow, so he turned to the imp bow instead, a simple bow, short on range, but easy to use. At once he put an arrow into an imp trying to get through the door. It was trodden down from behind by a bewk, which burst the doors apart and tumbled in. It barely regained its balance before Bazil walloped it with the bench, and it staggered back out the doors. Two more took its place. He slammed them with the table too, but they rode it out behind their shields. Their swords glittered.

Bazil pulled back, grabbed the bench by two of its legs, and drove forward, catching the bewks' shields and propelling them back by brute strength until they crashed through the ruins of the doors.

Arrows studded Baz's hide for that, but the bewks were a little slow getting up.

Bazil grunted with an obscure satisfaction. These things weren't as tough as that damned horror he'd fought in Mirchaz. Thing like a giant carrot, with rubber flesh and a strong sword arm, almost unkillable. No, these beasties weren't that tough.

His thoughts were cut off by a sudden flash of that damned green light. With the light came that hateful figure in the suit of armor. It raised a hand and froze its minions in place.

Bazil wasn't inclined to mince words with this sorcerer any further. He slammed the table down with all his might.

The knight took the blow and was hurled back several paces, but unharmed. He gave a great bray of laughter.

"Behold the shield of Waakzaam! This is a shield of Granite, foolish wyvern!"

He dodged forward, Bazil swung and missed and could not recover quickly enough to do more than hold up the bench as a shield. The great knight cut through part of the bench with his first stroke. Bazil drew Ecator just in time, as the bench was smashed in the next moment.

Relkin peppered the knight with arrows, aiming always for the eye slits in that armored head, but the magic was strong and all arrows ricocheted away.

The knight struck for Bazil's belly, but the wyvern had his sword there in time. The parry sent off huge sparks. Bazil exerted himself and heaved forward.

The knight was thrust back. He raised a hand and hurled a blue-white bolt of fire directly into Bazil's face.

Bazil was blinded momentarily, but training and instinct kept him moving. He jerked back, stumbled, then steadied himself with the sword at the ready. There were spots in front of his eyes, his head rang as if he'd been kicked by a mule, but he could see just enough to fight.

The knight came on with a shriek of cold triumph, certain that he had mastered the wyvern. He swung, but found himself checked once more by Ecator, which gave out a tiny scream of hatred.

Waakzaam's attention was deflected by this minute noise for a moment too long. Bazil's hand caught the side of his helmet with a heavy slap.

He staggered back, the dragonsword flashed around and broke the knight's fell blade in a flash of flame. Ecator screamed again, this time in triumph. Waakzaam gave a peculiar groan of frustration and impotent rage, and lurched backward, but not far enough. A moment later he was driven hard by a backhand from the dragon and went back through the door, arms pinwheeling for balance. He slammed up against a bewk and bowled it over.

Arrows flicked in and began to find the target on Bazil. Relkin kept up a steady rate of return fire, but his arrow stock ran low. Bazil lifted a table as a shelter from the arrows. They waited for the end.

It did not come. Instead the lull continued. They stared at the ruined doors, and the imps at the door continued to shoot at them. Relkin soon had plenty of arrows, and he started shooting back.

While he shot, he tried to think of some way out of this trap, but it seemed they were finally done for. At the back there was only the air vent, which was way too small for a dragon. Nor could they conceivably charge the enemy and hope to break through. There were just too many of them, and Bazil would die speared.

Suddenly there came a horn blast, and Waakzaam appeared at the door, bewkmen stepping in around him in a protective circle.

Relkin's heart skipped a beat.

The sorcerer held Eilsa at his side. Her face was bloody, her clothes ripped. She had put up a hell of a fight, but now she was chained by the neck, and Waakzaam held the chain. He tugged hard and forced her forward onto her knees.

"Well, well, look what we found!" There was a tone of malicious glee in the giant knight's voice.

Relkin swung up the bow, but Waakzaam's knife was pressed against the back of her neck.

"Do that and she dies."

Relkin could not shoot. Bazil stood back. The imps were getting fired up again for another attack.

"You will have to surrender. You will make superb experimental specimens. I have much to learn. Perhaps I should breed dragons of my own. They are remarkable beasts."

"Dragon never kill for such as you," growled Bazil.

"I don't know, perhaps with the right education they might."

Eilsa looked up, her eyes cleared at the sight of the dragon and his boy.

"Relkin, kill this thing, no matter what he might do to me."

"Hah! Foolish wench!"

The sorcerer made a fist and projected a bolt of blue-white energy at Relkin that knocked him off his feet.

Bazil looked for a chance to wield Ecator, but the sorcerer was holding Eilsa out in front of him by the scruff of her neck.

"Go ahead, kill his love, break his heart, great worm!"

"Put her down and take up the sword. This dragon fight you to the end."

"Oh, I'm sure you would. You are a creature of enormous heart. But I've had enough of this fight. I'm just going to order you to be speared if you don't surrender."

Bazil had just enough room to swing the sword. He waited, sword poised in both hands for a killing blow. Relkin rolled over and crawled out of range, still shaking his head after receiving that bolt of energy. There were spots in front of his eyes and a roaring sound in his ears, but he kept his grip on the bow. When he was behind the dragon, he pulled himself back together, pulled another arrow, and took aim. He was feeling a little wobbly, but his strength was returning. The sorcerer glared at them.

"Very well, I can't be bothered with you anymore." He raised a hand to unleash his minions.

At which point they all noticed something different in the air. A kind of rumble, a low vibration. It grew louder. Suddenly there was a shockingly loud scream, and then came the sound of doors somewhere being smashed to pieces very quickly. More shouts and a distant clattering. A few moments passed, and there came a roar-scream of shattering power.

Bazil and Relkin looked to each other with wonder in their eyes.

They knew the perpetrator of that particular noise.

"How?"

"Who care how?"

Bazil roared back, and there came a chorus of roars from beyond and an immediate sound of battle. Tremendous blows were being delivered. Screams and roars became indistinguishable above the clatter of weapons.

The sorcerer hesitated a moment, and then pulled Eilsa behind him and summoned his mount. The steed knelt, and he climbed into the saddle, hauling Eilsa up behind him.

Relkin sprang forward, dodged a bewkman's blade, rolled under another swinging sword, and scrambled up through the ruins of the door. The steed was accelerating to a gallop down the passageway.

Meanwhile in the other direction all hell had broken loose. Down the wide passage came dragons, the whole 109th Fighting Marneri from what he could see, with the Purple Green in the lead.

Ahead of them fled a mass of men, imps, and bewkmen.

And far ahead of it all sprang the great white steed.

Relkin didn't hesitate, but simply joined the rout of men and imps that was already in full flight down the passage. Behind lumbered the Purple Green and behind him was everyone else. The huge passage had suddenly become very full. Relkin reminded himself not to trip and fall. The dragons wouldn't be too choosy about what they stepped on in a situation like this.

The passage split in two. To the right were lights and a line of guards. To the left was dim light and a strange, earthy smell. Relkin sensed that the knight had gone to the left and took that passage. He immediately found himself alone. The imps and everyone else were running to the right.

He shrugged. He knew the enemy had passed this way. He ran on and emerged into a large chamber. A tiny spark of hot blue energy blazed in the center of the high ceiling, and lit the place with an eldritch glow around every edge.

Here grew a forest of plants with wide, round leaves and thick bulbous stems. Things that looked like enormous melons were spaced out around the room. Through the melons ran a path. Relkin felt certain that his foe lay nearby. He didn't know how or why, but he was damned certain he could sense the Dominator.

The path led to a stoutly build door guarded by a bewkman with spear and shield. Relkin noticed with a thrill of unease that the melon things were actually carnivorous pods, and they were feeding on men. Several men half-devoured, projected from the pods, some feetfirst, some headfirst. A few moved weakly.

Relkin got within range, knelt down, and took aim. The guard charged him. He released and his first arrow nicked the side of the bewkman's cheek, but bounced off the helmet. The critter was still coming. Relkin fumbled another arrow out, drew, and took careful aim. It wasn't his crossbow, of course, but he practiced with simple bows of all styles. It was just a matter of ignoring the huge, hog-faced brute that was a second or so away and aim. A miss now was likely to be fatal.

This release found its target. The guard pulled up all of a sudden and toppled over with the arrow through the eye. Relkin dodged out of the way.

Back on his feet, he ran to the door. An iron ring controlled the mechanism. He reached up to turn it and grasped hold.

Abruptly his hand was gripped by the iron, pulled in close to the metal, and then pulled in harder yet. Heat began to seep up from the iron, that heat intensifying quickly. He tried to pull his hand free, but found it glued to the iron. He got both feet up on the door, heaved till the veins throbbed in his temples and his arm turned numb, but could not pull it free. The heat was rising now into the discomfort level, soon it was extreme.

With his feet back on the ground, he tried to study the situation, while the heat rose to the unbearable level. He was close to screaming. It felt as if his hand was wrapped around a red-hot piece of steel.

"Open the door," whispered a voice in his ear.

He took hold of the iron with his other hand, and felt that too sucked in tight against the burning hot metal. While a shriek fled from his lips, he yanked down hard on the iron ring, turned it, and the door swung open.

The spell was broken, and his hands fell free. He stumbled through, tripping and falling onto his hands and knees. He put out his palms to absorb the shock and was amazed to find that they did. What should have been crisped flesh and smoking bones were unharmed.

Relkin made a note to think carefully before touching anything else while he was down here in this gloomy labyrinth.

He entered a curving gallery, with doors on the right-hand wall that opened into rooms which appeared to be filled with stores. He picked up his pace and ran.

At the end of the gallery was a final room, and here he found the white steed. He skidded to a halt in front of it, and it rose up from a crouch with a venomous hiss. Relkin darted a few steps back, notched an arrow, and brought up the bow. The huge white horse sprang forward, reared, and flailed at him with those immense, steel-tipped hooves. He shot for the eye and missed, his arrow going clean past the brute's head. The hooves swept past less than an inch from his nose.

He ran for it, dropping the bow and drawing his sword. The hall came to an end, and he skidded to a stop. The steed was on him. It reared up to crush him, and he drove his sword into its belly.

It gave a scream, and its eyes flashed red fire. Relkin was knocked to the ground, getting back to his feet just in time to save himself from those hooves, and he raked the sword across its face. Again it rose up to crush him, and he leapt in and thrust home with the sword once more, this time into the chest cavity. The beast screamed, then gurgled suddenly on black blood, toppled sideways, and fell. It twitched and shuddered, and an evil smoke filled the air with an excremental stench. The deadly glow in its eyes went out. The flesh withered quickly, right before his eyes, to reveal the gleaming white skeleton.

Shaking, Relkin got to his feet, then pulled the blade out of the huge, empty rib cage, and turned back to the room at the end of the hall with murder in his eyes.

There he found the sorcerer in the middle of conjuring, while Eilsa was slumped on the floor at his feet. The long hands wavered through the air and thick syllables warped the very fabric of the world. A moment later a black mirror sizzled out of the air. The bizarre flickering glare threw crazy quilt shadows across the room. It sounded as if a side of beef had been dropped into boiling oil.

The last time Relkin had seen one of these things was in Heruta's foundry on the Isle of the Bone in the heart of the dark continent, Eigo. On that occasion some kind of monstrous creature had come to the mirror and seized men, trolls, imps, and anything else it could catch with its tentacles of green fire. That memory made him keep a watchful eye on the weird disk.

Relkin's presence in the room had not gone unnoticed. The tall knight whirled around. Eilsa was bound in chains and unable to move.

"You!" An evil smile spread across the ancient face with its perfect elfin features.

"So you dog my footsteps still. But this time you are without your dragon. A mistake, I think. Well, well, I will take you with me as well. You can amuse me by torturing the girl to death. Then I will start on you."

Relkin made no response, but edged closer. He had lost the bow, but he still had the sword. If he could just get close enough.

The sorcerer's hand came up and another blue bolt of fire shot from his fist.

Instinctively Relkin put up a hand, as if to ward off a thrown weapon, but instead of being blown off his feet, there was a green flash and a pleasant tingling sensation on his chest and arm.

Instantly he felt imbued with tremendous strength. He thrust forward with the sword and almost caught the knight napping. Waakzaam the Great was forced to dodge a dragonboy's sword lest it take him in the throat.

Waakzaam hurled a second bolt of blue fire. The green flash followed in the same moment, and Relkin absorbed the bolt. He thrust again and slashed and cut with inhuman speed and power. Waakzaam was forced to draw sword and defend himself.

"You have come to die, then. So be it."

Relkin brought his sword up and met the stroke from the mighty sorcerer. His sword was notched, but his arms held and turned aside the blow from the Dominator of Twelve Worlds. Again and then again Waakzaam swung, and each blow was parried. Filled with the strength of a giant, Relkin thrust back at him and forced him to dodge aside.

Waakzaam hissed and leveled a look of hatred at him.

"What are you?" he snarled. "You are no man!"

"Just a dragonboy of the legion, that's all."

"You think I will believe that?"

Blades clashed again.

"He is a man," said a voice from the door, quiet but inescapable. Lessis had entered the room. Beside her was Mirk, a throwing knife in his hand. The mirror continued to float nearby, casting the flickerings of chaos.

"He is a man, and he is greater than you, with your foul habits and your contempt for the beauty of the world you helped create."

"The damned hag too! Will nothing cease your infernal bleating?"

"Why not ask that question of yourself? You ignore your duty and diminish yourself with every stroke. Why do you refuse to see the truth?"

"Bah, I will not trade words with such as you!" A bolt of blue fire was hurled at Lessis, and she put up her arms expecting to be hammered flat, but the blue fire was deflected.

Mirk's throwing knife flew by in the other direction and caromed off Waakzaam's great helmet the next moment.

Relkin darted in, and Waakzaam was forced back to the edge of the mirror, the glare of chaos flickered madly.

Waakzaam spoke thick syllables of power, and Relkin felt himself freeze. Glued to the ground, unable to even move an eyeball.

Waakzaam relaxed. This youth had exhibited most unusual powers. He would have to be investigated most closely.

He seized the chains and hauled Eilsa to her feet.

"And now we shall take our leave."

Lessis tried to disable him with a potent little spell. Waakzaam shrugged it off.

"You have no power over me, hag!" he snarled.

Relkin's hate blazed enormous. He felt it reach down to his toes and shake in his bones. Something snapped, he knew not what, but the next moment he was free of the Dominator's spell.

"Awake!" cried a voice in his mind. "As ye called unto Us, so We call unto You. Awake!"

Relkin felt the difference in the chamber the very next moment. They were joined by another presence, enormous, many-eyed, deep as the seas, the forerunner, the speaker of souls. Its presence wafted over them like a gentle breeze, but it brought with it a stinging spray of awareness. He sensed ten thousand minds linked in one great purpose, the very thing he had set free in faraway Mirchaz. It was with them now, at least in part, for Relkin sensed that it was also active in other places, even other times. Wherever the great dance went on.

Waakzaam sensed the lofty vastness of the intruder. He snarled with rage and strove with it for mastery, and the room filled with enormous expectant energy. Rage lines crawled slowly up the walls of the dark chamber. Sudden noises exploded in the walls.

A glowing mass, roughly the size and shape of a man, began to form in the room. Waakzaam struggled to prevent it, but could not. It grew remorselessly, and with it came more power. In desperation he concentrated everything on it once more. Thus he lost any control over Relkin.

Completely free now, Relkin dove across the space and brought his sword down on Waakzaam's wrist. The sorcerer jerked back his broken limb with a howl. The chains fell free.

The glowing presence intensified dramatically. Waakzaam gave a scream of rage mingled with fear. Relkin drove him back again with another thrust at his face.

At that point the great Dominator of Twelve Worlds looked up and saw that another figure had entered the room, the battledragon bearing that fell sword. The sword sparkled with hate, and he knew it thirsted for his soul. The dragon was just three steps away.

Waakzaam realized he had lost. This situation was untenable. The fact that it was unthinkable was beside the point. Analysis could come later, but first there had to be escape. He tottered toward the mirror.

Relkin saw the move and put himself in the way. Bazil was coming. The perfect elf features were contorted in a scream of hatred. Despite his broken wrist, Waakzaam swung two-handed with his mighty sword, and this time Relkin's sword broke asunder. Waakzaam pulled back for the killing stroke, and Relkin rolled forward in desperation, slid under the sword, and came up against the giant's steel greaves with a thump that knocked the breath out of him.

Waakzaam couldn't spare the time to kill him. The giant stumbled over his legs, and in the split second before Ecator could cut him down, hurled himself headfirst into the mirror and vanished into the seething matrices of chaos.

Instantly the mirror snapped shut with a final blast of harsh scraping noise. They were left with a deafening silence.

"It is done," said Lessis in a small voice.

Relkin wrapped Eilsa in his arms. Lessis stood behind them and put her hands on their shoulders.

The glowing mass began to diminish.

"No, don't go," said Relkin. "There are questions."

The enormity was unmoved by this plea. Relkin sensed coolness, detachment, almost amusement, but no further response. There were other events that were more interesting to it elsewhere.

The glow dwindled swiftly and was gone. For a long moment there was silence in the chamber.

"So that was what you released from Mirchaz," said Lessis. "The world is a different place as a result."

Relkin stared at her and groaned. They were going to ask him questions until hell froze over after this.

He felt the heavy tread of the dragon and looked up. Their eyes met.

"Boy's trouble only just begin."

Epilogue

After a huge meal out of the kitchens of Deer Lodge, the 109th turned about and began the march back to Posila. With them they took Wexenne of Champery, who'd been winkled out of a closet dressed in a washerwoman's smock, and also Kosoke, who was captured on the roof. They did not apprehend Porteous Glaves, who escaped during the fighting in the house when the dragons first surged up from Waakzaam's subterranean realm.

They commandeered horses and wagons for the children, and moved up the valley at a steady pace that took them out of Nellin within a day. The curious procession, nine great battledragons, two dozen wagons filled with children, a number of horsemen and some prisoners chained up in another cart, brought out the people as they passed. Many of them knew Wexenne. Few cheered him now. There were a few insults thrown their way, and one incident of sniping, which the dragonboys suppressed with lethal effect, but for the most part the people they passed seemed to have little sympathy for Wexenne or the cause of free Aubinas.

At Lake Torenz, the 109th picked up some of General Cerius's men who'd been captured at Redhill. They had been badly treated: starved, beaten, and in several cases, mutilated.

That night, and the next morning, the dragonboys torched a few fine houses and let pillars of smoke send a warning ahead of them. Lessis scolded them, but to little avail, and indeed even she found it hard to sympathize with the wealthy landholders who had mistreated Cerius's men. More pillars of smoke went up every time they passed some overly great farmhouse.

As they drew closer to Posila, the word of their coming

reached the town on the heels of the news that Deer Lodge had been sacked and Wexenne arrested. A wave of panic swept over the Aubinan. General Neth struggled to retain control. His force started to melt away as men spurred for their homes. If dragons were sacking Deer Lodge, right under the Sunberg in the heart of Nellin, then what might be going on in their own farms? After fully a third of his troops had deserted, Neth himself withdrew. Morale inside Posila disintegrated. When General Tregor on the Imperial side put in a surprise attack at dawn, he broke through. Dragons from the 155th got into Posila. By noon the Aubinans were in flight, and Posila was taken.

The next day the 109th marched up the Posila Road with the wagons in tow, and found General Tregor waiting at the head of the small legion force, drawn up in parade formation to welcome them back.

No mention was made of the fact that they had gone off without permission. Lessis had sent a message tied to a hawk's leg to Tregor the previous day to explain what had happened. She took full responsibility for their actions. It would all be explained later, or so she wrote. Charges of mutiny, desertion, dereliction of duty, all were to be dropped forthwith.

Other messages were winging their way to Marneri, from whence they would go on to Andiquant. The Empire of the Rose had had a lucky escape. The Dominator was defeated and driven from Ryetelth.

Temple bells rang loudly throughout the Argonath cities that day and the next. The Aubinan revolt had hung over the entire Argonath like a dark cloud. Now it was dispelled. In Antiquant the emperor proclaimed an Imperial holiday and sent a list of medal commendations to the legion headquarters in Kadein.

A month later, at a grand ceremony in the plaza in front of the Tower of Guard in Marneri, the campaign was commemorated and honors awarded.

The 109th were given medals of honor, battle stars, and a fresh campaign star. Commander Urmin was also honored, along with most of his officers and many individual soldiers. So too was the village of Quosh. Farmer Pigget and several other men from the village were present to receive a special Imperial medal of honor. In addition, it was announced that the Emperor Pascal had undertaken to raise the funds to rebuild the village.

A day of celebration was declared for the city of Marneri.

Lagdalen and Hollein spent most of the day with their daughter, together again in quiet bliss, thankful to have survived.

Relkin and Eilsa were also together for much of that day, albeit with her Aunt Kiri as chaperon. However, the medal ceremonies had done something to Aunt Kiri. She was actually smiling at Relkin now.

Eilsa was soon to take up a place at the temple school in Widarf, on the coast near Kadein. There she would receive counseling to help dispel the evil dreams that had troubled her since the fight at Wexenne's house.

That evening Relkin and the rest of the 109th were treated to a grand dinner by the Merchant's Association of Marneri, who had also taken on the burden of feeding the dragons. Relkin and the other dragonboys tucked into the best meal they'd had in ages, and washed it down with excellent ale.

As for their enormous charges, they were busy raising the roof of the Dragon House with song as they drained their kegs. They sang so loudly that they woke Wexenne of Champery in his prison cell in the Tower of Guard.